# Innocent Gestures

## Sharleen Cooper Cohen

**HEADLINE**

First published in Great Britain in 1994
by HEADLINE BOOK PUBLISHING

First published in paperback in 1994
by HEADLINE BOOK PUBLISHING

10 9 8 7 6 5 4 3 2 1

ISBN 0 7472 4430 8

Typeset by
Letterpart Limited, Reigate, Surrey

Printed and bound in Great Britain by
HarperCollins Manufacturing, Glasgow

HEADLINE BOOK PUBLISHING
A division of Hodder Headline PLC
338 Euston Road
London NW1 3BH

For Howard and Micah
my son and my grandson

This book is a work of fiction. All characters are fictitious and any resemblance to real persons, living or dead, is purely coincidental. However, it could not have been written without the generosity of the following people who opened their homes, their offices and their hearts to me. Their knowledge and love of France brought life to this material.

Paris:
Alan G. Ringgold
Patrick Riou
Patrick Baudot
Sylvan Desirée
Catherine Driguet
Joelle Berrebi

Lyon:
Rabbi S. Gurewitz & Madame Sarah Gurewitz

Toulouse:
Judy Grynfogel
Anolie Hadjedz

Village de Camon:
Dominique du Pont

Eugénie les Bains:
David Landerger
Pascale Pradines
Oliver Des Bois
Marcel 'Junior' Van Der Sluis
Isabel Gachet

California:
Kathy Reges
Neil Cohen

Houston:
John A. Leggio

And a special, loving thanks to Sandi Gelles-Cole for her sterling expertise and to my wonderful husband, Martin L. Cohen M.D., for his devotion above and beyond the call!

# Prologue

Pierre Fontelle was an important man. Chairman of Etoile Industries, he supplied the French government with their copying machines, their telephones, and half of their computers. But since his wife had died he was lonely; life had lost its excitement except for an occasional visit to a prostitute. But one had to be so careful of disease these days. That was why when he received the tape, it was such a surprise.

It came in the mail, marked 'Personal'. Curious, he opened it and began to watch. It was the most incredible gift anyone had ever sent him, and anonymous. There was no one to thank and he couldn't bring it up in conversation. He waited, but no one claimed the credit.

At first he'd watched it in amazement, after locking his door. Now he'd seen it so many times, he knew it by heart. But it never failed to drive him wild with pleasure.

Then he got a phone call from a woman. Her mature voice was low, soothing, intimate. 'Pierre? Did you like my gift?'

He knew immediately what she meant. 'Who are you?' he demanded.

'A good friend,' she told him.

'What gift do you mean?'

'The tape.'

1

'It's extraordinary,' he admitted.

'Would you like an appointment to meet her?'

'Possibly.' He had so many questions. Why had she sent it to him? How did she know his most intimate fantasies? His hand trembled on the phone. Never in his life had he felt such conflicting emotions: a fever of anticipation and terror of the consequences. He ought to walk away, but the possibility of pleasure overwhelmed him.

'Did you look at it, Pierre?'

'Yes.'

'Wouldn't you like to see more, to fulfil all the promises she made?'

He wanted to say yes, mortified by the raw ache of his desire, thrilled by the response of his body; yet his heart pounded so wildly in his chest he feared an attack. And that wasn't the only danger.

He shoved aside his better judgement. There was always danger in life, wasn't there? Where would he be if he'd let danger stop him. No more would he accept the leftovers of the elderly, nothing but the bitter dregs of ageing. This tape made him feel young again, in the full flush of youth where forbidden games were a matter of course.

Still, that voice of reason whispered: How did she get your name? Why did she single you out? What does she really want?

'Have you decided?' she asked.

'I'd like to see her in person,' he heard himself say.

'Then listen carefully.' She gave him a list of instructions. Be at his office by 11 pm on 23 December. Tell no one where he was going. Bring nothing but himself and the tape. Take off his tie, and unbutton his shirt collar for comfort.

'What is this going to cost?'

'There is no charge unless you are fully satisfied.

2

Then you may pay me what you wish. I depend on your generosity.'

Perfect, he thought, knowing how firmly he hung on to his money.

'Be discreet,' she warned him, as though he would tell anyone.

And now the adventure had begun, beyond his wildest dreams. He was more excited than he'd been in decades. And he'd kept it from those who knew his every move.

Nobody could know about this; they would want it for themselves.

At 11 pm he sat in his office, behind his desk, waiting. The throbbing in his groin pulsated like an engine pumping back his youth. This encounter would re-ignite him, spread warmth through his body, infuse him with new life. He could hardly wait.

The phone rang and he picked it up. '*Oui*?'

'*Bonsoir*, Pierre,' the woman's voice spoke, low, controlled, cultured. 'Are you ready?'

'Yes,' he whispered, his throat dry with anticipation.

'Good,' she said. 'We've come to take you to paradise.'

By the time the elevator door opened his heart was pounding so hard he thought it would break through his chest. The lights were dim in the foyer so he couldn't see her clearly as she entered. But she was beautiful. A tall slim blonde, wearing a man's overcoat. Her make-up was perfect, her hair falling over one eye like Veronica Lake. She removed her coat and dropped it to the floor revealing a tall slim body in a tight black dress, a diamond pin on the shoulder. Sheer class.

'Good evening, Pierre,' she said, offering her hand. She wore black leather gloves to the elbow. Then she walked over to the VCR and turned it on. Instantly the other image he knew so well appeared,

3

and like Pavlov's dog, his erection sprang up begging to be released. But before he could unzip himself, the blonde woman stepped aside and beckoned to her companion; he held his breath.

She stepped through the door and stood there as he'd imagined, only more breathtaking. He couldn't take his eyes off her.

The blonde spoke to him from behind his chair. 'Isn't she wonderful?' the voice whispered in his ear. 'And she's here just for you. Show her how you feel, Pierre. Take it out so we can see it.'

But he suddenly grew shy, willing only to rub himself on the outside of his pants. He wanted the girl on the tape to do something first.

'Aren't you going to take it out?' the blonde asked in his ear. Her warm breath sent shivers down his spine.

'Maybe later,' he said, breathlessly.

'All right, there's no hurry,' she agreed.

The tape was still playing and it had reached his favourite part. He rubbed himself harder in anticipation.

Then suddenly an iron grip grabbed his forehead, yanking his head back against the chair, exposing his neck. He gasped in shock. But before he could utter a sound, his throat had been slit from ear to ear.

# *Chapter 1*

'Jimmy, come down from that tree!'

Below me, my mother's face glowed like a puffy moon. My brothers and I seldom minded her, though we hopped to our father's commands. I climbed higher into the walnut tree until the white sky shone through the lacy green leaves above me. One branch higher and I could stick my head into the clouds; then I'd float right into space.

The voice became Victoria's. 'Come down right now, James. Or else . . .'

The jolt of the airplane wheels touching down awoke me. My mouth was dry and I moistened my lips. I'd finally managed to fall asleep on this interminable flight from Houston to Paris, and now it was time to get up.

The retro engines of the Delta airbus pitched my cramped and exhausted body forward as though Victoria's voice pushed me.

'If you go to France without me, James, don't expect me to be here when you get back!'

'Fine, you won't be here,' I said, intending to go anyway. But I was keeping the real reasons to myself. Somehow I had to break through the deadness surrounding me so I could see if she was the one causing it.

'Stay here and go to a shrink with me,' she'd pleaded, the last thing I wanted to do.

'I'm not taking this trip for pleasure. Emile needs me on this case. I owe him.'

'And what do you owe me?' she'd countered.

A lot. Enough to use up all my credit. But I wouldn't admit it.

'Running away won't solve anything, James. We have to deal with the distance between us.' She spoke softly when she wanted to convince.

'I am dealing with it,' I said, losing my temper. 'Just not your way!'

When she was hurt, her eyes filled with tears and I was the asshole. Again.

'I'll be working all the time I'm there. And we can't both afford to go. Next time, okay?'

Excuses. Sure I wanted to help Emile, and yes, his daughter was getting married. But I was running away.

Dazed, I gathered up my belongings and stepped over the enormous amount of rubbish that had accumulated underfoot during these nine torturous forgettable hours. And then I heard French being spoken over the loudspeakers welcoming me; it was heady, like a long swallow of Glenlivet. At last I was in France.

A haze of cigarette smoke engulfed me in the terminal as passengers from the plane lit up and mingled with other smokers. Most Europeans have no concept of life without cigarettes.

After customs and passport control I walked through the passage way to baggage claim past advertisements for Chanel, Cabochard, Cartier. How opulent life is here, and how they flaunt it.

Claudine's familiar face was all smiles as she waved and beckoned. 'James, *ici*!' I pushed my baggage trolley towards her marvelling that she had a daughter old enough to be getting married; she looked almost as good as she had in the summer of 1974, when Anne Marie was only four.

I smelled something flowery behind each ear as she kissed my cheeks then drew away to inspect me.

'What an 'andsome man you are – so tall, with those blue eyes and that dark hair! And successful. Special Agent with the FBI.' She gazed at me as I pushed the trolley along. 'Emile couldn't get away from the Prefecture but 'e can't wait to see you.' Her hs were non-existent. 'We're so 'appy you could come to the wedding. If only your Vickie was 'ere too!'

'You mean *Victoria*.' I had married a Vickie who now preferred Victoria. It had happened when the playfulness left our relationship. She stopped calling me Jimmy, too.

I hid my expression from Claudine who was watching me as I hefted my suitcase into the boot of her car. I had a thing about sharing my troubles.

As we drove into the city, she chatted about the wedding plans, the joining of two families. I nodded and listened, ignoring the traffic as I drank in the sights I hadn't seen for nineteen years: the voluptuous shapes of the buildings, the chestnut trees in full leaf – trimmed to perfection, golden domes shining in the sun, the total difference of the place. Paris was breath-taking, a willing lover waiting to embrace me. I just might let her.

I listened to Claudine describing Anne Marie's intended. But when the discussion turned to my own marriage, I changed the subject.

'How is Emile's case going?'

She sighed. 'Better for 'im to tell you,' she said. From that, I guessed things weren't going well.

Claudine dropped me at a hotel not far from their home in Maison Alfort, a suburb about twenty minutes outside the city. I promised to join them for dinner, checked in, left a wake-up call for three hours hence, and, before I fell into an exhausted sleep, reassembled

7

my .44 Special from my luggage and holstered it.

By the time I reached the Laurents' home that evening I was ravenous, but when I saw Emile grinning at me, I forgot my hunger.

'There you are!' he exclaimed as he opened the front door and then gave me kisses on both cheeks, the French sign of true affection. The difference of opinion that had nearly ruined our friendship was settled long ago because he'd written and apologized and asked for my forgiveness. Since then, we'd corresponded regularly. But there was a time I thought I'd never speak to him again, when he'd taken *their* side instead of mine. Now, I was really glad to see him and realized how much I'd missed him all these years.

I slugged him in the arm, uncomfortable with male displays of affection until I recalled how he and not my own father had inspired me to join law enforcement. Seeing his grin, I could tell how much he cared for me. Damned if it didn't feel good.

Emile had aged more than Claudine, the lines in his face were deeper, but he looked fit and handsome still with his square jaw and piercing grey eyes. I had forgotten the scar above his lip and the way his wavy hair grew to a point on his forehead. It was nearly all grey now.

'You look good, James.' He held my shoulders and studied me. 'We're so pleased that you could come – to the wedding,' he added, pretending it was the primary reason I was here, and not to help solve his multiple murder case.

'Do you want to get to it?' I asked.

'Later,' he promised me, then handed me a glass of wine and led me into the living room where I was introduced to the groom and his family. The groom, a young man with a thin face and heavy eyebrows that met in the centre, watched as I kissed Anne Marie, whom I'd last seen when she was four years old. She'd matured into a lovely woman, but not as beautiful as her mother.

'We've all followed your career,' Anne Marie told me.

Claudine put her arm around her daughter. 'Your parents must be proud of you, just as Emile and I are,' she said, beaming at me. 'Not only Special Agent for the FBI, but one of the best in the country. We have a scrapbook of your articles: the time you convinced that gunman to surrender his hostages, and when you found that kidnapped child. You have so many commendations.' Her glance at her husband seemed to say, 'Some people manage to be recognized and advance within their field.'

I was flattered. It reminded me how much I had loved my work when I believed I could make a difference.

My parents are unimpressed by my career. If I'd ever seen the admiring look in my father's eyes I now saw in Emile's, things might have been different. My dad's grudging acknowledgement of my accomplishments was always less than his resentment that first, I'd gone to college, and second, had risen higher on the ladder of law enforcement than he had – with commendations, as if I'd done it to better him. In fact, I stayed away from the Bureau at first because I didn't want to be like my father, though I'd always wanted to be in law enforcement. After I met Emile, and realized I could have such a career and not resemble my father, it changed my mind.

Now, in the presence of warm-hearted people, I felt my protective shell begin to dissolve. Not only was I smiling, but even the tension in my shoulders had relaxed. Maybe I could rediscover the kid I used to be, when life was an adventure and love songs didn't embarrass me. If I could fill this emptiness inside, maybe sunlight would once again flood my soul.

No one noticed my forced enthusiasm as they chatted amicably, Claudine describing to the groom's parents how I'd spent the summer of 1974 as companion to Anne Marie and Guillaume.

'My cousin Annette's son, Charles, met James in college. Charles told James to contact us when he came to France after graduation. So James wrote to us, asking if we could get him a job, and we hired him for the summer to teach the children English.'

'That was you, Froggy,' I teased Guillaume. He had been Froggy-the-Gremlin No. 1, and Anne Marie was Froggy-the-Gremlin No. 2. Suddenly I could feel the frustration of those years again like the pimples of adolescence on my face.

'Dad was only a detective inspector then. Now he's chief inspector of his group,' Anne Marie stated proudly. Evidently she didn't mind that her father had never made superintendent.

'Guillaume and I thought you were so strange,' Anne Marie laughed. 'You'd never tasted café-au-lait or croissant before and you wanted bacon and eggs for breakfast – until you ate our bacon.'

'Well, it was more like ham,' I laughed with her, thinking of Claudine's breakfasts: freshly baked croissants, sliced fresh fruit and brewed coffee. Victoria wouldn't even put those limp-wrist waffles in the toaster for me any more.

'James became fascinated by police work,' Claudine explained. 'And Emile monopolized him completely, took him to the Prefecture every day. The children hardly saw him, until we went on holiday, then James spent more time with them.' She patted my cheek and smiled, but I recalled how tough she'd been with me at the end of the summer, compared to how nice she was now. I was really pissed at them then. A lot of what happened was their fault. And they hadn't stood by me when I'd needed an ally.

Thinking about the past threatened to stir up the dust that had settled. If I allowed painful memories to resurface, they might choke me. So I forced myself to be calm.

'Go to France,' Victoria had said. 'You need to get away from me as much as I need time away from you. We can't go on like this. Sometimes I feel as though your sadness is suffocating me, and yet you won't share it with me. Well, enough. Just go. Maybe I'll smile again.'

Then, in the next breath, she generously presented me with her air miles.

That day, holding the ticket in my hand, I thought about staying in France for good. Why shouldn't I chuck everything and be the bastard Victoria's clenched jaw accused me of being? Would she care? Maybe.

But I couldn't leave my children. My daughter Lindsay had enormous green eyes that could melt steel. When she climbed on the monkey bars and yelled, 'Daddy, watch,' it was better than any accomplishment of my own. I couldn't believe she'd outgrown baby-hood already, all of five years old.

And my son Adam's smile could get me to do anything he wanted. He looked just like my brother Rob who was killed in Vietnam. At seven, he had my build and my face, but he played T-ball better than I ever did.

'I'll wait 'til you get back, Dad,' he promised: a major sacrifice, not to see the latest Disney movie with his friends the moment it was released. It made me want to eliminate everything that could ever threaten them. But Daddy-the-all-powerful had an intimate

11

acquaintanceship with what waited out there – like this case of Emile's. Every ounce of me wanted to protect my kids. But how could I? Sometimes the bad guys win.

If only their mother meant as much to me as the children did. She had once, but now there was a chasm between us that widened every day.

What should I do? Get a divorce? That's one of the major contributions to society's troubles; that, and teenage pregnancies. I could not add to those statistics. To me, my children's world is a clean, innocent place in an otherwise blood-soaked life. I ingest their hopeful smiles with my morning cup of coffee. And at night, when I sing or read to them, I am more soothed by Pippy Longstocking or the Purple Prince of Oz than they are. Nothing gets my mind further away from the grisly obscenities human beings devise for one another than they do. When I see the unspeakable things people do to each other, it helps to think of my kids.

Emile beckoned me and I joined him in the garden, fragrant in the late twilight. We sat at a patio table and I could feel that familiar rush that a new case brings to me, like a narcotic. It's the only thing that gets a rise from me lately.

A filter of moonlight dappled the flagstoned patio. We could see the rest of the family inside, enjoying their conversation.

'This is a tough one,' Emile started. 'It's keeping me awake at night.'

'Tell me about it.'

'There have been three murders so far. Murders? More like massacres.' He put his head in his hands and I received a brief mental picture of a blood-spattered room. 'They've all had their throats cut.'

'Who are they?'

'Pierre Fontelle was the first. A man I've known all

12

my life. They found him in his office last December a few hours after he was killed.' Despair underlined his words. 'Pierre was born in Aquitaine not far from where I grew up – the same age as my father. His son Jacques and I went to school together.'

I put my hand on his shoulder. 'That's really tough, Emile.'

'In all my years with the Prefecture this was the first time I've known the victim. Have you ever?' he asked me.

I shook my head. 'I get to know them afterwards, through the grief of their families.'

'Well, knowing them in person makes a difference. It makes me that much more anxious to find the killer. But so far I haven't come up with a damned thing, not even a suspect. I can barely face Jacques and his family; they're counting on me and I'm letting them down.'

'Tell me more about Fontelle.'

'We didn't travel in the same social circles – he's rich, I'm a *flic*. But they are like family. Pierre left Aquitaine after the war, moved to Paris and got a job as a typewriter salesman. He worked his way from manager to vice-president and bought out his partners. Then he expanded the company into business machines and computers and founded Etoile Industries. They even supply the government. Besides his son Jacques, he has another named Bernard, and two daughters. His wife died two years ago. Both brothers were in business with their father. Jacques and I spent our summers together as boys. When I moved to Paris, the Fontelle family watched over me.' He stopped talking, overcome with emotion. 'Like I did with you.'

'I'm really sorry, Emile.'

'And now, with these other two killings, my boss has come down on me hard. He's under pressure from the Minister. But I'm no closer now than I was last year.

13

Three prominent businessmen have had their throats cut. Believe me, the whole country is affected.'

'How can I help?'

'First thing in the morning we'll go to the Prefecture and look at the files.'

'Isn't tomorrow the wedding?' I reminded him.

He gave me a wan smile. 'You see what this is doing to me?'

'We'll go the day after,' I assured him.

He sighed with relief.

'You know I'm glad to do this for you, Emile.'

'And I'm grateful. But, James, don't tell anyone at work that you are helping me. They think you are here only for the wedding.'

'Why?'

'I have enemies in the department who have wanted to discredit me for years.'

'What do you mean?'

'There are factions here, like everywhere else. And I'm past my retirement. They could force me out before the case is over. It is very cut-throat. Everyone wants this case, especially the rookies who want to be stars. I have to be careful.'

'I've been through it myself,' I told him.

'Then you understand. There's an ultraconservative element at the Prefecture that wants to control the Brigade, and they'll do anything to get it. Recently I took out a warrant to question a suspect and someone in the department warned him I was coming. When I got there the suspect was gone.'

'Jesus!' I exclaimed. 'It's tough enough without being sabotaged from within.'

'Calling in an outsider, especially an American, makes me look weak; if I lose face I lose power. And I can't let that happen. No one's going to take this case away from me!'

14

'No they won't,' I assured him, 'not while I'm here.'

'Listen, I have some of the files at home with me. Want to see them?'

'Lead the way,' I told him.

Emile had commandeered a corner of the master bedroom into a work space. As we entered, I was struck by how similar intimate territories are; no matter if they are used for happy conjugality, committing a crime or as a battle field, they all contain the odour of failed dreams.

I sat on the bed and opened the first file, glancing through the forensic photos of Pierre Fontelle slumped in his chair. A well-dressed elderly man in a three-piece suit, his upper body was covered with blood from a knife wound to the throat. The measurements taken by the crime scene experts were attached to the photos – so many centimetres from here, so many centimetres from there. The blood from his cut throat spread out like a fan. Death was still death.

'His office is on the Boulevard Richard Lenoir, in the centre of the city. The janitor found him about six am. Died sometime after midnight.' Emile's voice was subdued. Violent death did that to you.

'What have you come up with?'

'The killer is right-handed, nearly six feet, judging by the position of the finger prints. And strong enough to hold someone's head and kill him quickly. He knows anatomy, cut straight through the carotid arteries. And the prints are all smooth glove.' He pointed to a signature at the bottom of one of the reports. 'The same *juge d'instruction* has been assigned to the Paris cases. There's a different *juge* on the third case in Bordeaux.'

'Are you sharing jurisdiction with the Gendarmes?'

'No, the National Police have full control.'

I remembered details of the French criminal system

15

of investigation, different from the American. In some ways they have it easier. They can keep a suspect under wraps for two days – no phone calls, no visitors, no lawyers, no nothing. The French figure that if you let a suspect make a phone call, he'll just get rid of evidence. On the other hand, the amount of documentation required would drive me crazy.

The French police rely primarily on written reports taken by investigators at the scene to solve their cases; the report is their bible. Once an arrest is made, the report is the basis of every trial and carries more weight than live testimony. So, whenever a crime occurs in France, you can be sure that the documentation will be mountainous.

And jurisdiction over a crime isn't automatic; sometimes it's a local matter and other times it's federal, depending on the severity of the case and the profile of the victim. Once jurisdiction is established, a *juge d'instruction* is assigned to each case. His function is to oversee every activity of the police, down to minute details, and ensure that proper legal procedure is followed to the letter.

Still, there have been times in my career in America when civil rights laws have curtailed me from making a case against a real scumbag and I've wished I were in France where things are more geared towards the police. Except that having to inform the *juge d'instruction* of every step and ask his permission to take action would really slow me down. Emile's current files weighed several pounds at least.

Jet lag was making me bleary. 'Condense this for me. Whom did you question, what did they say, and who are the possible suspects?'

'We've eliminated family members and business associates in the Fontelle case. They all had alibis.'

'Tell me about the family.'

16

'One daughter was a model, never married, a bit eccentric – you know the type. Lots of cats and flowered dresses, lives in Provence. The other is married to the Malfils Mustard heir.'

'The one from Dijon?'

'That's it. Both sons are married. Jacques has two children, his brother Bernard has three. Everybody is Catholic, nobody's in trouble.'

'Was Fontelle a good guy or a bad guy?'

'Good. Only one brush with the law two years ago when he was investigated on suspicion of smuggling. He was fully cleared.'

'I see. That might lead somewhere.'

'I checked it out myself,' Emile assured me. 'There was no evidence, only an anonymous tip. The incident took something out of Fontelle. He withdrew from the business, aged rapidly. And when his wife died it hit him hard.'

'Women?'

'No mistress, but after his wife's death he frequented brothels until recently.'

'What made him stop? His age?'

'No, his sons say the AIDS scare got to him.'

'You buy that?'

'Why not?'

'I don't know, a guy his age. What was he doing for sex?'

'Maybe nothing?'

'Not if he's French! Did you check with his doctor?'

'The autopsy report showed that his health was good for his age, nothing dysfunctional.'

'Then his doctor might know about his sex life?'

'You think it's important?'

'Don't you?' I winked.

'You haven't changed,' he said.

But I had.

17

'We investigated the hell out of it and came up with nothing. I had to let it go and move on, though we kept the files open. And then, six months later, there was another one with the same modus.' He handed me a second file.

'Exactly the same?'

'Close enough. Only this man died with his prick in his hand and there were more suspects.'

'His prick in his hand? That's intriguing.' I flipped through the second file, thicker than the first. 'What are the possibilities here?' I started listing. 'His assailant talked dirty to him, but wouldn't follow through. The assailant thinks masturbating is something to kill for, or the victim was forced to perform a sex act upon threat of death.'

'Maybe he was surprised in the act,' Emile offered.

'Unlikely,' I stated. 'Imagine sitting there whacking off while someone sneaks up behind you and slits your throat. That could really take the pleasure out of it.'

Emile smiled.

I read. François Sourais, 69 years old, widowed, remarried, third-generation liquor distributor based in Paris, with offices in New York and Bordeaux. His two brothers were in charge in those cities. Two daughters, one son in the business, and a stepson who owned a photo developing store in the Marais.

'Did Fontelle and Sourais know each other?' I asked.

'No evidence that they did,' Emile insisted. 'But this time we suspected the wife's former husband, a volatile Spaniard who had threatened her. He fought the divorce and told her if she remarried he'd slice her face.'

'So he was good with knives?'

'Then we suspected the stepson who resented his stepfather for not inviting him into the family business. The Spanish wife, Maria Theresa, complained that her husband's friends and family never accepted her. Everyone accused someone else of killing him – a very different group of people from the unified Fontelle family. There was even a business competitor who wanted to buy the company and tried to force the deal.'

'Any arrests?'

'I got close. Our theory was that Sourais' killer made this one look like Fontelle's. But I never found any physical evidence to link anyone to the crime – no matching fibres or hair. None of them was as tall or as strong as the killer. And the similarity to the Fontelle case had to be considered. It could have been a copy. Until the third one happened.'

By now, my head was throbbing and my eyes burned from jet lag. For me, it was the middle of the night and all that wine on an empty stomach was getting to me. I couldn't stifle my yawns. Emile noticed. 'I am a terrible host. You are tired and I want to solve everything immediately. We'll finish another time.'

'I would like something to eat,' I told him, following him out of the bedroom.

But he couldn't let it go. I knew the feeling.

'If I could just establish a connection between the victims,' he said as we entered the dining room. Delicious smells were making my stomach contract.

'We'll find it,' I told him, spreading pâté on a piece of bread and popping it into my mouth. 'The killer knows what it is and so will we.'

But he wasn't convinced. He knew that true serial killers chose their victims by the twisted reasoning of a psychopathic brain. Hard to figure.

'There could be a joint business venture between these men, or a political connection,' I suggested.

'The only element they have in common is their age and their wealth. What kind of a pervert kills rich old men?'

19

'A psychologist would say, someone who hates his father.' I got a flash of my own dad lying drunk in front of the television. How would I feel if someone slashed his throat? Not as bad as a son should feel. There were even times when I'd wished him dead. At least I didn't hate him any more.

Emile was thoughtful, 'Our behavioural psychiatrist said that was possible.'

'Don't discount it. You need crazy scenarios when you're profiling serial killers,' I told him. 'It takes ingenuity to think like a sicko. I have a buddy with the Bureau in Houston who's good at it. Afterwards he can't shake the feelings. Puts him right on the edge. But Hal Markham, a trainer I know at Quantico, is excellent. He'll be glad to consult with us. There's also a good FBI man right here in Paris. I could fax them the sheets on your cases.'

'This is strictly between us,' Emile cautioned.

'Okay,' I agreed, alerted by his concern. But I had the feeling his ego was involved, and threatened to hinder progress. 'Serial killers are a grisly group. And you've had little experience to guide you. Lucky guy.'

He nodded.

I had investigated two serial killers in my career and both cases brought me commendations. One turned out to be a high school student, quiet and introverted, who'd murdered four children in his neighbourhood and six in another. It was all I could do to keep from tearing the eyes out of the guy when we caught him. We did save one child, the one he was about to kill at the time. She was alive, but he'd already raped her. Four years old. After that, I stayed close to home for weeks, taking my children to school myself and picking them up.

Then there was a clever, good-looking psychopath whose current girlfriend couldn't believe he had killed her roommate, two of his ex-girlfriends, and a middle-aged couple down the hall by bludgeoning them to death. She stood by him, even when we found the murder weapon in his trunk and other damning evidence in his apartment that tied him to six other murders in other states. Sometimes I just don't understand people.

Most of the homicides that come across my desk are drug-related. Houston has a thriving drug trade and at one time was a major clearing house for Mexico, South America and the US east to Florida. Lately, the drug enforcement units of the FBI and the Houston police have made some headway in the 'war against drugs', as former President Bush named it. And there is consolation in the fact that the ranks of drug dealers are thinning themselves by attrition; but not enough to suit me. As Special Agents we also handle bank robberies, extortions and kidnappings, and Houston has as much of that kind of crime as any city in America. It's changed since I was a kid. We Texans always liked to party and fight, but I'll never get used to those killings for no reason.

Recently I had handled a hostage situation in an Arby's restaurant where a crazed asshole, wanted in Kentucky for murder, killed four people, including a three-year-old boy, before blowing himself away. When I was a rookie there were three killings a week. Now the Houston police handle three a day and the FBI isn't far behind.

'Where should we start?' Emile asked.

'I'll know better when I review the cases and work out how they reflect your society.'

'What do you mean?'

'Crimes are particular to the individual societies in which they're committed; they're a product of that culture. For instance, Americans, as a rule, are afraid

21

of the IRS. If we tangle with Uncle Sam we know we'll be hounded for the rest of our lives.'

'You mean nobody cheats on their taxes?'

'Sure we cheat: we don't declare income, we hide assets, we have plenty of ways.'

'Then what are you saying?'

'I'll give you an example. Recently, a group of Nigerians were able to defraud the IRS because they had no qualms about doing it; there was no cultural background to cause them concern over what the IRS does to your life.

'People were recruited off the street, and taught how to get rapid tax refunds from the new computer system. Billions of dollars will never be recovered because these immigrants weren't afraid of the big boys. Americans just don't dream these things up. That's what I mean by cultural difference.'

'I don't agree,' Emile said. 'These killings prove it; our psychopaths are as crazy as yours.'

'For different reasons,' I insisted. 'The motive in your case is peculiar to one stratum of French society. This killer has something in common with these victims, even if it's only their social class. Like tends to kill like. We have to find out what the link is.'

'But the victims are chosen randomly.'

'I'm not so sure. It seems planned to me.'

'Why do you say that?'

'Look at the victims – wealthy men in their late-sixties. Unusual. Every victim, like every witness, gives you information, if considered within their social context. Take the choice of a weapon . . . why not a gun? Too noisy? Easily traced? No. The weapon is part of the killer's scenario, it's tied to his motive. What I want to know is why he hasn't used these bodies sexually or mutilated them more.'

'Isn't slicing their throats enough for you?'

'Perhaps not. Give me a list of typical French crimes,' I asked.

He listed them. 'Burglary, robbery, murder, drug dealing, smuggling, illegal arms, technological espionage, embezzlement.'

'You see! You never mentioned gang violence; it would be first on my list. You French have a more homogeneous society so you don't have as much racial tension as we do, even with your immigrant population. Your divorce rate is lower than ours which makes your families more stable. You don't have gangs because your society isn't as angry.'

'But something made this man kill. Are serial killers made or born?' Emile asked.

'Both,' I told him.

Suddenly, his shoulders sagged. 'I'm asking too much of you. This is truly an imposition.'

'No way, Emile,' I insisted. 'I'm glad to be your white knight.' I couldn't tell him that my helping him was saving me from my own hell right now. And it felt good to be needed. I was reminded of the hero worship I'd felt when I'd followed him around the Prefecture. At twenty-two I wanted to be just like him. I had hung on his words as he explained procedure, fascinated and eager.

'Stop worrying,' I told him. 'We're going to ace this one. You'll see.'

His grin matched my own and I was determined for him to keep it. I made a vow to the demented psychopath out there: *I'm after you, Shithead. You're gonna be dead meat.*

# *Chapter 2*

Being in France should have been fun, but it wasn't without Victoria. Her enthusiasm used to invest even the mundane with excitement. Alone I found myself having to make an effort.

The wedding of Anne Marie and Roger Cohen took place in a grand orthodox Synagogue on Rue de Victoire, the women separated from the men. As a frugal Frenchwoman, Claudine booked Anne Marie's wedding to follow an earlier one where they'd decorated the temple, so the flowers were profuse without the Laurents having had to pay.

I was sensitive to Jewish issues because of conversations I've had with my friend, Sam Lebenthal, a cop in the Jewish neighbourhood of Beachnut. But I'd never attended a Jewish wedding before. The chanting in Hebrew was like a priest chanting in Latin, and the *yarmulke* on the Rabbi's head reminded me of the priest's hat. Judaism was a precursor to Christianity so we've borrowed much of their rituals. Even the blessing over the bride and groom is the same: May the Lord Bless and keep you, etc. But Christian weddings don't have cantors. As he sang, I could hear the suffering of his people in his voice. It made me think of Claudine's story, how she was born in North Africa after her family escaped from Paris to avoid the Nazis during the war.

I watched Emile during the ceremony and wondered what it was like being married to a Jew. If the mother is Jewish, so are the children and that adds a whole set of other problems, like marrying out of your race. But Emile seemed comfortable with it, even though he didn't convert. When I stayed with them that summer, Claudine had become more open about her religion and it was causing a stir in the family. Evidently, hitherto she had been keeping it a secret and only observed at her mother's house.

During the years since then, she'd practised more openly and taught her children about their heritage. In his letters Emile had told me that his own family had not reacted well. Obviously, though, he respected her choice for I saw him reciting the prayers in Hebrew along with the other men. Several times during the ceremony he even wiped tears from his eyes.

But he had paid a price for his mixed marriage. The Laurents never fully accepted Claudine, and as I observed them in the rows ahead of me, I could see how stiffly they sat. Emile's father had died but his two brothers and their wives were here. They'd travelled all the way from the south-west to attend the wedding and yet never smiled. Seeing them again, I recalled the way their disapproval had made me feel – small and insignificant. I had not been a favourite of theirs that summer of 1974.

I glanced over at Claudine's family, by comparison a friendly, demonstrative group. All the women were dabbing their eyes. Perhaps they could make up for the coldness of the Laurents.

Anne Marie circled her groom seven times and they each drank from a cup of wine, then Roger broke a glass with his heel, signifying the fragility of life and the destruction of the second temple, and everybody shouted: '*Mazel Tov*!'

Victoria would have loved it.

The reception was at the Brasserie Zebra on the Left Bank, owned by a friend of Emile's who gave him a special price on the food and liquor. The menu was lavish, and even at a discount, I couldn't imagine how he was going to pay for it. No wonder he hadn't retired yet.

Most of the music at the wedding was Israeli and everyone except Emile's family participated in the festivities. The women danced separately from the men, in their own circle, while the bride and groom sat at a table and greeted their friends. Then the young guests yanked the newly married couple from their seats, placed them on chairs and lifted them up above the heads of the crowd, marching them around. The bride and groom each gripped their chairs with one hand and then took opposite ends of a handkerchief with the other. Anne Marie was terrified that she might fall but Roger loved it.

The celebration was boisterous, but I wondered what life held in store for them. Would they turn out like Victoria and me?

Seeing Emile's family holding on to their prejudice dampened my spirits and I left the wedding early, took a taxi to the Champs Elysée and walked the boulevard, staring at the strollers and tourists who stared back at me. Then, for old times' sake, I took the Metro to Les Halles, and watched the street performers and mimes, mingling with the Sunday crowds.

I bought a paper, thinking I might catch a movie later in the underground cinema of the enormous shopping pavilion, and was about to choose a café to sit down in when a busload of girls wearing private school uniforms unloaded in front of me and headed for the Musée Pompidou.

I watched them descend one by one, their navy skirts

27

swinging around their knees. Each one was wearing some personal accessory which declared her individuality: a scarf, a cap, a bracelet, a plait. I wondered how Lindsay would look at that age; probably a knockout like her mother.

Several girls were oriental, one was black, some were tall, some overweight, some had short hair, others curly. They chatted among themselves; it was clear that they believed they owned the world. And flashes of memory began to stir, of another girl and another time . . . but I shut them out until the last girl came down the stairs and our eyes met.

Turquoise blue was all I saw, and blonde hair. She was walking straight ahead, striding with confidence and staring at me, her head turned my way, her eyes holding mine in a timeless moment. Heat suffused my body as I watched her, thinking she would bump into someone if she didn't pay attention. But something protected her and no one got in her way. Still, she watched me. What is it? What do you see? I wanted to ask, feeling a stirring in my loins for the first time in months.

Someone called her name. 'Chloe, hurry up.' But she didn't hurry.

All the way to the door of the museum our eyes held until she finally rejoined her group and entered the revolving door. With a terrible disappointment I watched the back of her shiny flaxen hair and shapely calves disappear into the gloom, and then, oh so briefly, her right hand, at the hem of her skirt, waved to me behind her back.

I almost laughed out loud and felt myself grinning. I looked around, embarrassed, to see if anyone was watching. But no one was.

That precocious girl had lifted my spirits and I almost followed her inside. But I couldn't trail after a schoolgirl so I forced myself in the opposite direction. With a newfound spring in my step, I sauntered down the row of cafés between the Forum des Halles and the museum and chose the Café de la Cotes, the only modern-looking café in the row. I felt like a million bucks.

Still seeing her eyes and feeling a lightness in my heart, I ordered an espresso. The area had changed since I'd seen it last. Formerly the red light district, a major gentrification had now taken place, though massage parlours and peep shows were still around. And the modern decor of Café de la Cotes was nothing like the other turn-of-the-century cafés with their rococo furniture and panelling. In fact, it reminded me of a restaurant in Houston with its sleek metal furniture and caramel wood interior. The sink in the men's room was really unusual; the tap water poured into a triangular glass shelf with a drain in it, the shelf placed at an angle so the water flowed to its apex.

When I came back to my table, the one next to me was occupied by a group of young people involved in an intense conversation. One of them, a slender woman in her early-twenties, medium build, with a short boyish haircut and pale skin, looked up and winked at me. This must be my day, I thought, wondering why I was getting all this attention. But this time I didn't respond, and pulled out my pad to write a note to Emile. 'Where was the night watchman?'

She pressed her leg against mine and for a brief moment I let it stay, wishing she was the girl from the bus. Then I shifted my weight, and damn if she didn't follow me, continuing to press against me. Our eyes met and she smiled, speaking in rapid French. I fumbled my reply. Usually I turn off women who approach me, but I was in a carefree mood, primed by my encounter with the young girl, so I thought: What the hell?

29

'American?'

'What else?'

'I'm Jeanette,' she said, extending her hand. She introduced me to her friends, Michel, Lisanne, Sophie, who continued their conversation.

Then she leaned over and whispered in my ear, 'Want to get laid?'

'No thanks,' I told her, uninterested in hookers.

'I have plenty of condoms,' she said, running her hand lightly up my leg almost to my prick. 'My speciality is putting them on for you, two at a time. I'm very sexy when I'm careful.' She smelled of some expensive perfume. The tips of her fingers continued to move lightly over me and I'll be damned if I didn't respond. She gave a satisfied smile. But I was the one who was grinning – the second grin in less than half-an-hour. I hadn't had a hard on like this in months and I was enjoying the hell out of it.

'Are you sure?' she asked. 'I only charge for sex when I need extra money. I'm a filmmaker.'

Sure, I thought. But my hard on was keeping me interested.

I told her I was a computer salesman, and as we talked and her friends joined the conversation, I began to believe her story. They used technical jargon and were familiar with details of European and American films in production. Soon we were playing, 'Have you seen this?' speaking the universal language of the movies.

When I told them I rarely saw French films, they insisted that I rent a video of a film called 'Mama, There's a Man in Your Bed'; I was sure to love it. Then they discussed some Danish director named Lars von Trier and his film 'Zentropa' which was supposed to be a hypnotic train journey into the scarred nightscape of Germany after the war.

'The man is a fraud. He's not a Jew and he's not innovative.'

'I say he is!' Jeanette defended the director. 'Though a seriously pretentious person!'

I'd never heard of him.

We switched from coffee to vodka, and after a few more drinks she was looking better to me. In the twelve years since my marriage I've never played around, though I've had plenty of opportunities. But things were so bad between Victoria and me that I hadn't been able to sustain a hard on during sex in months. And it was eating me alive. I kept telling myself things would get better, but they hadn't. I'd resolved not to think about it, but I thought of it ten times a day. Every time a sexy woman walked by, it reminded me of my failure. Until now. The young woman in front of the museum had stirred me up. Maybe this one would prove the problem wasn't mine?

Feeling my palms starting to sweat, I said to Jeanette, 'Were you serious about the two condoms?'

'But of course,' she smiled. 'A doctor friend of mine told me about it.'

I wondered if I would feel anything incased in all that rubber. She looked into my eyes and an agreement passed between us. We said goodbye to her friends and took the Metro to an apartment near Montmartre.

All the way there I kept telling myself I could back out any time. And then that I-dare-you voice goaded me on. I noted the Metro stops so I could get home later.

The closer we got to her apartment, the easier it seemed to cheat on my wife when I considered it an experiment.

As we walked up the narrow hilly streets to her apartment she came around behind me and put her

31

hands in my suit pockets, caressing my thighs. My immediate reaction made me feel young and carefree. 'Do all American computer salesmen wear blue suits on Sunday?' she teased.

'I went to a wedding on the Rue de Victoire,' I told her. 'The daughter of an associate.' I never tell strangers what I do for a living, especially hookers I'm about to fuck.

'There's no church on the Rue de Victoire or an Hôtel de Ville,' she said, running her hands up my chest under my jacket, walking behind me single file, like a kid trying to stay in my shadow.

'I didn't go to a church or a Marie, I went to the Chas Laube synagogue.' In France, all weddings are performed in a civil ceremony at the Hôtel de Ville in a magistrate's office, and then they have a religious ceremony later or the following day.

'I would never feel married if it didn't take place in a church with the blessing of Jesus, would you?' she asked.

'No,' I agreed.

She had her head on my shoulder as if we were on a real date. I put my arm around her.

'How do you know these people? Are you Jewish?' Jeanette asked me. She reached into her bag, pulled out her cigarettes and lit one. I stepped on the other side of her to be downwind.

I explained how I had met the Laurents, leaving out the part about law enforcement.

'The Jews are too tough with the Arabs.'

'Oh, you think so?'

'Yes and they shouldn't have left France during the war.'

'That's an odd thing to say,' I commented, unable to keep my eyes off her behind as we climbed a narrow staircase between two buildings that ascended an impossibly steep hill. 'What should they have done?' I asked. I had no desire to educate her on the plight of the French Jews during the war, but I felt protective of Claudine. Especially after the way Emile's family treated her.

'Stayed in France and fought like the rest of us,' Jeanette said, looking back over her shoulder.

'The rest of us?' I said, smacking her on the behind a bit harder than I needed to. 'You weren't even born. And if they'd stayed in France, they would have died. Thousands did.'

'Jews only died in other countries, not here,' she insisted, responding to my hostile tone. We had reached the top of the steps and were on a narrow street of old-fashioned apartment buildings. I had to stop to catch my breath.

'Don't you know about the concentration camps in France?' I asked. 'My friend's relatives died there. I saw their pictures.' I remembered how Claudine had cried when she looked at them.

That seemed to make her pause. 'That was the Nazis' fault.'

That set my teeth on edge. It wasn't all the fault of the Nazis; the French had collaborated in deporting the Jews of France with more vigour than the Pétain government had admitted, but if I kept arguing with her, I wasn't going to get laid.

'Forget about that and look at this,' she said, pointing behind me. I turned and saw that we were above the Sacré-Coeur and the whole of Paris was spread out before us, glistening in the sun.

'God!' I exclaimed, feeling as though she'd given me an incredible gift. My hostility abated as the grandeur soothed my anger. In a gesture of reconciliation, I put my arm around her and drew her to me.

'There's a book you could read by Antelme, the

French anthropologist. He describes how he fought with the resistance, was captured by the Nazis and spent time in the French camps.'

She raised an eyebrow as she glanced at me. I could see she was making a mental note. Maybe there was a film in it. 'How do you know about such things?' she asked, taking my hand and leading me into her building.

'I read,' I told her. 'It's a habit I got into when I was a kid. When I was ten, I was hit by a car while riding my bicycle and spent six weeks in a body cast. I couldn't get out of bed to watch television, so I read. My father made fun of me, but my mother brought me books from the library: *The Hardy Boys*, *Black Beauty*, *Treasure Island*. Even now, I love to read, especially books about World War II, or the Russian classics, and I like French authors. For a brief moment in college I considered being an English teacher, but my current work suits me better.'

'Computers,' she said, as though she didn't believe me.

Her entire apartment reeked of cigarette smoke. I almost turned around and left. The girl at the museum wouldn't have smoked.

She plopped on to the bed and patted a place beside her, but I wasn't ready for that yet. The liquor was wearing off and I was beginning to regret being here, especially when she reached over and picked up a burned-out butt and added it to an overflowing ashtray next to the bed.

Contrary to what Americans tell you, not everybody in Europe speaks English. My French became fluent after the summer in France with the Laurents and then nearly a year with the Peace Corps in Senegal. But I've lost it from disuse.

'How did you learn to speak English?' I asked,

34

attempting to stave off the moment and to overcome my distaste.

'In school. And I perfected it when I worked on several American films shot here in Paris.' She was watching me, wondering how much longer until we got to it. I pretended to be interested in her apartment.

It was a studio affair with a view of the neighbouring roofs and chimneys. She had covered the garret with photos of her on location and I took my time looking at them, stalling until I could figure out some excuse. Now that I was out of time, I just wanted to get out gracefully.

The room had a sloping ceiling; a double-sized mattress pushed against the wall served as both sofa and bed. The flowered wallpaper was faded and streaked with large yellow spots from a leak that could have occurred twenty years ago or yesterday. The whole place was stark and terribly sad.

She had called ahead to be sure that her roommate had vacated the place and when she saw I wasn't going to make a move, she got up from the bed, came over and kissed me, pressing hard against me. Her hands skimmed my body, touching my gun, and she pulled away and looked at me.

'For computers?' she asked.

'I carry cash sometimes,' I answered, removing my jacket and my holster. We went at it again. Her thin body was surprisingly strong. But the taste of nicotine on her tongue was a turn-off.

I was about to pull away when she reached down between our grinding hips and began to caress me. I felt the glimmer of a reaction so I began to touch her, first the nape of her neck where the hair was cut short, feeling it rough against my hand, and then down her neck to her shoulders and inside her cotton top. She had small breasts and a boyish body, but she was turning me on.

See, Barton, I told myself, feeling those wonderful stirrings. You can do it! Her tongue was inside my ear and then mine was in hers. We began to undress one another and she was getting excited, but my hard-on was only fair. It's the nicotine, I thought. And then I got an image of Victoria's lush body compared to Jeanette's and realized that I didn't want to be doing this; but I had to prove myself. I kissed her again, probing her mouth with my tongue, trying to ignore the hot-acid shot of fear running through me that maybe this time wouldn't be any better than the others.

An image of Victoria's sympathetic expression flashed in my brain. Every time I failed, her understanding turned to disappointment. This time will be different, I told myself. You'll see. I knew my problems with sex were a result of having been with the same woman for twelve years, who did not excite me any more, who had changed. All I needed was one good fuck, and that's exactly what I was getting. The fact that I wished she was the girl from the museum would not make any difference.

The condoms were ready, but I wasn't. Jeanette set them down on the bedside table, moving aside the overflowing ashtray and three pairs of worn socks.

Her body was white, dotted with occasional dark moles. Her rib cage stood out prominently from her thin waist and she had dark hair that grew in a line from her navel to her pubis. Her legs needed shaving. I ran my hands up her thighs and she arched her back, breathing more rapidly. It might have been an act, but it turned me on. I felt myself getting harder.

See, it's working, I told myself. Now concentrate. Her cunt had a pungent female smell, and the odour grew stronger as I tongued my way down her body. She

36

grabbed my head and held it there until the smell of her filled my senses. I'd needed this for so long. It was totally therapeutic. My breathing matched hers as I moved up the length of her and rubbed myself against her thigh. She reached to stroke me.

Nothing.

I pressed harder against her, rubbing, pumping, letting the taste of her and the smell of her fill me again. She was moaning and ready for me. I reached to touch her with my fingers, but she pushed my hand away and reached for my prick. It wasn't there!

Oh God, please not again. Don't let this happen! But all the pleading in the world never gave anyone a hard on, least of all me.

'James,' she whispered my name, running her hands down my back to my ass, pulling on the cheeks, caressing my asshole. That's it, baby, I thought. The sensation I longed for shot through my balls and up my prick and I pumped against her vigorously, caressing her so she'd remain ready. My mind reached for images to keep me going and I thought of the girl at the museum. Things were starting to happen. I reached for a condom and moved over to put it on. The moment I took myself in hand, my erection went limp.

Jeanette noticed what was happening and pushed my hand away to sit up, leaning over me. I lay back on the bed and she came forward and took me in her mouth. A memory from my past came floating to the surface, a memory of the most incredible blow job in the world, but I pushed it away and concentrated on the woman I was with. It didn't help. Why wouldn't it work? I wanted to smash somebody's face.

Eventually Jeanette gave up, rolled on to her back and stared up at the ceiling. Then she reached for a package of cigarettes that materialized from somewhere within the bedcovers. It must have been under her pillow. Disgusting.

'If it's the money, you don't have to pay me. We can do it as friends. Would that help?'

I was touched. Some women are so damned helpful. Victoria was always too understanding. It made things worse when she tried to assure me that it was only temporary. She'd even tried doing what she thought I wanted, wearing see-through negligées, talking sex talk, things like that. But it wasn't the answer. What did I want them to do? Slug me in the gut for not performing? Point their finger at me and laugh, tell me I'm a piece of shit for not getting it up? I was already doing that.

I sat up and started putting on my clothes.

She gave a sigh of resignation. 'Can I ask you a personal question?'

'Has this ever happened before?' I supplied. 'Yeah,' I admitted.

'Is it because you're gay? If you are, I know someone who'd really like you.'

'Hell, no,' I laughed. 'Sometimes I wish I were. Maybe I wouldn't be having these problems.'

She nodded politely and watched me reach for my clothes, her hands lightly caressing her own body. As I holstered my gun and put on my clothes, her caresses became more deliberate, exciting herself even more until she was really into it. Then, as I reached the door, she drew up her legs and continued to masturbate, exposing her pink inner lips, moist and inviting. I stood there staring as she brought herself to a climax, which seemed as satisfying as anything I might have done, her eyes glassy and her mouth slack as her vagina vibrated.

I'd never seen anything like this before except in a porno flick, a fantasy come to life. And though the

38

blood was throbbing in my temples, where it counted I didn't get a goddamned rise!

I opened the door and let myself out, leaving her there along with my self-esteem.

# Chapter 3

After the fiasco with Jeanette, I felt lower than I'd ever felt in my life. Paris had lost its charm and there were no more school girls giving me the eye. Maybe I'd never be able to have sex again. Jesus, Barton, I told myself. Get a grip. Go to work!

Emile was depending on me. And without his support, where would I be? His letter of recommendation helped me get into the FBI. My father never wrote one. So now it was my turn to help him.

Eddie Barton, my father, was an old-fashioned cop. Before the social revolution of the sixties labelled him 'pig', he took his job seriously. He still does, but he doesn't talk about it as much. A love of police work is one of the few positive traits I inherited from him. The minus column contains more entries. For instance: any man who lets you know how he feels is a wimp, loyalty to a buddy is sacred, when in doubt hit first and ask later, and women are only good for fucking. It used to be that women were good for cooking *and* fucking, but since the invention of frozen dinners and take-out pizza, nobody cooks any more, so now it's only fucking.

With a background like that, it's amazing that I ended up as mild-mannered as I am, and married to a feminist. Not that Victoria is a bra-burner, but she's newly arrived at consciousness raising so she's gung-ho.

I admit that I agree with some of what she says, like equal pay for equal jobs, fair treatment under the law. But whatever her definition, I can barely swallow it when she talks about women being victims of men, and men's rage against women. According to her, men never understand women's needs. And when she gets started, my mouth pulls to the side in that same derisive smirk my father gets when my mother voices her lame opinions. Even though my mother asks for it, I hate that smirk of his; yet I can't stop myself from doing it. My mother is the gentler side of me, but there's more of my father's fury in me than I'd like to admit.

To this day, my father says, 'Women are always bellyaching about something.' And he ignores my mother's requests until she stops making them. As we were growing up he'd continually be pointing out to us how inept we were, or else saying it to her; she was beneath his concern, her wants of little consequence.

Defeated by his attitude, she'd stand at the kitchen sink, her shoulders hunched forward, her arms to their elbows in suds. The only reprimand she dared make was to turn her back on him, which went unnoticed except by me. Her posture was the only way she expressed sorrow, or resignation, or anger, as though the faded apron with the frayed red piping was her protection. What an ancient apron could do, with its one button at the neck and a sorry sash that tied in a haphazard bow at the waist, was never apparent to me. Yet she wrapped herself in it daily like a swaddling cloth, the way patriots wrap themselves in their country's flag. And we dismissed her, relieved to have his negative attention turned on to her and not on us. We'd collude with him by absorbing ourselves in some sporting event on the radio or television, ignoring her completely. And if the department called my father to work in the middle of the game, my brothers and I

42

would continue to ignore her, as though behaving like our father kept us safe from his wrath. It was a cinch, she wouldn't protect us.

Yet, no matter how badly we treated her, she always took it. If only she'd stood up for herself, we'd all have been better off. Treating her that way is a major regret of mine. But there are so many others piled on the rubbish heap since then that I rarely think about it. It's enough just to keep my head above it.

Victoria has taught Adam not to be like me. He helps in the kitchen, makes the salad, clears the dinner table. When Lindsay asks if she can help, Victoria tells her, 'This is a man's job, honey. You have to get good grades so you can go to law school.' Then she winks at me. I don't fight her on this, I want my daughter to be President. And she makes a helluva point. But deep down I fear that Adam will turn into an introspective type who talks about relationships and rarely fucks anybody. Victoria says if I would help in the kitchen, it would set an example for the kids, especially for Lindsay who has to choose a mate someday. (Over my dead body!) Even without my example, Adam's become pretty good at tearing lettuce and chopping vegetables.

I think all Victoria's training is bullshit. Adam has to grow up in the real world of male supremacy and she's confusing his loyalties – his desire to please her and his love for me. She knows nothing about the shared male experiences I have with my son. I hate watching Monday night football by myself while he's in the kitchen with her (if I'm home, which is rare). I don't mean to say that men shouldn't help their wives, but we should carry in the groceries or carry out the rubbish or mow the lawn – not wash the stupid watercress for an organic salad.

In France, men cook because they choose to, it's

43

honourable, not because women nag them. I can't explain it, it's just different. There's a comfortable delineation of roles.

I was waiting in front of my hotel the next morning when Emile picked me up, eager to get started.

'I made a note to ask you about the night watchmen,' I asked Emile. 'Where were they? What did they see?'

'None of the buildings employed a watchman,' he told me.

I shook my head. Almost every office building in Houston has someone sitting in the lobby after hours to check you in and out. It's so different here, and their Federal headquarters is an example. The Prefecture at 36 Quai Des Orfèvres is several hundred years old, built in the Mansard style and designated a national monument which means they're not allowed to modernize it. We parked in the official area and checked in with the guards at the gate where I reported my weapon. Then we continued through a dark stone tunnel which opens into a sunlit courtyard, nothing like our modern glass and steel building in Houston.

The offices of the Brigade Criminelle are four flights up a circular staircase whose marble steps under the linoleum are worn from centuries of use. Just climbing them made me think about the history of the place, a thought that would never have occurred to me while taking the lift to my own office. But then, there's no lift in this wing of the building and no air conditioning, making the atmosphere humid and thick.

At the top of the fourth staircase, we were buzzed through a door in a wall of bulletproof glass (our bulletproof glass has no distortions), and there just ahead was the famous collection of policemen's hats from all over the world, gathered by French police who steal them right off the heads of other officers.

'I see many additions to the collection since my first visit,' I commented.

Emile smiled. 'The ones from the Soviet Union are real collector's items.'

We turned left and continued down the hall past the Chef's office whose door bore a special insignia. Emile's shoulders stiffened. Employees are always intimidated by the men who run their lives.

Emile's domain, a small square office with metal desks and a sitting area, is nicer than mine. He took off his jacket and loosened his tie as soon as we entered, and introduced me to four members of his group. The five others were out on assignments. He had given me a rundown of his group, most of whom he trusted, these four in particular.

Every group of ten investigators in the Prefecture takes the name of its leader, like we did at summer camp: I'm from Jack Sprat's Cabin, I'm from Billy Bob's, etc. I shook hands with the two men, Georges Maran and Lucien Beaulieu, and then two women, Solange Monod and Lillianne Reneau.

Emile told his co-workers about the wedding while I looked around the office. It was decorated with posters of classical concerts, a lecture series, an art exhibition, and no pinups – politically correct and squeaky clean. Only a poster of Clint Eastwood and a memorial plaque to a compatriot killed in action hinted at law enforcement. The name on the memorial plaque was that of a French officer who'd been assassinated by a Libyan terrorist who shot him from the Libyan Embassy and then claimed immunity. The French couldn't prosecute. Another reason to hate the Libyans.

Finally we got down to it.

'I told James about the case, and he asked to see the files. Does anybody object?'

No one did – to my face.

'Our group wants to keep jurisdiction over the Boardroom Killings,' Emile explained, as he placed the file on the table. 'That's why we need results.'

'It's the biggest case in French history,' said Georges Maran, a tall muscular blond with a youthful face. 'And we'll break it. We're the best in the Brigade!' A real team player.

'He's right,' Emile assured me, proud of his man. 'Of course, the Chef is closely involved.'

I could see they admired Emile. And I recognized a quality I see only in rookies – eyes alive with eagerness, enthusiastic optimism. In America, too many of us look defeated. And why not? By comparison, their caseloads were a piece of cake.

I caught a look between Solange Monod and Emile and knew in an instant that he was sleeping with her. A part of me didn't blame him. Solange Monod, in her early-thirties, was extremely tall and well built, with long legs and short brown hair that swung when she moved, and a lower lip that quivered. Her eyes held an expression of lust mixed with hero worship when she looked at him. What a turn on.

But screwing a co-worker is a bad idea. Work comes first and sex clouds judgement. Secondly, Emile and Claudine are hot together; he's always kissing her neck or touching her, as though they've just done it or are about to. Maybe that's the secret of infidelity: keep each woman thinking she's the one driving you crazy. She'll never suspect you're getting it elsewhere.

Sexual tension twanged between Emile and Solange like a guitar string playing one note. *Now! I want you now! I want you now!* I was jealous as hell.

'Assistant Inspector Monod has the reports on the third killing,' Emile said, taking the files from her. His eyes met mine and I saw several things. 'Don't tell

Claudine,' as if I would. 'Envy me a little,' which I did. And, 'if you even look at her, I'll rip your balls off.' He needn't have worried. As great-looking as she was, there was something calculating there too, and I feared she was with Emile because he was group leader. She assessed me to see if I was worth pursuing so I toned down my chemistry and raised a wall between us. She got the message. Men and women do things like that, use 'off limits' signs to let the other know there's no chance. She looked away.

Emile handed me the file. The pictures of a death scene are universal. A dead grandfather sprawled back in a swivel desk chair with his throat cut, blood all over him, on the floor and the desk. He too had been masturbating, fly open, semi-erect penis flopped to the side. It had remained engorged even after death. It reminded me of a snuff killing, almost as if it had been staged. Only victims of snuff killings were usually women or gay men.

'We've ruled out burglary as a motive in all three cases; nothing was taken,' Emile said.

'In Pierre Fontelle's office, the safe was open,' Georges Maran said. 'But according to the records, no important papers were missing.' They were eager to show off to me. I was circumspect for Emile's sake.

'I'll bet the killer took a souvenir,' I commented. 'They usually do.'

'We've been hoping an informant would come forward,' Lillianne Reneau told me. 'But none has.' She was short and athletic with a cleanly scrubbed face and sandy blonde hair in a pony tail.

'You won't get informants,' I told her. 'Psychopaths operate alone or with one accomplice, like the Hillside Strangler in Los Angeles. It makes your work more difficult not to have stoolies. In other cases, they're invaluable. We're always looking for new ones – people

47

on the periphery of an investigation who are unhappy and want to change their life. They'll become informers to get away from destructive influences. It also helps when I have something to bargain with. But not in cases like this.'

'There is no evidence that any of the victims was involved in drugs or the drug world,' Emile said.

'It figures,' I told him. 'These sickos don't need narcotics to make them crazy.'

The fourth member of the group spoke up, Lucien Beaulieu, dark-complexioned with thick straight black hair and a short stocky body. 'Do you think this man kills for pleasure like Americans?'

I shrugged. 'In America we've had even more sordid cases than this one, Jeffery Dahmer ate his homosexual victims and Chase drank their blood. Most serial killers will deface or decapitate their victims, or cut off their fingers to avoid identification, or for other reasons. Your killer hasn't gone over the edge yet, but he could at any moment.' I made a note of it for myself. 'He's fastidious and brilliantly careful. He doesn't get himself messy, he doesn't touch the victim afterwards, he covers his tracks like a trained spy.'

Emile sat up straighter. 'Maybe he's had military training?'

'Could be,' I agreed. 'He approaches this with diabolical intelligence. I'd say he's well educated.'

'Killing for pleasure is not the French way,' Reneau said.

'Except for the Mourmelon killings of young military officers, and the Old Lady murders in Paris,' I commented.

Beaulieu was surprised that I knew about French crimes.

'What kind of suspect should we look for with this

third victim?' Solange asked. She had a sexy voice, gravelly like an actress's.

'Go down your list. The killer is comfortable with office buildings, not intimidated by them. He blends into a cityscape. He travels easily. How did he get from Paris to Bordeaux? Cross match airline reservations and car rentals in both cities. Keep the pressure on; you have to break through the killer's deadly patience.'

She nodded.

Lucien spoke up. 'In the first two cases, the killer gained access to the victim's private office. Now he's entered a private residence without breaking in.'

'Someone opened the door,' I concluded.

He nodded.

'We've checked all the cleaning people at each location,' Emile said. 'Especially new employees.'

'Any leads?'

He shook his head.

'What about that smuggling case?' I asked. 'Wasn't one of the victims involved?'

'Pierre Fontelle,' Solange said. 'I questioned him two years ago, when I was with the Michel Leveque team. Customs in Marseille discovered a shipment of nuclear trigger devices stolen from the Soviet Union. They were being shipped through France to the Middle East. My partner Marcel Duroc and I spoke to Fontelle. He had government contracts and did business with Moscow. He was clean, but I wasn't fully convinced.'

'That's interesting,' I said. 'What made you suspicious?'

'Intuition,' she shrugged.

'Did you ever find out who smuggled the devices?'

'No.' She looked away but I saw an expression of pain in her eyes.

Emile continued, 'Solange's partner, Duroc, was killed in an automobile accident at that time.'

'That's when I transferred to the Emile Laurent group,' she said quietly.

'I'm sorry for your loss,' I told her. 'If I ever lost my partner, Ben, I don't know what I'd do. We rely on one another, finish each other's sentences.'

I thumbed once more through the photographs of the third killing. The victim was seated in front of a window that looked out on to a park-sized lawn. The room, a library, was handsome, typical French *boiserie* lining the walls.

'Before the murder in Bordeaux, we assumed the killer was Parisian,' said Lillianne. 'But why go to Bordeaux to kill elderly men when we have plenty here?'

'A good question.'

'And why this man? Patrick Richard is from an old Bordeaux family, one of France's leading business-men.'

That term set my teeth on edge. *Leading business-man* . . . everything I despised. To me it meant narrow-minded, fiercely clannish, autocratic, self-absorbed, and cruel. My exposure to one particular leading family had formed my opinion.

'A Richard has been head of their import-export company for generations,' Solange told me. 'Patrick Richard helped rebuild the export business after the war.'

Emile continued. 'He was honoured by the Association of Righteous Christians for rescuing the Jews of France during the war. Claudine and I attended the dinner. Richard and his father funded thousands of false passports for people escaping the Nazis.'

So there were a few good aristocrats in the world, but I hadn't met them.

'Any medications or drugs?' I asked.

'Beta blockers for his heart. And he had the same

50

mistress for thirty years; her family runs an inn near the coast. He left her money in his will, but I don't think she killed him for it by slitting his throat. There are easier ways. He had no known enemies.'

'What about his children?' I asked.

'Four sons and one daughter who lives in Switzerland. One son lives in Chicago, the other three had just arrived at the Richard summer home near St Moritz with their children for the summer. Richard was with them when he received a call. He said it was from his wife's nurse. She told him Madame had taken a turn for the worse. His children offered to go with him, but Richard said no, to stay with their families. If their mother died, they'd be needed at the funeral. But the nurse denies ever calling him. Madame was not worse.'

'He lied about it? That means that someone called him and he came all the way home because of it.'

'The killer?' Emile asked.

'Maybe. But serial killers don't usually know their victims. Unless he lured them to their deaths.'

'The Richard family lost both parents within a short time,' Solange said.

'But the wife was still alive right after the murder,' Emile told me. 'She died just last week. The nurse claims she never called Richard in St Moritz or asked him to come home, and the phone records show that no calls were made from Bordeaux to St Moritz that day.'

'Maybe someone impersonated the nurse,' I said.

'Or she lied and actually called Switzerland on a payphone?' Charles asked.

Emile checked the report. 'She has nothing to gain from his death. And she didn't have a car. The nearest phone is several miles away; besides, she couldn't leave her patient.'

'Who supplied the household with food?' I asked.

'The cook.'

'And how did Richard get to Bordeaux from St Moritz?'

'Took the train and then a taxi to his house. He arrived about nine o'clock, looked in on his wife, greeted the nurse, told her he was going to his office and not to disturb him. She was surprised to see him again so soon. Assumed he just didn't want to leave his wife. She found him dead in his office the next morning.'

In the photos, the exterior of the house was like a Texas mansion, a huge stone structure, three storeys tall, with a large front porch, situated in the wine country of Bordeaux behind iron gates on several acres of landscaped property.

'Are there groundskeepers?'

'Been with the family for years. They were off for the week while the family was away. The cook and her husband were in the servants' quarters. The nurse was with Madame Richard.'

'Anybody hear anything?'

'The nurse said she heard the television downstairs around midnight.'

'How did she know it was television and not people?'

'She heard music along with voices.'

'Anybody else hear or see anything?'

'The nearest neighbours are two kilometres away. But one of them heard a car drive past his house and turn up the road to the Richards' house, sometime around eleven.'

'Anybody see the car?'

'No. And there are no tyre prints or footprints either, coming or going.'

'Do you have the scientific report on hair samples, body fluids and fibres?'

Solange handed me the report. There were several samples of unidentified male and female hair found on the body. However, they didn't match in type and texture those found on the other victims. Leather and wood fibres had been scraped from under the finger-nails where Richard had dug them into the arms of the chair. The medical report noted that he was in a state of cadaveric spasm from dying so suddenly. They'd had difficulty prying his hand away from his penis. Must have been quite a surprise.

'One of his friends, or associates, or his mistress, knows something that could help you. What did the wife say?'

'Being ill, she didn't notice any change in routine. Her husband was in a good mood, he smiled and kissed her and told her about the grandchildren. She was glad to see him and didn't question him,' Emile said.

'Then he showed no signs of being called back to an emergency. You should talk to the nurse again,' I suggested. 'Keep digging.'

Lucien Beaulieu bristled. 'Do you think we've been sitting on our thumbs? We have witness testimony from the Richard case alone that fills five boxes. We are running out of storage space.'

'Then move the files to larger quarters, like a ware-house,' I said, shutting him up. 'All the evidence should be in one controlled location. Is it?'

'As of tomorrow,' Emile said apologetically. I guessed there were office politics at work.

'I'd like to see it all, when you have it assembled,' I told him. 'The clothing, the fibres, the hair.'

'Is there anything we haven't considered?' Emile asked, smoothing things over. 'What kind of psycho-path are we dealing with?'

'The classic profile is white male, mid- to late-twenties, educated, with probable mental instability. But this killer doesn't fit that description for several reasons. The primary one is that he's so controlled, he never goes beyond his plan.'

'He must be charming enough so that his victims let their guards down,' Solange stated.

Emile agreed. 'Otherwise there would be forced entries and signs of a struggle.'

'Most psychopaths kill to make themselves feel powerful. But this killer is physically strong,' I said, 'already powerful.'

'What about the sexual aspect?' Solange asked.

'The connection isn't clear, but it's there,' I told her. 'In this case, he uses the victim's pleasure to trap him. I've never seen that before. Yet he doesn't molest, either before or after.'

Emile concurred. 'There's been no semen samples present, other than the victim's, or pubic hairs found at the sites. Oral and anal swabs show no signs of sexual activity.'

'And why a steel scalpel as the murder weapon?' Lucien asked.

'You're sure it's a scalpel and not an artist's tool or architect's knife?' I asked.

'The metal fragments are refined steel,' Lillianne told me, 'the kind used in medical instruments.'

'Can you narrow down the manufacturer?'

'We're trying. Many companies use this steel for scalpels and sell them all over the world,' she replied.

'Keep at it,' I told her. 'It's good information.' Her expression softened with my praise. 'And remember, sexual fantasies are what drive multiple murderers to act,' I said. 'After a while the killer needs to elaborate on his fantasies, so he moves from straight killings to more horrible tortures to increase his kicks.'

'Why?' asked Solange, her voice subdued.

'Because the reality is never as great as the fantasy. Deranged minds can control themselves only for a while; their sick needs build up over time until they

54

explode and act out their horrible fantasies. I'm afraid these murders will continue and get worse.'

'Not if we stop him,' Lucien insisted.

Everyone was silent for a moment and I felt their collective determination as something real. If my presence focused their efforts, it was worth the trip.

Then I had an idea. 'How about if I check out Richard's nurse? I was planning to go to Bordeaux for some wine tasting, I could see her then.'

Emile went along. 'You mustn't give up your vacation for us.'

'I'd be glad to.'

His group was all for it. 'Well, if it isn't too much trouble,' he said, giving in.

'I'll need official sanction. Is there an officer in Bordeaux who speaks English?'

'Of course,' he said.

'In the meantime, I suggest you request additional officers from other groups in the Prefecture to help you cross reference all the victims' phone numbers. It's a big job.'

He nodded. 'We plan to do that, going back five years.'

'That's a good start,' I told him. 'Maybe you'll be lucky and turn up duplicate numbers.'

He agreed.

'Be sure to check all unsolved homicide records for at least five years back. You may find a matching phone number or a similar crime.'

Lillianne Reneau made a note in her personal notebook.

But even if some of the same numbers turned up, it didn't prove anything. We needed a common bond between the victims; that would be the key: their business associates, organisations, charities, church affiliation, real estate brokers, investment counsellors, employees, sexual partners. We had to narrow the field. In criminal investigations, the narrower the field, the more likely one was to solve the crime.

Suddenly my stomach told me it was time for lunch. I shook everyone's hand, and they wished me good luck.

Georges Maran seemed the most enthused about my trip to Bordeaux. 'Check in with us if you find anything.'

I agreed.

Clouds had gathered, cooling the humid air as Emile and I walked over the bridge to the Left Bank to have lunch at Chez Papa. We helped ourselves from the cold buffet. It reminded me of home.

'If I ask the department to pay for your trip, they will know I needed your help.'

'It's okay,' I told him, thinking I'd really have to stretch the budget now. 'I'll rent a car and drive down. I can use the time to clear my head.'

He nodded.

'How are you going to pay for the wedding?' I asked.

'I've been saving for years, and Claudine has been working in a boutique. It was worth it,' he announced, as though convincing himself.

'And what about Solange?'

He had that pleased-with-himself grin that says, Aren't I something? 'At first we just worked together, then I would see her at the gym. God, is she built! Then one day she looked at me with those eyes.' He shrugged. 'You know how it is. It won't last forever. Right now, it's wonderful. And I rely on her. She's sharp. If she wasn't a woman, she'd move up faster in the department.'

'Maybe she's using you to further her career.'

'Thanks a lot! Couldn't she want me for myself?'

I grinned. 'Sure, old fella.'

He laughed.

'Why didn't you find someone away from the job?'

'I work all the time.'

That was true. 'Is it hot with her?' I asked, feeling envious.

'What do you think?' He saw my expression. 'How is it with you and Victoria?'

Now it was my turn to shrug.

'That bad, eh? Doesn't she want to?'

'That's not it.' This was difficult to say. 'It's me. I've been having some problems lately.'

The look of shock in his eyes pierced me to the core. I never should have told him. 'Try someone else,' he said.

'I did. Yesterday. Same problem.'

He signalled to the waiter for more coffee, not meeting my eyes. Then he looked back at me. 'Swear to God you'll never repeat this?'

I nodded.

'It happened to me once, with Claudine.'

'What did you do?'

'It went on for months. I was okay with other women, but not with her. We tried everything. Nothing worked.'

'What happened?'

'I figured out that I was angry with her.'

'Why?'

'Because of the damned religion. I let her raise the children as Jews, but I was enraged at her for not being Catholic.'

'How did you get over it?'

'We fought it out, a terrible argument, both of us yelling, throwing things. Then she told me she understood how hard it had been for me, with my family against us and me not advancing in my job. She understood and she didn't blame me. I was the one blaming myself. What a relief it was to get it all out.

57

After that, we were better than ever, and that's saying something.'

'Victoria and I are both Methodists,' I told him.

'So it isn't religion. But you're angry about something else. Find out what it is.'

I didn't put any store by what he was saying. 'If you and Claudine are so hot, why Solange?'

'I'm not dead yet,' he laughed, as if that explained it. But I understood. Men craved sex from other women for many reasons, mostly for ego, to compete with other guys, to show how great they are because of who they can nail, and because they're conditioned to it from childhood. Especially when a woman as attractive as Solange comes on to them. Women are trophies. At least they are to my father's generation. But who was I to analyze it?

As we were waiting for the bill a silence grew between us. I looked away, conscious that Emile was watching me.

'Leave it alone,' I told him, turning back.

'I have no intention of bringing it up,' he insisted.

If only the damn bill had come right then and interrupted us, but it didn't. Instead, the unspoken subject sat between us like a pink elephant until my mouth formed the words I'd never planned. 'How is she, Emile? What have you heard?'

He looked me straight in the eyes and said, 'Nothing in years.'

Neither of us said her name, but it clamoured in the silence. *Catherine*. A hot flush crept up my face, turning my ears red, and something dormant awakened.

'You never heard from her?' he asked.

'You know I didn't!' I said, too sharply. 'Only from her brother, years ago.' This was the subject I had buried long ago, the one that being here in France was

58

bringing to the surface especially when I saw young, beautiful, blonde schoolgirls. If I hadn't buried it and kept it there, it would have destroyed me. It nearly ruined my friendship with Emile and Claudine when they took sides against me. I'd been screwed up for a year afterwards, first bumming around Europe and then in Senegal, haunted by what had happened. I only put it to rest when I came back to the States and joined the Bureau. There was no way I'd let it resurface now, though it was threatening to.

'I wrote to tell you that she married the heir to a barony.'

'Someone more suitable than I,' I couldn't resist. My guts twisted in spite of my resolve.

' . . .And that her parents were killed.'

'Yes.'

'I was never sure if I should tell you about it or not.'

'No, I appreciated the news.' Something in his face made me ask, 'Was there anything you left out?'

'No,' he said, turning down the corners of his mouth to indicate, Not at all. But still I wondered.

'What happened between her family and yours after I left France?'

'Now that's a subject *I* don't care to discuss, only that it was a relief that it hadn't been worse.'

'*A relief*?' I said, feeling my temper flare. As much as I liked him, in that moment I wanted to smash his face. There was no relief for me. Only a pain that ached so long, a part of me had mercifully gone numb. I was loth to let it regenerate.

'Listen, Emile,' I said, with great control. 'I'll help you with your case. I'll pay my own way. I'll even keep my work a fucking secret. But let's agree never to discuss Catherine d'Aumant again, okay?' I forced the words out through clenched teeth, pushing the memories back.

'Never again,' he said, holding up his hands in surrender and then offering to shake on it.

We shook.

He thanked me again for my help. But as I drove away in my rental car, that awful metallic sickness of loss washed over me again and I wished to hell I'd never brought up her name.

# Chapter 4

In July of 1974, the air was humid over south-western France; storm clouds gathered. I had only just arrived with the Laurents at their family's farm in Aquitaine when I first saw Catherine d'Aumant, a water nymph swimming in the river. It was after one of those five-course Provençal lunches; Claudine and Emile had supposedly gone to sleep, the children were with their relatives, so I went exploring.

The moist air was heavy with the sound of crickets, buzzing insects and an occasional combine driving along the road. There was a farm next to the Laurents' that advertised *foie gras*, this being the *foie gras* capital of the world. I walked past fields of sunflowers that reminded me of Van Gogh; in fact there were enough sunflowers growing in France to drive anybody crazy. But I felt more like Tom Sawyer than Van Gogh as I kicked up dirt in the country roads. Houston in the summer was like this, forests and farms teeming with verdant richness. But in my own backyard I knew what to expect: who would be blasting at cans, who would be fishing in the stream, who would be shooting hoops, who would be drinking beer and playing pool. Here I was alone with no point of reference, thousands of miles from home on a lazy summer afternoon and at a crossroads in my life. I had stayed out of the draft by drawing a fairly high lottery number, but I was torn about not going to Vietnam. I had wanted to join up right out of high school like so many of my buddies, but my brother Rob's death changed everything for me. Rob had died two years before, in 1972, and until then I'd never known the meaning of pain. Even two years later, I still wasn't over it.

Texas was hardly what you'd call liberal or anti-war in the late-sixties. In fact, I don't think the social revolution made an impact on us. We watched the rest of the country going crazy and shook our heads. We didn't have any hippies but we hated them anyway. And pot was for long hairs. Hell, we'd been drinking whisky since we were kids. Getting stoned didn't mean a thing.

What I was going to do with my life was a question I could not answer so I used all my savings from my jobs during college and came to Europe to postpone the decision, not for the culture. I needed to take my mind off my troubles.

I heard the river and smelled the water before I saw the Adour. And I remember feeling excited by the possibility of activities on the water, boating or swimming. For up 'til now this had not been a great French vacation: there were no topless women.

The drive from Paris had been interminable. Emile and Claudine bickered with Anne Marie and Guillaume as only families on vacation can do. I got carsick from sitting in the back seat between two squirming children on winding D roads; the only thing keeping up my hopes was the promise that I'd love the village of Eugénie les Bains. When I saw it, my heart sank with disappointment. It was the smallest town I'd ever seen, two short streets bisecting one another in the middle of farmland.

The local hotel, built that year, Prés d'Eugénie, was set back from the road down a long driveway; it was a huge fancy place that reminded me of a Southern plantation. Surrounded by a small forest of tall trees, it stuck out among the fields of vegetables like the top of a wedding cake. The rest of the town consisted of two *charcuteries*, a *coiffeur*, a *patisserie*, a *tabac*, a church, one café and a few pensions. Nothing else. Here I was, just out of college with the world ahead of me and stuck in nowheresville with no movies, no arcades, no stores, no schools, and no people, let alone women.

But as I stood on the bank of that river and watched a girl with long blonde hair swimming in the water, my disappointment vanished. Especially when she walked up the embankment to her towel and lay down in the sun, topless. My hard on shot up so fast it was like the ears of my German shepherd, Pottsie, when he heard a noise. 'All right,' I whispered.

I shaded my eyes and stared at her across the green water, aware that a family of swans floated by making the scene look like something out of 'Cinderella', which added to the enchantment.

Oblivious to me, she lay there sunning herself. I watched her, cursing my luck for being stranded on the other side of the river. But if I let her out of my sight long enough to find a way across the river, I was afraid she'd vanish and I'd lose her forever; if I swam across, I'd look ridiculous meeting her for the first time in wet clothes or my underwear. Little did I know that in this tiny hamlet of France, everyone knew everyone else; if she lived around here, I would see her again. But at that moment, I was in an agony of suspense. I vowed that if I was ever given a second chance with this vision, I'd be wearing my swim suit under my clothes. Finally, as the sun began to move and the shadows lengthened on the river bank, she got up, wrapped herself in her towel and disappeared into the undergrowth. One moment she was there and the next she was gone, an instant of sheer beauty vanished. I was transformed into total misery.

My mother used to sing a song, 'Have You Ever Seen a Dream Walking? Well, I Have'. Now I found myself singing it too.

I didn't ask anyone about her, thinking no one would know who she was. And the next day I went back again, to her side of the river this time. But first I familiarized myself with the area, the town, the surrounding fields, the farms, while I explored ways to get across the water. Being stuck in the sticks bothered me no more, I was going to meet a princess from a fairytale.

She didn't show up that day or the next. And then it rained. There is less than nothing to do in the country when it rains; by mid-afternoon the Laurent children were battering their heads against the farmhouse walls with frustrated energy and I wasn't much better. I played Monopoly with them and a French board game I didn't know, all the games of cards we could remember or invent, and then Claudine decided to teach us ballroom dancing. Even though she was a good ten years older than I was, dancing close to her turned me on. I was that desperate.

Even with my American Express discount travel coupons, the only car I could afford was a Renault with no radio and no air conditioning. But I'd brought my Walkman with me so I would be sweaty but accompanied by music.

Armed with a complete copy of Emile's files next to me on the seat, I took the autoroute south out of Paris through Orleans, the birthplace of St Joan, and then through Tours, the centre of château country. And I thought about the case.

*Why are you slitting the throats of old men, Shithead?*

*How did you find these victims? Did you drive around the city looking for them or did you find them while you were walking? How did you get them to let you in?*

I pictured him carrying a briefcase like an ordinary businessman, while he decided the fate of his victims. It must have made him feel powerful, like a god. Maybe he chose them from the financial section of the paper, or read about them in corporate reports. That meant he was smart enough to read corporate reports. He followed them to their offices late at night. But how the hell did he get them to masturbate in front of him?

Nothing about this case fit my expectations of serial killers, except that there were three dead victims. I felt I was swimming underwater in murky depths and at any moment I might run out of air. Just work this one like you work all the others, I told myself. Stick to the process. Tedium pays off. Have faith in your experience, it's all you've got. Remember: a killer is a killer in any language.

When I reached the city famous for its red wine, it was late-afternoon. I was so impressed with its stately beauty that I almost wished I could stay here and be a tourist. Caught up in the architecture and the difference between Bordeaux and Paris, I immediately got lost among the winding streets of the city and stopped to ask directions from everyone I could find while angry drivers honked behind me. Finally, I located the Prefecture and introduced myself to the officer on duty.

He pointed me to the third door on the right where I met Hector Berrault, my interpreter, a man in his late-fifties, trim and bald, with a moustache.

'Emile Laurent told me to expect you, Monsieur Barton,' he said. 'But it is very late. Perhaps we wait until tomorrow, no?'

'No,' I insisted. 'Chief Inspector Laurent is anxious for us to get to work.'

He nodded sadly, knowing his dinner would be late tonight.

He directed us out of town to the D1 road and within a few minutes we were in the vineyards of Margaux where we stopped to ask directions to the Richard residence.

The house was at the end of a long road among vineyards where enormous châteaux with world famous, exotic names dotted the miles of lush greenery. Iron gates stood at the end of a long gravel drive lined with tall hornbeam hedges. The driveway circled around a fountain in front of the enormous Mansard house of the photographs.

No one answered the bell so we circled the house. I took one direction, Hector took the other, and we converged on a back terrace that overlooked a garden shaded by weeping willows. The place was deserted.

We got back in the car and drove to the closest residence, a small house with a tiled roof, slightly set back from the road.

But when Berrault enquired about Madame Richard's nurse, we were told she had left after Madame died.

'The house is empty,' the neighbour told us, shaking his head sadly. 'The Richard family is planning to sell.'

These neighbours had been questioned by the police but had slept through the murder of Richard and didn't find out about it until morning. Being of a different social class, they were only acquainted with the family and knew nothing of their personal life.

'Where did the nurse go?' I asked, repeating the question twice because the man couldn't understand my pronunciation.

'Vivienne Doré?' the neighbour said. 'After the

funeral, she went home to Mont de Marsan.'

Berrault shrugged as if to say, A typical policeman's luck. 'Mont de Marsan is only a few hours from here,' he informed me.

It was too late to go there tonight. 'Can we get into Richard's house?' I asked Berrault.

The neighbour spoke up. 'I have a key,' he said, going to get it.

'We'll drop it off on our way back,' I told him.

We drove back up the long gravel drive and parked by the front door. The key was difficult to turn in the lock, but then we were inside the front hall where a smell like old cheese permeated the air and dust particles shone in the light streaming in from the lead glass transom above the doors. The electricity had been turned off but there were still several hours of daylight.

'The library is that way,' I said, orienting myself from the photographs and the outside tour of the house. We headed across the hall. There were the bay windows of the room I had admired in the pictures. I tried to imagine that I was the killer entering the room. Was I wearing gloves or did I put them on now? Was Richard seated already? Did we talk? What about? If Richard wasn't gay, how did I get him to masturbate? By talking dirty?

The desk and chair had been removed and the rug stripped from the floor. A black blood stain had soaked through the carpet and discoloured the oak boards. The view from the window was the same as in the photograph. Standing in the room, I was surrounded by tradition.

The books lining the wall smelled of old attics. Everything was dusty and the shelves needed polishing. But it was a handsome room. Everything was original, from the carved edges on the shelves to the plasterwork on the ceiling, to the brass chandelier. Framed family

67

portraits stood on a glass-fronted cabinet filled with more books. The fireplace contained an iron grate, the kind I'd seen in England. A set of brass utensils stood nearby. There was evidence of the police investigation; the bookcases had been dusted for prints. Areas were still circled in chalk where patient prints had been removed, including the controls on the television. But I noticed the VCR hadn't been dusted.

I took out my miniature magnifying glass, the one I always carry, with the plastic ring that attaches to my keychain. It's probably from a Cracker Jack box but it works. I'm starting to need glasses so I find myself using it more often.

I felt that familiar rush as I spotted something others had missed and motioned to Berrault to join me. There on the VCR eject button was a fingerprint outlined in blood. It was a smooth glove print, probably the right index finger, and attached to it was a piece of hair.

'This is the victim's blood and hair,' I said, not wanting to breathe on it lest I dislodge the hair which hung precariously. 'The killer's hands were bloody when he removed a videotape from the machine after he killed Richard. That's how he got the man to masturbate; a videotape.'

'I can't believe we missed that!' Berrault said.

'Send someone over right away,' I told him.

He nodded.

I was thrilled to have found something. But it meant the French police weren't doing their job, hardly reassuring.

We continued to check the house until the outside light began to fade.

'We could visit Richard's mistress now,' I suggested, and Berrault agreed. We dropped off the key at the neighbour's house and told him the police would be back later.

Anne Duxelle owned an inn on a hill overlooking the village of Taussat, on a bay just inland from the Atlantic Ocean. Sitting on her terrace we sipped aperitifs of peach liqueur and champagne while she talked about her former lover.

'Patrick and I were involved for over eighteen years,' she said, brushing a strand of once red hair off her forehead. Madame Duxelle was in her late-sixties with a plump body that was still lush and green eyes that had not forgotten how to flirt. 'He was not the type to experiment, but he had passion. Then I got too old to interest him any more.'

'Did he take up with younger women?' I asked.

She shook her head and turned away to hide the tears that had sprung to her eyes. 'No, he was too old to find someone else. And so was I. It was a sad time for us. I miss him. He was generous with me.'

'Madame,' I said, 'please don't be offended by this next question, but I must ask it. Did Monsieur Richard ever watch sexual tapes or masturbate in front of you?'

A heightened colour rose to her cheeks. 'By the saints, *non*!' And then she added slyly, 'He didn't need that when I was around.'

I smiled at the twinkle in her eyes. 'I'm sure he didn't,' I told her. And then added, 'I have a feeling he missed you too.'

There was something sad about an old man watching a porno tape and using the old right hand as the only act of pleasure left to him. And then to die in the middle of it was really cruel. I still had the feeling that something about it was staged. Maybe Shithead was involved in the theatre or films. I made a note of it.

Hector Berrault and I drove back to Bordeaux. He recommended a hotel and we arranged to meet in the morning.

At Café L'Hydelis I ordered a first course of snails

and then a brochette of shrimp, and was asleep in my hotel by ten o'clock. But somewhere around three in the morning I woke up sweating. A dream had awakened me – a dream about Catherine d'Aumant. It was obvious why. Tomorrow I was going to Mont de Marsan to see Richard's nurse, and that's where Catherine and I used to go. Even though I fought it, I was being drawn back.

When I finally saw her again, she was on what I now thought of as my side of the river while I was on hers. But this time I was prepared; I'd left towels on both sides, just in case.

I stripped down to my suit and waded into the water, hoping that the noise would draw her attention. But she either slept or ignored me. I swam across the river, trying to look cool as I climbed out, slipping on the mud and the reeds at the water's edge.

What would she think of me? I wondered. Would she find me appealing? The girls back home always did, said my blue eyes were like Paul Newman's and that I had a killer smile. I'm tall like my father, just over six foot, and I have his square jaw and wavy black hair; my nose is short like my mother's, though mine is wider across the bridge. And right then, as I looked down at my flat stomach, I was glad I'd carried on distance running instead of giving it up my last year.

The sight of her breasts made the heat rush to my groin. To keep my hard on from embarrassing me, I filled my mind with disgusting thoughts like rotten food or vomit.

She heard me approaching and sat up, gazing at me with eyes the colour of the sky above the Caribbean. She was young, but a nude girl without makeup could be any age at all, either sixteen or twenty-five. I wasn't good at judging.

'*Bonjour*,' I said.

'*Bonjour, ça va?*'

'May I sit down?' I asked, in English.

She nodded, looking up and shading her eyes. 'You are the *Américain* staying at the Laurents'?' Everybody knew everybody around here. She spoke perfect English with an accent. I forced myself to stare at her face and not at her chest, to appear nonchalant, but I couldn't take my eyes off her breasts. They were so there, like two small creamy pears with peach-coloured nipples. Her body was gorgeous too, I couldn't avoid it, not that I wanted to. How do the men in this country keep their sanity with these naked women around all the time? I wondered. What are the statistics on rape? Surely this casual nudity encouraged depraved behaviour? Before I arrived in France, I'd heard that there were topless women all over the beaches on the Riviera so I was dying to go there, and when I discovered that the Laurents weren't going to that part of France, I was bitterly disappointed. I assumed that toplessness was exclusive to the area between Monte Carlo and St Tropez and that I'd never see any of it. I never dreamed that nudity was endemic to all of France. Was I delighted!

I had never conversed with a nearly nude stranger before. (Her bikini bottom barely covered her.) Part of me knew she was just a nice, gorgeous, ordinary French girl, and the other part of me thought she'd been placed on this earth solely for my raging hormones and to relieve my boredom. Like a gift from God.

'You know who I am but I don't know who you are,' I said. An asinine approach. I went to retrieve my towel where I'd left it in the crook of a tree and spread it on the wild grass next to her, staring at the river instead of her.

'I'm Catherine d'Aumant,' she said, offering her hand.

We shook. I looked at the trees over her head, she avoided my eyes altogether. I thought she said '*Charmant*'. To the unpractised ear, they were close.

'*Charmant* to meet you, Miss Charmant,' I said.

She turned away unamused; my heart sank. 'Do you come here often?' As if I didn't know.

'Yes, it's my spot for the summer.'

'Exclusive?' I asked.

'This part of the river is ours.'

'Oh.' I assumed she meant her farm was the one beyond the trees.

I had no idea what to say to a naked girl. My cheeks burned with desire. All I wanted to do was reach out and touch those upturned breasts with the peach-coloured nipples. I'd never seen such a beautiful girl before. She was Catherine Deneuve, with a mole above her left breast that my mouth watered to kiss. 'Have you lived here long?'

'Of course.'

We had nothing in common but our hormones.

'What are you reading?' she asked, assuming that I, like everyone else in France, read. At least I was literate. '*The Greening of America* and *The French Lieutenant's Woman*, by John Fowles. He wrote *The Magus*.'

'It's a mystery, isn't it?'

I nodded. 'Of sorts.'

'While you're in France, you should read Georges Simenon, the Maigret series,' she offered.

'I have,' I admitted. 'I like reading about detectives. The family I'm staying with, he's with the French police.'

'I know,' she said.

'Is there a cinema near here?'

72

'In Aire sur L'Adour,' she told me. 'They're playing Truffaut's "The Wild Child". I really want to see it.'

'Perhaps I could take you?' I suggested.

'You're quick, just like an American,' she said, laughing. It sounded like little bells.

Sitting on a French provincial river bank and talking about shared experiences with a nearly nude girl was the most sophisticated thing I'd ever done. 'Are you in school?'

'*Au Suisse*,' she said. 'Near Lausanne. I go to university next year, perhaps in Avignon. Right now, I'm in first year of Terminale.'

*Oh God, she was in high school. Jailbait!*

'When I'm in school I get homesick for Eugénie les Bains. Then, when I'm here, I miss my friends at school.'

'What is there to do around here for fun?'

'There are dances and parties and a disco at Mont de Marsan. A group of my friends and I go there sometimes. And there are many villages nearby, each with their own character. Some have summer fêtes.' She noticed that I hadn't stopped staring at her and her expression grew wary. I tore my eyes away.

'In America it is different, yes? They do not sunbathe.'

'Not topless they don't,' I told her, sounding both boastful and pejorative which was not what I felt. In fact, sitting here like this, I could see how stupidly we Americans behaved. The whole world should be topless. Especially if they all looked like Catherine.

She reached into a basket by her side, pulled out a white T-shirt, drew it over her head and stuck her arms into the armholes.

'You didn't have to do that,' I insisted, crushed with disappointment and hating myself.

'I think it is better.'

'My name is James,' I told her. 'James Barton. But some of my friends call me Jimmy.'

'I like James better. Like 007.'

We both thought that was terribly funny.

And then I wasn't sorry she'd put on her shirt, for now I could look into those incredible blue eyes without distraction. Her long blonde lashes lay across her cheeks when she blinked and her mouth had a pouty bottom lip that begged to be chewed on. My eyes travelled over her slender muscular body and I appreciated every inch of her. She was like a gazelle. Then I met her gaze and she gave me a Madonna smile, quiet, peaceful, serene. She reached out and touched my nose.

'You're getting sunburned.'

Out of her bag she produced a bottle of Ambre Solaire, offering it to me.

'Can you see where I need it?' I asked, opening it and handing it back to her. *Cool move, Barton.* For the next moment her small delicate hand was filled with fragrant oil and touching my body, my shoulders, my forehead, my back. Already, this was the best summer of my life.

# Chapter 5

The next morning, Berrault and I visited the offices of Richard Import-Export to re-question everyone on the chance that they'd remembered something new since the murder. Three secretaries, two vice-presidents, four sales managers, and an account executive had no knowledge that Patrick Richard watched porno tapes. To some, he was a kind old gentleman, to others a son-of-a bitch. But no one could understand why he was killed nor offer a suspect.

On our way out, Berrault said, 'Speculation at the Prefecture is that a pimp killed Richard, or a whore, or a crazy person.' He gave me a smile of apology. 'I'm not being much help.'

It was lunchtime when we left Bordeaux and drove through the pine forests with their strangely denuded and slender trunks, joining the autoroute which turned into the N134.

Mont de Marsan hadn't changed much since I was there in 1974. But that's not unusual. There are parts of France that haven't changed since the Middle Ages. And neither have the people. There is still a strong delineation between the classes here. It's nearly impossible for the low-born to rise in the social hierarchy. The old rich are different from you and me.

As far as small French cities go Mont de Marsan is unremarkable except for its modern museum in an ancient abbey and its Roman ruins. But suddenly, like Proust from the bottom of a teacup, my memories were awakened by the scent of the nearby pine forest where they tap resin from the trees. It brought Catherine back so clearly my heart contracted. This time I couldn't force her away.

Everywhere I turned, I saw her: sitting in a café, standing in front of the bullring in her yellow summer dress, clapping her hands with excitement as a straggling brass band of boys in red shirts marched by. To her that band was a big deal, to me it was a sorry little display; after all, I'd been to New Orleans at Mardi Gras and the Superbowl at the Dome. But that insignificant little parade became grand to me through her eyes. Everything seemed new.

The air was misty and cool after a day of rain, the city quiet before the summer influx of tourists arrived. By mid-July there would be parades of people dressed in medieval costumes, and brass bands of boys trying to please the crowd. Tickets to the horse races or the bull fights in the local modern arena would be hard to get.

It had surprised me to discover that there were bull fights in France, I'd thought it an activity exclusive to Spain. But the region had an ancient history and an interesting mix of people as well as pastimes, even though in France they don't actually kill the bull the way they do in Spain, merely pick at it. The day we went to the fights, Catherine had stood with the crowd and shouted 'Olé' with each veronica; I had been so proud to have her by my side.

'Anything wrong?' Hector asked when I stopped abruptly and stood still.

'I'm fine,' I told him. But my hands were shaking.

Hector insisted we eat lunch before visiting Vivienne Doré and I agreed. We ate at the Hôtel Le Midou, named for the local river, a typical French meal of *pâté*,

76

*Andouillet* in wine sauce, a selection of cheese, a half litre of wine, and *Mousse au Chocolat*. After that heavy meal, I could feel my eyes drooping, so we sat in the lobby for a brief rest and both of us fell asleep.

I dreamed of Catherine again. The two of us were swimming underwater in the depths of a bottle green river, encircling one another like a pair of dolphins. We kissed; her submerged body felt cold and clammy. Then she became entangled in the reeds and I lost her. I swam towards her trying to reach her; again and again I tried to free her until my lungs were bursting. She was always out of reach. I could see her limbs, stark and white, diffused by the murky water and reeds, her blonde hair waving in the current, the look of terror in her green eyes which were the colour of the water. She was terrified because a man was looking down at us from above the water, his features enlarged and distorted. *It was Shithead.* He was going to cut my throat. I heard his laughter, saw his cold grin. But I couldn't see his face.

I awoke with a shudder, forgetting where I was, and then that awful sick feeling washed over me, the sickest feeling I've ever known – that someone had just died.

*Forget it, Barton! She's in the past, long gone. Keep your mind on business.*

I could not let her haunt me again.

We found Vivienne Doré, Madame Richard's former nurse, working in a local hospital. She was on duty so we had a cup of coffee in a nearby café until she could see us.

'You have many new technical advances in America, yes?' asked Berrault, stirring his espresso.

I nodded. 'But you have a MiniTel informational computer in every home.'

'That's nothing compared to your new program for re-creating testimony. I was reading about it,' he said.

'You mean the one that illustrates on screen what the witness has described? You're right, it's amazing. The murder scene is pictured from every angle,' I told him. 'It's helpful in front of juries.'

The idea impressed him so, he wouldn't let me pay for our coffee.

Vivienne Doré was in her early-sixties, plump, grey hair pulled back behind her ears, wearing a French nurse's uniform of white with blue trim.

At the mention of Madame Richard, her eyes filled with tears. 'It is better she's with God than living with the memory of that terrible murder. How could such a thing happen to Monsieur Richard? The work of a demon! Every day I see people who are sick. I see them bleeding, too. But this was different. Just hours before, I spoke to him. And then I found him with blood all over his body, all over the floor. *Mon Dieu*, so much blood! I shall never forget it.' She wiped her eyes with a handkerchief.

'Mr Richard paid you well?'

'Oh, yes,' she insisted. 'Private jobs pay better than regular nursing, especially for a woman my age who cannot work long hours. Madame Richard was such a dear woman.'

'What were your duties?'

'To care for her, poor soul. I brought her meals from the kitchen, gave her medication, a bath. She liked me to brush her hair.'

'Do you know that Monsieur Richard told his family you called him in Switzerland and asked him to return to Bordeaux because of Madame?'

'I didn't call him,' she said, her eyes growing wider. 'Poor man, he needed a rest. But he couldn't stay away. His conscience, you know. He was devoted to her. The Richard house was a quiet place to work.'

'Except for the television. Do you watch television?' I asked.

'Sometimes.' She shrugged. 'The night of the murder, Monsieur was watching a tape.'

'How do you know that?' I asked, glancing at Berrault in triumph.

'There were no advertisements. I don't like advertisements, they interrupt the programme and they are too loud. I have to turn down my hearing aid.' She pointed to the flesh-coloured amplifier in her ear.

'Did Monsieur Richard often watch his VCR?'

She nodded. 'He bought it several months ago.'

'Do you know what he watched?'

She shook her head.

I referred to her statement. 'You told the police that you went to sleep after midnight.'

'I gave Madame her medication at midnight and then I retired in the next room from Madame.'

'One of the neighbours heard a car approach the house at eleven. Did you hear it?'

She shook her head. 'I might have been dozing in my chair,' she said with embarrassment. 'But then something woke me up. Like a door closing.'

'Describe the sound,' I asked her.

'It sounded like a car door, an expensive car,' she said. 'A solid sound. *Whunk*!' She smiled as though this was a game. 'I could have been dreaming. I've always wanted a car to sound like that.'

'Don't we all?' I agreed. 'But you didn't see a car?'

'No.' I could tell she wanted to help me.

I thanked her for her time and instructed her to contact Emile if she remembered anything else.

As I closed the door of my Renault, I realized how different car doors sound, especially cheap ones compared to expensive models.

And then something popped to the surface of my brain. I reached into the box and read the fibre reports again. Fibre samples not belonging to the victims were found on each of the bodies. The perpetrator always leaves some evidence on the victim and takes some away with him. But a careful killer will wear coveralls over his clothes so as not to leave microscopic evidence behind.

But Shithead didn't wear coveralls. On Fontelle's body, they found dark brown wool fibres that didn't belong. On François Sourais, they found beige wool gabardine fibres as from a Burberry raincoat, and on Richard they found black wool mohair fibres commonly used in men's overcoats. All were from expensive clothing. More proof that the killer was wealthy. And well dressed. He'd worn a different outfit each time. I would too, if I'd got blood on my clothes. Had he taken those bloody clothes to the cleaners or could he afford to toss them? I made a note to tell Emile to check with all the dry cleaners in Paris and Bordeaux with a description of the three items of clothing.

Shithead had killed all three people; we knew because the modus operandi was the same. Poor people did not wear Burberry or mohair overcoats and their cars did not make a solid sound when the doors closed. The profile was getting narrower.

Hector Berrault planned to stay overnight in Mont de Marsan and I was going back to Paris so we parted company. But as I approached the autoroute, I somehow took a wrong turn and found myself heading in the opposite direction. When I saw the sign to Aire sur L'Adour, my heart started to pound.

It's only an hour from here to Eugénie les Bains, I thought. Why not take a look?

*Turn around!* A voice shouted in my head, and I tried to slam on my brakes in the middle of the road –

but the car kept going. *Don't do this, James. Don't do it.* I kept on driving.

The familiar landscape made my pulse race as though I was in an action movie accompanied by a musical score that added to the suspense. There's no danger on these country roads, I kept telling myself. But my pulse pounded in my ears as the miles clicked by.

I was driving much too fast through unfamiliar hamlets and landmarks. I was lost. You're not supposed to find it, I told myself. Fate is protecting you.

Then, unexpectedly, I came over the crest of a hill, dropped down an incline, and there was the miniature village of Eugénie les Bains before me – sleepy, innocent, and evil. The location of my personal hell.

Hyperventilating, I shot down the hill and on an impulse yanked the car left and into the gate of Prés d'Eugénie, my tyres squealing. Serenity surrounded me as I applied the brakes, driving more slowly down the tree-lined driveway of Michel Guerard's famous auberge and restaurant.

The place had changed; it was even bigger and more sparkling than when I'd first seen it. It had intimidated me then and I'd gaped at the magnificent grounds and the stately columns of the chalk white buildings. It didn't intimidate me any more, but the memories did.

Christ, I was terrified.

I sat there facing the entrance watching handsome guests at outdoor tables sipping aperitifs, walking through the lobby in towelling robes after the spa or the pool. I envied them their prosperity and privilege. Money still separated us.

I parked my car and took a deep breath before walking down that long flagstoned walkway to the front entrance. At the desk I asked for a brochure of the rooms, pretending to be a legitimate guest. The sweet

81

smile of the clerk in her starched pink dress made it seem possible, until I read the prices. Then I became an imposter and headed for town, such as it was. One and a half streets in all.

Walking back down the long wooded driveway wasn't too difficult. No ghosts jumped out, no pain twisted my guts until I reached the town. The driveway ended at the centre which now sported two cafés on the minuscule main street; civilization had arrived. I walked over to the one I remembered and went inside. Nothing had changed; even the man behind the bar with the droopy handlebar moustache was the same, only older.

It was a small whitewashed room with a mahogany bar, a case of pastries, liquor on display and a few tables, some of them occupied. I half expected the six people sitting there to turn and say the French equivalent of: 'He's ba-ck!' But no one did.

I ordered coffee at the bar. The man with the handlebar gave it to me and I carried it to a table. *Now what?*

*Prove that this place has no hold on you.*

Well, here I was where I'd found my greatest pleasure and most agonizing pain. And I was meeting it head on, putting it to rest.

What if Catherine walked through that door right now? My heart leaped at the thought. What would she be like? Seventeen years old, wearing a light summer cotton dress, and she'd sit down opposite me. Then, in a breathy Melanie Griffith voice (which she didn't have, but I now attributed to her), tell me she'd never stopped thinking of me, missing me, wanting me back. Seeing me again made her delirious with happiness. Somehow her husband had conveniently disappeared along with my wife, and there was no obstacle in our way. The two of us would walk off

82

into the sunset, after fucking our brains out.

I sat there for an hour but Catherine never came.

Finally, I called Emile on the payphone in the small hotel next-door and told him about my conversation with the nurse and what I'd found at Richard's house. And also my rich man theory.

'You've come up with more in two days than we have in a year,' he told me. I didn't believe him, but it helped the ego.

'It's excruciating to know there will be more deaths before we've fitted the pieces together. There was a meeting this morning with the Chef and the Minister about warning the public. They discussed issuing a bulletin to men over sixty not to go to their offices alone at night.'

'You would panic the cities, and he would change his pattern, Emile,' I cautioned.

'I said so too. We decided to wait a bit longer.'

Something else was at the corner of my mind, just out of reach. Hopefully, it would come. 'If you don't need me in Paris, I'd like to stay here overnight,' I told him, letting him think I was still in Mont de Marsan while I was really spending the night in my own haunted house.

'Just keep in touch,' he said as he hung up.

Monsieur Alfonse Larousse, *proprieteur*, the man with the handlebar moustache, knew of a room to let in the home of a relative down the road. '*Pas cher*,' he assured me. Cheap! My kind of place.

Madame Cretier lived at the end of the main street in a converted stable. She was at home and showed me a room above her garage, formerly the carriage house. The thick walls, made of the same brick and plaster as all the buildings in this area, kept the room cool even though the weather was warm. It had a new bath and its own entrance down a narrow wooden staircase. A crucifix above the bed, a dresser and a table were the only furnishings.

She didn't seem curious about me. It was customary for her to rent this room to strangers. There weren't many inexpensive places to stay in this hamlet and Europeans are always on a budget, especially the English.

The natural baths at Eugénie are a popular attraction though I have no idea why and personally would avoid those foul-smelling, muddy pits reeking of sulphur. The average visitor to the area couldn't afford the prices at Prés d'Eugénie, any more than I could, a hotel that looked like an expensive country villa and charged as much. Except for the new inn next door which Guerard also owned, Le Couvent des Herbes, the hotel had no competition for miles around.

The town had been made famous by the Empress Eugénie who used to come with her entourage for her *fortifiant*. But I could see by the wine bearing his name, the cookbooks on sale, the ownership of the two local hotels, and the *charcuteries* proclaiming his method of preparation, that the fame of Monsieur Guerard's cuisine and his persona was well on the way to supplanting that of a former empress.

I went to sleep easily, fatigued after so much tension, but awoke intermittently, feeling Catherine's presence more strongly than I'd allowed it in years.

The next morning I took a jog and then a long drive over familiar lush country roads which brought back more memories of the two of us bicycling along side by side, or picnicking in these fields.

I passed through the village of Duhort-Bachen on the way to Aire sur l'Adour and then circled back. Without meaning to, I found myself at the entrance to Castelle d'Aumant and stopped the car, looking up the long road which eventually ended at the *castelle*. Just seeing the gates twisted my guts. It was the most I'd allowed myself to feel in years and I discovered tears on my cheeks. Jesus, what an idiot, sitting here like some old lady and bawling. But my stubborn streak ignored the derisive voice inside. *Are you just going to sit here?* I asked myself.

*Yes*, came reply.

And remember.

What would she be like now? She'd been married longer than I. Any children? Was she happy? Probably. And nothing like I remembered; maybe she was fat with a hairy mole on her chin. No way. Catherine d'Aumant would still be gorgeous, she was only thirty-five. And I bet her brother Paul was still running her life. I tested the sore place to see if I still hated him. Yes. A stab of rage rushed through me. He was more to blame than anyone for keeping us apart.

Then I drove back to my room, parked my car and walked to the café to call Emile.

'We got the report on the blood and hair sample taken from the VCR,' he announced right away. 'They were Richard's. We're checking with all the porno dealers in Paris and Bordeaux, cross matching credit card payments.'

'I'd give anything to know what tape he was watching,' I told Emile. 'I'll bet it wasn't rented from a legitimate dealer.'

'Black market?'

'Yes. Maybe even a snuff film,' I told him.

'How are you doing?' he asked me.

'I'm okay. Doing some catching up.'

'There's no need for you to hurry back until we have something on a porno tape,' he said. 'And we're still checking the phone records.'

'I'll call in the morning,' I told him, disconnecting. Then I went inside the café and ordered the plat du

85

jour, *Carré d'Agneau*. This was actually becoming a vacation; I was winding down. Maybe I should stay another day and think about Victoria, come to some conclusions about our lives.

I gazed out of the side window of the café that looked out over the fields behind the town, waiting for my salad to be served. And then the most extraordinary thing happened.

Through the open window I caught a whiff of strawberries so fragrant and fresh I could almost taste them. My mouth began to water just as a teenage girl carrying a box of berries walked by. She glanced in at me and our eyes met. My heart stopped. It was the girl from the museum in Paris! But it couldn't be! This time I saw how extraordinarily beautiful she was. She had long flaxen hair, eyes the colour of morning glories and a mouth shaped like one of the berries in her box. Just a glimpse of her made my blood pressure shoot up, and then she was gone. *Catherine!* I thought, and almost called out her name.

But she wasn't Catherine. Catherine was a woman now. And their features were not the same, neither was their hair. Catherine's hair was honey blonde, this girl's was the colour of moonlight. Being in this town again was making me hallucinate, creating Catherine out of every French girl in the province, and every French girl into the one who had flirted with me. *Barton, you're an asshole!*

Voices from the kitchen interrupted my thoughts. A woman, probably the wife of the owner, and the girl. I caught the words '*fraises des bois*', those tiny wild strawberries, one of my favourite dishes, and something I'd only eaten here in France. The girl must be from a local farm, making her delivery. A young man brought me my wine and I asked him if he had *fraises des bois* on the menu tonight.

86

He nodded.

I had an urge to sneak into the kitchen for another look at the girl, but of course I didn't. Instead I looked out the window, expecting her to walk by, when something made me turn.

She was standing in the doorway looking at me exactly as she had in Paris, her head tilted to the side, one arm behind her back holding the elbow of the other, her feet planted apart. This time there was no mistake and I marvelled at the coincidence. The odds must be incredible that I'd see the same girl in Paris and here in this tiny town. But it had happened. And she recognized me too, finding it also surprising and intriguing.

The setting sun was directly behind her, shading her face, but I could see her body clearly through the cotton of her white dress – too clearly: the long slender legs, the delicate bone structure, a wisp of a waist and small breasts. She was in her mid-teens, achingly young, her whole life ahead of her, just as Catherine's had been.

Then she turned sideways, blocking part of the light, and I could see her face. It was oval-shaped with a slightly pointed chin, high cheek bones, a button of a nose and widely set eyes which held the most startling expression, both innocent and knowing. She lowered her chin and gazed at me, moving her blonde hair back over her shoulder in a movement women have made since they were created. She was exquisite, even more beautiful than Catherine. She gave me the kind of smile that unnerved me. Either she was flirting with me or I wanted her to. And I remembered how she'd affected me before.

And then she was gone.

The moment was so intense, so personal, so mysterious, I suspected that I had conjured her up. Except that later on, after my dinner, the waiter brought me a delectable bowl of *fraises des bois*, and with each delicious bite I could see her face, gazing at me.

That night as I lay in bed the memories would not stop. I had not allowed them in for eighteen years. Maybe it was time.

Catherine and I fell into the habit of spending our afternoons together, since my mornings were spent with the children giving them their English lessons. Or else I'd sit at the Laurents' kitchen table and help Emile tie fishing lures. Early each morning he went fishing and then again, late in the afternoon, rain or shine, but he couldn't interest me in it because all I could think about was seeing Catherine.

The Laurent farm had been in the family for generations. Emile's two brothers ran it, along with their ageing father. Wives, cousins and relatives made up their extended family. At first they seemed proud of their Parisian connections. Within days, old prejudices came forth, however, and all was not so cordial.

Sometimes I'd stop by the café on my way to see Catherine where Emile held court with his boyhood friends and his brothers, talking about the cases he had solved or the ones he was working on. I was always struck by the differences between these Frenchmen and us Texans. We slap each other on the back while the French kiss a lot; and in the provinces they kiss even more, three or four times as they greet you, instead of twice.

Their rapid conversations went over my head so I'd study their body language, the way they used their fingers for emphasis, tapping on the chest to get attention or wagging a finger to point out foolishness. And both hands gestured as they talked, mostly about politics. If they passed one another in the car, they'd hold their hand to their jaw, thumb at the ear, little finger to the mouth, three middle fingers pulled in tight, mimicking a phone receiver to say, 'Call me.'

Other mornings I'd take the children for a walk or we'd go riding, then I'd raid the refrigerator, pack a picnic lunch and set out for the river. Somedays Catherine would bring the picnic. And always we shared a bottle of wine. Bless the French.

The wine that Catherine brought rarely had a label on it, merely a number; I assumed it was from her family cellar. But no wine since has ever tasted that good. The food I brought was pedestrian, *saucisson*, sliced rabbit or leftover lamb, fruit and cheese, preferably grapes or peaches. Nothing elaborate. When she brought lunch it was prepared exquisitely, and usually she'd have to explain what it was: open-faced sandwiches of cold lobster *en gêlée* with arugula on rich light brown bread served with three kinds of mustards in earthenware crocks; vegetable or goose *pâtés*; slices of white stuffed veal; pieces of endive filled with chopped wild mushrooms and goat's cheese; and exotic fruits like mango, kiwi, figs or blood oranges. And *fraises des bois*. Many of these foods were new to me, but I took to them right away, assuming this was how her mother cooked, with five star quality.

We had been meeting for a week before I noticed how often I heard not only the Laurents but the townspeople mentioning the name d'Aumant. Usually it was in reference to crops or percentages of payment on the harvest. I assumed the d'Aumants were part of a co-op.

I suppose it's typical for a young man in love, especially one as cocky as I was, to assume that the object of his infatuation shares his social and cultural background, or else he would feel threatened. So I ignored the signs that she was more cultured than I, and assumed she had been put on this earth merely for my delectation. I was superior, but I also aspired to her attentions.

And what attentions they were. Her smile made me feel invincible and the touch of her hand sent shivers through me and a throbbing sensation to my prick. And any opinion we didn't share, she'd drop immediately. The girl was perfection. I was one lucky man.

It felt as if everything we did had never been done before. No one but us had ever swum in a river, climbed up a hillside, jumped on the back of a hay truck just to see where it would take us. I appropriated a bicycle from Emile's brother and we rode for miles, past the fields of sunflowers which eventually became fields of corn, past the vineyards filled with ripening grapes that traversed the hillsides, by the pastures filled with gentle pale Charolais cows who ambled over to see us, and through small villages of no more than ten houses and a church. Catherine had biked all of her life and kept up with me no matter how steep the terrain.

As we spent more time together without making love, tension mounted along with my desire. All I had dared to do so far was to give her lingering looks, shy smiles, chaste kisses on the cheeks, and hold her hand, reminding myself that she was young. Of course, every centimetre of her body was etched in my brain, especially her breasts, since I studied them in detail whenever we went swimming; they were all I dreamed about at night. Anticipating the moment each day when she'd pull off her T-shirt and I'd see them gave me blue balls. And the thought of touching them made me come.

I ached to hold her, to taste her kisses, to lick the salt off her skin slick with sweat after a long bike ride, to stick my tongue into her mouth right at the moment when she came up for air after swimming under water.

And most of all, I wanted to be inside her, feel that miraculous sensation, become one with her. I'd even picked out the perfect spot, behind the Laurent barn. The ideal time would be when everyone was taking their afternoon nap.

And then I'd remember that none of this was possible. Catherine was only seventeen – in America, that was definitely illegal. For Christ's sake, what was I to do?

It was she who finally settled the problem a few weeks after we'd met. That particular day we had ridden north to have a picnic among the trees and had chosen a hilly region, wild and untamed, where tall trees grew in profusion. We spread our blanket on the soft grass and decomposing leaves, and after lunch I put 'our song' in the tape deck: 'I Feel Like Making Love', by Roberta Flack. Portable tape players were larger and more cumbersome then; I dragged my ghetto blaster everywhere. That summer we listened to Elton John's 'Greatest Hits', and 'Band On The Run' by Paul McCartney and Wings. But it was Roberta's love song that expressed what I felt for Catherine.

As the notes faded away we gazed into each other's eyes, trying to show each other how we felt. Then, out of nowhere, Catherine said, 'Is there something wrong with you, James?'

'What do you mean?'

'You don't want to make love to me.'

I was so stunned, I couldn't reply. And as I sat there stupefied, searching for something to say, her eyes filled with tears and she turned away.

Quickly, I took her hand. 'You'll never know how much I want to, more than anything in the world. But you're too young. You're still at school and I've graduated from college.'

'Here the age of consent is sixteen,' she said, which

made hope shoot through my heart. 'And you're not an old man,' she said, smiling, as though it was the silliest thing she'd ever heard. 'In Houston, nobody makes love when they're seventeen?'

'Sure they do,' I told her, thinking, If we're lucky, we did it as young as possible. 'I just don't want to take advantage of you,' I explained.

'What if I want you to?' she said, standing up and lifting off her T-shirt. Then she hooked her thumbs inside the elastic of her shorts, pulled them off and stepped out of her shoes. I was ready in an instant and could hardly breathe as I gazed up at the beauty of her standing there. Her pale skin glowed in the afternoon sunlight, her long smooth legs seemed carved from marble, the appendectomy scar on her stomach was like a punctuation or a caress, and my eyes were drawn like magnets to the dusting of light hair between her legs.

I don't know what I'd imagined, but until that moment I'd been sure she was a virgin. And yet, what I saw standing before me was a woman, not a girl with a child's innocence, though she had a rare kind of purity I'd seldom found in the girls back home. They were crass by comparison; they acted differently, sure of themselves, more worldly. Their language was harder, their attitudes more sophisticated, and except for a few who stayed virgins or went steady, a lot of them slept around.

If I were the first for Catherine, I could handle the responsibility, but I wouldn't take it lightly.

I gazed at her with an expression of desire and wonder. She looked at me with a challenge.

'Are you sure?' I said.

'Yes,' she whispered.

I yanked off my polo shirt, wiggled out of my shorts, and was about to stand up when she motioned for me to stay where I was. Then she approached me, leaning over to kiss me, tasting of the *fraises des bois* we'd eaten for lunch and a trace of the Tursan wine we'd drunk. Her kiss was tender and loving at first and then she grew more passionate, nibbling on my lips and tongue as our breathing quickened along with our heartbeats. The pine trees and the sky above whirled around my head and I closed my eyes, lost in that first kiss, breathless, excited, and madly in love. I reached up and cupped her perfect breasts in my hands, sighing with the relief of finally touching them, gently rubbing my thumbs over her nipples. She moaned into me, dripping saliva into my mouth.

*Oh, God, I thought, if this is all she'll let me do, it's enough.*

I hated letting go of her breasts but there was so much more to touch. I ran my hands up her silky legs from her ankles to her thighs, brushing between her legs. Her body trembled and a matching tremor ran through me. She thrust against my hands and pulled her head back, gasping with pleasure. I was looking up at a goddess, more beautiful than any Greek had ever imagined.

When she leaned forward again, her hair engulfed us both in a golden halo. 'Do you have any protection?' she asked me.

With that question my heart plunged from the delight where it had been soaring into complete despair. 'No,' I told her, nearly wild with disappointment, thinking, *Barton, you are the stupidest, most simple-minded asshole in creation*! My condoms were back at the farm house in my duffel bag. Who would ever have thought this would happen?

'Next time, when you bring protection, we will do it,' she whispered, leaning forward to kiss me again.

I was dying. My disappointment was so intense it

93

threatened to choke me. I would never survive until next time. I had to have her this minute, right now! Paradise was within my grasp! God, the frustration of having to wait even one more moment for the dream of a lifetime to come true cut me to the core. And that's what she was, a dream of a lifetime. What could I do? Certainly not travel miles for a condom; not while I was right here with her and she was so willing. My mind searched for alternatives. But there weren't any. Girls like Catherine didn't give blow jobs or hand jobs. I couldn't even ask something like that of a girl who quoted Flaubert and Sartre, Mallarmé and Malraux, who knew every aspect of France's economic problems including the causes of double digit inflation, and had a definite opinion on whether France ought to make a deal with the Arabs to buy oil in this current market.

'When we make love it will be my first time,' she whispered, sending a chill up my spine. 'So we must be careful, all right?' I nodded, hoping against hope that she wasn't going to stop kissing me, stop letting me touch her. As long as she remained where she was and let me do what I wanted, all was not lost. My prick never ached like this before. If she merely touched me, I would shoot off in an instant.

This time when she pulled away, I groaned. *Oh God, please save me.* I wanted to yank her down next to me and make love to her this instant. But I was helpless; my life hung on a whim, like a breeze toying with a leaf that barely clung to its branch. Would she let me touch her, or stop me?

When she didn't pull away and stayed where she was still kissing me, I held my breath, sensing a difference in the air. The winds had changed, the precarious leaf still held its own. Not only was she continuing, she was taking control.

She leaned forward again, only this time she thrust

her hips forward, placing herself level with my mouth to give me easy access. When I realized what she wanted me to do, I nearly fainted. I couldn't believe my luck! As if somehow I had missed her cue, she made certain I understood by curling her fingers in my hair and bringing my head towards her so I could tongue her to my heart's content – which I did – the feeling of those petal soft lips filling my mouth was like the first taste of whipped cream on a hot cup of bittersweet chocolate. Her inner juices were a mixture of maple syrup, sweet figs and pure sex. I wanted to eat her up, to drive my tongue in so far I'd reach heaven and she'd belong to me. But instead, I worshipped at her fountain, lapping up her nectar, tracing those delectable folds with my tongue, searching for her magic button and circling it to show her how adept I was, how adoring. And all the while I was doing this, transported by the experience, I could not believe it was happening. The reality was a million times better than my fantasy.

After heart-stopping moments of her holding me exactly where she wanted me, and my body showered with sensations I had never known before, she reached a climax, crying out my name for all the forest to hear as her body shuddered against me. I was in ecstasy. My brain exploded with the wonder of her gift, with amazement at my incredible fortune, and with the knowledge that the rest of my summer was going to be filled with miracles.

Somehow, during the throes of her passion, I had found the strength to hold off my own pleasure, hoping that if she was uninhibited enough to do this, she might reciprocate.

I was right. She collapsed over my shoulders sliding down my body into my lap, covering my face, my neck, my chest with kisses on the way. Her smile was dreamy

95

when she said, 'I want to rest a bit and then it's your turn, all right?'

Shaking with anticipation, not daring to make a move lest it be the wrong one, I was thinking, *Anything you do is all right with me, even if you grew wings and flew off into a tree*.

I waited breathlessly, proud of my adult-like control, sitting there with my legs outstretched, her body in my lap, my prick at attention. Her cheek was resting on my thigh, her breasts pressed into my groin, and I caressed her long golden hair, pulling it back off her face so I could trace my fingers along the shape of her cheek where her eyelashes lay, the pink seashell edges of her nostrils, the rounded tip of her nose, and that mouth, that incredible mouth that had kissed me only moments before. The taste and smell of her filled my head, better than I'd ever dreamed, better than any girl in my life – not that there had been that many, but six women wasn't bad for someone who was only twenty-two. I licked my lips, tasting her, smelling her, ignoring my throbbing penis.

I didn't actually sleep – in that position and considering the state of excitement I was in, it wasn't possible – but I day-dreamed. I imagined us years from now, here in this pine forest, high on wine and drunk on love, doing exactly what we'd just been doing, over and over, until we'd gotten so good at it we could make it last for hours, even days.

Finally, she stirred and my excitement, barely quiescent, shot up again as her hand fluttered over my leg up to my thigh. *This is it*, I thought, with enormous delight. I was hovering on the edge again, staring at freefall, and anticipating the plunge with my entire being.

She moved her body down until I felt her breath on me, like a butterfly's kiss. The heat in me could have

96

started a fire, one touch would make me lose control. But when I finally felt that touch, the cannon didn't explode because I wanted more touches and more and more. No matter what, I would not ruin this for myself by coming too fast.

She obliged me with her nose, with her lips, with her cheeks and with her hands. Gently, as though worshipful, she touched me the way I'd touched her, breathing along my length, exploring the tender skin once convoluted and now taut and stretched to the limit. I imagined a dry forest on fire, the flames licking at the base of a tree, teasing, flicking their heat-filled feathery edges up the trunk, but not consuming it, building, stoking, increasing the fire. She indicated for me to lie back, but if I did, then I couldn't see her, and I had to see her while she was doing this. The visual images of her filled my brain as though it might explode. She was every centrefold ever conceived and she was all mine. I would never forget the picture of her blonde hair as it caught the tree-filtered sunlight, see the outline of her porcelain profile with her mouth on me. She alone breathed life into my fire dragon. It was as if I'd created her for this moment; I had to see it happen, see her breasts, which now were mine, though I hadn't yet claimed them, hadn't sucked on them, hadn't yet nursed them as ownership would allow. If the sensation of what she was doing wasn't sending me to heights I'd never before experienced, I'd have stopped her so I could suck on those tender tips and then slide myself into the silky velvet of her. Another time.

She looked up and saw me watching her, but she didn't shy away, or flinch, or lower her eyes. Instead she returned my look with a strong steady gaze not only of love but calculation. It was as if she could tell what I wanted by watching me; my smile, my grimace of pleasure, the glazing of my eyes, these were her signposts. And she read them. Even better than she read poetry. For with the slightest altering of my expression her pressure on me increased or decreased according to my desire; even before I knew what I wanted, she anticipated me. Incredible! Her mouth, her tongue, her lips, her lashes, her cheeks, her breasts, even her hair trailing across my body caressed me. She made a spiral of her tongue and it felt like a tiny golden snake had wound itself around me, undulating. She controlled the amount of moisture, the pressure she exerted, oriental in her skill. Not that I knew anything about the mysteries of the orient, but where else had these techniques been perfected? And they were techniques. Lucky me. And then I thought, *Has someone else been this lucky?* The thought drove a knife through my heart. *She had to have done this before. Nobody could do these things without practice.*

I wanted to die.

But my body had a mind of its own.

I was nearly over the edge now, pumping wildly, begging to be released, for I could not do it alone. I, who whacked off five times a day, who came on a dime, was unable to climax without her. She was that much in control. I cried out, 'Now, please God, Catherine! Now! Now!'

And now was beyond my imagining. For suddenly she tightened her grip an infinitesimal amount, running her hand from the tip to the shaft in one swift motion followed by her mouth, which nearly swallowed me whole. Then she lifted my knees and hips in a sudden movement that stunned me and thrust her index finger up my ass, pressing on some sweet button I didn't know I had until I exploded into heaven. Again and again, I released twenty-two years of need all at once. I swear to God, nothing in my life had ever prepared me for that experience. It was close to sublime.

Afterwards I stunned myself by finding that my cheeks were wet with tears. I was crying from the glimpse of beauty I had seen, the sheer wonder of it, and the realization that if I didn't have this experience through the rest of my life, I would never be the same.

'I love you,' I told her, knowing how inadequate those words were for what I felt. She lay next to me, our bodies sticky and hot and totally satiated.

'*Je t'aime aussi*,' she whispered as we both fell asleep.

# Chapter 6

The face of the girl I'd now seen twice haunted me, reminding me of Catherine. But Catherine was a closed chapter in my life and I would not hunger for a substitute. Then it occurred to me that Catherine might possibly be at Castelle d'Aumant right now. I could even see her! A chill went through me as though a ghost had appeared before me. For I had buried her in my past.

No! I'd never see her again or go to the *castelle*. Especially not there. Why relive the way her family made me feel? They detested me with the kind of hatred reserved not for those who've earned it but a virulent strain only unleashed on the innocent. Throughout history, the innocent are often the most vilified, I don't know why. Except that those who hate practise cognitive dissonance, convincing themselves that the object of their hatred has asked for it.

Obviously I represented a threat or the d'Aumants wouldn't have treated me the way they did, but at the time I could not comprehend it. Their hatred made me feel worthless. Later, I found out it was her brother Paul who'd fomented the trouble, when I'd thought he was my friend.

Thinking back, it's still difficult to understand the degree of opposition I encountered. I was a good-looking kid of twenty-two, just out of college, who fell in love with a beautiful girl of seventeen. Not so unusual, not so terrible. I didn't know she was the daughter of a duke from an aristocratic line that went back to the court of King Louis XIII – the king whose mother was Marie de Medici, whose chief minister was Cardinal Richelieu, and who turned France into an absolute monarchy. Perhaps Catherine's father had inherited traits from his ancestors who in turn learned them at court, like how to maintain the status quo by despising everyone different from you.

The d'Aumant family had owned the majority of this valley and everything in it since the mid-1600s. Even the village next to Eugénie was on their property. If I had known this when I fell in love with Catherine, it would not have made any difference but I might have stepped more cautiously. I had no idea what the magnitude of that kind of power meant, I had never been exposed to class differences, only racial ones. In Texas, the nouveaux riches were *de rigueur* and vulgarity had reached a pinnacle of glorified proportions. How could I understand the subtleties here, the undercurrents? Like a clumsy animal it was in my genes to lumber through flowerbeds treading on delicate blooms and barely noticing them being crushed beneath my oafish hooves.

My explanation? I was an American, it was my right to do whatever I wanted, take whatever I saw. Americans did things like that, especially Texans. Still do. Texans will tell you to your face they can't stand you. We have a special way of saying, 'Hey, Boy', that lets you know. We insult you openly, curse you out loud, run you off the road, chase you off, or punch you in the jaw on a whim. These upper-class French smile and shake your hand politely, and in the meantime they've cut you off at the knees.

My hosts, the Laurents, had no idea they'd invited a

destroyer into their midst. To them, I was brash and coltish, eager to please, good with the children, unsophisticated and harmless. To Catherine's family, and then later to every person in the village who opposed me, I was a fungus to eliminate, an infestation of vermin sent by God as a plague, a noxious pest to be got rid of before I completely devoured the land and laid spoil its fruitfulness forever.

That was why I ducked my head whenever I saw someone in town who might recognize me, like Madame Larousse, the nosy wife of Alfonse, the owner of the café. So, like some former sheriff in a second-rate western who'd let the town's people down and been run out on a rail, I was back without a fanfare, trying to remain incognito. Few people hereabouts would be glad to recognize me.

In the meantime, Emile's murder case had worked its way under my skin and I thought about it constantly, reviewing the files, hoping to come up with ideas for him.

'Where are you?' he asked, when I called again that afternoon.

'Near Chenonceaux,' I told him. 'Not far from Tours.'

'I've always wanted to go there,' he said, sounding as though anywhere was preferable to where he was now.

I disliked lying to him. 'I've got some ideas for you,' I said.

'Wait, I'll put you on the speaker.' His voice came back with a hollow sound. 'Georges is here with me and Lillianne. We were just reviewing the case.'

'Are you enjoying the wax museum at Chenonceaux?' Lillianne asked.

I had no idea what she was talking about. 'It's great,' I said, which seemed to satisfy her.

'What have you got for us?' Georges asked.

103

'Some ideas on the connection between the victims,' I said, 'new areas in which to dig. If there's anything you haven't covered, feed it into the computer and cross reference it against any unsolved cases from the past. For instance: are there any unsolved murders of older men in the files?'

'Not with this modus operandi,' Emile replied, sounding discouraged.

'Well, then, I've got a list of other possibilities,' I told him.

'I'll take notes as you talk,' Lillianne said.

I continued. 'Check out the following: religious affiliation; terms of inheritance; heirs and beneficiaries; involvement in radical or controversial organizations; police records. Were their companies ever cited for infractions? Did they have a common illness, or holiday in the same place? What excuse did they use on the day of their death for being in their offices late at night? Were they threatened, blackmailed, extortioned? What were they doing during WWII and the Algerian conflict? Were they involved in politically sensitive activities with the government? Do they have friends or associates in common? What were their sexual preferences? Did they use the same brothel, madam or pimp?'

'We have dealt with most of these,' Georges Maran told me.

'But some of them are new,' Emile said. He picked up the phone so we could speak privately. 'I appreciate the help, James. I am not going to lose the biggest case in French history. It's the one I want to go out on.'

'I hear you,' I told him. 'I'll be waiting to see the computer reports.'

'I'll fax them,' he offered. 'Give me a number.'

'I'm moving around too much,' I hedged. 'I'll see

104

them when I get back to Paris.'

'Okay,' he said, ending the call.

I was frustrated. I should be there helping him with those leads. But I wasn't finished here yet. Though still hesitant about opening too many wounds, I had to settle with my past.

I borrowed some fishing gear from my landlady and set out for the river. I rented a boat and rowed for a while before dropping anchor. It was hot and humid, and as the rhythm of the water rocked me, another memory flooded back. The day Catherine finally took me home to meet her parents, and I learned that my blissful world could be shattered.

After declaring our love, Catherine and I were rarely apart. Time seemed endless, except that the summer was slipping away while we enjoyed ourselves. At night we'd sneak out of our houses and sleep in sleeping bags under the stars. Each morning at five, we'd awaken, make love again and go back to our respective houses, mess up our beds and pretend that we had slept in them. I wasn't fooling anyone; when I appeared at breakfast, Claudine would nudge Emile with her elbow and they'd smile. That was before they knew who I was seeing.

I assumed that Catherine's house was similar to the Laurent farm and kept pestering her to take me there. But she'd say her parents were away or busy, or give me some other excuse. I'm the kind of guy who never gives up, but no matter how many times I asked, she wouldn't do it.

Then I met her brother Paul, who was five years older than I, ten years older than his sister. He was tall, like Catherine, and slender, only with dark hair not blond like hers. He had some of her features, widely set blue eyes and thick lashes; his nose was longer and more prominent, his eyebrows heavier, his mouth not soft like hers, more haughty, showing a hint of dissipation. He invited us to dinner in Aire-sur-l'Adour; a restaurant with white tablecloths and waiters in black coats.

At first I thought him rather cold but as the evening went on I found him not only friendly but likeable. I couldn't figure him out, though. I'd never seen anyone so perfectly starched before; even the comb marks stayed in his hair. The creases on his trousers were razor sharp, and during dinner he'd align his fork and knife in perfect symmetry whenever he set them down. Yet under the sophistication was sensitivity. I saw it every time he looked at Catherine.

He studied me intently, watching the two of us, picking up nuances in my conversation. Sometimes he was gracious about them, other times he'd pounce, making me clarify or reveal the exact truth.

Especially when he asked about my family.

'My mom's okay,' I hedged.

'Is she a housewife?' He said it as though it was alien to him, as though he wanted to understand.

'Yes. She's not a particularly interesting woman, but she's always there when we need her. She cooks all the meals, she cleans the house, mends our clothes, grows tomatoes, things like that.'

'How fortunate for you,' he exclaimed. 'A real mother. And your father?'

'I don't get along with my dad. He's a cop.'

He nodded and poured me another glass of wine. 'I know what it's like not to get along with one's father.' His sympathy seemed real. 'Does he bully you, physically or verbally?'

'Both,' I said, surprised to find myself revealing so much.

'And your brothers?' He reached over to hold Catherine's free hand, since I was holding the other one. I envied the affection between them. His face softened when he looked at her.

'My younger brother's in high school, my elder brother was killed in Vietnam two years ago,' I said.

'How terrible for you. If anything ever happened to my sister, I don't know what I would do.'

I felt the tearing pain of Rob's death stab me again and steeled myself against it until it passed.

I'd never told Catherine the details. I couldn't. My brother had stepped on a land mine which blew him to bits. They sent us parts of his body to bury. Rob's death was the most painful thing that had ever happened to me. He was the closest person in my life, my best friend as well as my brother. After his discharge and my graduation, we were going to get a house together, maybe a small ranch out of town where we could keep horses. And we vowed never to marry a girl the other one didn't like. How I wished Rob could have met Catherine; not only would he have liked her, he'd have been as jealous as hell.

What made us so close was that we were allies against Dad. When we were younger, Dad would catch us and punch us around. When we were older, we'd run off together and stay away until he sobered up. In high school we both played football and added some muscle, so Dad stopped hitting us. Phil, my baby brother, is five years younger and never got the crap from Dad that Rob and I did, though Dad's drinking grew worse after his retirement. Living on campus, I saw Dad as little as possible. Rob and I were eighteen months apart, almost like twins, and I guess we raised some hell in our time. But not enough to deserve what Dad dished out.

When Rob was drafted, he wanted to get away from home but he also believed in the war. I was going to join him when I graduated. After he died, I didn't want

107

to go to Vietnam any more.

Paul's voice interrupted my thoughts. 'Our parents don't approve of Catherine seeing boys. They could forbid her to see you, you know.'

'I hope you will tell them how much I respect her,' I insisted.

'Then you will make sure she remains a virgin,' he said.

'Paul!' she exclaimed, indignant and embarrassed.

'Catherine, this is not open to discussion. You promised!' he said, staring at her until she looked away.

My heart nearly stopped. I couldn't look at Catherine. 'You have nothing to worry about,' I told him, thinking, They'd shoot my balls off if they found out.

He turned his gaze on me as though he could read my mind. I held my breath. 'I believe you, James,' he said with a disarming smile. 'But they're old fashioned, even in these modern times. It's foolish of them, isn't it? If it were up to me, I wouldn't care what you did. But you know how parents are when they love their children? I can see you are a man of your word, so don't worry. I will make sure they do not bother you.'

I was grateful to him. I'd misjudged him. He was all right.

When I questioned Catherine about what he'd said, she seemed unimpressed. 'Love? They don't know what it means. My parents are cold, unfeeling people. They are cordial to me only when I do what they want, which is never. Only Paul loves me, in his own way. Do you think I care what they say?'

'I don't like lying to your brother.'

'We must,' she insisted. 'Or he won't be on our side. I know Paul better than anyone – you don't want him angry with you. But he likes you, he told me so. My father and my brother have never got along, but my

108

mother adores Paul. She'll do anything he asks. It makes me sick.'

I offered to stop having sex with her if she wanted it that way.

'Frenchwomen don't wear chastity belts any more, James. It's nobody's business what goes on between the two of us. Just don't tell Paul. Making love to you is the most beautiful thing I've ever done, and it's all I want to do,' she said, wrapping her arms around me, touching me so that fire consumed me again, blotting out all caution. God, I loved her. Besides, what was done couldn't be undone. And it would have killed me to stop.

Eventually I insisted, 'Your parents can't be as bad as you've described. I want to meet them myself,' I told her.

She gave me a strange look. 'I suppose it must happen.' Then she mounted her bike and took off as though demons were chasing her.

I followed her and was amazed when we arrived at the huge ornate wrought-iron gates we'd passed so many times before. She'd never once acknowledged that this was where she lived.

'Here?' I said.

Without a reply she turned in and I followed.

I'd assumed that these gates guarded the entry to a vineyard or monastery; both were correct. The vineyard manufactured one of the world's great wines, Castelle d'Aumant. But still I didn't get it. We passed an ancient monastery on the left and Catherine told me it housed an order of nuns dating back to the Middle Ages. A pope had visited them once. Then we passed six more farmhouses with land surrounding them, all larger than the Laurents'. I expected her to stop at one of them and when she didn't, I really began to wonder what was going on.

But nothing prepared me for the *castelle*. It loomed ahead like something out of Disneyland, white and sparkling in the sunlight. And Catherine headed straight for it.

'Jesus,' I whispered under my breath, pedalling after her. I was nearly struck dumb by what I saw. *She couldn't live here*, I thought. And yet I knew she wasn't the daughter of a servant. And then it hit me that she belonged to this place. She was an honest-to-god princess.

The L-shaped structure – I could hardly call it a house – was an acre wide and three storeys high above its basement, complete with turrets and battlements. It stood at the edge of a lake and on three sides was surrounded by the indentation of a moat. Grassy embankments surrounded the lake, larger than golf greens, overhung with weeping willows. It had a tall, steeply pitched roof covered in blue-grey slate tiles and from this angle, five chimneys were visible at the top; I was sure there were more on the other side. Pointed spires rose at each corner and a large round turret graced the east end.

'I thought all these places had been turned into monuments or hotels,' I said.

'Our own Relais et Château,' she commented, dropping her bike on the lawn. 'Some people think it's beautiful.'

'Don't you?' I asked.

'I guess so. It was built in 1674 for the first Duc d'Aumant.'

I dropped my bike next to hers and we walked over a real honest-to-God drawbridge and up the wide sweeping front stairs. 'It's been in our family for three hundred and seventeen years.'

When she said 'our family' my hands began to sweat. I was beginning to understand her reluctance now.

The arch-shaped front doors were made of glass which surprised me. I'd expected them to be solid wooden planks embedded with iron studs, like in the movies.

A footman, whose sole job was to open the door, greeted her. '*Bonjour, Mademoiselle.*' I was so awestruck, I could only follow her inside, staring.

The entry hall had to be forty feet across, with a floor of inlaid marble that started with a central design and circled outward in a perfect pattern of black and white diamonds. The walls were panelled in light green-painted wood, ornate and impressive, though the colour was a bit dim. In fact, compared to the outside, the interior had a slight air of shabbiness to it. On the left stood a grand staircase, ascending to the second and third floors.

'Look at that!' I commented.

'It was added after the house was built,' Catherine replied, 'when sweeping staircases came into vogue. The original one was circular stone encased in its own stairwell. More in keeping. They should have kept it.'

The paintings on the walls and up the staircase looked as if they belonged in the Louvre and the staircase itself was carpeted regally. On each tread, the carpet was held in place by a stanchioned brass rod. There were two formal rooms on either side of the staircase.

'These are the morning and afternoon rooms,' Catherine explained, pointing to right and left. They were furnished like rooms I'd seen at Versailles in brilliant colours and hung with silks and tapestries. The place smelled slightly musty and I half expected to hear a harpsichord playing.

'Those are called *niche à toit*,' Catherine said, pointing to cupboard-like structures in the corners of the entry that jutted out at right angles, with glass-paned doors and their own roofs.

'They're servants' entrances leading to corridors inside the walls. Servants used them to perform their duties while staying out of sight. The presence of servants can be tiring, you know. Until their masters called them, they would stand in these little cupboards for hours.'

'Did you play hide and seek in there when you were a kid?'

'Never,' she said, without smiling.

'I would,' I told her.

'You didn't have my parents.'

Straight ahead was the library, and on our way we passed a dining hall with a banqueting table you could have skated on; it had at least thirty chairs around it. And I'd thought Texans were rich! The only place I'd ever seen that came close to this was Bunker Hunt's mansion and it was piddling by comparison.

In a smaller room off the library, which was also book-lined and with a bar in it, sat the family: the Duc and Duchesse d'Aumant and Paul. The parents were wearing riding gear. Paul was in cream linen slacks with that razor sharp crease, a white linen shirt and a silk ascot. The man didn't sweat. Out of a fucking movie! I was grateful when he gave a slight wave to put me at ease.

The Duc and Duchesse were equally tall. The mother had Catherine's colouring; her blonde hair was worn tied back in a black ribbon. She also had Catherine's brilliant blue eyes, but her chin was hard and her expression haughty. By now, I was intensely nervous.

'So you're the American boy,' the father said, ignoring my proffered hand. The mother barely nodded as Catherine murmured my name to them. The look she gave Catherine was marble cold. I couldn't tell whom she disliked more, me or her daughter. But when she turned her gaze to her son she radiated adoration, which he accepted as his due. The undercurrents in this room were treacherous.

I was taken aback. Never had the parents of my friends greeted me like this. Mostly, I made a good impression; they wished their sons were more like me. But the cold-eyed stares from the d'Aumants made me squirm. They were like actors on a stage in a play I didn't understand, the parts known only to themselves.

What really sent a chill through me on this hot summer day was the way Catherine changed the moment we came into the room. Her brilliant light faded and the lustre of my shining girl dimmed before my eyes. Even her body trembled, as if holding back fear or anger. I recognized her distress. It was exactly the way I felt in the presence of my own family, for different reasons. My father would be brutal; hers was carved in stone. My mother would try to placate; hers showed blatant preference for the son over the daughter. No wonder Catherine and I were drawn together, we were kindred spirits.

Catherine couldn't be my ally in front of her parents so she went over to her brother and glued herself to his side, something she must have been doing all her life. He put his arm around her in a protective way I found disconcerting, for it erected a wall between us thicker than this *castelle*.

'*Monsieur, 'dame,*' I began, 'I'm so happy to meet you. Your home is overwhelming. I'm a visitor here, but your daughter has extended French hospitality to me.'

From their expressions I might have been a frog who'd escaped from the kitchen, leapt in uninvited, but would be caught and returned to his place as the main course for lunch. And the look on the Duchesse's face,

113

when she turned towards Catherine, said that she was lowlier even than that for having brought me.

'Catherine . . .' Her mother spoke rapidly in French, with tightly pursed mouth. I made out the words '*ce soir*' and '*ce garçon horrible*' – this awful boy – and '*vitement*', which I took to mean that Catherine was commanded to attend some event that evening so she'd better get rid of this disgusting boy fast.

'He speaks French, Mother,' she snapped, trying to be brave, but her voice trembled. Her mother had the decency to look discomfited when she glanced back at me. But it was only a fleeting look and then all conversation just stopped as though I was unworthy of further notice. The silence was oppressive. Our meeting was over. I was dismissed.

I didn't know what to do, how to back out gracefully, though they didn't deserve any grace. From the look on Catherine's face, she might become hysterical or scratch her mother's eyes out. I bitterly regretted that we'd come and I wanted to murder these people for hurting her so. Catherine's cheeks were flushed as she clung to her brother.

Finally he spoke, measuring his words for emphasis. 'You two are unbelievable,' he said. *Incroyable.* 'Sometimes you make me ashamed.' Then he accompanied us out of the library, one arm around Catherine, his other hand on my shoulder protectively, while two pairs of eyes bored into our backs. Only his calmness and restraining hand kept me from running.

Back through the grand hall we went, heads held high in defiance. I took my cue from brother and sister, old hands at this. Seemingly calm, Paul guided us into a round-shaped room with a domed ceiling and frescos on the walls. I expected his parents to come charging after us any minute to throw me out.

The relief when they didn't was intense enough for

114

me to relax. I looked around.

More opulence. Between the frescos were niches filled with marble statues of Greek gods and goddesses. I recognized Diana. Three round tables were set with crystal, silver and peach-coloured linen. I guessed this was the family dining room for there was a long buffet laden with hot chafing dishes and cold salads, an amazingly normal contrast to the bleakness of my audience with the duc and duchesse.

'Sometimes they are despicable,' Catherine said, letting go of Paul.

I wanted to put my arm around her but felt constrained in front of her brother. 'At least Maman can be human,' Paul said.

'Only to you,' Catherine countered.

It was like a play by Edward Albee – *Who's Afraid of the Duc d'Aumant?*

White spots of anger appeared on Catherine's flushed cheeks. 'I don't want to discuss it,' she told him. Then to me she said, 'You wanted to come here, you might as well enjoy it.' She pointed to the ceiling. 'Everyone finds this interesting.'

I raised my eyes to the ornate chandelier I assumed was Venetian, hanging from star-shaped stones embedded in the centre of the dome. Around the star was a circle of stone, and from that a semi-circular pattern radiated out to become a diamond chequerboard pattern of light and dark marble.

'It's called stereotomy,' Catherine explained, her voice still shaking. 'See how the stones are cut with absolute precision to fit the dome shape and make the design at an angle. They all revolve around the keystone and match the design on the floor. Precision and order was crucial in architecture as well as design, an extension of religious beliefs. It amazes me that it doesn't come crashing down on our heads. Maybe it will someday. I can hope, can't I?'

Before I could reply, she said to her brother, 'Are you having lunch with us?' Her voice sounded desperate.

Paul patted her head as though he were an indulgent father. 'I can't, *chérie*. I have an appointment. But you have another protector now. You'll be fine.'

He turned to me. 'So what do you think of us, James? Are we what you expected?'

He wanted me to know that only his parents thought I was a specimen to be chloroformed. I relaxed my guard.

'You were right. They're very old fashioned. But I had no idea Catherine was so . . .' I couldn't say the word 'rich'. It sounded wrong. But that's what I meant. 'That she had such an impressive history.'

'She does,' Paul said. 'Our ancestors' legacies surround us. We know where all the skeletons are buried, as you say. We've read their diaries, and lived with their portraits in every room. Some of them were good and others evil, some were victims and others victimized. But there were no saints that I've been able to find,' he added. 'I find it interesting that generations who come after us will know our little secrets too.' He smiled at Catherine who looked away.

He continued, 'One of our ancestors is from Serrières, a town on the Rhône. Our mother looks a lot like her.'

'You're not going to tell that story again, are you?' Catherine interrupted.

'Wouldn't you like to hear it?' he asked me.

'Sure,' I replied.

'It's quite my favourite. Serrières turned their local cathedral into a mariners' museum,' he told me. 'For good reason. It had become desecrated ground.'

'How?'

'About a hundred years ago the parishioners discovered a secret room in the church that had been walled in. In that room they found the skeletons of four hundred people. Evidently all of them had been locked away and left to die, packed in so closely that four of them mummified in an upright position.'

'My God,' I said. 'Who were they?'

'Either victims of the plague or Protestants,' he said. 'What intrigues me most about it is this: what were the good Catholics like our ancestor Eleanor doing while those people were imprisoned right above them? Did they go to church and pray as usual? They must have known what was going on in their stone attic, maybe even heard the screaming. One can only imagine.' He gave a quirky smile. 'Our country's history is rich in *anomolie*, wouldn't you say? And the d'Aumants are part of it all.'

I wonder now what he was trying to tell me. That his generation also was capable of walling up four hundred innocent people and leaving them to die? I wish I'd understood his subtlety.

Catherine tried to smooth over the ghoulishness of this tale. 'I never understood why our family was given so much privilege that we didn't deserve. But we were. Maman and Papa don't question it, nor do they understand the world you live in. They would be just as happy if you'd never come here. They think Americans are terrible. I'm sorry.'

How dumb was I? I honestly believed it didn't matter what they thought. I didn't know the influence they wielded. I'd grown up on Texas history where land barons ruled the territory; I'd even seen it in the movies. But this was different. The parents I knew yelled at their kids, got drunk and sometimes beat each other. More often they ran out on their families or went berserk. But most of them were okay. A brother had

117

been an ally against them. And parents didn't control our futures, thank God. If they did, I'd end up a drunk like my father.

All this meant to me was that Catherine would be difficult to support. But love would conquer all, right? Love and McDonald's. We could work there and eat there too. What do kids know? I underestimated the d'Aumants. They weren't actors. They were living their parts. I had no idea what iron strength ran in the veins of the Duchesse d'Aumant. Or that her son was just like her.

We filled our plates with items from the buffet, the like of which I'd never seen before except on the pages of a gourmet magazine, then joined Paul at one of the tables.

'Sure you won't eat?' I asked him, resenting him for being so handsome and self-confident. At the same time, I was grateful that he'd been a buffer between us and his parents.

'Thanks for offering, but I can't.'

'When do the other lunch guests arrive?' I wondered. There were eighteen places set and enough food for twenty.

'This is just for us,' Catherine told me, lowering her eyes. 'It's what they do when I bring a guest home, whether they like him or not. My parents will eat later.'

She was calmer now, but embarrassed by the flagrant display. Then I caught a smile hiding at the corners of her mouth. She was playing it cool for her brother's benefit. It endeared her to me even more. I was so in love and she was the dearest, smartest, most gorgeous, sexiest, and now richest girl in the world. And she was all mine.

'You never told me what you do, Paul?' I asked, being polite. It had not come up when we'd had dinner together.

118

'Do you mean what do I do sexually, how my bowels function, or how I clothe myself? Or perhaps you mean how do I amuse myself?' This was the facetious side of him I'd suspected was there.

'Paul,' Catherine said, laughing as though he was funny, 'nobody cares about that. My brother is a superb vintner,' she told me. 'He works with Father on the estate.'

After meeting the Duc I couldn't imagine working with the man.

'Every award d'Aumant Vinyards has won in the last few years is because of Paul,' Catherine explained. Then, to her brother, she said, 'Papa must not keep you from making the changes you've planned. I too want our wine to be even better.'

'You're so right,' he said, wrapping his arms around her and then leaning over to kiss her neck. To me he said, 'We need to modernize and expand, but our father is completely opposed to my plans.' With those words I saw the same steel-eyed determination in him as in his father.

'You'll convince him,' said Catherine, encouraging him the way she did me.

'Isn't she delicious?' he asked. 'You are a lucky man.'

My stomach turned and my neck reddened with a flash of jealousy more intense than I've ever known. The heat rose up to my face and I could have strangled him for merely touching her, her own brother. What kind of people could make me feel this way?

'Yes, she is,' I countered, staking my own claim. He looked at me then with one raised eyebrow and smiled. His eyes narrowed.

'But, of course, she's too young to be serious. You remember what I told you?' he added, wagging a finger.

119

I kept silent.

'Well, you two, I'm off.' He turned to go. 'How about a game of tennis, sometime, James?' he offered.

I was really flattered. At least one member of the family accepted me. 'I'd like to. Any time.'

Catherine was pleased too. 'I love you,' she called as Paul left.

He waved a hand over his head without turning.

I couldn't help liking him, except for his proprietary manner with his sister.

Now that we were alone, I wanted to talk about Catherine's parents but she held up her hand as if to stop me so we ate mostly in silence with four servants waiting on us. When I asked her about Paul, all she said was, 'He's on our side.'

'Why isn't he married?'

'He's too busy.'

After lunch I asked her to take me on a tour.

She hung back. 'I'd rather go back to the river or into town. Anywhere but stay here.'

'I want to see your room,' I insisted. Actually, I wanted to make love to her on her bed, so she'd always remember me there, like a canine in the wild who stakes out his territory by urinating in a circle as a warning to other predators.

Reluctantly, she led the way up the grand staircase to the second floor where her wing was located, and again I was overwhelmed. Catherine had a suite of rooms all to herself with furnishings that had belonged to the family for centuries: a sitting room, a small kitchen, a study and bedroom, complete with one of those corner closet *niches* for the maids. It was hardly the kind of bedroom that I'd seen back home: no football banners, rock posters, stuffed animals or patchwork quilts. Instead a collection of dolls that belonged in a museum, a Victorian-style baby carriage and a miniature sterling

120

silver tea set. I lost the desire to stake my claim. And for the first time since I'd met her, I lost the desire to make love to her. It was then that I got an inkling of what I was up against.

From the moment we entered that room, Catherine kept her distance from me. We sat awkwardly on her uncomfortable antique sofa with its silk upholstery and four matching chairs, and looked out at the view through the French doors over the balcony to the lake below. White swans floated on the water. It could have been paradise.

I had wanted to picture her in her surroundings, but this wasn't what I'd expected. Neither did our usual topics of conversation seem appropriate.

'Why didn't you ever tell me you lived in a *castelle*?' I said, trying not to feel betrayed.

'I didn't know how you would take it. You're the first person I've been close to in my life who isn't rich. At school, all my friends are wealthy, and in Eugénie everybody knows who I am.'

'Do I make you feel uncomfortable about being rich?'

'A little,' she admitted.

'That's absurd,' I insisted. 'Nobody feels that way.' Suddenly, I began to feel used. The joke was on me. I'd thought I was the one taking advantage of her. What a fool I'd been. She was so far above me I could never reach her level and was suddenly ashamed of where I came from.

And yet there was a part of me that refused to be defeated by all of this. I remembered how she'd made love to me, given herself to me completely, in defiance of her family. Wasn't that important? Didn't that count? Maybe the rest was bullshit. A helluva of a lot of bullshit to be sure, but it was only money. And I'd be rich someday, too. Maybe not this rich, but rich enough. Besides, we'd be living in Texas where nobody would know that her parents lived in a *castelle*; it wouldn't matter.

'Do you love me?' I asked.

'Yes,' she whispered. 'With all my heart. More than anyone in my whole life. Enough to lie to my parents, even to my brother. I only began to live when I met you. I would die without you.'

I put my arms around her. 'I love you too,' I repeated, overwhelmed by her devotion, so much more than I deserved.

'I'm sorry for not telling you,' she said. 'Can you forgive me?'

'Of course I do,' I assured her. 'And I never want you to apologise for what you are.'

'You're so good,' she said, and then pulled away from me to look into my eyes. 'Do you believe in God?'

'I guess so.' It wasn't a subject I liked to discuss. In college, discussions about it generally ended in fights. My God is better than yours. 'I was born a Methodist,' I told her. 'But I don't follow the religion. Do you?'

'Of course,' she replied. 'I'm a good Catholic. I believe in heaven and hell.'

'A hell with fire and the devil?'

She nodded, as though she wanted to say more but couldn't. A tear ran down her cheek.

'What is it?' I reached out for her hand, wanting to soothe her pain; religious fervour was beyond me. When I was a kid I couldn't figure out why God had given me such a bully for a father, and when I grew older I decided that the concept of God and Jesus had so many inconsistencies, it was too much trouble to bother with. 'Why are you crying?'

'Because of what you said.'

'You mean about not being ashamed of what you are, or about hell?

122

She didn't reply, but suddenly burst into tears which rapidly became sobs. I moved over and put my arm around her, holding her in bewilderment. Such pain over a little question?

'You're not afraid of hell, are you?'

She nodded, unable to stop crying.

'Because of us?'

When she cried even harder, I knew I was right. But why, all of a sudden?

'Catherine, we love each other. What we do together isn't wrong. You never thought it was before, did you?'

No reply.

'Is it because of your parents?'

'No.'

'Why are you so upset?'

She finally got control of herself and looked at me with a terribly sad expression. 'It's nothing,' she said.

But I knew there was something she couldn't say and I had to make her tell me, convince her (and myself too) that we were all right, that we had something pure and special between us. If I couldn't, we were lost. I felt my temper rising; this house, these people, had done this to her. They scared the hell out of me and my first defence was anger. If I couldn't annihilate them, I would hang on to her with all my might. I'd get her away from them.

'Catherine, there isn't anything in the world you can't tell me. I'm here for you. You know that.'

'James, you're so good for me.'

Then I blurted out, 'Will you marry me? You can come back to the States and live with me!'

'Marry you? It's impossible!' She saw my face fall. 'But I want to more than anything in the world. I'm just too young. My parents would never let me.'

'I know exactly how young you are, but I'll take care of you. We won't ask your parents' permission, we'll just do it. And when we're married you'll never have to be with your parents again, or be afraid of going to hell. Married people can make love any way they want to and not worry about damnation, can't they?' I was desperate to put that smile back in her eyes again.

'It's impossible.'

'It isn't,' I insisted. 'We could get married next week; you can finish school in America and then go to college.'

She smiled as though I was crazy, which was how I felt. 'You know I can't.'

I wasn't giving up on the idea. But there was something else bothering me. 'Catherine, I have to ask you this and I want you to tell me. Are you afraid of going to hell because of things you've done with me or with other guys?' I steeled myself to hear her reply. I was unprepared for it.

She turned to me with those sky blue eyes and said, 'Other guys, *non*! You are my first! You must know that. I never did it with any boy before you. But we mustn't tell! You mustn't ever tell.'

'You know I wouldn't,' I promised. I'd never known her to lie, so I was thoroughly confused. 'Are you telling me the truth? You've never had sex with anyone before me?'

'That's what I said.'

'But there's more to sex than intercourse. What about the other things we do . . . you know?'

'Oh, that.' Her smile implied that I was being silly.

'Yes, that. How did you know how to do it so well? You're so experienced for a girl your age.'

'I just knew,' she told me, as sincere as I've ever seen her.

And though I really wanted to question her further, something in her expression stopped me. I had the feeling that the more I pressed, the more evasive she'd

124

become and I would be the loser. The last thing I wanted to do was kill the goose who'd laid the golden egg. True, curiosity was spreading inside me, but did it really matter how she knew what she knew? I was her one true love, and nobody but me would ever share the things we did. That would have to satisfy me. At least for now.

That night she said she had a surprise for me and took me to her parents' barge where for the first time we made love in a cabin in a real bed, lulled by the sound of water slapping against the sides and the gentle movement of the river beneath us. Somehow that night was different, and it wasn't because there were no rocks in my back and crawling insects to worry about. We were serious about one another. From the way she loved me, I could tell she was committed. And I vowed, no matter what, I would never let her go.

# Chapter 7

I sat there in the boat remembering the night Catherine and I spent on the barge, how wonderful it had been not to be cramped by a sleeping bag or poked in the back by rocks. It was like the first time all over again.

If only I hadn't seized on the idea of getting married, maybe things would have worked out differently; but I couldn't let it go. It was all I thought about and talked about, until finally I convinced Catherine. The day she agreed, I was so excited it was all I could do to keep from telling Paul when we played tennis. My game showed my excitement and I beat him three sets to one. It felt strange not telling him, I was used to confiding in my own brothers, but I decided to wait.

Then I set about trying to make it happen. In today's world, marriage among the upper class in France isn't exactly arranged, but young people tend to marry within their peer group to someone of whom their parents approve. They inherit their attitudes along with the family holdings, the titles, the jewels, and the Chanel suits. Catherine and I would prove the exception.

Just out of college, I had no idea what I wanted to do with my life. I had saved enough money to bum around Europe while I was waiting for my application to the Peace Corps to be processed. I was sure I would be accepted – I had gained experience as a plumber working for my Uncle Ben from the time I was sixteen, and I spoke French too. But if Catherine was with me, I'd change my plans. Either she'd go with me to Senegal, or we'd go home and she could continue with school. I'd get a job. Other couples managed to be married and go to school or college. Of course, their parents helped; mine would be unable to. Hell, there was always pizza delivery.

I had it all figured out. Catherine would move into my apartment with me and my two roommates and we'd take over the bedroom. She could enrol in my old high school, Miltby, and maybe work part-time at Gulfgate Mall across the street. I could just see her behind a counter at Sakowitz. Eventually I'd find something I wanted to do. True the economy was sluggish because of the Watergate scandal which filled the newspapers all summer. It looked as though Nixon would be impeached or made to resign any time now. The jerk! I knew something was up the minute they caught those guys breaking into Democratic Headquarters at the Watergate. The President had to know what his re-election committee was doing, and if not, he was even worse for not knowing.

But what the French government required of a foreigner who wanted to marry a French citizen was worse than applying for the Israeli Secret Service. The American consul was in Paris and wouldn't tell me anything on the phone. The French were no better. My presence was required. In fact, every government requirement was daunting; we needed proof of our citizenship and passports weren't enough. They demanded birth certificates, and something called a *certificate de coutume* – proof that I was legally free to marry. There was other bureaucratic tripe as well, though easier to obtain. It meant I'd have to take the train back to Paris, be shunted from one official to the next, and still not get any satisfaction. A wrenching thought to be spending what precious time we had away from each other.

If only Rob had been alive, he would have helped me get all the information I needed. So I did the next best thing – I went to Catherine's brother. I didn't tell him our plans, only asked for the name of a good lawyer. It was a calculated risk, but he and I were becoming friends, especially when I let him beat me at tennis.

'Why do you want a lawyer?' he asked.

'I want to know what it takes to go into business in France.'

'What kind of business?'

'I don't know yet. But I like it here. Maybe I'll come back, after I've been in the Peace Corps. I have to return to the States, of course, and set up something. A business investment would be the best way to get me back here, right? Maybe I could import your wine into Texas. Do you have a distributor there?'

'No.' He studied me carefully. 'Texas is not one of our markets. Is that your true intention?'

'*Bien sûr*,' I assured him, wishing I could tell him the truth. He was in a position to cut corners for us if he was willing to help. But I didn't tell him. He gave me the name of a lawyer who spoke English, in Mont de Marsan.

Then I called home and asked my roommates Beau and Haskell to get me what I needed from the States. They agreed with a lot of grumbling; my new lawyer did the rest.

Rather than deter me, the obstacles strengthened my resolve. Catherine was not as enthusiastic but she went along. The formalities were daunting, yet I forged ahead. Even when I learned that we needed her parents' permission. Fat chance! I practised forging signatures. The cost of all this paperwork and legal advice was using up what little money I had, and we needed some to get back to the States. But my buddies came through and wired me some cash.

Another major problem was religion. We were required to be counselled by a priest and I had to convert to Catholicism or agree to allow our children to be raised as Catholics. For a non-believing Methodist, it felt oppressive. The orthodoxy of the Catholic church was to me just short of Muslim fanaticism, something I didn't want for myself or my children. I didn't approve of their rigid doctrines and had trouble believing in the immaculate conception. In order for me to come to terms with it, I would need months of study and soul searching, which I did not have. Catherine agreed to a civil ceremony if we could have a religious one later on. I agreed.

The obstacles which had loomed ahead were beginning to peel away. But time was passing. Only two more weeks of August and my job would end. Catherine would be going back to school and I was supposed to meet some friends from college in Amsterdam. If my application to the Peace Corps came through I'd have to make a decision as to whether to take it. We had to make plans.

I picked the date 27 August. Catherine was due back at school on 1 September and I would return to Paris with the Laurents. She would take the train to Paris instead of to Zurich and meet me. We'd get married in Paris and then go to Amsterdam and wait for my confirmation or rejection by the Peace Corps. If I was accepted, I'd ask permission for her to come with me. If they refused, we'd go back to the States right away. She had enough money to pay for her own ticket, but not much more. I was marrying an heiress without funds.

In the meantime, we tried to behave normally. But

130

the atmosphere around us had changed. Ever since my visit to the *castelle*, things were difficult, as though someone had put out the word: The princess is dating Quasimodo. Everyone disapproved. Before then, people beamed at us. The townspeople and the local farmers knew us as *les jeunes amoureux* – the young lovers. Madame Larousse delighted in serving us sorbet in the afternoon. Gaston, the caretaker of the family barge, would take us for a cruise. And wherever we walked, or biked, or hitched a ride on a combine, someone would wave or call out, '*Ça va?*'

Now, suddenly, all we got were glowering looks and cold shoulders. And the provincial French are experts at disapproval since they are by nature opinionated.

Catherine was affected by the pressure. If we were in the presence of others, she'd let go of my hand or pull out of my embrace; our sneaking around grew even sneakier. Worst of all, when we made love it wasn't the same any more. I was heartsick but unable to change things. I kept promising myself things would be different once we were married. But the pressure made her doubt this.

'We should wait a year,' she'd say. 'You don't know what my parents can do. They will find us wherever we go. I'm afraid.'

I'd soothe her and reassure her, until the next time.

And then Paul found out about our plans. Catherine rode over immediately to tell me. She was shaking with terror.

'This could ruin everything,' she cried, clinging to me.

'Who told him? Did you?'

'I would never be that stupid!' she insisted.

'Well, he won't do anything. He's on our side,' I assured her, trying not to panic. But Paul was a loose cannon that could shoot in any direction.

'He's only on our side if he controls things. As long as he believed you were leaving at the end of the month and I was going back to school, he left us alone. But now!' She threw up her hands in despair. 'He knows what you mean to me.'

'That shouldn't matter. He and I are friends. He's been kind to me, Catherine.'

'Paul is many things, but not kind. He was furious. I begged him not to tell our parents. I swore that I would never marry you. I told him it was a crazy idea, that you were filled with romantic notions that I don't share.'

It hurt me to hear that. 'Did he believe you?'

'One never knows what Paul is thinking.'

'You're his sister, you have to do something. Are you sure you didn't tell him?' I shouted, fearful of losing her.

'Don't blame me! This is *your* fault,' she shouted back. 'Your lawyer told him.'

'He wouldn't do that. Our relationship is confidential.' I could not believe I'd been betrayed by my lawyer. That would have been illegal, unethical.

She looked at me with tears in her eyes and shook her head as if I had no conception of what was going on.

'Paul doesn't know we're lovers, does he?' I was feeling some of her fear myself, remembering how adamant he'd been.

'I'd *never* tell him that,' she insisted. 'Unless you told your lawyer.'

'Of course not!' I reached for her and held her to me to stop her trembling. Everything was falling apart. I had to make it work. 'Don't worry. We won't take any chances. We'll leave tonight.'

'We can't leave without your documents from America.'

'I'll have them sent to us wherever we go.'

'But if I sneak out of the *castelle* now, I can't take anything with me. We agreed I would pretend I'm leaving for school, then I can take all my luggage.'

I heard the note of panic in her voice. She had to have something to hang on to. I was asking her to give up her family, her country, and now everything she owned. But I could see that we couldn't wait a moment longer. 'We have to go right now,' I insisted. 'Before Paul has a chance to do anything to stop us. Don't worry about your clothes. You won't need more than a few pairs of jeans. Tonight, before you leave, put on several layers of clothing under your coat. Everything else of importance, carry in your picnic basket.'

She gave me a look as if to say I knew nothing about women. I suppose I didn't.

'We'll meet at the barge at eleven tonight,' I told her, rushing on with my plan. 'Then we'll hitch a ride to the station and be out of France in a few hours.'

Heady with excitement and nervousness, I shoved aside my doubts. She was very young, and though I loved her, I had no idea how I would feel in ten years. And now, I didn't have the luxury of finding out.

'I don't know if I have the courage to do this,' she said. 'To run away, to leave everything behind.'

I held her face between my hands and gazed into her eyes, certain enough for both of us. 'If you love me, it's the only way. Do you love me?'

I held my breath until she nodded.

'Shall I come back to the *castelle* with you and stay until it's time to go?'

Her eyes were filled with fear. 'I wish you could, I'm so afraid. But if anyone sees you, they could try and stop us.'

'It will be all right,' I promised, reassuring myself as well as her.

She tore herself out of my arms, climbed on her bike

133

and rode off. As I watched her retreating figure disappear around the bend in the road, I had a feeling of despair. I wanted to run after her and tell her we should go right that minute. But I knew she needed time to prepare.

That evening at dinner, Claudine and Emile confronted me.

'What's going on between you and Catherine d'Aumant?' Emile began, looking more uncomfortable than I'd ever seen him, but determined to get this unpleasant business out of the way. Anne Marie and Guillaume stared at me with frank curiosity.

'You know it's unsuitable, James,' Claudine cut in, speaking in a short clipped manner uncharacteristic of her usual maternal demeanour. 'A girl like Catherine d'Aumant is off limits for you.'

'Why are you saying this?' I asked, on alert. *This couldn't be a coincidence. And if they knew, maybe Catherine's parents knew also*. My pulse began to race.

'It is not proper for you to see her any more. It must stop at once!' Her raised voice made Guillaume's head snap to attention and he stared at his mother, perversely interested in how I would handle her wrath. Usually he took the brunt of it, being a mischievous six year old.

'Not proper?' I said, barely keeping my temper. 'What are we living in, the Feudal Age?'

'*Ecoute-moi!*' Claudine demanded. 'We have treated you like a member of our family, but you are our employee. While you are under our roof, you do as we say.'

'Your behaviour reflects on us,' Emile countered.

'You must not see her any more,' Claudine said. 'From now on it is over. Is that clear?'

Before I could reply, the phone rang. Guillaume got up to answer it and called out, '*C'est Oncle Marius*.'

'I'll speak to him,' Claudine said, getting up with such force that her ladder-back chair teetered on edge on the uneven ceramic tile floor and nearly fell over.

I glanced at the clock as I tried to collect my thoughts. Half-past eight. Only two and a half hours before we were to meet. My heart pounded.

'*Non, Marius,*' I heard Claudine say. '*Je suis en train de lui dire.*' I'm telling him now. '*Oui, il comprend!*' He'll understand!

Great, the whole damned family knew my business! The town must know too. I could see what might happen later tonight. We'd be two waifs on a lonely road, trying to hitch a ride, and suddenly a crowd of pitchfork-wielding farmers would jump in front of our path and drive us back. No matter. I would fight the world if I had to.

Claudine returned to the table, her movements abrupt, her mouth pursed in a disapproving line. Anne Marie and Guillaume, usually boisterous and noisy kids, were absolutely silent except for drinking their soup and clicking their spoons against the crockery bowls.

'Listen,' I began, 'I had no intention of offending anyone. But Catherine is the girl I love. I plan to marry her and there's nothing you can do about it. I love her, man,' I said to Emile, who glared at me from under thick eyebrows forming a continuous line of disapproval.

'*Marr-i-age? Absolument, non!*' Claudine sputtered. 'You cannot think of such a thing, James. Who do you think will pay the consequences for what you do? We will! This is not America, this is France! Here, we are taught to honour our family. Emile's father and his brothers depend on *Monsieur le duc* for their living. We cannot defy him! This house,' she gestured around at the modest but homely cottage, 'the vineyards, the

135

farmland, all belong to the d'Aumants. You cannot jeopardise this because of your overactive cock!'

'Claudine!' Emile said.

'I won't stand for it,' she insisted. 'Besides, she's too young.'

'You weren't much older when I met you,' Emile said, making my hopes soar.

'Oh,' she sputtered, '*je m'en fou*.' I don't give a damn. 'This is different. Why do you compare us to them? It is not the same.'

He shrugged and made an obscene gesture by tapping his thumb against his upper teeth. Shut the fuck up. 'It's the truth, you know. You were eighteen, she is seventeen. Only one year, Claudine. James is a healthy man, the girl is willing.'

'Now who's being gross, and in front of the children?' Claudine said, and both of the children laughed behind their hands.

I could see how upset they were. If I could calm their fears, make them think I'd changed my mind, they'd ease up. Tomorrow we'd be gone. 'I didn't mean to cause you trouble. Catherine and I met by accident and fell in love. But maybe you're right. We've been too hasty. It would be better if we waited. It's just that she's the most wonderful girl I've ever known, intelligent and beautiful.'

'And rich, eh?' Emile said. I wondered again if I had an ally in him.

Claudine suddenly shouted, 'Enough, *c'est fini*! If you don't tell him, I will.'

'Tell me what?'

'You must agree this moment not to see her again, or we will leave here tomorrow and go back to Paris. If you refuse to come with us, no one in this province will give you a room. Not a hotel, not a stable, not even a pile of straw. You will be cast out by the entire village.

136

I would not advise that! Everyone here feels as we do. It would be a terrible way to end our *vacances*, but so be it! I keep my word, James. You know I do. Is that clear? You will stop this right now? Emile and I cannot allow your behaviour to interfere with our family. This is a *scandale*, James.'

I wondered why she was so protective of Emile's family who didn't give a damn about her.

He interjected, as if to soften her harsh words, '*Chut!* Let me speak.' He turned to me. 'James, we have opened our home to you, treated you like family. And you must repay us. Catherine d'Aumant is off limits to you, *ça c'est clair*?'

I was thinking, *Go along with it, tell them you won't see her any more. Write an apology later.* My temper flared but I contained it. People I barely knew were trying to run my life. They weren't my fucking parents, for Christ's sake!

Then I recalled the letters of recommendation I'd asked them to write for my Peace Corps application. I was supposed to conduct myself as a credit to the Corps, a representative of the United States. I had promised to stay out of trouble, no drugs, no misbehaving and so on. My elopement with Catherine came under the category of 'and so on'.

If the Laurents gave me a negative evaluation it could ruin my record. And they might. In a way, I had corrupted a minor. And in their eyes, what was even worse, I had ceased being a team player. Now a scandal was threatening. I was causing the suffering of an entire family.

So I gave them my most repentant expression and servile nod, the kind I gave to my dad to avoid a punch when he found no more beer in the refrigerator. 'I hear you,' I said. 'You're absolutely right! We'll cool it, okay? It's frozen as we speak.'

'Not cool it,' Emile insisted. 'Not frozen. You will not see her at all. I'm truly sorry,' he added.

'There is no more of this girl for you. *C'est tout!*' Claudine said. 'I know it hurts, but that is final!'

'I'll tell her goodbye tonight,' I said, willing myself not to look at the clock.

Claudine covered my hand with hers, squeezing me too tightly. 'Right now! You will call her and tell her that you can't see her any more, and you will mean it!'

This was archaic, it was Shakespearean, it was outrageous. Call her without any warning? What if she believed me? I could not hurt her like that. I might really lose her. She might think I was changing the plan. I wished we'd worked out some kind of code, but who would have thought this could happen?

The pain in my guts tore at me, searing my stomach, grabbing my heart. It was suffocating pain, as though cancer had exploded into being and was eating at my flesh. 'Oh God,' I moaned, finally understanding the impact of what they were saying. There was no way out.

Both of them stood up and, like guards at a prisoner's elbow, escorted me from the table to the telephone and watched while I picked it up. Then they stayed by my side while I made the call. I felt I was facing my own execution. My hands were clammy, my stomach lurched, and I was shaking as I tried to think of what to say so she'd understand I didn't mean it.

Some secretary answered the phone. I asked for Catherine. 'She's out of town,' the voice told me. I stood there stupidly staring into space. *Out of town?* I thought. *She can't be. We're leaving later. Maybe there are people standing there making her do something she doesn't want to either.* Then I realized that they might have whisked her away somewhere, without letting her speak to me. She could be going through the same hell

138

as I, frantically wondering what I was thinking, what they were telling me. I had to find her, to get her away from them. Everything was closing in on me.

I looked at the clock. Two-and-a-half hours before we were supposed to meet. She might be at the barge now, waiting for me.

'May I leave a message?' I choked out the words.

The secretary pretended efficiency. '*Bien sûr.*'

'Tell her that Monsieur Barton regrets that he cannot see her any more.'

The woman replied, '*Vraiment. A bientôt,*' and hung up before I could even say, 'Tell her I love her.'

I ran out of the house with Emile and Claudine shouting for me to come back, jumped on my bike and tore over to the barge. I covered the forty-minute ride to Aire sur L'Adour in twenty-eight, hoping against hope that I'd find her. Everything looked exactly the same, but she wasn't there.

Then I tore over the country roads looking for her, but I couldn't find her. I went back to the barge at the appointed time and waited for two hours but Catherine didn't come. As the minutes ticked by I felt something inside me dying. Finally, I realized there was no sense in waiting any longer so I rode the long way back, heading towards the *castelle*. It was pitch dark and I only had a small flashlight to guide me. I was determined to storm those walls and force them to tell me where she had gone. But the gates were locked against me. If I climbed them and trespassed on their property, they might have me shot.

I rode down to our special place by the pond and called out her name, screaming my anguish. But only the crickets and night birds answered me. I was in shock; I still thought there was something I could do. Aimlessly, I rode around under the starlight, exhausting myself, hitting bumps in the road invisible in the dark, falling off my bike and hardly caring if I broke my neck or where I was going, just praying that I'd find her around the next corner or around the next, that somehow she'd escaped and was looking for me too.

The town was deserted, the stores and the café boarded up for the night. I raised my fist against the August moon and railed against a power greater than mine. 'God,' I cried. 'Why did you do this to me?' But God hadn't done it, her parents had. They were the ones I hated. And Paul. He had told them.

I went all the way back to the barge and sat on the deserted deck until the early hours of the morning when exhaustion overtook me. Then I let myself in, using the key in its hiding place, and made my way below.

An eerie echo greeted me of water slapping against the sides of the boat. 'Catherine!' I called, my voice reverberating against the boarding below deck. What came back to me was my own anguish. No reply. I went forward to the cabin where we'd made love that one night. It was deserted. I flung myself across the narrow bed and held on with all my might. The pain was so intense I didn't think I could stand it; it was as if I was being torn in two.

Eventually I fell asleep and dreamed of Catherine, her scent, the touch of her hand, the feel of her beneath me, the sound of her laughter, her quiet serenity. My subconscious played with the vision of her, over and over, so that the very essence of her ran in my blood like fatal bubbles of nitrogen.

Something woke me. A sound, a touch. I froze and turned.

It was Catherine.

I've never felt such joy in my life. I grabbed her and held her to me. 'Oh, thank God. What did they do to you, what did they tell you? Whatever they said, it isn't

140

true. I didn't mean it. I love you, you know that, don't you? I love you forever. We have to go now, immediately.' I grabbed her hand but she held back, and then put her arms around me as though she'd never let me go while she whispered, 'I love you, you know I love you, I love you.'

'How did you get away from them?' I asked. But she didn't answer.

'Where have you been all this time. How did you find me?'

'I didn't know you'd still be here.' She was crying now. 'But I prayed you would, that you would wait for me.'

I started to say something but she put her hand over my mouth. 'I can't go with you now. My parents are sending me to my aunt's in Switzerland. I'm leaving from here. It's a remote village near Gstaad. I'm to wait there until school starts or they'll lock me in my room. Oh, I hate them!' she said, putting her head on my shoulder.

Her body was so slender, so defenceless. I felt an overwhelming fury that I couldn't make all this better for her, eradicate her pain. And then my body responded to hers. Desire shot through me like fire. I had thought I would never touch her again. I wanted to devour her. I buried my head in her hair, breathed her in.

'I've been desperate all night. I thought I'd never see you again. They made me call you and leave that goddamned message.'

'I never had any message from you. They told me you had gone back to Paris. That you didn't want to see me any more but you didn't have the courage to tell me. I called your house. They said you were gone. Oh, they are so cruel, the Laurents and my parents. I hate them all! But I knew you wouldn't do that.'

141

'Never,' I swore. 'We can't let them destroy us. We have to outsmart them. I'll come to you in Switzerland. We'll go to Spain, to Morocco. We'll find a way. I can't lose you, Catherine. I can't!'

She was crying again. I could tell she'd cried a lot in the last few hours.

'I gave my word that I would go back to school and not marry you.'

'To whom?'

'To my brother.'

'I don't give a damn about him! He told your parents.'

'It wasn't Paul. He swore to me. He knows how much I love you. I was desperate. I threatened to kill myself if I couldn't see you one more time.'

'Kill yourself? You didn't mean it, did you?'

'Yes, I did,' she said. And from the look in her eyes, I believed her. It was almost the beginning of madness. I held her to me and stroked her hair, not knowing what frightened me the most, what they were doing to us or her reaction to it.

'Paul agreed to sneak me out of the house and bring me here only if I would tell you goodbye. I promised him. If I don't go back with him, my parents will make him pay. He will help us find a way later when everything has calmed down.'

'I don't care what you promised him. You can't go back! We may never see each other again.' If this pain tearing my guts wasn't so real, I'd never have believed it was happening.

'Catherine,' Paul called from the dock. His insistent voice struck another blow for their side. '*Dépeche-toi.*' Hurry up!

I held on to her, not knowing what else to do, boiling with a fury I had no way to express.

'Here.' She pressed a piece of paper into my hand.

142

'It's the address of my school and my aunt's home in Switzerland. I've also written the phone numbers. Come to me there. We'll find a way, James, we have to.'

At least she was resourceful. I hadn't thought of these things. 'My phone number is listed in the Houston directory,' I told her. 'If anything happens, leave a message for me there. I'll see you in Switzerland, I promise. Don't worry.' I kissed her mouth; our tongues intertwined. I cupped her breasts one more time and thrust myself against her, telling her I loved her.

'I love you too, James,' she said. And then she was gone.

I screamed with the agony of that parting.

I never saw or heard from her again. The phone numbers were all disconnected, my letters to her all returned – addressee unknown. She never returned to school, nor did she leave any messages in Houston, though I spent a lot of money trying to find out.

I blamed Claudine and Emile. We had a terrible fight and I swore I'd never speak to them again. Eventually, when Emile apologized, I forgave them. And I wrote to Paul who answered back.

His first reply was sympathetic, full of declarations of friendship and a few excuses. He hinted that I would only find her if she wanted to be found; but she needed time for herself.

I poured out my heart to him, telling him how I adored her, telling him how we'd planned to be married, that I'd do anything to be worthy of her, wait years if it was necessary, make my fortune before asking her again.

In his next letter there were no more hints of friendship, only underlying fury. Now that he knew the extent of our love he was sorry for me. Catherine was glad that she'd waited because she'd changed her mind.

She'd never cared for me at all. She realized she needed someone from her own class.

I didn't believe him. They must have done something to her to keep her from me. She never would have changed her mind on her own. I begged him to let me speak to her. It did no good.

In the third and final letter Paul wrote to me, he said I was ridiculous to think I could ever marry his sister. He admitted that of course he'd told his parents about us. The lawyer to whom he'd referred me was loyal to him not to me, and had told him of my plans. The son-of-a-bitch! Paul would always protect his family and never let his sister marry someone like me. In closing, he said I would never find her so must forget about her. She would get over it, and so would I.

The wound left by my brother's death had not yet healed. Losing Catherine on top of it was more than I could bear. I shut away that pain and mourned only for Rob. I told myself that there would be other women for me. And with a skill I'd perfected from living with my father, I set thoughts of Catherine aside. During the months I was in Amsterdam and then in Senegal, I screwed as many women as I could find and stayed stoned as much as possible. I rarely thought about her.

Years later, when I was with the FBI and Emile wrote to tell me that she'd married some nobleman, the son of a family friend, and was living in Italy, it barely registered with me.

Now, suddenly, all these years later, the pain was back again, as excruciating as if it had just happened. I couldn't believe how much agony there was that I had never let myself feel.

# Chapter 8

I had fallen asleep in the boat and awoke to discover tears in my eyes. Disoriented, I looked around to see that I'd drifted downriver where the water widens into a small lake. I knew the place; Castelle d'Aumant was just around the bend. If one ignores the teachings of Freud, I had arrived here without planning to. As though sharpshooters were aiming at my head, I dipped the oars in the water and rowed back as fast as I could. By the time I reached the dock, I was breathing hard, my hands were blistered and my muscles begged for relief.

Feeling like a fool, I reached the landing, tied the boat to the dock and gathered up my belongings, glad no one had seen me. But someone had. The girl from the museum and the café. I marvelled at the way she kept appearing in my life like a dream that I could actually hang on to. I raised my hand to wave, feeling that by now we knew one another, and called out, 'Hello.'

She just stood there regarding me coolly as though she knew all my secrets.

I climbed out of the boat on to the pier and our eyes met; something about her calm gaze unnerved me. There was an innocence about her body but not her eyes. They had seen too much. Today she was wearing khaki shorts and a cotton tank top which delicately outlined her breasts; the strap on one side hung casually over her shoulder. One arm was bent at the elbow and crossed her waist, the other elbow rested on a raised hip. Her posture said, 'I'm giving you an opening if you want to take it.' But I was at a loss to know what kind.

We stared at one another silently, waiting for the other's move. I expected her to falter but she stood her ground. We were the only two people in the world and I was mesmerized, nearly lost in her gaze, unable to tear my eyes away. How exquisite she was, like some enchanted forest nymph come to life. I wondered if she'd been following me, but it was wishful thinking though she fascinated me.

Then she parted her lips and slowly stuck out the luminous tip of her pink tongue. It sparkled in the sunlight as she licked her lower lip, tasting something wonderful. Her blank, knowing expression and the deliberate action of her tongue made my prick go hard as a rock and it scared me. *Jesus!* How could a teenager be turning me on? *That's great, Barton. Proud of yourself? Something to write home about.*

I could swear her eyes strayed down to my shorts and she noticed me pointing towards her like a sword. My face flushed which made the corners of her mouth twitch into a smile. Damn her! She knew exactly what she was doing. Or I thought she did.

Then she lowered her arms to her sides, turned on her heel and walked away without a backward glance, her hips swaying from side to side. I let out a low whistle under my breath. If girls like that had been around when I was young, life would have been different. This girl was a heart breaker. But she wouldn't be breaking mine.

The moment she turned, the spell was gone, as if someone had thrown cold water on me. Now I saw her vulnerability, her youth, her defencelessness. If she came up against an adult who wanted to take advantage (and who wouldn't, in those shorts and tank top?) she'd be in trouble. That such a young girl had entranced me, made me ashamed.

And why was she always alone? Even with her school friends in Paris she'd stayed behind, kept herself separate, though kids her age generally travelled in packs. There was an illusory aspect about these encounters as though I'd created them out of my own need. It brought to mind others associated with nymphets: Roman Polanski, Jerry Lee Lewis, Errol Flynn, and of course Humbert Humbert. *I could never be one of them!*

Fully humiliated now, I carried both my rods to the car and slammed the door. As I drove past her on the road I didn't give her a backward glance, even in the rear view mirror, though I knew she was watching me. This place was getting the better of me. It was time to get back to work.

When I arrived at my rooming house and turned into the gravel driveway, who should be standing there with my landlady but her relatives, Monsieur and Madame Larousse? I wanted to turn around and drive away but they had seen me.

As I got out of the car the light dawned on Madame Larousse's face and her eyes studied my face.

'*C'est toi!*'

'*Bonjour, Madame.*' I offered my hand. 'You remember me?'

'But of course,' she insisted, giving her husband a look. *Muet!* Idiot, it said, for not recognizing the visitor.

Larousse took it coolly. 'How was I to know? He was only a boy then.'

Madame shook a finger under my chin. 'So you are

147

staying here? We haven't seen you for such a long time. Do *they* know you are here?'

She was referring to the d'Aumants. 'It's just a holiday,' I told her.

'You were the cause of much trouble for Mademoiselle Catherine, yes? Tell me, she was *enceinte*?' Pregnant. 'We always wanted to know.'

'No!' I insisted, realizing that must be what the family had told them.

'You took advantage. She went back to school in disgrace.'

'But she wasn't pregnant!' I repeated, remembering how careful I'd been.

'*Hah!* It's good they kicked you out. André Laurent nearly lost his farm because of you. The Duc was very angry. He made them pay, believe me.'

I was stunned. 'How did he make them pay? Emile never told me.' I recalled our conversation in Paris the other day when he'd said, '*It was a relief that it wasn't worse for us.*' That bastard d'Aumant must have done something to Emile's family.

'*Pauvre Mademoiselle*,' the woman said, forgetting the Laurents, her bottom lip turned down in a scowl as she shook her head. 'Such a shame. *Tragique. Très tragique.*'

'What is?' My heart leaped to my throat.

'The parents died, and then the husband was killed in an accident.'

'The husband too?' Emile hadn't told me that either! He'd written about the barge explosion that took the lives of the Duc and Duchesse d'Aumant, and the caretaker, sweet old Gaston. But not that her husband had died; why not something that important?

'How did the husband die?' I asked.

Larousse sucked in air and shook his fingers up and down as though the information was hot. 'His car went over the Corniche near Nice, many years ago. More than ten.'

*Ten years and Emile never told me.* 'Was Catherine with him? Was she hurt?'

'*Non!*' They looked at each other for corroboration and decided that she wasn't.

'What happened to her?'

'*Je ne sais pas.* She was ill, *non*?' Larousse said to his wife.

'Poor thing,' Madame said with a sigh. '*Quel tragédie.* So young, so beautiful.' Her head shook from side to side.

'What do you mean?' I asked. They were torturing me with this stretched-out story. Emile had said she was fine. *Wait till I get my hands on him!* 'Is Catherine living at the *castelle*?' I asked.

'*Non, ne plus ans!*' Not for years, he said, as though I were stupid to ask.

'Where does she live?' A sense of apprehension was beginning to grow.

'*Qui sait?*' Madame Cretier, my landlady, spoke up sharply to shut them up. Obviously her relatives had said enough. 'We don't know, do we, Marie?'

'*Non!*' Monsieur Larousse answered for his wife, playing innocent.

I wanted to grab someone's neck and wring it.

'*C'est tout!*' Madame Cretier said with a shrug. 'After the husband died, *rien.*' Nothing.

Something was going on.

I left them and went into the house to place a credit card call to Emile. Why hadn't he told me these things?

'Where are you?' he demanded, coming on the line immediately. 'You were supposed to call me!'

'I'm in the south-west,' I told him. 'I got distracted. Now tell me what you know about Catherine.'

'Never mind about her – there's been another

149

murder, in Toulouse! I'm on my way now. Meet me there.'

Instantly my attention shifted. 'How long ago? Have they moved the body?'

'I think so, but the scene is fresh. You can be in on this one from the start!'

Toulouse was several hours to the east. It would take me a while to get there. Adrenaline was rushing through me at the idea of working again. 'I'll leave right away.'

'I'll see you there,' he said, about to hang up.

'Wait, Emile!' I barely stopped him. 'Did anything tragic happen to Catherine d'Aumant besides the death of her husband? And why didn't you tell me he died?'

'How did you find out?' he asked.

'Never mind. You lied to me. You sat across from me at lunch and insisted there was nothing left to tell about her. Why?'

'I was afraid of what you'd do if you knew she was a widow. You suffered over her, James. When her husband died you were happily married to Victoria. What good would it have done to tell you? Only stir up old feelings.'

'So you were protecting me?'

'Why give you more trouble?'

'She might have wanted to hear from me, Emile. I could have sent condolences.'

'Would you?'

'Probably not.'

'She didn't contact you, did she?'

'No,' I agreed.

Suspicion came into his voice. 'Where exactly are you in the south-west?'

'Eugénie,' I replied.

'Oh, Christ. This is all I need.'

'Then it's true. Your family did have trouble. Was it because of me?'

'It's been over for years, James. Drop it.'

'For God's sake, tell me,' I insisted.

'I've got to get to Toulouse.'

'It won't take long.'

'Oh, Christ!' he sighed. 'It just gets me upset to talk about it. But that bastard d'Aumant blamed the Laurent family for bringing you to Eugénie and letting you mess around with his daughter.'

'But you didn't let me! You tried to stop me.'

'It didn't matter to him. That October, when the family's leases were due on the farm, the Duc refused to renew them. My family had leased their farmland for generations, but it made no difference. He threatened to turn us out of our house! My father and my brothers had to beg. Finally he agreed to let us stay, but he raised the price of the lease. It took everything we had, nearly ruined the family. Thank God there was rain for the next few years and good crops. But my father worried all the time, and then he died. The aggravation and worry wore him down. I didn't shed a tear for Monsieur le Duc when he was killed.'

'Emile, I'm so sorry,' I said, recalling how Claudine had warned me there would be consequences. 'I don't know what to say.'

'It wasn't your fault, James. He was a despicable man. It's over now.'

No wonder Emile's family had glared at me at the wedding.

'The helicopter is waiting, James. I'll see you in Toulouse. Check in at the Prefecture and have them call me.' And he hung up. There was more about Catherine I wanted to ask him, but it would have to wait.

I felt awful. Especially learning that he had protected

151

me and stayed my friend. I might not have been so generous. Now I really owed him. At least I had a way to make it up to him by solving his case.

I packed my belongings, so I could return to Paris with Emile after Toulouse. I wasn't finished here yet but it would have to wait until Shithead was captured.

As I drove out of town along the route to the highway, I saw her again – my teenage fantasy. She was riding bareback on a caramel-coloured horse, still wearing the shorts and tank top from earlier in the day. The blonde hair that streamed out behind her matched the colour of the horse's tail. Joyously she bounded over the fields, the setting sun behind her, as if one with the horse; and yet, something about it felt staged for my benefit.

Impossible. She had no way of knowing I would be driving on this road. I was really off the deep end being haunted by a sexy poltergeist.

After I passed her, I concentrated on the case ahead of me. But Catherine and this girl were intertwined in my mind. The girl enticed and ignored me, the same as Catherine, who enticed me by existing out there in the world and never contacting me, even after her parents and her husband died. I was surprised at how much that hurt.

It was the first time I'd driven at night since I'd arrived in France; I always forget that headlights on French cars are yellow instead of white. It rained all the way to Toulouse and the journey took longer than I expected. I made one pit stop at a Total station where I filled up the tank for a small fortune and grabbed something to eat while I checked the dates of the murders to see if the days of the month matched, or they coincided with cycles of the moon. But they didn't.

The Europeans have well-equipped road stops on

their highways with clean lavatories and sometimes a full service restaurant. But this place only had filled baguettes.

When I arrived at the outskirts of the city just past midnight, my Guide Michelin helped me locate *le centre ville*. Then I asked directions until I found the Prefecture of Police on Rue Fermat.

Emile had set up a command post. I found him conferring with Chief Inspector Didier, who'd been called in by local police when the body was discovered earlier that night. Electricity charged through me to be working again.

Emile introduced me to Didier, a short stocky man with hooded eyelids in his late-thirties. Outside his Paris Prefecture, Emile didn't have to keep my presence a secret.

'FBI?' Didier implied, *Who gives a shit?* His arrogance annoyed me after my long drive, but I understood his resentment. This was the biggest case he'd ever had and he wanted to keep it. Once the similarities to the Boardroom Killings were established, Emile had yanked it away. Didier could only hope that the *Juge d'instruction* in Toulouse, deciding on procedure, would keep him informed. Tough break.

Now there were four different investigative teams and three separate judges. As the cases grew more complicated, details could get overlooked. And this case could be lost on such details. It was my job to see that didn't happen.

I was disappointed to discover that the victim's body had already been photographed, measured and taken to the morgue. So the scene wouldn't be as fresh as I liked. The autopsy would not be completed until morning. Still, I was anxious to see the scene myself. It was the first time I'd been close to a partially fresh crime scene. But Emile was in no hurry to go there.

On the desk were plastic bags filled with evidence and the files from the other three cases. None of the forensic reports was back yet from the Scientific Police lab and probably wouldn't be until morning. When I heard that, I assumed we'd go to the scene for a quick look but no one was leaving. This was not the time to ask Emile about Catherine. I took off my coat and hung it on a chair.

The air in the Chef's office was thick with smoke and there was strong coffee. I glanced through the preliminary reports feeling right at home. This case was almost identical to the other three.

I studied the photographs, hoping to see something different, but there were no defensive cuts on the hands. This victim hadn't defended himself either. Another poor sucker taken unaware. How do you do it, Shithead? How do you keep these men so mesmerized that you kill them without a struggle?

'What about the VCR?' I asked Emile.

He nodded. 'Similar evidence of use. This time they found prints on it. The same as before: smooth finger type.'

Someone called him to the phone. It was Solange. He grabbed the phone as though desperate to speak to her. 'I've been waiting for you to call me back. Where are you?' He listened to her reply. 'I called you in Marseille and they told me you'd left yesterday. Are they wrong? Are you still there?'

I cleared my throat to let him know people were listening but he didn't care.

'Then I guess it was a mix-up.' He listened to her question. 'Yes, I'm waiting for the lab reports. James has just arrived.' He turned to one of the local people and said, 'Officer Monod is faxing me a witness report from Paris. Please bring it to me when it arrives.' He went back to the phone. 'I'll call you later.' He paused

154

and listened again. 'If you had been there when I called, you could have joined me here. Yes, it's too bad we missed each other.'

He hung up, obviously annoyed with her, and turned to me, his mind in two places at once.

'What's with Solange?' I asked.

He gestured me aside and lowered his voice. 'She tells me one thing and does another, you know how it is. She was supposed to be in Marseille following up a lead, but when I tried to reach her, she wasn't there. I don't know where the hell she was. As her commanding officer, I'm supposed to know every minute. She's taking advantage.'

'Lovers do that,' I said.

It sounded like he didn't trust her – an unfortunate distraction at a time like this. He said to Didier, 'Is it true that your people found a blood sample by the door?'

'Yes,' he confirmed.

'It can't be the victim's blood,' he said to me. 'The man never got out of his chair.'

'We'll know whose it is when the reports come back,' Didier replied.

'If it's the killer's blood, that's evidence you can use to prove your case in court,' I said to Emile.

'If we ever get to court.'

'There was also a sample of semen,' Didier pointed out.

'From intercourse?'

'No, masturbation.'

'Like the previous guy,' I said to Emile.

He nodded. 'At least this one got off. The other one was right in the middle.'

'The killer's timing is improving,' I commented, marvelling at the iron will and cold calculation it took to wait until a man is about to come and then kill him.

*Shithead, I want to get you.* I got a flash of these elderly victims kissing their wives, lifting their grandchildren high into the air, and it nearly made me gag. I usually keep myself from feeling emotional over victims or I lose my objectivity, but at the moment I couldn't do it, as though a part of me had been opened up. Because of Catherine. Letting those memories back was making me vulnerable.

'It seems our killer has a compassionate side,' Didier interrupted. 'Pleasure before dying.'

'You stupid ass,' I blurted out, wanting to kill him. 'Compassionate? Never! This son-of-a-bitch toys with his victims just to perfect his timing.'

'James.' Emile put his arm on mine to calm me. Didier's face was turning purple, his fists clenched. The other officers in the room were staring at me.

I took a deep breath and let it out. 'I'm sorry,' I told him and everyone else. 'It's been a long night.'

Didier glanced at his people. Everyone relaxed.

'I think he's really getting cocky,' Emile said. 'He murdered the victim, de Saint Robert, in the height of a summer evening, without waiting for people to be asleep.'

'Maybe we'll get an eyewitness,' I said.

'Marcel de Saint Robert was a friend of mine,' Didier said. 'He was sixty-six years old, born here in Toulouse. A respected man. I was the one who had to tell his wife.' He looked away and I saw how upset he was. I was sorry I'd snapped at him.

'I know how you feel,' Emile told him. 'Pierre Fontelle, who was murdered last year, was a friend of mine.'

Didier nodded sympathetically.

'Any fingerprints?' I asked.

'A great many, none identified as yet,' Didier said. 'Both latent and patent and, of course, smoothglove.'

156

He was still annoyed that we were there.

'I'd give anything to find a duplicate print from one of the other cases,' Emile said.

'Any physical evidence would do, blood or hair,' I added.

'He is the one who wears the gloves, *c'est vrai*?' Didier asked.

'Yes,' I agreed. 'But sometimes we've taken fingerprints through gloves, if the finger has pronounced fiction ridges.'

Emile shot me a look, warning me not to challenge him. 'It can depend on who's doing the lifting,' he said. 'That's why I brought one of our experts from Paris.'

'Maybe someone noticed a man wearing gloves on a warm summer evening,' I commented.

'He could have put them on in the office and removed them before he left the building,' Didier countered.

'Yes,' I agreed, willing to soothe him for the moment. I knew what it was like to be invaded by the higher-ups. I was glad I was one of them.

'But if he put them on in front of the victim, it could be because he knew the victim, and the victim was comfortable in his presence, not alerted to any danger.'

'Oh, *c'est fou*!' That's ridiculous. 'De Saint Robert would not be acquainted with a killer!'

He subscribed to the myth that the upper class is above reproach. Anyone who's wealthy cannot be culpable. If so, to what can one aspire? Whom can one envy? The social hierarchy is accepted in France, especially by the working class. They pay deference to their social betters while denying that they do it. It's the same at home, too. The wealthy get away with things. I thought of the way Catherine's parents treated me and Emile's family.

'James is right,' Emile insisted. 'The victim had to know the killer.'

'How could the same man know all these people when they didn't know each other and lived in different cities?' Didier said.

'We don't know what the connection is yet,' I answered. 'We're searching for it.'

Emile's patience was thin too. 'I want to see the statements from his friends and family.'

'The killer won't be among them,' I insisted.

Emile shrugged. We'd had no luck with that so far.

'The killer drives the kind of car that won't break down when he travels to distant cities.' I repeated what Patrick Richard's nurse had told me about the sound of a car door closing. 'I wish we knew whether he lives in Paris, Bordeaux or Toulouse, how he arranges to meet the victim, and what kind of video tape he brings.'

Emile said, 'I'd like to know when it is during the scenario that he puts on his gloves, whether he takes the elevator or the stairs, and where he parks his car.' We looked at each other in frustration. We still had so far to go.

'Maybe he took a plane or a train,' Didier said.

'Too easy to trace,' I snapped.

A light went on for Didier. 'One witness reported seeing a four-door, dark-coloured new model Mercedes coming out of the underground parking garage beneath the square across from the building. It nearly ran him over,' Didier said.

'A Mercedes in the public garage could belong to anyone,' Emile said.

'Let's assume it was our killer,' I said. 'To afford a car like that he's either a professional or a skilled worker, probably educated, not a social misfit or he would stand out, somebody would notice. We've established that he's articulate and clever – a match for the police – and he doesn't arouse suspicion when dealing with wealthy people. That eliminates all suspects who aren't upmarket.'

Emile was pleased with my conclusions.

'Be sure to check the rental agencies and stolen car reports. Serial killers use their own cars or steal them,' I told Didier.

He nodded curtly. I'd stepped on his toes again, but I didn't give a damn.

'What about the video machine?' he asked. 'The VCR in de Saint Robert's office was on and the tape slot empty.'

'The other three victims watched a video before they were killed,' I told him. 'The killer removes the tape after he murders them.'

'I don't want that leaked to the press,' Emile told Didier, who nodded.

'I think it's more significant that the safe was open,' Didier said.

'Everything's significant,' I said.

'It wasn't a robbery,' Emile told him. 'Stock certificates and cash were still in the safe, and so was the jewellery.'

'I'd wager something is missing,' I said. 'Killers take souvenirs.'

'Especially if it's a woman,' Didier said, looking smug.

'Unlikely,' I replied. 'In spite of what you see in the movies, women don't commit crimes like this.'

'How do you explain this?' He held up a photograph of a woman's shoeprint, clearly outlined by the victim's blood. 'It's not from a cleaning woman, we've checked them all.'

Emile was furious. 'Why didn't you show me this before?' He snatched it.

'I thought the great detective would find it himself.'

Emile was livid as he looked at the photo. It showed a woman's clear print. She'd stepped in the victim's blood on her way out of the door. The print faced the door which meant it came from behind the victim – anyone coming into the room would make prints that faced the victim.

Emile and I exchanged a look. This was a new twist.

'I don't buy it,' I said. 'A woman slitting men's throats?'

'The clothing fibres we've found on the previous victims have all been from men's clothes,' Emile said. 'Hair samples are from both men and women, but they don't match.'

'Our hair samples are from a woman,' Didier said.

'A cross dresser,' I offered. I couldn't stand Didier. 'What size is this shoe?'

'Large,' Didier informed me. 'According to our measurements it's a size forty.'

'What's the equivalent in the US?'

'I think it's about a size nine,' Emile said.

'That is large!' I exclaimed.

'The right size for a tall killer.' The photo of the shoe print showed that it had a wide stacked heel worn for comfort, not a stiletto type worn for style.

'Let's speculate,' Emile said. 'We know the killer is tall and strong enough to cut from this angle.' He demonstrated with a finger across his throat in an upward slash. 'It takes powerful muscles to slice through a living body, especially one that's struggling even slightly.'

'Okay,' I said, trying to make the image fit. 'A strong, diabolical woman makes an appointment with the victim. To do what? A manicure? A strip tease? A dance?'

'She puts a tape in the VCR,' Emile said.

'Maybe it's a tape of her. First she gets him excited.

160

Then, while he's whacking off to the tape, she sneaks up behind him and slits his throat as he's about to reach orgasm.' It made a crazy kind of sense.

'Not many women are tall and strong enough to do it,' Emile said. 'With a bald man like de Saint Robert, she had to hold him by the forehead. The other victims were held by their head or their hair. It's got to be a man dressed as a woman.'

'Let's reserve judgement on gender 'til we find more evidence,' I told him.

'Why?' Didier challenged me.

'Because women rarely commit multiple murders.'

'That's not enough of a reason,' he scoffed.

'Do you know anything about serial killers?' I asked. He stared at me. Obviously, he didn't.

'There are usually two categories, organized and disorganized. The disorganized killer isn't careful about his actions, he's overwhelmed by his fantasies or hears voices telling him what to do. He acts spontaneously. Usually he's suffering from extreme mental illness. Disorganized killers are the ones who grab random strangers off the street.

'The organized killer will stalk his victim, take time to plan his crime, and usually bring along a kit to kill with – weapons, ropes, torture devices, clothing. He'll pick a familiar location and have a place to take his victims. Afterwards, he'll find a place to hide the body.'

In his clean little city, Didier had never encountered people like this. 'That doesn't fit this killer, does it?' he asked.

'No,' I admitted. 'The Boardroom Killer makes no attempt to hide anything. Usually multiple killers not only obscure the identity of their victim by decapitating them or cutting off their fingers, things like that, they'll dump the body where it's not easily found.'

161

Emile was thinking out loud. 'Each time this killer leaves the body for us to find as though he disdains us. He doesn't believe we are smart enough to catch him. Or *her*.'

'He's probably been committing crimes for a long time and has never been caught,' I added.

'What else do you know?' Didier was getting interested.

'If multiple murderers travel distances to commit their crimes, they kill along the way. Mostly, they opt for convenience. But a woman might not be bound by the same behaviour patterns. We don't know enough about female killers. Suppose her job takes her on the road. She might be choosing victims in each city she visits.'

'But you said she knows them,' Didier said.

'Maybe she sold them something, like a typewriter or a computer. Emile, did you find out if any of the victims owned things in common?'

'Yes, but it hasn't led anywhere.'

'My deputy inspectors are gathering samples of hair from the office staff and family members for comparison.'

'The FBI rule is, over three samples of hair found on the victim belongs to the killer,' I said.

'At least we have DNA testing now,' Emile said.

'Were there other shoeprints?' I asked Didier.

'Latent ones by the elevator and one leaving the building heading towards the parking structure across the street.'

'Where the Mercedes came from?' Emile asked.

Didier nodded.

'Any weapon found?' I asked.

'No,' Emile replied. 'But we're combing the building and the neighbourhood, checking all the litter bins and any lowslung roofs for a four-mile radius. I'm not too

162

hopeful. None of the weapons has ever been recovered.'

'Is it the same type of weapon as was used in the other killings?' I asked.

'We'll know when the lab reports come back, but the photographs of the wound look the same.' Emile removed his glasses and wiped his eyes. If I was tired, he must be too. He was nearly fifty-three. I wouldn't want to be doing this at his age. But if I didn't plan something for my future, I'd have little choice later on. I wondered if I'd still be married to Victoria.

'Any drugs involved?' I asked.

'Only a heart medication like Richard in Bordeaux was taking,' Emile replied. 'Beta blockers.'

I yawned. It was now about two-thirty in the morning and my eyes felt dry and gritty. But the French police never take a break on an investigation during the first forty-eight hours. They gather all the data they can and question every witness while the trail is hot. So I drank another cup of coffee strong enough to dissolve a spoon in and said, 'Let's review the witnesses' statements.'

'We're still compiling them,' Didier told us.

'What amazes me,' Emile said, 'is that the murder occurred in such a public place, a building in the middle of the city, with thousands of people on the streets below.'

Shithead knew how to blend right into the crowd, I thought.

'Let's check out the scene,' I suggested.

'It's near the Place President Wilson, in the entertainment centre of the city,' Emile said.

'About that Mercedes,' I asked Didier, slipping back into my jacket. 'Did anyone get a look at the licence? Your French licence plates tell you where the car is from, city and district.'

'No one got a number. However, the witness who

163

saw the car claims there were two blonde women in it, one driving, the other a passenger.'

'Could we get a composite?' Emile asked.

'We're trying,' he said.

'Two women!' I said. 'Of course. The killer has an accomplice who distracts the victim while she kills him.'

Emile nodded slowly. 'That would work.'

I studied the photographs in the file again and saw something on the carpet of de Saint Robert's office. 'What's this?' I asked, pointing to a small circular indentation in the carpet.

'It looks like a scuff mark,' Emile said.

'No, it's too perfectly shaped. We'll check it out when we get there.'

I wanted to ditch Didier, but he trailed along with two members of his group.

'What's with Solange?' I managed to ask Emile.

'She's not where she's supposed to be,' he said. 'Drives me crazy. I can never locate her.' He glanced sideways at me. 'I shouldn't mix business with sex, but it's rare for us to be together when the government is paying.' Then he sighed. 'Hotel bills are expensive. Maybe it's better this way.'

The office building was only a few blocks from the Prefecture. There was a restaurant across the street which I eyed longingly. I was hungry and tired, and wanted to ask Emile about Catherine.

The high-rise where de Saint Robert's import-export business had its headquarters was surrounded by people, even at this hour of the morning.

We crossed the street at the corner of Boulevard Strasbourg and Allée President Roosevelt and entered the ceramic-lined entryway. The lift was typically European, tiny and impractical even though the building was modern. I tried to picture Shithead taking this same elevator earlier tonight. I could almost feel him breathing in my ear. 'Have all the elevator buttons dusted, the interior hand rails and the stairwells,' I told Emile, who nodded. 'And check the cloakrooms on all floors.'

Didier got off with his entourage to follow my suggestions and Emile and I sighed with relief as we continued to the office alone.

The mahogany doors to the suite were cordoned off with red caution tape and a guard stood at the door. Emile showed his badge and he let us by. Just like home.

We went through the reception area, down a hall and into the executive offices. On the way I saw chalk marks encircling the faint outline of a bloody footprint on the carpet. Modern technology provides law enforcement with helpful tools to use in investigative work, but it's still the hard slog of human beings that solves the crime. Victoria complains that women don't have equality in a man's world. Well, here was a female killer who had become the equal of any male psychopath.

The executive office itself was large and luxurious, with a view of the wide divided boulevard below and the city beyond. I looked up the boulevard and saw where it crossed Le Canal du Midi. If I craned my neck to the east, I could see the Garonne.

On the left side of the room was a sitting area consisting of a sofa and three chairs, and in the centre, in front of the window, was an enormous fruitwood desk flanked by two club chairs; a large swivel chair sat behind, still covered in blood. I hated the smell of death in that room, distinctive and unmistakable, excrement mixed with blood and the sickening sweet odour of slightly rotten flesh. Even after a long shower and shampoo, I would still be able to smell it.

I looked around. To the right of the door was an

entertainment cabinet built into a bookcase. The doors to the television were open, the set partially extended and swivelled towards the desk. The VCR was still on, but the slot was empty. I saw where they'd lifted a print on the eject button. A drawer beneath the console revealed a row of video tapes all labelled with the company logo. An adjacent cabinet housed the safe, its door ajar.

'When people use a safe, they generally close and lock it afterwards.' I was thinking out loud. 'De Saint Robert was killed before he could do that and so was Richard. I have a feeling that whatever was in the safe is now missing.'

'More valuable than stocks or money?'

'More private – a porno tape.'

'That's what I was thinking,' Emile said.

'So he had it in advance. That means the killer sent it to him. If only we had the package. Have them check the rubbish here and at his home.' Emile made a note.

'Has anyone looked at these?' I pointed to the video tapes in the drawer.

Emile looked through his notes. 'They've been checked. They're all videos of the company's products being unloaded on to docks and delivered to their destinations. De Saint Robert thought this kind of record keeping was a good use of modern technology. Older people who haven't grown up with mechanical devices overuse them or ignore them. His methods were redundant. There are descriptions of the same transactions in the files.'

I approached the area I had seen in the photograph, a small indentation in the carpet in front of the desk between the two club chairs.

I knelt down and laid my cheek on the floor so I could see the carpet pile from a side angle. I had learned this trick from a girl I used to date who sometimes lost her contact lens. Crouching to eye level with the object was the best way to find it.

It worked now, too – an indentation in the tight pile of the expensive wool carpet popped into my line of vision. And then I found three more just like it forming the shape of a square. I stood up and looked down to see four small circles in the carpet, the kind made by chair legs. Two armless chairs stood on either side of an antique console table against the wall. Using a Kleenex so as not to leave my own fingerprints, I picked up one of them and carried it over to the four indentations. Its legs fit perfectly into the four circles.

'Someone brought this chair over here and sat on it facing the desk. Someone who didn't weigh much,' I said, 'or the indentations would have been deeper.'

'I'll have the chairs gone over again,' Emile promised.

'Why did someone use that chair instead of these two in front of the desk?' I wondered.

'Perhaps his secretary takes dictation from a straight-backed chair, preferring it to these soft leather ones.'

'If the secretary used it, there would be more marks like this in the carpet.'

I was starting to get a picture of what might have happened. 'The killer brought over the chair for the accomplice to sit in. The accomplice faces the victim who's watching a porno tape. While he's occupied, the killer moves around behind him, and when the victim is ready to come, she slashes his throat. Afterwards, the accomplice puts the chair back and the killer removes the tape.'

'That would fit. Anyone who wears a size nine shoe would leave a heavier indentation in the carpet.'

Emile was catching on fast. 'We may find something when we have these chairs dusted,' he said. There were prints all over them. We turned to each other and smiled.

'Two people are easier to catch than one,' I said. 'The chances of making mistakes are greater. I'll bet our killer is more careful than the accomplice.'

It wasn't until we had stopped off to say goodbye to Didier two floors down, and were walking back to Emile's hotel, that I brought up the subject of Catherine.

'We agreed not to talk about her again, isn't that enough?'

'But there's still more to tell. So spill the rest,' I insisted.

'You'd better brace yourself,' he said.

'Is she alive?' I could not stand the suspense.

'Yes. But she's in a *maison de repos* – a private sanatarium. She had a complete mental breakdown.'

My throat closed involuntarily. 'When did that happen?'

'At least ten years ago, after her husband was killed. He was a Jolibois, one of those old families we provincials love to hate. I think his name was Antoine, quite a playboy. He had girlfriends after their marriage, not discreet at all, he raced cars, spent money. They lived near his family on the Riviera. I suppose losing both her parents, her husband, and you as well, was too much for her. She became violent, attacked her brother with a knife. I heard she scratched off her own skin.'

I shuddered to think of it.

'I saw her at her parents' funeral. We were in Eugénie when the barge exploded. What a sound! It broke windows for miles around.'

'Was it a fuel leak?'

'I don't know, it wasn't my case. But a lot of people hated the Duc. Anyone could have done it.'

'It wasn't an accident?'

He shrugged, 'Who knows? If my father wasn't already dead, I'd have suspected him.'

I had a crazy thought. 'You don't think Catherine did it, do you?'

'She wasn't there when it happened. Only showed up afterwards for the funeral.'

'Emile, you knew her all her life. Did you ever think she'd become mentally ill?'

'It's hard to say. You knew her too. Did you?'

I shook my head, trying to remember.

'As a girl she seemed normal, except for being so seductive. She wasn't just beautiful, she was aware of men, how she affected them. Everyone in town had a hard on for her. We were all jealous of you when you got her.' Emile smiled at me. 'Some of us were relieved that we didn't have to dream about her any more.' That didn't sound like the Catherine I knew; it sounded more like the other girl, the one from the village.

'With me, she was just a sensual young woman,' I said.

'At the funeral, she looked sad, withdrawn,' Emile said. 'But she was in shock.'

I tried to remember any signs I'd missed. There was the time she was afraid of going to hell. And the night we parted, she'd talked about suicide. I'd believed she was serious. Right now, I was overwhelmed with sadness that her life had been ruined.

'How long has she been in a sanatarium?'

'At least ten years, maybe longer.'

'Do they keep people locked up that long?'

'She can't function in the world, James. Be comforted that she has excellent care.'

I felt sick to think of all the years she'd spent locked away, that beautiful, sensitive girl. Somehow it was my fault. I should have prevented this.

169

Emile's hand patted my shoulder. 'These things happen, son. There's no one to blame. Think of it as an illness.'

If only I'd stayed with her. But I had no power to fight her family; I too had been caught in a prison of sorts. But, oh God, Catherine. I was sunk in despair as though I had just lost her and there was a knife in my heart. In that moment, all the love I'd once felt came flooding back and I almost cried out from the pain.

If only I hadn't been so helpless, if only I'd been older, smarter, stronger. If only I'd found a way to be with her, none of this would have happened, I knew it with dead certainty. We should have been married.

And then it hit me. When Catherine and I were together, I had been impotent, not sexually but lacking the power to determine my life. And now I was impotent again, only for real. Maybe Catherine was the reason. I had to see her. If I didn't, I might be impotent for the rest of my life.

We reached the hotel. 'Emile,' I said, 'I have to go back to Eugénie and find out where Catherine is. But I'm not deserting you. I'll call you twice a day and be there the instant you need me.'

'I understand,' he told me. 'But don't go yet. Stay until I've interviewed the family.'

I couldn't say no.

# Chapter 9

When we arrived at Emile's hotel, I looked longingly at the bed, but instead we showered, put on clean shirts, and were off again to interview Madame de Saint Robert and her family. Deputy Inspector Berthelot (complete with typewriter) accompanied us to record the interview.

The de Saint Robert home was on the Place Ste Scarbes, a street too narrow for parking, even for police, so we left the car in a public lot under the Church of St Sernin half a block away.

The apartment was in a *hôtel particulier*, meaning that the building had once been a single residence for wealthy people and had now been remodelled and divided into apartments for wealthy people who could do with less space. Not that they were roughing it in this antique stone and brick edifice with its spanking new plaster, paned glass windows, shiny marble and guarded entry. Each apartment had a separate entrance off the stone courtyard and a garden off to the side. One garden was decorated with a Roman arch unearthed during the renovations, something that would have impressed Victoria. I could hear her saying, 'Imagine having your own Roman arch.'

'Won't they be asleep at four in the morning?' I asked, as we turned the timer light on and climbed the wide circular staircase to the second floor, hurrying so we'd reach the top before the light went out.

'If your husband was murdered earlier tonight, would you sleep?' Emile replied.

A young maid in uniform ushered us into the circular foyer. Even I could see that the pale marble floor complemented the fruitwood panelling. In the living room the brocade draperies were drawn over tall french windows and the light was dim. I didn't know how I would keep from falling asleep.

A woman sat facing us on a Louis-something chair, the kind with a wooden frame and curved legs. She was in her late-sixties, elegant white hair swept up on her head and a string of pearls contrasting with her black dress. Next to her on a footstool sat her daughter, a woman in her late-forties. They looked alike, except that the daughter's hair was dark, worn short and straight to her jaw line. Three grandchildren sat on the sofa, in their late teens or early-twenties. Their father was in his shirt sleeves, wearing navy braces and light grey trousers. In other circumstances he would have been a handsome man, but with the shadows deepening the grief lines in his face he looked ghoulish. He came over to shake our hands.

'I'm Arnaud DuPont,' he said. 'Please, come in. We are expecting the bishop and a priest momentarily. I thought you were them.'

We introduced ourselves and offered our condolences.

Madame de Saint Robert nodded her thanks. Her daughter stared at some spot on the carpet.

'What should we say to the press?' DuPont asked. '*Le Figaro* and *La Dépêche du Midi* have both been asking for statements, so have the Paris papers and the international press. Reporters have been outside the gates all night. Did you see them?'

'They're not there now,' I told him.

'They haven't left us alone all night.'

'They'll pursue you until they get a story. And they will exaggerate whatever you tell them,' Emile replied. 'Always, they exaggerate.'

This family was truly in mourning. Their pain hung in the air so thickly it was difficult to breathe. The widow's face had a greyish tinge to it. Only with an effort of will was she keeping her body erect. Her daughter sat by her side unmoving, except to stroke her mother's hand.

The third generation was also suffering. The slender, attractive granddaughter, in her early-twenties, was crying on her brother's shoulder while he tried to be strong. The elder son's eyes were glued to his father, ready to leap to his aid. Their restless movements reminded me of an abandoned litter of kittens, mewing for relief, jittery and without focus. I was struck by their bravery; we human beings endure unbelievable suffering and still go on. But what choice do we have?

Emile took the chair offered him by DuPont next to Madame de Saint Robert; I stood slightly apart. We seated Inspector Berthelot at a table. He opened his typewriter and began immediately.

'I'm so sorry for your loss,' Emile began. 'But we need to question you. Inspector Berthelot will carefully record all of your interviews and you must sign them once they are completed, so read them carefully. They are legal documents so please be as truthful and complete as possible.'

He turned to me. 'Monsieur James Barton is a Special Agent with the American FBI. He's here as my guest, and to question you also. I'd appreciate your cooperation.'

They were hoping that we could alleviate their helplessness. No one could do that.

'Tell me everything that happened this evening until

173

the time you were notified of your husband's death,' Emile said to the widow.

Her voice was low and controlled from centuries of breeding. 'He came home just before eight and we dined in the garden, an early dinner. We were finished by nine-thirty.'

'What did he eat for dinner?'

Emile wrote down everything she said even though Berthelot was getting it too. If the autopsy showed different food in his stomach, we could assume he'd eaten somewhere else, perhaps in a café. And that would mean witnesses.

'After dinner, he went to take a walk. I should have gone with him. If I had, this wouldn't have happened. I never would have let him walk as far as the office. He works too hard, you see.'

'Do you know why he went to the office tonight?'

'No.'

'Did he often go there after dinner?'

'Sometimes.'

'Inspector,' DuPont interrupted, 'my wife and I work with my father-in-law. We often go back to the office in the evenings, especially in summer when the days are longer, to discuss certain problems. Our business is subject to government regulations, not only the French government but other countries as well. And regulations change every day. Sometimes we don't have the time to discuss them until after hours.'

'What is your job?' Emile asked him.

'I'm executive vice-president, in charge of sales. When Marcel retired, I was to take over the company jointly with my wife. Yvette is head of customs regulations. Our elder son, Louis, has a master's degree in business and handles marketing. He also works with us.' He glanced at his son with pride and the young man sat even straighter.

'Was there something the three of you needed to discuss tonight?' Emile asked.

'No,' Yvette answered. It was the first time she spoke. I saw the agony in her eyes before she lowered her head again. 'Why would someone do this?' she whispered.

'We're going to find out and stop him,' I told her.

'Did the same man kill my grandfather as killed those men in Bordeaux and Paris?' the grandson, Louis, asked.

'We think so.' Emile's reply was gentle.

'*Merde, merde!*' he repeated, pounding the sofa with his fist. 'And you do nothing!'

The other grandson, a boy of about eighteen, suddenly shouted, 'When are you assholes going to find this crazy man?'

'Victor, Louis!' his grandmother said sternly. '*C'est tout!*' The younger one bolted up from the sofa and headed for the door.

'Where are you going?' his father asked.

'*Pissoir,*' he replied, angrily.

DuPont raised his eyes to the ceiling. Teenagers were the same everywhere. And that made me think about the girl from the village. If I were to have a conversation with her, would she too have an attitude of hostility?

Emile spoke to the daughter. 'Was there anything unusual in your father's behaviour lately? Was he troubled, or agitated or excited?'

'No,' she replied.

Emile asked her husband, 'Did your father-in-law ever close his office door to watch the VCR?'

'Sometimes,' he said. 'But it's noisy in the office and his hearing is not what it used to be.'

'Did he receive any threatening letters or phone calls, or unusual visitors? Any large amounts of money

175

withdrawn from the accounts, any strange packages?'

Before Arnaud DuPont could answer, his wife, Yvette, said, 'I thought this killer murdered people because they were older or wealthy. Why do you ask these questions?'

'We think this killer picks his victims and plans his murders carefully,' I interrupted, fearful that Emile might say it was a woman, something I wanted to keep from the press. We might flush out the killer if they thought their gender had not been detected. If we appeared stupid, the killer might make a mistake.

'What do you mean, plans them carefully?' Madame de Saint Robert asked. 'Nobody has threatened Marcel, no one has tried to intimidate him. I would know!'

This was the hard part, telling the family that their murdered loved one might have contributed to his own death.

'It's entirely possible that your husband knew the person who killed him. Not that they were friends, but acquainted somehow through business or an organization.'

'Impossible!' DuPont exclaimed.

The younger son, Victor, came back in the room just then. 'Did the other men know the person who killed them?'

'It's possible,' Emile told him.

'Oh God,' the granddaughter cried. 'Will he kill us too?'

'Of course not,' Emile said, but she jumped up from the sofa and clung to her mother, sobbing.

'None of you is in danger,' Emile repeated, waiting for her to subside.

'Was your husband acquainted with any of the other victims?' he asked the widow.

'You're not accusing my father, are you?' the daughter, Yvette, interrupted.

'Please answer the question,' Emile insisted to Madame de Saint Robert.

'I think he knew one of them, Patrick Richard from Bordeaux,' DuPont replied for her. 'After Richard was murdered he called the man a poor bastard, as though it was a personal loss. Once he joked with me that he'd better watch out too, eh? But I never asked him if he knew the man well.'

'It's important for you to remember exactly what he said. Did he ever tell you where they met, how they knew each other?' I interjected. This might be the connection we needed! Any acquaintance between them would show up in daily calendars, phone records or other affiliations.

Madame de Saint Robert glared at her son-in-law. 'He never discussed it with me,' she said.

Emile glanced at me. *Wives don't know everything, do they?* 'What did he tell you about the Richard murder?' Emile turned back to her.

'That it was a national tragedy; someone was killing the best men in France and the police were fools, nothing but a bunch of Clouseaus.'

I hid a smile. I had always wondered what the French thought of the Peter Sellers character. Berthelot was smiling too.

'I understand your anger,' Emile said. 'But we will catch the person who killed your husband.'

Her energy seemed to leave her and she collapsed on her daughter's shoulder. The two of them wept. I would rather have been any place but there.

Emile turned to DuPont. 'I need to speak to Madame alone.'

DuPont ushered everyone out.

'You want to ask me about sex, don't you?'

I was surprised by her candour.

'Yes,' Emile told her. 'I need to know if your

husband had any unusual habits?'

'He did not. And there was no mistress, though I have had two lovers in my life. Marcel and I were open with each other and he knew about my friends. Lately, intercourse was difficult for me and Marcel has been watching movies. You know.'

'What kind of movies?' I asked.

'Don't be naive, young man,' she snapped, pulling herself back from that awful place she'd been.

'I mean, what kind of sex tapes did he prefer? Men and women, women and women, animals . . .'

She had not thought of that. 'I never watched them, but he told me about some. One in particular he disliked because of the woman's anatomy. He liked women to be in proportion.'

'Where did he get the tapes he watched?'

'He bought them or rented them, they are not difficult to find.'

'Do you know whom he patronized? Any particular shop or many shops?'

She shook her head. 'I don't know. But he didn't keep them. Once he looked at them, he gave them back or threw them away.'

'All of them?' I asked.

She looked startled as though I'd caught her keeping a secret. 'All except one. He said he'd never send it back, that it was a classic. I was curious and asked to see it, but he said it was his alone. I didn't give a damn.'

I could tell that she did.

'Did he actually say, *send* it back?' Emile asked. 'As though he would mail it. Is that how he got it?'

'I don't know. It's a figure of speech, isn't it?'

'Perhaps not. Your husband was killed while he was masturbating. We think he was looking at a tape.'

Her eyes filled with tears but she smiled. 'He was doing what he liked.'

'Was he adventuresome in sex?' Emile asked.

'Not particularly,' she admitted. 'That's why I took lovers. He was fastidious, you know, methodical. And it was usually the same. But there could not have been a kinder, more loving man in the world than Marcel. Do you think someone killed him over a sex tape?'

'We don't know, Madame,' Emile said.

She was overcome with grief again and he went to her side. I told the family to come back.

They all trooped in again and resumed their former places, except for Yvette who stood next to her mother.

Emile continued the questioning until mid-morning. Finally, when I found myself nodding off where I stood, we parted company with Inspector Berthelot and left.

It was a clear and sunny morning, already warm and humid. My stomach was rumbling as I dragged after Emile who headed back to the scene of the murder like a spaniel to a downed fowl. I marvelled at his energy. He would not have stopped if I hadn't insisted. And so we sat down in a café called Hippopotamus across the street from de Saint Robert's office.

I let Emile order for us.

'We'll try the prosciutto of duck and melon,' he told the waiter. 'It's a Toulousian speciality,' he explained. 'And the brochette of lamb and beef, with the potatoes *au volante*, and a salad of string beans. What do you want for dessert?'

'*Iles Flôtante*,' I said. I love Floating Islands. Luckily, the plat du jour had been prepared early or we'd only have been given an omelette.

It wasn't until I'd eaten something that I found the energy to talk.

'It's good that Solange didn't come after all,' Emile said. 'You and I got some good work done. De Saint Robert's acquaintance with Patrick Richard, and the porno tape angle is a real break,' he said, drinking yet another cup of coffee.

I made so many trips to the bathroom in the de Saint Robert apartment it was embarrassing, but he hardly ever had to go.

'Start with the local porno dealers. I'm sure there aren't many of them,' I said. 'Mail order will take longer to check. Interpol can take the other European countries. Maybe one company sent the tapes to all the victims.'

'The killer sent the tape,' Emile said. 'And then killed his victims while they were watching it. But why?'

I yawned, even sleepier after the heavy meal. 'If it's really a woman, maybe she's punishing men who watch pornography, like some men kill prostitutes for being whores.' I couldn't stifle another yawn. 'I'm going back to the hotel to sleep. If you want me to stick around and help question the porno tape dealers, I will.'

'No, we can handle it.' He studied me for a moment. 'You're going to try and find Catherine, aren't you?'

'I have to,' I insisted. 'Even if I have to go through Paul to do it.'

'Why don't you leave it alone, go home to your wife?' He placed his credit card on the bill and gave it to the waiter.

'Do as I say, not as I do?' I commented.

He shrugged. 'We are pair, aren't we? Risking everything for romance.'

'I'm not after romance. I just want to heal the wound in my gut.'

He clapped me on the back and watched me walk away.

# Chapter 10

I slept a few hours in Toulouse, but was anxious to get back to Eugénie. So I roused myself and got on the road. On the drive back I thought about seeing Paul again. How could I keep myself from tearing his heart out? All this suffering was his fault, even more than mine, for keeping Catherine and me apart. I recalled how happy she'd been when I knew her, incredibly sexy, full of life, not unstable. And there had been a hidden secret or deep hurt within her which she wouldn't reveal, something elusive I could never catch. And she had cried easily, laughed inappropriately sometimes. Was that mental illness? More likely a premonition of the disasters that lay ahead.

We always try to find explanations for why something terrible has happened, as though we could have prevented it. *What did I miss? What didn't I know?* Real reasons give us a sense of control, like blocked arteries after a heart attack or a clue that solves a murder; like a man watching a porno tape he kept locked in his safe. The evidence confirms our omnipotence – the need for it confirms our stupidity. And we grab for it even more desperately when our lives are off kilter from some terrifying intrusion. How egocentric and helpless we are to affect anything at all about our lives; we stumble through, thinking we're making progress. If we make any at all it's a miracle.

And so, within the greater context of Emile's case with its myriad loose ends, the mystery of Catherine simultaneously occupied my brain. Especially since my sexual feelings had been aroused by that girl who kept appearing in my life and haunted my fantasies along with my lost love, like my own porno tape.

When I arrived back at Eugénie les Bains, I was still exhausted and fell into bed, only to awaken at three in the morning with my prick in my hand, as hard as the bed post behind my head.

A deep groan of pleasure came pouring out of me as I continued what had been started; a groan that echoed off the walls of my pristine cell. The stiff bedpost was in my left hand, an even stiffer prick in my right, which was doing the job. Four men had been killed doing what I was doing. And I deserved to be punished more than they, for I was thinking about *her*, the girl with the strawberry lips, the girl who was innocent yet knowing. But it didn't stop me.

I imagined what would have happened if she hadn't disappeared into the museum that day. If I'd been with her instead of Jeanette. I saw her staring at me, her tongue darting from between her lips, shiny saliva on her mouth staining it as red as the wild strawberries in her basket. Then she started to make love to me the way Catherine had, that pink tongue licking me again and again, around and around, sucking, tasting, applying perfect pressure, bottomless heaven, in and out, up and down, faster and faster, harder and harder. My hand applied its friction. and then my back arched and my hips bounced with the wild joy of an incredibly intense climax.

'Oh God, James Barton,' I swore to myself as I lay there panting, letting the image of the girl fade away. 'You are one sorry bastard!' But just the same, I was in working order again.

The next day, I called for an appointment with Paul d'Aumant. Surprise! He would see me. At the appointed hour, I drove directly through the ornate gateway of Castelle d'Aumant. Only this time I wasn't a frightened boy in need of approval. I was a man seeking vengeance.

Changes had taken place. A profusion of flowerbeds lined the road, all manicured to perfection. No longer were the antique farmhouses quaint, *au natural*, the fields bisected by imperfect roads. Now the roads were smoothly surfaced, the fences repaired, the houses white-washed, their shutters painted green or blue or salmon, and the windows underscored by boxes overflowing with flowers.

And the plane trees lining the road were smartly trimmed and standing to attention to welcome visitors over the miles of approach. A new sign announced the opening hours of a tasting room open to the public by appointment. '*Dégustation*' it proclaimed.

Paul d'Aumant had improved things. But if he didn't tell me where his sister was, this time I would beat the shit out of him.

The same footman from nineteen years ago, tottering but still imposing, greeted me at the door.

'Monsieur Barton to see Paul d'Aumant,' I told him, handing him my card. 'I have an appointment.' My hands were steady.

'This way,' he said, leading me back down the front steps and around the *castelle*. We traversed formal rose gardens, each section separated by precision cut hedges, 'til we arrived at the former stables, now converted into offices. The footman held open the door for me.

I entered the large reception area and approached a girl at the desk who smiled sweetly and directed me to a sofa with soft down cushions, upholstered in some country French pattern.

'Monsieur le Duc will be with you soon,' she explained.

The next person to greet me was a male secretary who shook my hand and offered me refreshments: wine or mineral water. I declined. I was too revved up for these niceties. *Let me at him*, I thought. But he kept me waiting. Naturally.

The reception room floor, which ran down the hall and into the other offices, was distressed oak that had been bleached and polished to a pale blond patina. Victoria would have killed for floors like it. The place was newly decorated, but with a homely quality the *castelle* never had.

At last the secretary came back and ushered me into Paul's office, furnished like a huge living room with the same blond oak floors, a stone fireplace in the far corner, comfortable sofas, chairs covered in linen prints, and magnificent pine cabinets.

He was on the phone with his back to me. Just looking at him made the bile rise in my throat. To keep myself from grabbing him by the neck and lifting him out of his chair, I concentrated on the room. To my right, a wallful of photos of prize-winning horses with blue ribbons attached to them caught the morning light. On the wall behind me hung *certificats d'excellence* with gold seals from wine associations, awarded to Castelle d'Aumant. To my left, french doors opened on to a stone patio, with steps leading down to a sloping lawn and the lake beyond. And behind Paul's desk stood the pine cabinets filled with books and an entertainment centre. I stepped out on to the patio and took a deep breath, hoping to calm the anger inside me.

From here, I could see the window of Catherine's room where we'd sat that day planning our future. This building had been the stables then. I wished I could turn back time.

Paul's voice interrupted me. 'James Barton. I heard you were in town. What are you doing here after all this time?'

I turned to face him as he came towards me with outstretched hand. I itched to punch away that supercilious smile. Instead we shook hands and I followed him back inside without smiling.

'It's been a long time.' He wore designer clothes, probably Armani, six hundred dollar trousers and a fine linen shirt. His hair was longer, worn with an off centre parting, his face more lined around the eyes but with that same intense stare. As we came back into the room he turned to face me and moved abruptly forward, invading my space. I'd forgotten it was a quirk of his. I held my ground.

'What brings you to Eugénie after all this time?'

'I'm here about Catherine. I want to know where she is.'

My directness startled him. He stepped back. I was not the boy he'd remembered. 'And to show us a thing or two, I'd wager. If anyone treated me the way we treated you, I'd want to rub his face in it! *N'est ce pas?*'

'Do you mean you regret betraying me after pretending to be my friend?' I watched him closely.

'Sometimes,' he admitted. 'I wanted to be your friend. But I was a d'Aumant, you see.'

'And Catherine paid the price. Are you happy?'

'Never. I ache for her every day. I'm not a person who likes to admit he was wrong, but I was wrong about you. You might have made things different for her. She has suffered so much.'

I was speechless for the moment, hating him a little less. Then I remembered what a liar he was, saying whatever I wanted to hear – that I could be the d'Aumant wine distributor in America, for instance, when he had no intention of letting that happen. He'd been so understanding about my relationship with my father, deeply sympathetic over the loss of my brother; he'd referred me to a lawyer whom I'd trusted, and then paid the man to tell him all my plans. He pretended to be my ally while he made sure I'd never see his sister again. 'How convenient to be sorry when you've ruined our lives! Now Catherine is in a sanatarium. Was it worth it, keeping us apart?'

There was pain in his eyes. 'I cannot bear to think of it. Having her there is worse than when my parents were killed. They lived their lives. But my poor Catherine, my precious darling, has had no life at all.'

'How long?'

'Years,' he replied. 'They do what they can. Each time a new drug is invented they give it to her. Nothing works. She has moments when she's all right. She even goes on outings with her companion.' Another shake of the head. 'We bring her home, but she always goes back again.'

The thought of her pain pierced me sharply.

Paul was holding my business card. 'American FBI.' He raised an eyebrow. 'It makes one feel guilty, even when there's nothing to hide.'

'A man with nothing to hide is a dead man,' I said, glancing around. 'You've made a lot of changes.'

'In myself as well. Regret is a cruel adjunct to ageing. I've kept busy. I modernized the vineyard after my father's death; he'd never allowed it. Now things are up to standard. It helped me get over the shock. Would you like to see?'

I wanted to tell him to fuck himself. Because of him I was denied a chance at true love, forced to choose a life different from everything I'd wanted. I might have saved Catherine . . . Instead I followed him out. The feeling of being treated as an equal, of being accorded respect, was too heady. Especially since I hadn't expected it. But one wrong twist of his mouth and I would take pleasure in beating him senseless.

He seemed eager to please. Perhaps it was true that he'd changed, stopped being the asshole he was when his parents died, or maybe he'd finally grown up.

The horse ranch was magnificent, filled with prize-winning Arabians. Then he showed me some new equipment that de-stemmed and hulled the grapes without bruising the fruit, and the enormous stainless steel vats of the *chais* where the grapes are vinified or fermented.

The first-year cellar – I would have called it a warehouse – held miles of spotless oak wine barrels arrayed in perfect lines, the air heady with the smell of yeast. We were enveloped by a dark coolness, surrounded by the scents of spices and woods.

'All the first-year barrels are new, made from white oak that's two hundred years old and dried in the open for five or six years. Younger oak has too much sap which makes the wood porous and absorbs the wine.'

We were like two gentlemen observing the niceties of acquaintance. My hatred was hard to sustain and I could almost see how Catherine had loved him. But he should not have kept us apart.

'The government restricts the number of barrels we produce per hectare, which is the equivalent of two-and-a-half acres. Ours is three thousand litres per hectare, or four hundred thousand bottles a year for this estate.' I wondered if his expansion had cost the Laurent family any land.

The second-year cellar was cooler than the first but just as big, another mile-long room with a vaulted ceiling and enormous pillars holding up the roof. The

187

scent of yeast was even stronger here. You could get high on the fumes.

'These barrels don't have to be new,' he told me. 'We pick the grapes when the sugar content reaches its peak, usually late-August or early-September, depending on the weather. Even in a drought there's always enough humidity in the air to moisten the roots and the vines will produce great fruit.

'But December and January is when we taste the first barrels and do the *Assemblage*, the blending of flavours.

'Come this way.'

He led me into a side room where crystal glasses were standing ready. My first tasting. A servant handed me a glass etched with the family crest that had been rinsed with wine – *avine*.

'This bottle came directly from the barrel,' Paul told me. 'It's a '91 that's about to go into bottles. I think it's one of the best Tursan wines since '67.'

I raised the glass to my lips, but he stopped me.

'When this vintage is bottled, it will not taste as it does now for years. You are tasting the future.'

The flavour was a mixture of many things, smoke and peaches and even sex. Or else I had sex on my mind. We cleansed our palates with a bite of goat's cheese. These people really knew how to live. If he was doing this to impress me, it was working. I got a glimpse of the young Paul who had faced me across the tennis court.

We emerged from the darkened *chais* to find electric carts at our disposal, and for the first time since I'd arrived in France, I thought how much Victoria would have loved all this. We hadn't spoken in over a week; it seemed like a lifetime.

'Will you join me for lunch?'

I glanced over and saw servants dressed in formal

clothes setting up a glass-topped table on the lawn, under a weeping willow tree. Nearby the lake sparkled in the sunlight. A maid set out individual place mats, a silver-domed luncheon cart came wheeling out of a side door of the *castelle*.

'I'll stay if you'll tell me how to find Catherine,' I said.

'Of course I will,' he agreed.

'All right then,' I said.

'Does everyone ask you what it's like to be an FBI agent?' he said, as we walked down the lawn towards the table.

'Yes. They think we have shootouts every week like you see on television. In truth, our work is mainly a tedious following up of details. No one wants to know about the drudgery of searching through five years of phone numbers, or how your stomach feels after no sleep and quick greasy meals.' I decided not to tell him about the pee bottle we keep in the car for stakeouts and the extra miles I jog to burn up fat from eating pizza and sitting on my ass. Then there's the twisting icy fear when I'm approaching a suspect who could shoot me in the head or slam his fist into the bridge of my nose and drive the bone into my brain. And even worse is the fear of being maimed for life.

'The best part of the job, besides catching assholes,' I said, taking a seat at the table facing the lake, 'is when my buddies and I have a few drinks after hours and tell each other stories. We're so full of bull you can't tell the truth from the lies.'

Paul gave an interested smile.

'What keeps me sane is the creative work, like profiling. It's similar to plotting a novel, except that the stakes are different. In one the results are life and death. In the other you end up on a local talk show.'

'I heard from Emile Laurent's brother that you're

189

helping him with this Boardroom Killer.'

I was surprised that he knew, but before I could answer someone slipped into the seat next to mine and I turned. When I saw who it was I nearly gasped out loud. *It was her*. The girl of my wet dreams. Heat rushed to my face and I coughed into my napkin. *Jesus H. Christ. She was everywhere.* She gave me a shocked look, as surprised to find me here as I was to see her, and then cast her eyes down as though denying our brief encounters.

'Are you all right?' Paul asked me.

'You didn't tell me someone was joining us,' I managed to say.

A smile played on her lips, damn her! Now I was the one at a loss. I couldn't have felt more stupid. This was crazy!

'I've seen you before,' I said, daring her to look at me. 'We've run into each other,' I told Paul. 'A lot.'

'Oh?' He seemed surprised.

Having her so near made my blood race. Every ounce of me wanted to reach out and trace the shape of her face with my fingers, brush the silky lashes where they lay delicately on her cheek – like touching paradise. *Get a grip, asshole.*

'Did you know she was my niece, Chloe?' Paul asked.

*His niece?* 'You mean, this girl is Catherine's daughter?' I couldn't keep the shock out of my voice. Now I really wanted her to look at me. How dense of me not to have realised! That's why I'd been so drawn to her, I'd recognised the similarity to Catherine when I'd first seen her in Paris. And then again, that first night in the café. Suddenly it hit me. I'd been lusting after someone who could have been my own child! My heart dropped into my stomach and I felt sick.

'Chloe, don't be rude,' Paul chided. 'Monsieur

Barton was a friend of your mother's.'

'Oh,' she said, still keeping her eyes averted.

'I knew her a long time ago,' I said, staring openly in spite of shame, drinking her in, searching for Catherine's face. The resemblance was obvious now. I couldn't find my voice.

Suddenly, Chloe looked at her uncle, as if realizing something. 'Is *he* the one?' she asked.

'Why, yes,' he replied mildly.

That infuriated her. 'I don't believe this. It's not possible!'

'Am I what one?' I asked.

'Our guest for lunch,' Paul replied and gave her a look so malevolent it frightened even me. She trembled but didn't cower. *Good girl!* I thought. This was one person he didn't fully control.

When he next spoke to me, he was smooth and charming. 'Chloe is even more beautiful than Catherine, isn't she? She has her father's mouth and chin. He was a very handsome man.' He lifted her face so that she was forced to look at me, then he winked. She pushed his hand away harshly which only made him laugh. Obviously she gave him more trouble than Catherine ever had.

Chloe was painfully real now, in her shorts and top and chipped red nail polish. Much too young for me. Not some beguiling nymph. God, the shame! I wanted to flay my own flesh.

'Don't you think you should change for luncheon?' Paul asked.

'I wish to speak to you!' she demanded, getting up from the table and marching a few steps away, waiting until he got up to follow her.

'I'll be right back,' he said, and I had a sudden insight into how difficult teenagers could be.

He followed her across the grass to the path leading

191

to his office. They climbed the stairs, crossed the patio and disappeared inside. But the french doors were open and I could see reflections in the panes of glass. Unaware that I was watching, they launched into a battle that fascinated me.

Chloe shoved her face up to his, only inches away, shouting and pointing in my direction. 'No!' she repeated, over and over. While he insisted, 'Yes!' and pointed at her, shaking his finger, arguing for all he was worth.

I couldn't help thinking they were arguing about me. I had no idea why. Except that she didn't want to have lunch with me, and he insisted she must. If only I could hear them. When she kept refusing, Paul got so furious he slapped her right across the face. *The bastard!* I was out of my seat in an instant and starting across the lawn, but I didn't get two feet before I saw Chloe knee him in the groin. *Good going, kid!* I thought, as Paul let out a yell and doubled over.

She stood there watching him writhe. It took a moment for him to catch his breath. And then, to my amazement, he lifted his head and looked at her, and they both started laughing.

Carefully, he straightened up, pulled her to him and hugged her, still clutching himself between the legs.

Quickly, I turned around and sat down again before they saw me watching. What a relationship this was. Certainly not one in which I wanted to be involved.

Paul returned moments later and took his seat. 'She'll be joining us,' he said, the victor.

'Is she always difficult?'

He sighed. 'She's at that age; doesn't do as I ask, just to defy me. All her friends are the same. I do my best, but I'm not the fatherly type. She needs a mother. I think she was surprised that I knew you. She thought you were a stranger.'

If my previous encounters were how she treated strangers, I wondered how she treated her friends? Waiting for her to return was excruciating. I longed to have her near me, yet never wanted to see her again. These forbidden feelings I harboured for someone who could have been my daughter made me no better than the scum I arrested. Well, the feelings would stop right now.

Paul broke into my thoughts. 'Are you and Emile getting closer to solving these horrible killings?'

'We're making progress,' I told him. 'I was with him in Toulouse. I just got back.'

'The death of de Saint Robert was in all the papers. Who would want to kill these men?'

'I never discuss a case I'm working on,' I told him, enjoying the way his lips compressed with annoyance.

'Of course,' he said. 'But there must be something you can tell me that won't break a confidence?'

'No,' I said with a sly smile. 'Except that we'll get him. You can be sure of that!'

'I feel better already,' he said, matching my tone.

When Chloe returned she was wearing a demure white summer dress, a touch of lipstick, and her hair was freshly combed. She took her seat. 'I'm sorry for being rude before,' she told her uncle, the perfect young lady.

She placed her napkin in her lap and, still ignoring me, ate her soup with one of those huge soup spoons we rarely see at home. It was a sweet carrot purée, cool and refreshing. I couldn't eat. I missed her former combativeness.

Next came a mixed salad of endive, tomatoes and arugula, those strange greens the French use, and oil and vinegar to pour over it – something I'm hopeless at. I either get it too oily or too tart.

Chloe saw me hesitate, and with amused authority

took the bottles out of my hands and doused my salad with just the right balance of the two. Then she placed the bottles back in their silver cruet as if I was a child.

'You are so much like your mother,' I told her. The blank stare she gave me made me wonder if she understood English.

'Chloe doesn't know Catherine very well. She was too young to remember her before she got sick. And now she is so changed.'

'Your mother was wonderful,' I said, finding the words inadequate. I was not equipped to re-create Catherine's brilliance, her vibrant essence. In that moment my heart softened towards Paul. All their wealth and privilege hadn't prevented the d'Aumants from suffering; my own problems seem mundane by comparison.

'Do you have a family, James?' Paul asked.

'My wife Victoria and I have two children. Lindsay is five and Adam seven.' I turned to Chloe, trying to make friends. 'My children would love to have a lake in their own back-yard as you do.'

My conversation didn't interest her. In fact, I realized with a growing sense of embarrassment that she was not interested in me at all. I had only imagined it out of my own sick needs. This typical teenage girl had none of the sensuality I'd attributed to her; her gestures were innocent.

By the time we were served our main course, I was more comfortable in her presence and enjoyed the leg of veal, seasoned with lemon peel and sharp olives.

As the servants cleared, Paul received a phone call and got up from the table, taking the cellular phone out of our hearing. I watched him pace by the lake.

'Didn't I see you in Paris with your school class? You were going into the Pompidou.'

A shrug. 'It was our last outing of the year. That evening each of us returned to our homes from Paris.' She kept her eyes averted.

'And you live here? What a coincidence that I saw you there and here too.'

No reply.

'What subjects do you study in school?' I asked.

'Biology and literature,' she replied. 'I'm second in my class. Why?'

'I'd like to get to know you.' I gave her a friendly smile. 'I knew your mother when she was about your age. I could tell you about her.'

'If you like,' she said, turning to look at me as if she was thinking about what I'd said. Then, without warning, she reached over and touched the back of my hand, her fingertips running over it in a featherlight caress.

An electric jolt went through me and I grabbed my hand back as if I'd been burned, praying Paul hadn't noticed. He was on the phone, yards away from us. No one had ever touched me like that, so deliberately yet clandestinely.

Then she finally gave me a smile, full of mischief; it lit up her face with such an infectious glow, it melted my reserve. I smiled back.

I shouldn't have.

For she moved. Almost like a cat stretching. And then gave me that look again – the one I'd first seen in Paris, the one I told myself I'd imagined, that I'd berated myself for responding to – the one that was purely sexual. I felt mesmerized. My heart leaping wildly. *Not again*, I thought, unable to tear my eyes away.

Ever so slightly, she shifted in her seat so that she was facing me. I didn't move.

She placed her hands in her lap, palms up, as if she

was readying herself for something, like an animal going into heat or a cobra in the thrall of a fakir. Her eyelids closed halfway, just enough to hood her eyes and intensify her gaze as she stared at me. My eyes were glued to hers as my pulse pounded in my ears. Perhaps the danger of having Paul so near, or seeing her transform herself into another aspect, had hypnotized me, but I was caught in her spell.

And then something made me look down. What I saw amazed me; the lower half of her body was visible through the glass table top as if it were magic. I knew the table was solid since I'd been leaning my elbows on it, but when she drew my attention to it, I realised it was transparent and I could see her.

She shifted in her chair, placing the sunlight behind her so that it illuminated her body the same way it had that evening in the café. She was wearing the same dress then too, of soft white cotton.

I swallowed hard, willing myself to tear my eyes away, yet unable. I should stop her. But I couldn't. Like an insect caught in a web, I was enmeshed in her plot even though my brain screamed, *Don't do it!*

I glanced down into her lap and held my breath, watching to see what she would do.

Slowly, with her palms upraised and her eyelids lowered, she parted her legs in an infinitesimally small yet maddening movement calculated to drive me wild. She knew exactly what she was doing. I was completely in her spell. All she did was move her thighs an inch apart, but the gesture was unmistakable. She was flashing me. And I could see what she was revealing. Outlined by the light, the transparent fabric, the position of her body and the lack of underwear, was the delicate pink of her vagina bordered by light brown hair. God help me, I looked.

Without realizing it, my hand reached out, or had

she taken it? My fingers burned to touch her. A kettle drum pounded in my ears.

If her uncle hadn't returned at that moment, I don't know what would have happened.

# Chapter 11

My experience with Chloe shook me so that I was nearly immobilized.

'Stop that!' I said, just as Paul reached his seat.

'Is something wrong?' he asked.

'No,' Chloe answered, instantly crossing her legs, and dropping her napkin in her lap. Then she smiled up at him.

The women in this family were sex-crazed and this girl a changeling. To my shame, she'd affected me. I shifted in my seat to relieve the pressure on my balls while she smirked.

And yet she'd brought me back to life. I was grateful for that, but for all the wrong reasons. She played a dangerous game.

And she was Catherine's child, I felt a responsibility to stop her. But how? If I told her uncle what had happened, he would never believe me. Look at her now, for instance, acting like a typical teen in front of him, the blatant sexuality gone. Only my pounding heart, and flushed face, indicated something had happened. Twilight Zone time. If I brought this to Paul's attention, he could accuse me of child abuse! It could ruin my life.

Chloe was chattering about snorkelling equipment and video games, ignoring me completely. Her uncle listened intently, doting on her, as fascinated by her girlishness as I was by her blatancy. Idiot that I was, I felt a stab of betrayal, as though I'd been discarded for another lover. Ridiculous!

When lunch was over I got out of there as quickly as I could, mumbling my appreciation and running away.

But I couldn't stop thinking about Chloe's power to bewitch. What in hell possessed a girl her age to behave like that? Maybe it was common in this country, but I doubted it. It made me wonder all the more about Catherine. Perhaps her overdeveloped sexuality was the basis for her psychosis? That could mean Chloe was headed in the same direction. I'd heard that mental illness was inherited.

I went right from lunch to the nearest bar in Duhort-Bachen and ordered a whisky. It took two, straight up, before I rid myself of the last vestiges of that encounter.

I'd been planning to call Victoria that afternoon, but didn't trust myself to talk to her. I'd wait until after I saw Catherine.

Paul had given me the name of Catherine's clinic in Lourdes and offered to call ahead, tell them I was coming. So I set out the next morning.

Lourdes was several hours away from Eugénie les Bains and as I drove my tension mounted. My ability to block Catherine from my mind was no longer operational and I was afraid of what would happen when I saw her. I didn't know what would be worse, to feel nothing or too much. If I'd gone to a shrink as Victoria had urged me to, maybe I'd be better prepared.

Underneath my mild manner, I have a temper that flares on occasion. I dislike that part of me; it's too much like my father. Once I badly beat a guy for flirting with Victoria. He didn't press charges because he'd thrown the first punch, but I was reprimanded by the Bureau.

As I got nearer to Catherine, my apprehension grew. I told myself not to expect too much from this visit, but I was in a state of high anticipation and couldn't calm down.

I knew what I wanted to happen – sheer magic. I wanted all the years to roll away and for us to be kids again, all the love to be restored, and I wanted to be healed.

Paul had told me that Catherine suffered from schizophrenia. Often she was withdrawn, terribly sad or completely out of touch with reality. 'And then, sometimes, she'll recognize me and we talk the way we used to,' he explained. 'Other times, she makes no sense at all. She might start to cry and not stop for hours.'

I couldn't bear the thought.

When I arrived in Lourdes, I was surprised to find so much activity, the streets crowded with people. Glad of an excuse to postpone the visit, I gawked at the circus.

Famous for sightings of the Virgin Mary by Saint Bernadette, the entire economy of Lourdes revolves around this miracle. Tourists and pilgrims from all over the world come here in their polyester outfits, miniskirts, designer clothes, blue jeans or religious habits, making the city into a huge carnival.

The main event is the never ending stream of visitors to the grotto where the Virgin supposedly appeared. The side shows are the merchants hawking their wares, and the continuous showing of the film 'Song of Bernadette', seven days a week. Many people who come here think Jennifer Jones is the saint herself.

The stars of the show are the churches and the hospitals, more in Lourdes than I've ever seen in my life. (These are for the millions of people who weren't cured by a miracle.)

My cynicism grew as I followed a continual wave of humanity down the paved step incline to the grotto where they commemorate the miracle, as though we were cattle behind a feed truck. There were hand rails on either side like a ride at Disneyland, and at the bottom vendors sold candles to the faithful.

On a wide paved section of the riverbank, a priest officiated in front of the shrine. Wheelchairs took up the front row, while I stood behind with hundreds of others watching the show. Amazing. The shrine itself was a disappointment, a small cave with a plaster statue of the Virgin standing on a rock.

After the service we snaked back up the hill where I perused the rows of vendors selling every kind of religious paraphernalia: vials of water from the Gaves de Pau, objects blessed by priests, carvings made from the local trees. What made them sacred was the money they brought the local craftspeople who sold them along with rosaries, chess sets, icons, candle sticks, incense cups, drawings, replicas, jewellery, crosses, and other useless objects of every size, shape and price. Even in the Vatican there isn't this much religious crap for sale.

That Catherine was stuck here in this capital of hypocrisy infuriated me. What a sight to see when she walked out of her front door. I hoped these people didn't accost her when she went on an outing. Maybe, being Catholic, she found it a comfort.

When I located her *maison de repos* there were no busloads of pilgrims blocking my way. The sanatarium was in a small ancient building of a type common to France, three storeys high, slate roof, large windows with shutters and a wide double door at street level. Some scrawny flowers were planted in a small bed outside.

I stood there immobile, knowing she was inside.

Then someone came out of the front door, held it open for me, and I entered.

The place was as modern and cheerful as antique stone walls allowed it to be; the furniture had seen better days. The entry had a terracotta-tiled floor, and behind were french doors leading out to a walled courtyard with a square of glass in the middle and stone benches on it. I could see pink hydrangeas in bloom.

So far so good.

It was lunchtime and the patients were being served in the dining room, cafeteria-style. They were visible from where I stood. No one was at the front desk so I stopped a nurse in uniform and asked for Catherine Jolibois.

'She is at her meal, Monsieur,' the nurse told me, displeased that I was here.

'I've come all the way from America to see her,' I said, trying to smile, but my face was frozen.

She gave a sniff and told me to wait while she summoned Mademoiselle Véronique Desault, the person in charge of Madame.

An attractive young blonde came towards me, fashionably dressed and with short hair that curled around her face. She seemed too sophisticated to be stuck in a place like this with her expensive gold jewellery, the kind I wished I could buy for Victoria. But at least a capable woman was in charge of Catherine's care.

'Do you have permission from Monsieur le Duc?' she asked.

'I had lunch with him and Catherine's daughter, Chloe, yesterday at the *castelle*. He said he would call you. I didn't think it necessary to ask him for a note,' I chided.

'But I have never heard of you.'

'I'm an old friend from America,' I told her, flirting a bit. 'We were sweethearts.'

It worked for she said, 'Of course, I understand. Come with me.' And she escorted me to the dining room, stopping me at the door.

'Now, I warn you, she fabricates stories. It's difficult to know when she's telling the truth. She appears sincere. And her moods change. One minute she's happy, the next sad. It would be best to take your cue from her. She may not know who you are. If she becomes agitated, be soothing. Tell her everything is all right.'

'Won't she know if I'm pretending?'

'Monsieur Bart-on,' she pronounced my name with the accent on the last syllable, 'we who are blessed with mental health have no idea what the world is like to someone so confused. To them, our faces are distorted, our voices are too loud, as though someone sits at a sound console and varies the volume of our speech.' Seeing my concern, she touched my hand. 'It will be all right.'

We came into a room of men and women of all ages and sizes whose clothing hung on their bodies as if it were borrowed, involved in a world of their own, unrelated to mine. They had all acquired the same patina, like old wood rubbed to a shine. Or else they'd picked up one another's bad habits, like twisting their hair or wiping their faces, twirling their arms back and forth. And yet, some of them seemed normal, spoke to one another, ate their meals like people in a barracks, while cheery attendants dispensed encouragement as they passed out the food. 'Here you are, dear. Now be sure to eat all your vegetables.'

Mademoiselle Desault went to tell the two nursing attendants that I was visiting Catherine. I dreaded seeing her, yet searched the faces, looking for her sky blue eyes. When I finally saw them, they were no

204

longer clear and sharp, and they looked right through me. Even so, my heart skipped in my chest.

*There she is*, I thought, watching her. She was seated at a table with four other people, eating quietly. She glanced up at me and then continued eating without acknowledgement.

My whole body reacted and feelings from twenty years ago flooded through me. I was positive that if I just touched her, she would be my Catherine again.

'Catherine,' I said, softly.

She heard me and looked up. But I was only a voice in her dementia.

Mademoiselle Desault hung by my elbow, crowding me, until I gave her a look and she backed away. But she didn't leave; she stood nearby so she could hear our conversation.

Catherine's table manners were still precise; she took small bites and chewed slowly, keeping the fork in her left hand, European-style.

'Hello, Catherine,' I tried again.

Now she gave me a polite smile, closer to the one I remembered. I grinned back. Her beautiful honey blonde hair had been cut shoulder-length and hung without style. She wore it parted on the side and held with a slide. And she'd put on weight. But then, most of us don't weigh the same as we did at seventeen. Still, my heart was filled with love. When I looked at her, I saw her younger face superimposed over this one.

'Madame Jolibois,' Mademoiselle Desault called to her. 'You have a visitor, Monsieur Bart-on. Why don't you take him out to the solarium? I'll save your dinner for you.' She motioned to an attendant who came over and picked up her plate and put a cover over it.

Catherine rose docilely from the table and led the way while I followed. I was surprised to see how tall she was. I remembered her being shorter than I, in need of

205

my protection, but she was nearly my height. Maybe she'd had a late spurt of growth. Yet everything else about her was familiar.

Mademoiselle Desault stood guard in the doorway of the solarium. Wicker furniture was scattered about, upholstered in flowery prints, hanging ferns overflowed their mossy holders, and the room had a view of a garden with shady trees.

Catherine walked to the centre of the room and turned to look at me.

'Oh, Catherine,' I said, holding out my arms. She walked directly over to me and put her head on my shoulder, cuddling close, the way she used to. It broke my heart. And the ache only grew worse as she began to sob, her shoulders shaking while I held her.

'Shh,' I soothed, 'it's all right. I'm here now.' In the act of comforting her, I was comforted too. I had needed to do this for so long, hold her again in my arms.

But still she cried.

When she showed no signs of stopping, I realized it was the illness, not a normal sadness like that time in her room at the *castelle*. I could not imagine the kind of pain that sobbing could not relieve.

'Why don't we sit down?' I suggested, indicating a sofa. My concern was that if I upset Catherine too much, Mademoiselle Desault would cut short my visit. I led Catherine to the sofa while she glanced over her shoulder to check on the attendant who was still there.

'Are you James's father, Mr Barton?' she asked.

That hurt. In her mind James was still twenty-two. I seemed old enough to be my own father.

'No, I'm James. A lot older now. I came to see you.'

'Dr Barton?' she asked, trying to place me.

'No, I'm James. Your sweetheart from long ago. Don't you remember me?'

'James died. The boat blew up,' she said.

'I wasn't on that boat, Catherine. Only your parents died that night, not I.'

Her eyes grew wider as she stared, seeing the youthful me behind my current face. Then she reached out and touched me to see if I was real. 'I thought you were dead. You never came before,' she said. 'You never came, you never came!' The accusation pierced me.

'I tried,' I told her. 'I couldn't find you.'

'I was right here!' she said. Perfectly logical. She knew where she was, I didn't.

'I'm so sorry, I wanted to.'

'Did you?' she asked wistfully.

*Oh God, how I wanted to.* 'Catherine, I met Chloe. You have a beautiful daughter – she's just like you. She misses her mother.' There was no recognition of the name. I wanted to grab her shoulders and force her to see me clearly. If only I could make contact, she'd be well again.

She leaned forward as if she had an important secret to tell, speaking in a half whisper. 'I couldn't take care of her. I wasn't a good mother.'

'That can't be true,' I assured her, thinking how abnormal she seemed.

'It is!' she insisted. 'I saw him die,' she said, continuing the secret. 'The car hit the side wall and then it hit another car, and then it turned over and over and over.' She made a revolving motion with her hand. 'It smashed his head. I saw it. I ran over to the car before the explosion. I ran and ran. People were screaming. So much blood. And his brain.' She held out her hands as though holding a weighty object, then squeezed. I shuddered. It was grisly. Especially since I knew she hadn't been anywhere near her husband's car when he died.

'When the fire started they held me back and I

screamed some more. I couldn't cry then. Now I cry so much. I deserved it, you know. He didn't love me. Only James loved me. Not Paul. Do you like him? I don't. I shouldn't have married Antoine. Mama and Papa are dead because of me.'

She blamed herself for these accidents.

'Did you know I have a car? They don't let me drive.' Another secret. 'But *she* lets me when *she* comes with me.'

'Who, Mademoiselle Desault?'

She nodded. 'And Chloe.'

'Catherine, none of what happened was your fault! Not your parents' death or your husband's.'

'Yes, it was,' she said viciously. 'You don't know! I was bad. I did bad things on the barge and it blew up. Don't you remember what we did? They're dead, he's dead, because of me. Nobody can help me. Especially not you! You should have helped me, you should have helped me! Why didn't you help me?' she kept saying, pushing me away angrily, pounding her hands on my chest without control.

'Oh, Catherine, I wanted to,' I told her, holding her hands until she calmed down. 'I wanted to help you.'

She seemed to hear me. 'You did?' she asked, incredulous. 'That's not what he said. He said you didn't love me. That's why you went away. He couldn't find you.'

'No! It was the other way around. I looked for you!' That goddamned Paul again.

She shook her head violently from side to side and covered her ears with her hands, repeating, 'No! No! No!'

And then her expression changed as quickly as Chloe's. 'Oh, go to hell!' she snarled. I'd never seen her so filled with hatred and malevolence. 'Leave me the hell alone! Keep your filthy prick to yourself or I'll stick it in a meat grinder. I'll grind it and grind it and grind it. Or else I'll slice it. How would you like that? Sliced prick for breakfast. You have enough? You have enough? It's never enough. Catherine, I want you. Catherine, do it again. Suck me, Catherine. You do it so good, Catherine.' She stuck her tongue out and wagged it obscenely. 'I won't do that any more. I don't want to.'

My face was bright red as she shouted out our most intimate words, the things we'd whispered to each other. A knife twisted in me as I recalled how much I had wanted her to do those things.

The next instant she was contrite, touching my face, begging me, 'Oh, please don't be angry. I'm sorry, don't be angry. I can't believe you're here. You look old. How old are you? Can you take me away from here, to your apartment? I can't go back *there*, you know. I hate it here. They spy on me. They watch me. I wanted to come to you but they wouldn't let me. If only you could have saved me! It's too late. No one can save me now. I'm a coward. I'd never hurt your beautiful prick. It's so beautiful, so beautiful. So special. Do you remember? I do. We actually did it, you know. We weren't supposed to, but we did it. Paul found out.' Then she put her hand on my groin and gave me a coquettish smile. One moment she was raving, the next almost coherent.

These illogical scenarios made sense to her, but I was lost. Véronique Desault had told me Catherine made up stories and distorted reality so I pretended everything was normal. What I really wanted to do was howl at the moon like a wounded beast.

'When you come back I'll take you for a ride in my beautiful balloon,' she said.

'I'm not leaving, Catherine,' I assured her. 'I'm here

209

to visit you. It's been a long time.'

She stared at me, curious.

I took her hand and started talking as I'd seen people do to someone in a coma. 'They shouldn't have taken you away from me. We never had the time to understand each other. I loved you so much,' I told her as my eyes filled with tears. 'I only wanted to be with you and take care of you. If they had let me, maybe you wouldn't have suffered so much.'

She was listening closely.

'When they took you away, part of me died,' I told her. 'Seeing you now is bringing me back to life. You're so beautiful.'

'It's too late, James,' she whispered, really talking to me. 'The girl I was died that night on the barge. She died in your arms. You buried her.'

'Catherine, you're not dead. Maybe there's someone else who can help you, another doctor? I'd like to try. Would you let me?'

She just stared.

'When did you start to get sick? Was it that summer or after? Did I do this to you?'

Tears were streaming down her face. 'I don't remember. Was I like this then?' she asked. 'I don't remember. I had too much sex. The doctor knows.'

'With me?' I asked. That same question again. If we'd had too much sex, it was my fault. Paul had insisted that Catherine remain a virgin. Maybe he knew something I didn't know? Female hormones were a mystery. Maybe our having sex had unleashed this madness in her. Maybe it ran in the family. Chloe could be at risk then. I had to ask her doctor or Paul.

And then Catherine shut me out. Her eyes glazed over and she gave me a deadened look.

'Catherine, don't leave me again,' I pleaded. I took her hands and lifted her from the sofa, pulling her to me and holding her again, rocking her. This time she just stood there rigid.

'I'm going to try and help you,' I whispered. 'I know you understood me, I know you did.' If I hadn't seen that spark of the girl I'd know, this wouldn't be so hard.

I kissed her on the cheek and said goodbye. She remained standing where I'd left her.

I thanked Mademoiselle Desault and told her I wanted to speak to Catherine's doctor. She gave me his name. But when I called him, he wasn't there. I said I'd call back. And then I left.

When I reached the pavement, I leaned against the wall of the building, wishing I could tear out of my brain what I'd just seen. My eyes welled with tears and grief overcame me. I stood there sobbing, realizing that I was holding nothing back. All my feelings for Catherine had finally emerged from the dark hole of my psyche and hurt more than I'd imagined possible.

While I waited for Catherine's doctor to return to his office, I found a pension for the night with a telephone in the room where I could make credit card calls, and then a café nearby for a bite of dinner.

I ordered a meal and waited for it to come, reliving my visit, trying not to let the hopelessness overwhelm me. Perhaps Catherine's doctor would have something positive to say about her prognosis. I didn't have much hope but it was worth a try – part of the process of letting go.

Somewhere in the back of my mind, I had harboured a fantasy that Catherine was still waiting for me; somehow we would find each other and be together, fulfilling our ideal of love, somewhere we'd always be infatuated, never bored or tired with each other, and the sex would be forever hot. It wasn't a conscious fantasy, but it was there. Now, seeing her as she was, the fantasy faded like a wisp of smoke. If she could not be cured, I could give her up once and for all, not hold a part of myself back from Victoria. On the other hand, if the illness was reversible, maybe I could be with her. If the reality of being with her fulfilled even a fraction of my fantasy, life would be ecstasy.

As I was paying the bill, I glanced up to see a couple strolling by; they weren't holding hands, but from the way their heads were tilted towards each other I could tell they were lovers, that they shared intimacy. And I also recognized them as cops. The woman held her bag at the ready, a weapon inside, and strode purposefully, glancing right to left, checking details as good cops do. The man's short haircut, his shirt and tie and the bulge of a weapon under his arm, were easy to read. Two cops in love. Interesting! I congratulated myself on spotting them as they came abreast of me and considered introducing myself when I noticed something familiar about the blonde female cop.

It looked like Solange Monod, wearing a blonde wig. Instantly, I turned three-quarters away from her and lowered my head. If she was on a stake-out I didn't want to blow it. If she was with a lover, I didn't want her to know I'd seen her. But why the disguise?

I was amazed to have run into her at all. France is a big country. But here we were, in the same place, at the same time. I bet she didn't want to be seen here.

I turned my back even more, wondering why Emile had sent her to Lourdes when there was so much work to be done elsewhere.

She and her companion continued past me and I fell in behind them until they turned into a restaurant a few doors up. I slowed my pace so I could glance inside and saw them join a woman in her fifties, with reddish, well-coiffed hair, wearing a beige silk suit and jewellery – the rich, matronly type. The woman seemed furtive as she shook hands with them and nervously slipped into a booth. Solange and the other cop took the chairs facing the street.

Just then the male cop glanced up, but before our eyes met I moved along. Whatever was going on didn't look kosher to me. Damn! I sure as hell didn't want to tell Emile about this. Even if she was doing her job, she was sure as hell cheating on him.

Filled with the images of crazy women, I returned to my room and dialled the four thousand digits it takes to call overseas with a credit card.

It was mid-morning, Saturday, in Houston and Victoria wasn't at home. I knew she wouldn't be at Kennedy High where she worked as a guidance counsellor, so I tried her at Lindsay's dance class.

'James?' she said, when they'd called her to the phone. 'Are you all right? I've been worried sick. Why the hell didn't you call me before? You know I can't talk to you here.' Her southern drawl took the sting out of her words.

'It's nice to hear your voice, too,' I said. 'How are the kids?'

'Alive.'

'Why? Have they been in danger?'

'A lot you'd care.'

'Were they?' I insisted.

'No, they're fine.'

'Is this going to be a long-distance fight? At these prices, I'd like to pass.'

'No fighting,' she agreed. 'Just talk. We all miss you. How was the wedding?'

'Very nice. Your type of affair. Weepy and sentimental. Lots of dancing and hugging and kissing. You would have liked it.'

I could tell I'd made her smile. But then she said, 'The wedding's been over for a week, hasn't it?'

213

'I've been helping Emile. There was a fourth murder, in Toulouse.'

'Is that where you are?'

'No, I'm in Lourdes.'

'The city of the miracle? Have they converted you yet?'

'Not a chance. Actually, I came here to see a friend in a sanatarium.'

'What friend?'

'Catherine.'

She was so quiet I thought we'd been disconnected. 'Vickie,' I said, feeling that long distance between us.

'I'm here,' she replied. 'Processing information. You went to see Catherine, all the way to Lourdes from Toulouse. Are they close to one another?'

'No,' I admitted. 'I had to see her.'

'Is that the real reason you went to France?' She always got right to the heart. Damn, the woman was psychic.

'Of course not!' I insisted. A man caught in an untruth will deny it vehemently.

'So you went to see perfect Catherine, the love of your life. Does she still fire your piston, or did it misfire with her too?'

She knew how to get me. 'Damn it, Victoria, that stinks. I didn't fuck her. She's barely coherent. The woman's been in a mental hospital for years. It was rough seeing her that way. But I think it helped. I may have had what you shrinks call a breakthrough.'

'Really? Well, good for you.' Then she said, 'I'm sorry for what I said, honey, I was hurt. You haven't called, and you went to see her. It must have been horrible finding her like that.'

'It was. I hardly recognized her. And she said some strange things to me, talked a lot about sex, as though she was obsessed with it. As a professional, how would you explain that?'

'I'm not a therapist, but I know it can't be from sleeping with you,' she zapped me, unable to resist.

'Very funny. What do you think?'

'Honey, I can't analyze a perfect stranger's behaviour. I don't know her background, what's gone on in her life. It could be her medication or her hormones. Anything can trigger an obsession; she's disturbed.'

'She said she was being punished for having too much sex, like a sin or transgression.'

'She's Catholic, isn't she? You know how they spread around sin.'

It made sense – for Chloe too, who was even more seductive than her mother. Both women were caught in a vicious cycle; they were born beautiful and seductive, and men responded. But if they followed through, their religion made them feel guilty and they paid terrible consequences. You'd think, after the sexual revolution, things would be different but they weren't.

'James,' Victoria broke into my thoughts. 'I've been worried about you. I didn't know where you were and the kids ask me twenty times a day, "When's Daddy coming home?" I don't know what to tell them.'

'I'll be home soon,' I told her.

'Tomorrow? Or next week?'

'I wish I knew,' I admitted. 'It depends on Emile's case. The killings are getting closer together, which means the killer is escalating. Still it could be a while. You know how these things go.'

'Only too well. Are you going back to Paris?'

'Not until I speak to Catherine's doctor and see her brother Paul again. He lives in Eugénie les Bains. She has a daughter too, named Chloe, who lives with her uncle. I imagine it's difficult for her not having parents. I want to do something for her.'

'What are you going to do for us, Jimmy? We have a lot to settle.'

'I'm working on it.'

'I'll give you a week,' she said. 'And if you're not home by then, I won't be responsible for the consequences.'

'What's that supposed to mean?'

'I have to take care of myself too. You may be having a crisis but it also affects me. I'm the one at home with the kids while you're out there doing God knows what. Tomorrow's Father's Day, did you remember?'

I pretended to. 'Of course, why do you think I called?'

'The children made you presents.'

'Give them my love, will you?'

'James, why don't you let me help you.'

'You can't! Don't you know that?'

She took a deep furious breath and let it out slowly. 'Why the hell not? It's my job to help people.'

'Kids, maybe.' I knew how to get to her too.

'You can be maddening sometimes,' she said. I heard tears in her voice. 'The kids I help, as you pointed out, are more mature than you are.'

'I shouldn't have said that, I'm sorry. Don't cry.'

'I'm not, dammit.' But I knew she was and I felt terrible. I ought to be home with her now. But I had too much unfinished business.

'If you need to speak to me in the next two days, leave a message for me at the Hôtel Prés d'Eugénie. I'll check in regularly, okay? After that, you can find me with Emile. Tell the kid's I'll be missing them tomorrow.'

'Fine,' she said, empty of emotion. 'So long.' And she hung up. Her disappointment reached across the miles. I should have been more reassuring. But my

216

mind was in two places at once. And Catherine was taking precedence.

I met Victoria Wilson at a party right after I joined the FBI, in January of 1976. There was an instant attraction, the kind where your eyes meet and you let each other know there's potential. But when she came over to talk, I treated her as I'd treated all women since Catherine – a conquest or a one night stand. She wasn't impressed, so I moved on. I had plenty of other females.

A few weeks later, my roommate Buzz invited her and a friend to join a group of us watching the Superbowl at our apartment. When she walked in the chemistry was still there but she avoided me. And in that small apartment, it wasn't easy. She thought I was a neanderthal. I thought she was up-tight.

My girlfriend at the time was a beauty named Peaches, a bathing suit model – naturally. I hung all over her that night, trying to make Victoria jealous; really mature. Victoria kept her attention on the game. But I knew she wanted me.

During half-time I made another move. 'A girl as pretty as you must believe in giving a guy a second chance. How about it?' I extended my hand.

She took it and appraised me. 'Okay, we'll try again. What kind of work do you do?'

'Investigative agent with the FBI.' I couldn't help being defensive. Somehow I knew she wouldn't like it.

'I should have guessed.' She gave me a knowing smile.

'What's wrong, don't you approve of law enforcement?' I was bristling.

'Sure I do. With your lack of self-awareness, you've chosen the perfect profession.'

'What are you? A shrink or something?'

'Yes, as a matter of fact. I'm a psych major, I

graduate this spring and then I'm going for my Master's.'

'Aren't you a little young to be giving advice?'

'Maybe I am now, but when I get my Master's and put in my hours of supervision, I won't be.'

It was my turn to roll my eyes.

'Do you think shrinks are a waste of time?'

'Not when you have yourselves as patients. You're the ones who usually need the help.' She left before the game was over.

A year later I spotted her among the Masters' candidates at my cousin Kyle's graduation. I guess I was finally through with being a jackass and I'd screwed enough women to fade Catherine's memory to a dull ache.

This time I was determined not to be hostile to the gorgeous dark-haired woman with the brilliant smile.

My cousin reminded me I was on her hit list. 'She thinks you're a jerk.' He laughed and punched my arm.

'Don't worry, I'm irresistible,' I told him.

'Not to her,' he insisted, which piqued my interest. I could usually get any girl I wanted. Women were challenged by guys they couldn't conquer.

'Oh, it's you,' she said, one eyebrow arched. 'How's the broad-minded Special Agent doing these days?'

'Eating crow,' I admitted, remembering how obnoxious I'd been.

She gave me an up and down. 'Eating crow suits you. But you look as puffed up as the last time I saw you.'

'I'm really sorry,' I told her. 'I didn't mean whatever I said to you then.'

'The bad impression still lingers.'

'We got off to a wrong start. Want to try again?'

'In your dreams if you think I'll fall for that again,' she said, turning her back and walking away. But I had seen the spark of interest in her eyes.

I chased after her, intent on winning her over. 'Congratulations on getting your Master's,' I said. 'Pretty impressive for a dumb girl like you.'

She turned around with fists clenched and I swear she was ready to hit me until she saw that I was teasing, and then she laughed, a deep throaty sound that I've loved ever since. Her laughter has always lifted my spirits higher than I could ever lift them myself.

'I'm really sorry,' I told her, taking her hand. 'When I first met you, I was growling at every woman with a brain.'

'Don't tell me there's some self-awareness growing like a fungus under all those muscles,' she said, removing her hand. 'Maybe you should tell me all about it?' We both laughed.

I took her home that night and we've been together ever since. Once we got over the hostility, it was easy between us. We just fitted. We had similar backgrounds; her sister's husband had been killed in Vietnam like my brother and she had a deeper understanding of what loss means than most. When I told her about Rob, she listened. And I found myself opening up to her in a way I'd never done before.

I'd gone to Miltby High, and she'd gone to our rival, Austin. I played football and she was a songleader. We even had a political philosophy in common: we hated Nixon. Both of us liked to ride a bike and play tennis, and we rooted for the home teams. But what I liked best about Victoria was the joy she found in life. It was so infectious that I found myself feeling joyous too after such a long time. Basically, I was born with a heavy heart, the kind of guy who takes everything seriously; my brother Rob was the one who found everything funny. Losing both him and then Catherine had wounded my heart. Vickie made it light again.

Being from Texas, we both have accents, but

Victoria's is more pronounced since her mother's from Louisiana. She's the opposite of Catherine in looks. Where Catherine's is blonde, Vickie's hair is black; where Catherine's is pale, Vickie's skin tans to a coffee colour after five minutes in the sun. Her dark eyes see everything and still find humour whenever possible. Her hair is shorter these days than when I met her, but it's still thick and shiny. I always thought she could be in those commercials where the woman's hair swirls around like water flowing. Victoria's hair moves like that in one smooth action when she tosses her head.

But what kept me with her was her self-confidence and her optimism, exactly what I needed. With Victoria, everything was possible.

On our first date I took her to see a marathon of 'Godfather I and II'. Afterwards we parked and made out and I found out she had excellent tits, firm and full, as good as a guy could want.

'What are your goals in life, Jimmy?' she asked me after a few breathless kisses.

I mumbled something about coming home to kisses like that every night which stopped the discussion.

But on our third date she asked me again what I wanted out of life, and I could see she expected an answer. We were parked in front of her house and she was holding my hand, staring at me with her serious expression.

'I'm ambitious,' I admitted, finding it awkward at first, but having a woman like her interested in me was a privilege.

'I am too,' she said. 'Ambition's good, keeps the mosquitoes from biting.'

'I really love my work, but it's not enough. I want to advance in the Bureau, really make a difference in the world by getting rid of some of the scum.' I heard

220

myself say it out loud for the first time. 'If I could make Special Agent in Charge, I wouldn't be earning thirty thousand a year, five years from now.'

'And after retirement?'

'I don't know. Maybe stay on as special advisor, teach at Quantico. I might write a book about my bizarre cases.'

She nodded thoughtfully.

'What about you?'

'I've considered going into private practice where I would make a lot of money. But I'd rather help more people by being a counsellor, working with problem kids. The money's not as good, but it would be more satisfying.'

'That would suit you,' I told her, impressed.

'Is a career all you want? Don't you think there's more to life than your job?'

I didn't reply right away for I felt a painful stab. My family hadn't done much to build my self-esteem and Catherine's family had damaged it even further. So I'd never had the courage to reach too high. As for the possibility of a relationship, which is what I assumed Vickie meant, this was the first time I'd been close.

I depersonalized Catherine by calling her Frenchie. The only time I let myself think of her was when I had a blow job. Just the thought of what the tip of her tongue could do to me filled me with fire. I also stayed away from boats. The one time I went sailing and re-experienced the sensation of floating on water, I got alternately sad and horny. It was a toss up between going into the head to masturbate or crying.

'No,' I finally replied. 'My career isn't everything. I want to get married someday, have a family.' In my estimation, families weren't all that terrific.

'I want that too,' she said. 'When I'm ready. We have more in common than I ever expected. Both of us are in the helping professions, especially yours. Society couldn't exist without people like you. But it must be difficult dealing with criminals all the time, and dangerous?'

'Walking across the street is dangerous,' I told her, not wanting to be analyzed. A kiss ended the conversation, which was fine. Vickie turned me on more than any woman since Catherine. And I truly admired the reserves of strength within her, the way she smiled at people and made them feel special. When she gazed into my eyes and immersed me in her warmth, it made me feel like the most important person in the world. She was so firmly placed in her own orbit that after the ups and downs of my own life, it was a relief to know her. But I wasn't ready for marriage.

I was still bitter, like those obsessed people filled with fury whom nobody wants to know. And when my temper erupted it got me into trouble. Twice I was reprimanded for using excessive force while performing an arrest.

When I finally felt ready to confide in Vickie about Catherine, she listened without comment. It took several attempts before I got to the truth, that Catherine had abandoned me. I remember Vickie putting her head on my cheek and saying, 'It's okay now, James, I'm here,' and holding me. I think that's when I fell in love with her.

Once I said to her, 'Every guy you've ever been with drives me crazy, I can't stand the thought of anyone else touching you.'

She caught on right away. 'Are you asking me if I'm jealous of Catherine?'

'No way,' I insisted.

'Jealousy's a waste of time, darlin'. We've got better things to do with each other. The way I see it, you're with me, not Catherine. Her loss is my gain.'

'Who cares? She doesn't mean a thing to me.' I didn't know whether to be flattered or annoyed.

'Like hell,' she countered. 'If she didn't mean anything, something would be wrong.'

'I've dealt with it. It's over. Done. Finito.'

'No, Jimmy. It's eating at you. I can see it.'

'Don't give me that crap!' I protested.

'Okay,' she said, backing off. 'You'll get to it when you're ready. But don't tell me it doesn't bother you. It's my job to know when someone is blocking.'

'Why should I be blocking?'

'Why does anyone? Usually it's a legacy from childhood. In your case, the injuries to your soul then were worse than anything she did to you. I'm talking about Rob's death on top of your father's abuse. Catherine added the final blows.'

I knew the truth when I heard it, the way you know deep inside where you live. But I'd be damned if I'd admit it. So, I pretended to scoff. (The woman still reads me too well.) 'That's the stupidest thing I've ever heard.'

'Okay, Jimmy. You decide when to let go.' She was gentle, noting my resistance.

Now, after seeing Catherine, I realized how right she was. But every time she brought it up then, I denied it.

'There's no problem,' I'd say, frightened that she homed into the core of me, like a witch. So I suppressed the memories of Catherine – gentle, elusive, brilliant Catherine, creator of my passion. I wanted Vickie to say, 'I'm jealous as hell of the bitch. She was a stupid fool to let you go.' If Vickie and I had fought it out, if I'd admitted that the passion I felt for her was different from what I'd felt for Catherine, maybe things would be better now. But how could I have said such a thing? I hadn't let myself know it.

Instead, it's hung there between us all these years.

Victoria's been waiting for me to acknowledge and face it head on, and I've been too afraid. I wanted to be cured without working at it.

When we'd gone together for a year, Vickie asked me how I felt about her.

I gave her a sheepish grin. 'You know.'

'James,' she said in that quiet, southern voice of hers, 'if you're not serious enough by now to consider getting married, I'd like you to say so. I have to know if there's a future for us. If not, I'm going to break off with you and find someone who wants me as much as I want him.'

'You're gonna go and find someone, just like that?'

'Not just like that,' she said. 'It will hurt like hell and I will cry, and be tempted to beg you to take me back. I love you, darlin'. I don't want to lose you. But eventually the pain will lessen, and I will meet someone else. There has to be someone for me to love. I deserve that, James. I want it, and I'm willing to look for it. I need to be appreciated for what I am. And I won't settle for less than being cherished by the man I cherish.'

I admired her so much I couldn't let her go. So I proposed. After all, I did love her. With her I saw a life of shared experiences and the fulfilment of a family. Besides, her smile made my day. So I told myself that the fire Catherine ignited in my belly was unimportant.

But my body wouldn't let me forget.

I closed the wooden shutter over the single window in the room and lay on the bed staring into the pitch black, thinking about Catherine and Chloe and whether I could pull my marriage out of trouble. Before I had any answers, darkness engulfed me and I curled on my side and went to sleep.

# Chapter 12

First thing in the morning, I called Emile. 'What is Solange doing in Lourdes? I saw her last night. Is she on a stakeout, or questioning a witness?'

There was silence. 'Solange is right here with me, James. She never left Paris. She's been checking phone numbers for days.'

*I couldn't have been mistaken.* 'Are you sure? Ask her.'

'Of course.' He turned to her and told her what I'd said. She replied, and he came back to me. 'She was at the evidence warehouse most of yesterday, only took a break to visit her mother for a few hours. They had dinner together, then she went back to work. Right now she's reporting in before going off duty to get some sleep.'

*I could have sworn it was Solange. Maybe I was mistaken.* 'Emile,' I said, 'don't repeat this question out loud if she can hear you, but does she ever go under-cover wearing a blonde wig?'

'What are you implying?' he said, huffily.

'Nothing. Will you answer the question?'

'The answer is yes, and others as well. They're supplied by the department.'

'Because the woman I saw was wearing a wig.'

'So?'

There was nothing I could say. I changed the subject.

'I have an appointment to speak with Catherine's doctor this morning. Then I'm returning to Eugénie to see Paul, before I join you in Paris.'

'Fine, I'll see you then.'

Even though it was Sunday morning, Dr Guillaud met me at his office. I was surprised at how young he was. Or maybe I was getting old. He was about my height, with long wavy hair, an olive complexion and heavy glasses.

'I agreed to see you because you are in Lourdes for such a short while,' he told me. 'But I don't have much time. I have an in-patient practice, you see, which keeps me on call most of the time.

'Just to tell you about myself – I did my training in Switzerland and England and I prescribe the latest pharmaceuticals for schizophrenia. Some are so new they haven't been approved in the US yet.'

'Is there a chance that you can still help Catherine? Will she ever get better?'

'Do you know much about the disorder?' he asked me.

I shook my head.

'Well, no one can predict what will happen. Some patients have only one psychotic break and are never sick again. Others are helped a great deal by medication, and a small percentage are helped very little. It might be their chemistry, we really don't know. Several studies have shown that their recovery, or lack of it, might be the result of what's waiting for them outside the hospital. In Madame Jolibois' case, she has occasional moments of lucidity, but mostly she's acutely schizophrenic. Her parents' and her husband's deaths were traumatic for her. The schizophrenia helps her to avoid dealing with these tragedies. She knows that facing a great sadness awaits her.'

'What if she could deal with it? Would she get well?'

'It doesn't always work that way. In some people, once the chemical imbalance takes place, for whatever reason, it's nearly impossible to reverse.'

'Even if I were there for her?' I asked.

'I do not know if that would make a difference. She rarely speaks about you. However, given the gravity of her condition, I suspect it wouldn't change anything.'

'What about her daughter? Doesn't that give her an incentive to get well?'

'People who suffer psychotic breaks are not motivated by the same drives as you and I. Unfortunately, wanting to be a good mother would not help her overcome her illness.'

The next question was the most difficult. 'Why does she speak so violently about sex?'

'I'm not at liberty to discuss that with you.'

His refusal only made me more determined. 'I want to know if I did this to her, if having sex with me when she was seventeen caused her breakdown.'

He stared at me from over steepled fingers. 'I don't know exactly what caused her breakdown, Monsieur Barton. There were many factors, but I don't believe it was having sex with you.'

I could see I wouldn't get anywhere with him, but consoled myself that she was in competent hands. We said goodbye and he agreed to keep me apprised of her condition. But I wasn't ready to give up on her.

When I returned to Eugénie there were two messages for me. One from Paul, an invitation to join him for dinner at the hotel that evening. I confirmed the date.

The other was a fax from Emile and a request to call him immediately. I returned the call, thinking about his relationship with Solange. It could be blinding him to certain facts. In spite of her denial, I knew I'd seen her in Lourdes. And if it wasn't her, I

227

still didn't trust her. She was undependable, pursued her own agendas. And the way she looked at me made me realize she was using Emile. She might even be the person in the department who was working against him.

Emile was not in his office so I asked to speak to Lillianne Reneau. Maybe she could give me an objective opinion of her female co-worker. I swore her to secrecy and promised the same.

'What is your opinion of Solange?' I asked her.

'If you really want to know, Emile is my friend and I'm worried about him.' The frustration came pouring out. 'The woman takes advantage of us all. We do the work and she's gone half the time. She is using Emile to get her promotion, and will step on him if she needs to. But I do not hate her; maybe I'm jealous. I wish I could get away with what she does and not get caught.'

'Where was she last night?'

'She was supposed to be with us, on telephone detail, but she checked in and then left. She said she was going to see her mother, but when I called, no one was there. And we needed her, too. We have so much work to do. I wish someone would tell Emile. He doesn't see it.'

'Lillianne, could you run a private check to see if Solange was aboard any police, charter, or government flights to Lourdes last night? I thought I saw her there.'

'When I can,' she promised. 'The Boardroom case takes priority.'

I thanked her, glad to be in the business of investigating, feeling the urge to return to Paris. This was the first time I'd been removed from the centre of things and it was like being benched at the Big Game. My team needed me and I needed to be in the action. First of all, I felt possessive; call it ego, but I didn't trust anyone to do as good a job as I could. If my personal life wasn't consuming me, nothing could have pried me away.

I read Emile's fax eagerly. It answered some of my questions. A few common threads wove through the lives of the four victims: their age, their wealth, their way of life, their position in the community, and their sexual activities. Only Shithead knew the common denominator, but we would find it. So far, their religions were different, they did not belong to the same organizations, they did not know one another, except for de Saint Robert and Patrick Richard whose acquaintance had still not materialized into a proven relationship. They did not go to the same doctor, vacation in the same places, or buy merchandise from a particular source. But they beat their meat to video tapes.

I was still waiting for information on the political angle. Maybe it would be more helpful.

Dinner was hours away so I took a jog and then ended up at Alfonse Larousse's café. Sunday in provincial France is as one would imagine. The women go to church and the men sit in the cafés. In an adjacent park a game of *boules* was underway, with the better players attempting to make it to the end-of-summer *bouladrome* or playoffs.

'*Ah, le jeune Américain*,' Alfonse greeted me with a twitch of his handlebar moustache and a wave of his arm, inviting me to join him at the table with three of his cronies. My partner, Ben Chumway, and I often stop by after work for a couple of beers at McGintys', where we're sure to run into our buddies; being at this table of men felt just like that. Except that we five had nothing in common. They wore sleeveless undershirts, for God's sake, with scarves tied round their necks. Two of them wore berets. And they mistrusted me on

229

sight. No one spoke to me and they gave Alfonse dirty looks when I joined the table.

I had read somewhere that the French honour the boundaries of privacy; one doesn't speak unless properly introduced. In that way, Americans are superficial; we make friendships too easily, which are better developed over time. And we don't distinguish between close friends and acquaintances; the French language delineates with *vous* and *tu*.

I sat there quietly, not wanting to intrude, while I sipped my coffee and tried to decipher their political conversation. Nobody was agreeing and every comment was considered *trés stupide* by someone else. Nobody finished a sentence before someone jumped on his words.

I had a coffee and was ready to leave when three young Nordic-looking women in shorts, carrying back packs, pedalled into view, dismounted and went inside. Conversation stopped abruptly and we men bonded instantly, all lusting after the women.

These men were either farmers, small merchants, grape growers, mechanics, craftsmen, carpenters, or low level bureaucrats who sat here every Sunday of their lives, probably in the same chairs, waiting for just such an event: three beautiful women in revealing clothes to come riding by. Each man had his fantasy of what would happen next.

The women's conversation wafted through the open door as they laughed and joked with one another in Dutch, making us feel privileged to be part of the same scene. I assumed they were speaking Dutch, for there were a lot of *ogen pogen* sounds in their dialogue.

Too soon, they paid for their food, slung their packs on their backs, remounted their bikes and pedalled off, giving us a fine view of their behinds. They knew we were watching; two of them smiled and waved.

None of us waved back. But to a man we watched them go. Conversation did not resume until they were well out of sight. Then each of us smiled at one another and a few shifted in their seats to relieve the tension. The ice had been broken. I was now *un ami*.

Marcel the baker sighed. 'Girls in their twenties. It's the young ones who really get to me.'

'I know what you mean,' I replied, thinking of Chloe, my French sounding not half bad.

'Oh, you do?' Alfonse said, grinning, he punched the shoulder of the man next to him, as though they had a joke on me.

'What are you talking about?' I asked.

Everyone at the table chuckled knowingly, even a few at the table nearby.

'We've seen you noticing *her*,' Marcel said.

I felt my face flush, which caused more amusement.

Faustin, who repaired tractors, pointed to his crotch and then jerked his thumb skyward in an obscene gesture, implying that Chloe gave me a hard on.

And then, as though it was pre-arranged, Alfonse, Marcel and Faustin all leaned over the table to have a look between my legs to see if it was true.

This made them really hysterical.

Their laughter was good-natured and I couldn't help joining in, understanding that they too shared these feelings. It was a relief.

'Does she always act that way?' I asked.

To a man, they nodded.

Alfonse leaned over to confide in me. 'This one is even a little old. In France, the men are in love with "little girls". Especially when they wear their white cotton dresses and black shiny shoes. They tease us and we love it. But we don't do anything about it. *Les jeunes filles* grow up too fast. There are but a few moments of perfection between childhood and when they blossom into a woman. And then it is gone.' He made a gesture with both hands, cupping big imaginary breasts.

'Ach!' Marcel said, the corners of his mouth lowering. 'Then they want you to be rich and drive a Citroën and take them to the disco.'

'The little girls all love their papas, don't they?' Faustin said.

'Just once, I'd like to have one sitting on my lap,' Marcel said, a sly smile causing the corners of his mouth to rise now.

*What a bunch of dirty old men*, I thought, disgusted.

He saw my expression. 'Oh, we don't mean anything by it!'

'Of course not!' Alfonse insisted. 'We're French! Look at this.' He brought out an edition of the day's paper, *Sud-Ouest Dimanche*, *Sunday in the South-West*, and showed me an article entitled, '*La litterature du tendre*', exactly the subject we were discussing – seductive, nubile young girls.

A photograph showed a girl, younger than Chloe, lying on her stomach. You could only see her from the waist down, one knee bent, the other foot dangling over the edge of the mattress. She wore white socks and black patent-leather shoes with straps across the insteps; her dress was pulled up revealingly. Not only did she look appealing, but quite unconcerned.

The article itself chronicled a list of books currently being published in France which dealt with the subject of the nymphet. Evidently, the Nabokov legacy was alive and well and living in south-west France. But I didn't like it; it exploited children, set a tone for who knows what – for girls like Chloe to grow up and become women like Catherine.

I continued reading. Some of the writers, the review

said, had literary pretensions and tried to show that erotic work can be erudite, though they were often pedantic. One book had a theme that made me squirm, essentially saying that once a man succumbs to the attraction of little girls, 'whose eyes tell a lot about their secret appetites', he will always succumb.

I guess I wasn't the only one with a fixation; five books on the subject were being reviewed. What kind of people were these French? Catholics on weekdays and dirty old men on Sunday. I didn't want to be part of a conspiracy of men who fostered these fantasies. Certainly women didn't approve.

Alfonse saw my concern. 'In France we recognize these desires, but don't do anything about them, just enjoy the fantasy, the idea.'

'But some people take it further,' I said.

'Not in France,' he insisted.

I thought about the child porn cases I'd investigated in the US, the brutal beatings and sexual abuse of children; this was nothing like that. But my American ethics wouldn't allow me to shrug it off as they did.

Dining at Prés d'Eugénie is an experience. It was my first time at a Michelin three-star restaurant and I was aware of every detail. Hors d'oeuvres and cocktails were served on the verandah or in the garden under a canopy of tall leafy trees. The sound of chirping birds and the cascading water in the fountain made sighing sounds, and moist warm air caressed me as I watched the waiters serving fancy little tidbits they call *amuse gueules* from silver trays.

I took a seat on the patio and a waiter presented me with a menu of unbelievable descriptions. When I asked for explanations, he helped me make my choices and told me there was one sitting per evening, so I should wait until my name was called by the maître d'. He pointed her out to me an attractive blonde woman in a black suit.

Our reservation was for nine o'clock and I had arrived at five minutes past. But Paul was late. By nine-thirty I had eaten half-a-dozen tidbits.

I ordered another aperitif, a speciality of the house, sweet, fruity and lethal – one-third champagne, one-third peach Cassis, and one-third Armagnac. Then I ate more little goodies. French people generally keep to themselves, so I sat there alone, people-watching, until ten o'clock. The maître d' offered to call the *castelle* for me but I refused, feeling more foolish and angry by the minute. Either Paul had done this on purpose to further humiliate me, or he'd had an accident on the way. But there was hardly any traffic on these country roads. If one of his cars broke down he had a fleet of cars with which to replace it, or he could have walked and been here by now. Maybe he'd forgotten.

Finally, Michel Guerard himself came out to offer apologies for his errant friend.

'Please be seated, Monsieur Barton,' he told me. 'I'm certain Paul would want you to enjoy your dinner without him.'

With attention like that, I couldn't refuse. They showed me to my table and I sat there alone. Only one other diner was by himself, an elderly man who glanced my way and nodded.

My first course was just being served, *La Galette Feuilletée des Legumes Nouveaux Au Sabayon de Tursan*, layers of flaky pastry stuffed with country vegetables and truffles, in a sauce of foie gras, wine and cream, and I was engrossed in it when someone slipped into the chair opposite me. I looked up to see Chloe sitting there, smiling with her cat's eyes.

'What are you doing here? I'm supposed to meet your uncle.'

'It's my fault,' she told me, slightly out of breath. 'I didn't give you his message. Uncle Paul had to go to Bordeaux on business, and I forgot to tell you! I was watching "La Femme Nikita" and I went to sleep.'

'You fell asleep watching that violent movie?' I asked, realizing this was the first time she'd spoken to me directly, except to answer a few of my questions at lunch. The effect was powerful.

'Oh, it's my favourite, I've seen it many times,' she announced, brushing off my concern.

'La Femme Nikita', the one French film I'd actually seen, is about a young female assassin, too brutal to be anyone's heroine.

'When I woke up,' she continued to explain, 'I remembered you were waiting. So I got dressed and told André to drive me here. You won't tell Uncle Paul, will you?' She seemed only slightly worried that I'd tell him, and too well groomed to have dressed in a hurry. I suspected that Paul was ducking me.

Her behaviour tonight was different from before. Nobody was forcing her to be with me so she took the initiative. Until now, I was only someone to flirt with.

I appraised her. 'If you had called me, I would have told you not to come. I don't mind eating alone.'

The way she looked at me, made me think she'd arranged to get me alone. But I ignored her signals, only interested in helping her. I owed Catherine that much.

'I adore to eat Michel's food and will do it any chance I get,' she said, brushing aside comment. 'Uncle Paul doesn't let me; it's too public. When I'm home for *vacances*, he keeps me to himself.'

Her eyes took in the sights of the country-style decor. Two paintings of spaniels hung on either side of

235

the arch that separated the dining rooms. The dogs were returning pheasants to the table after the hunt as one would see on an English estate. In the room opposite were three-dimensional paintings of vegetables – squash, pumpkin, tomatoes. The food popped out of the canvas like a sculpture in a frieze. In any other location it would have been gaudy. Here, it worked.

'I'm glad they sat us in the blue room,' she said, her face full of animation, touching my hand and referring to the turquoise tablecloths draped to the floor. 'Though sometimes I like the white room, too.'

I looked through the arch following her gaze and noticed the other tables had white cloths and the wicker chairs were upholstered in beige, while our chairs were upholstered in turquoise gingham.

She touched my hand again and pointed to the flowers. 'Don't you love the way they arrange these in silver pitchers and baskets? Our flower arrangements at home belong in a museum,' she commented. The flowers on our table were large yellow roses; in the other room the roses were bright pink.

'Michel grows them in his garden. Feel how soft.' She guided my fingers to touch the butter-textured petal. I was being seduced again and withdrew my hand, giving her a look to stop her.

But her attention had shifted to the light of the candles in the antique silver candelabra on our table, making her eyes sparkle. Each table had candelabra on it and a bundle of wheat lying on its side, tied with a ribbon.

'Aren't they sweet?' she asked, fondling the ribbon. She was trying to act like a sensual woman, but she was still a young girl. She gave me a conspiratorial smile, and I couldn't help laughing.

But the man dining by himself was staring at her with

admiration and at me with envy. I didn't blame him. Chloe's hair fell in silky waves down her back. Her dress was light blue, like her eyes. Everyone in the room was looking at her.

'Is your hotel in Eugénie nice?' she asked.

'Not very.'

'Maybe I could visit you there sometimes.'

'Not a chance,' I told her.

She continued to smile as if she didn't believe me then raised her hand and summoned the waiter, ordering something in rapid French with an assurance and precision that dazzled me – a far cry from the way my young cousins ordered pizza or my own two children only ate peanut butter and jelly sandwiches no matter where they were. Upper-class children were bred to a different kind of life.

'I asked him to bring me *L'Oreiller Moelleux de Mousserons et de Morilles aux Truffes Noires*. I just love them, don't you?'

Whatever it was, it sounded delicious. I was bombarded by the full force of her attention until the wine steward hurried over to pour her wine from my bottle, and I held my hand over the glass.

'What are you doing?' she asked, getting huffy.

'You're under age!'

'What do you mean? I drink wine with every meal.' She couldn't believe it.

'Not with me, you don't.'

My determination stopped her and she gave me a glance of pure hatred. 'A meal without wine is like a day without sunshine,' she said.

I prayed I'd never see a look like that from my own children. 'Isn't the drinking age eighteen in France?'

'But no one follows it,' she insisted. 'You know I'm right, don't you?'

She was staring daggers, but I stood my ground and

continued to eat my first course. 'Chloe, as an officer of the law, I can't ignore the rules of your country or mine.'

'I feel sorry for your children with a father like you. In France, wine is not considered alcohol, we drink it when we are very young.' She tossed her head in a superior way as if to say, *You couldn't possibly understand*, and began to eat.

'Do you miss having a father and a mother?'

'Uncle Paul is all I need. He usually lets me do as I like.'

'That's what I was afraid of,' I replied, trying not to respond to her seductive behaviour.

'Tell me about your interests. What do you like to do?'

Her suggestive look made me sorry I'd asked. I ignored it.

'I study piano, I'm told I am good. And I raise show dogs, little ones.' She smiled. 'As for the future, I'd like to be a performer, possibly on the stage, that's why I must pursue my music. Uncle Paul doesn't agree. He thinks women are only for men's amusement.' Her expression was sombre and I sensed a major conflict.

'What do you like to read?' I asked.

She discussed the books she liked, both English classics and American literature, and for a moment lost her self-consciousness as though I was a person instead of a potential conquest. But it was short-lived.

'My favourites are the French, of course. Like Marguerite Duras. Her book *The Lover* became a film. I thought the girl they picked for the part was too old, or else the man was too young. In the book, the greater difference in their ages made it far more interesting.' Another sly glance.

'I'm not familiar with it,' I told her, but I was. Victoria had read it, about the author's love affair with

238

a much older oriental man when she was only fourteen. A subject I wasn't keen to discuss with Chloe.

'What other writers do you like?'

'Voltaire. I identify with Candide. I have to be positive, even when the whole world is disgusting.'

'Why do you say the world is disgusting when you have everything: beauty, position, wealth, intelligence?'

'Because it's a terrible burden.'

'Chloe, life is a precious gift and a joy.'

'I never read *Pollyanna*,' she stated. 'Are you strict with your little girl?'

'Only because I love her.'

She looked away. 'I saw your mother yesterday,' I told her. 'She sends her love.'

'Don't lie to me!' she snapped, with a fury more like Paul than Catherine. 'She doesn't even know me.'

'Why don't you visit her more often, then she would know you better? It would be good for both of you.'

'You don't have any idea what is good for me,' she said, raking my body suggestively with her eyes.

But I wouldn't play any more. 'Chloe, stay on the subject. Does your uncle let you visit your mother?'

'Of course! But I don't like to visit a crazy woman.' She paused, thinking about her mother, and then turned away to hide her tears. 'Whenever we go in my mother's car, Mademoiselle Desault has to go too. And there's no place to go. If we take Maman into a boutique, she pulls the dresses off the racks and acts strangely. So we go to the park and feed the ducks.'

I felt sorry for her. 'Was it better when you were younger?'

A brief nod. 'She held me on her lap then, and combed my hair.' How sad she looked. Perhaps she was right not to pine for a mother incapable of being one.

'Chloe, why do you flirt with me the way you do?'

'What do you mean?' she asked, straightening her back and lowering her chin.

'You know, like inviting yourself to my room, giving me looks, the way you're doing now. Is that how you act with your boyfriends?'

'What boyfriends?' she scoffed. There was a hardness to her that Catherine never had, and she was far more difficult to reach, even with Catherine's dementia.

'Don't tell me you don't have boyfriends, a beautiful girl like you?'

She was enormously pleased that I'd called her beautiful, then her expression became wary. 'You don't know my Uncle Paul.'

'Yes I do,' I told her. 'He didn't want your mother to have boyfriends either.'

'He didn't want her to have sex,' she retorted. 'There's a difference.'

I didn't like where this conversation was going. 'How do you know that?'

She gave me one of those maddening smiles and licked her lips as if tasting the last of something delicious. Damn, I wished she'd stop that.

'You were her first lover and look what happened to you. Pfft!'

'That's none of your business.'

'You're right,' she agreed. 'But it's true, isn't it?'

'Never mind about the past. I want to talk about the present. I don't like the way you act towards me, it's wrong. Do you understand? I want it to stop, Chloe. Like the games you've been playing all evening. Don't do it with me or anybody else. It isn't fun, it's dangerous. It can get you into trouble and you're too young to handle it. Is that clear?'

She looked at me stunned. This wasn't supposed to

happen. Nobody confronted or scolded her. I had seen the way she manipulated Paul.

Several emotions appeared simultaneously. Either she was going to throw a plate or burst into tears. But she did neither. Instead she grew frightened, as though she'd stepped into unknown territory.

'You think I'm playing games with you? Why would I do that? I would never do that.' I could see the fright in her eyes. 'You don't know anything about me. You're not even smart. If you were smart you'd be out catching the Boardroom Killer, wouldn't you? Instead, you're sitting here eating dinner with me.'

Now I was angry, damn her. She was right, I was wasting time.

'Why don't you stop telling me what to do, and I won't pay any more attention to you, all right?'

And then suddenly her eyes brimmed with tears. 'Oh, don't listen to me. I'm a terrible person,' she cried. 'I didn't mean it. I don't want to be crazy like Maman.'

'You're not,' I said, resisting the urge to hold her hand. 'Your mother's doctor would tell you that. Why don't you talk to him?' I handed her his card but she left it lying there. 'It will make you feel better. I know he'll reassure you. And if there's anything else you want to talk about, I'd be glad to listen.'

She looked at me then with stricken eyes, as though some kind of struggle was going on within her and it was too painful to withstand. Abruptly, she pushed herself away from the table and said, 'I'm not feeling well. I have to go home.' And she turned and walked out. I craned my neck and watched her go, through the lobby, down the walk and into the waiting limousine.

241

# *Chapter 13*

My dinner with Chloe dispelled my fascination with her because I could see how troubled and confused she was. Now I really wanted to talk to Paul about her. If Catherine had received help earlier, maybe her condition could have been avoided. I hoped the mental illness hadn't been passed from mother to daughter.

The phone rang as I was falling asleep, uncomfortably full from dinner and drunk on wine. It was Emile.

'I can't talk now, too tired. I got your fax, I'll call tomorrow,' I said, about to hang up.

'Wait!' he shouted. 'There's been another murder, in Lyon. It's just happened. They'll hold the body for us if we get there soon.'

I groaned. 'Emile, I'm too full and tired to drive all the way to Lyon. I'll have an accident.' I sat up, trying to focus, hating the idea of meeting him.

'I'll send a helicopter to pick you up. I've instructed Lyon to leave everything at the scene until we get there. I'm leaving Paris now. We'll be there at the same time.'

'Emile, it's one in the morning. If I don't get some sleep I won't be any good to anybody. I feel like a stuffed pheasant.'

'The victim's body was mutilated,' he said. 'A major escalation. Are you certain you don't want to be there?'

A mutilated body and a virgin crime scene. This changed everything. 'Are you sure they'll leave everything intact?'

'They promised.'

'Where's the heliport?'

'At the airport in Pau, charter terminal.'

'Okay, I'll meet you,' I said, hoping my sluggish body would get started. I dressed as quickly as I could, found my car in the dark street, and through bleary eyes followed the signs to Pau, hoping to sleep on the flight.

The helicopter was waiting and I fell asleep right away, but the flight to Lyon was short, so I got less than an hour. When I landed, yawning and nauseated, an officer was waiting to drive me to the crime scene in Dardilly, a modern suburb on the outskirts of Lyon.

The murder occurred in what I would call a motel, where you sign in at the office and park your car by the room. Only it had a restaurant like the other hotels on the row.

The Hôtel Coeur de Pays, or Heart of the Country, was a spanking new structure, unlike its elderly neighbours situated in this residential area. The streets were deserted at this hour of the morning except for the hotel guests milling around who'd been disturbed by the commotion. People in pyjamas were under foot; the press was out in force.

The main A-frame building housed a lobby, restaurant and conference room. The guest rooms were in separate two-storey buildings in the rear. The parking lot ran behind the U-shaped compound and was cordoned off, surrounded by blue and white French police cars. I spotted local Gendarmes, the National French Police and an ambulance to remove the body. The press was interviewing everyone. One of the hotel guests was shooting a video that would probably end up

244

on CNN. A police van had been utilized to take statements. My hope was that we'd get some valuable testimony tonight.

I made my way through the crowd. Emile had Lucien with him. They spotted me and hurried over.

'They've arrested a suspect, James,' Emile said. 'Found him in the bushes over there.' He pointed to some trees behind the parking lot. 'The suspect was covered with blood and had a scalpel. Bloody footprints led from the murder scene directly to him.'

'You mean it's a man, not a woman?' I said.

'That's right, and the evidence is overwhelming: the timing, the location, the opportunity are undeniable. Plus, he's deranged and violent. He tried to attack the local police. They had to sedate him. Come and have a look at the crime scene, then we'll go to the Prefecture and see him.'

Emile was understandably excited, and I caught some of his enthusiasm. But the minute I looked through the window and saw the carnage, I knew something was off. The Boardroom Killer was a controlled son-of-a-bitch. Whoever did this was completely mad. It must have been done by a copy-cat.

The room was tiny. Police investigators were on top of each other trying to do their jobs, grumbling as they moved aside for one another with no place to turn. The furniture was built into the walls, twin beds only twelve inches apart; it was like a cabin on a cruise ship. Obviously French building contractors didn't have to adhere to the strict building codes that we did at home where all rooms must be large enough to accommodate the handicapped.

Lucien cleared some space for me and I stepped over the body, unable to keep myself from stepping in blood. The blood-spattered room, which had green bedspreads and wall coverings, now looked like the belly of a gutted whale. The victim was lying in a pool of blood; there was blood on the walls, it dripped across the floor, soaked over the ends of the beds, and was smeared across the bathroom tiles. And all the handprints had been made without gloves – usable patents, our first! Maybe Shithead had lost it tonight!

Like the other murders, the victim had been killed in the chair that was placed between the beds, only this time he'd been dragged out of the chair and left by the door.

His throat had been cut but there were also multiple wounds to the body and about the face. The genitals had been cut off and were protruding from his mouth. The puncture wounds in the body had been made by a scalpel; that I could see, even without the science report. But there were no defensive wounds about the hands or forearms. Something about this crime was very different from the others.

'He was mutilated after he died,' I said. Emile looked at me in surprise. 'No defensive wounds,' I pointed out. 'Taken by surprise like the others.'

'Surprise is the Boardroom Killer's modus,' Emile said.

Footprints from a wide-tread rubber-soled shoe were everywhere, especially in the bathroom where the killer had tried to wash himself. And there, opposite the bed on a built-in desk, was a rented VCR hooked up to the television, the kind you get at a video store, bloody prints all over it, just like the other Boardroom Killings. But still . . .

Emile indicated the victim. 'His name is Henri Lepic, he's owner and chief operating officer of Lepic Industries. They manufacture silk fabrics, jacquards. He's sixty years old.'

That made him the youngest victim, but within our range.

'No ID, but the hotel clerk identified him. He registered under his own name.'

Emile introduced me to Inspector Chapelle, in charge of the National Police in Lyon, a man in his mid-thirties, tall, sandy-haired, with blue eyes and a large square jaw. He'd been called in by the local Gendarmes and notified Emile immediately. We shook hands before I turned my attention back to the body.

'The suspect we have in custody had Monsieur Lepic's wallet, his jacket, and one of his testicles,' Chapelle told me. 'No problem proving that he did it.'

The dead man was wearing a business suit, pants, vest, and shirt. His necktie had been cut into pieces.

'You predicted that it would escalate like this,' Lucien said, and I noticed how tired he looked.

Emile too. His eyes were dark-ringed, he needed a shave, his collar was open and I was surprised to detect body odour. They looked the way we all do when we're called to a scene in the middle of the night – beaten to exhaustion by the immensity of the encounter, weighed down by the enormous responsibility of needing to solve things before someone else ends up this way, and knowing we'd better do it fast. Except that Emile also looked euphoric. The end was in sight.

Not for me. Too many details bothered me.

'What's the ID on the suspect?' I asked Chapelle.

'We're checking his prints. He won't tell us his name and didn't have any ID except the victim's.'

'Did you see him?' I asked Emile.

'No. They'd already taken him in.'

'Describe him,' I asked Chapelle.

'He's dark, with a hairy body, slender, about 5'7", and he has a limp. He's been sleeping on some boxes in the woods nearby. That's where we found him.'

'That doesn't fit our profile,' I said to Emile. 'Our suspect is tall and rich and drives an expensive car, doesn't limp, and never makes mistakes. She wouldn't be sleeping in the woods.'

'She?' Chapelle said. 'You've been looking for a woman?'

Emile and I glanced at each other. That information hadn't been released to the public and was kept on a need-to-know basis.

'I had no idea,' Chapelle said thoughtfully. 'One of the witnesses saw a blonde woman in a dark-coloured car drive into the parking lot about two hours before the body was discovered. I didn't think it was important.'

'Any make on the car?'

'Expensive,' Chapelle told us. 'A Maserati sedan or a Jaguar. I'll get a police artist to work on the description right away.'

'Show him the partial drawing we got from Toulouse,' I told Lucien, and wondered why Emile hadn't brought Solange with him instead of Lucien.

'The witness who saw the woman, did he drink wine tonight?' I asked Chapelle.

'No more than a bottle.' Meaning, the usual, no problem. In the US, any witness who'd drunk a bottle of wine would not be allowed to testify. But as Chloe had told me, the French didn't consider wine alcohol.

'Did the clerk see anything?' I asked.

'No. The front desk faces the lobby, the clerk's back was to the door and there's no view of the street,' Emile replied.

'What do the footprints show?' I asked.

'Only the suspect's Reeboks, one heel worn down, indicating a spinal imbalance.'

'That is not the footprint of the Boardroom Killer,' I said.

'What about this,' Emile said, grabbing Lepic by the hair and lifting his head so I could see the slash across

248

the throat, exactly like the others. 'Explain the scalpel, the VCR, and the chair. No copy-cat would know that.'

'You're right,' I conceded. 'But everything else is out of character, typical of a disorganized killer.'

'I admit the elements are different,' he agreed. 'It happened in a hotel not an office, but the victim is a successful businessman in his sixties and he's had his throat cut while watching the VCR. Only this time the killer lost it!'

'There's no second chair for the accomplice,' I said.

'Maybe the room's too small.'

Why was I fighting this? I wanted the thing to be over too. Or maybe I wanted an excuse to stay in France.

Chapelle said, 'The desk clerk told me that Lepic brought the VCR with him when he checked in. He asked for instructions on how to attach it – said he was doing research for a documentary, as though he wanted to keep up appearances.'

'The Dardilly Gendarmarie is less than a block from here,' Emile said. 'And this murder was committed right under their noses; they are not too happy. It's as though he's giving us the finger, unless he didn't know the police were nearby.'

'He knew!' I insisted. 'That's why this mutilation doesn't compute. Anyone capable of luring a man like Lepic to a pre-arranged meeting, and murdering him under the shadow of a police station, wouldn't leave all this evidence. This hotel was chosen carefully. It's right off the main road, with easy access for a quick getaway, and plenty of traffic to blend with. It's the only one on the block with parking on a side street for privacy. And the police station is within spitting distance. It doesn't make sense that he would be so clear-headed and then suddenly alter his character like this, mutilate a body, sleep in the woods and behave like an animal.' Neither of us had an answer.

One of the policeman was placing plastic bags over the hands of the victim and securing them with rubber bands to protect the scrapings they would take from under the fingernails. Then he removed the genitalia from Lepic's mouth, showing us that there was a gonad missing.

'The suspect had it,' Chapelle said.

I leaned over and ran my hand over the surface of one of the beds. Then I placed my head down and looked sideways at the surface to see what I would find. It was easy to spot – on the opposite bed was an indentation at the edge where the killer had sat, placing her behind the victim sitting in the chair. Lepic would never have let a deranged bum, who'd been sleeping in the woods, come into his room and sit behind him on the bed.

'Look, Emile,' I showed him. 'She sat behind him, while he watched the tape. After killing him, she climbed over the bed and then straightened the bedspread. She never even came near the victim's blood. That's why she left no footprints, these belong to the deranged transient.'

*Her mind is still in control*, I thought. *She's still too careful to make this mess.* 'The suspect we have in custody may have mutilated the body, but he didn't kill him,' I said.

Emile was coming to the same conclusion and his face showed his dejection.

'Maybe we'll get some usable information from him.' I patted his arm.

Emile released the body to the medical examiner and the ambulance took off. We found Lucien who was taking witness statements and the three of us followed Chapelle into the city and then to the Prefecture on Rue Corneille, a peach-coloured lumpish building with huge antennae on the roof, set back from the street with grass around it.

Lucien got out with Chapelle at the Prefecture, but Emile held my arm. 'You and I can question the suspect in the morning. By then, he might be more coherent.' It was close to 4.30 am. 'We'll get a few hours sleep and come back first thing. The Scientific reports should be in by then, too. You need sleep, don't you?'

No argument there.

We checked into an Arcade Hotel not far from the Prefecture, located near the tallest building in Lyon, a lone obelisk of a highrise with a pitched roof that was the headquarters of Credit Lyonnaise, visible from anywhere in the city.

'The Lyonnais call it the erection,' Emile said.

Just what I needed to inspire me.

The Hotel Arcade was like a Holiday Inn with comfortable beds. We lay down in our clothes, but before we fell asleep I said, 'Chapelle is less hostile than Didier.'

Emile yawned. 'He's okay. But they all resent us when we swoop down on them from Paris and grab the glory. What they don't realize is that along with the glory comes the shit, plenty of it.'

'How is Solange?' I asked him.

'Lay off, will you?' he chided.

'Chapelle had better not withhold information,' I said.

'I'll get what I need,' Emile told me.

I slept 'til 7 am but Emile wasn't there when I awoke. He'd gone to the lab to look under the microscope at all the fibres and hair samples, to check the tags of every piece of evidence against the list he had made at the scene, obtain his own copies of photographs, as well as a list of all witnesses and their testimonies, their licence numbers, and names

251

and addresses of all residents in the vicinity. No piece of evidence was going to slip through his fingers. His briefcase was bulging when we met at Chapelle's office at 8.30 am.

Lucien had gone back to Paris but had left the artist's rendition of the woman in the dark car for us. She had long, blonde, straight hair and a hat pulled down over one eye; only the chin was visible. It had a vague similarity to the drawing of the witness's sighting in Toulouse.

'No one saw a second woman?' I asked.

Chapelle shook his head.

'What about the fingerprints of the suspect in custody?'

'His name is Alexandre Toussaint, he's twenty-two years old and he's been arrested before for defaecating in public. Some saint! Three hospitalizations since dropping out of school. His mother is also in an institution. He's been living in her apartment on the outskirts of Villeurbanne. The neighbours haven't seen him for a few days.'

'Inspector Chapelle, I want you to check the records for any animal mutilations in Toussaint's neighbourhood over the last five years – cats, dogs, horses, anything at all.' I told him, 'Often, psychotics will act out on animals before they escalate to humans.'

'That would fit the neighbours' description; they said he was strange,' Chapelle replied. 'The landlord once made him vacate the apartment because of a putrid smell. He had kept three dead animals in there until they were bloated and rotting.'

'Shall we go see him?' I asked.

Emile nodded and we followed Chapelle into the holding cells, small cubicles with glass doors. An officer sat at a desk watching the prisoner. We signed in.

252

Toussaint was pacing in the small space, mumbling to himself. His left foot dragged after the right, his arms flailed, his head hung low against his chest, shoulders thrust forward. As we drew close the stench hit us. Even the glass door couldn't contain it. He was covered all over with blood, dirt and faeces. Evidently, he'd been eating it too, for something awful was smeared on his face. God, what a smell.

'Didn't anyone clean him up?' Emile asked Chapelle in disgust.

'Of course. We took away his clothes, stuck him under the shower and gave him a uniform to wear. This has happened since yesterday.'

Blood still oozed from small cuts on his face and forearms. Defensive cuts. The wound in his shoulder was bleeding through his shirt.

'Shouldn't someone take care of that wound?' I asked.

'We did. But he pulled off the stitches and the bandages,' Chapelle said. 'He wants to bleed.'

'Hello, Alexandre,' Emile said, knocking on the glass. 'How are you?'

'Get the fuck out of here!' he screamed, pounding against the glass that separated us, leaving filthy smears on it.

'What about medication?' Emile said.

'You need him coherent to question him, don't you? If we drug him, his answers will be worthless.' Chapelle was annoyed with our criticism. 'The man hardly knows who he is.'

Seeing him like this, totally delusional, there wasn't the slightest hope that he was the Boardroom Killer or her accomplice. This pitiful specimen, whose stench permeated the area, could never have travelled to three other cities and pulled off sophisticated crimes; he had neither the means nor the mental capacity. No one who ever smelled him would have let him come close.

He began to cry now. 'Don't tell Maman about the animals, please, please, don't tell her,' he begged.

'We won't tell her,' Emile assured him.

'Who are you?' Toussaint asked.

Emile told him his name. 'I'm here to help you,' he said. 'Will you help me too?'

Toussaint stared at him. 'You're a liar, you don't want to help me. You told Maman where I was. Then she punished me.' He touched his injured shoulder.

'Who punished you?' I asked.

'Maman!' he repeated.

*His mother hadn't been near him, she was in the hospital.*

'Maybe he's referring to the killer,' I suggested.

'I want to help you,' Emile insisted. 'I'll get you medication so you'll feel better, something for the pain. Would you like that?'

Toussaint stood there trembling and crying, then he beat at the air as though bats were attacking him.

'Alexandre,' I called to him, 'sit down. Why don't we sit down, all right?' I pulled two chairs up to the glass, one for me and one for Emile.

'Let's all sit down.' Emile directed the two officers standing on either side of the cell. Toussaint copied us and sat on the bench, his head hanging down as though it was heavy.

Then one of the officers pulled his gun and slammed it against the glass, making Toussaint jump in terror. He screamed and leaped off the bench.

'Put that away,' Emile commanded, his tone implying, *You stupid ass.*

But the bully didn't pay attention to Emile; instead he stood there with his arms across his barrel chest staring at Toussaint, making faces, trying to intimidate him. The man was a loose cannon and I wanted to wipe the smirk off his face.

Toussaint reacted violently to the policeman, shouting expletives at him, spitting, crying, jumping up and down.

The man laughed and taunted him.

'Get the hell out of here!' Emile shouted, getting up and shoving the man away. 'This is a crucial witness in a major murder case and you behave like this? I'll have your badge, you bastard!'

The man backed off, but he didn't leave, just glared at us.

I looked at Chapelle who was staring at his officer. 'I apologize for officer Saint Jacques. *Tais-toi!*' he told him.

Emile spoke to Toussaint in a soothing voice, using great patience, until he had calmed down. Then Emile asked, 'Tell us about the hotel in Dardilly, Alexandre. Why did you go there?'

'I go places on the bus. I learned by myself,' he said proudly. 'But Maman followed me. She found me!' That made him angry.

*He had seen a woman at the scene*, I thought. *Our killer is a woman!*

'What colour is your mother's hair?' I asked.

'Green, like the car,' he replied. Behind me, officer Saint Jacques snickered. But I ignored him. 'Go on, Alexandre.'

'I saw her face in the shiny green car. It called my name: "Alexandre!" Yes it did! The car called me. The car wanted me to drive it. It wanted to be my car. But the man in the chair wouldn't let me have it; I asked him for the keys then Maman came after me. She didn't want me to have the car either. She wanted to keep it for herself.'

'What man, Alexandre?' Emile asked. 'Did you see a

255

man outside the room near the green car? Or a woman?'

He shook his head. 'I saw Maman and the man with the keys. The keys were inside the room. He wouldn't give me the keys. He wouldn't stop bleeding. I had to stop him bleeding. I put the sausage in his mouth.' He grinned as though this was funny. Then grew petulant. 'Maman doesn't like it when you bleed. She tried to stop me, but her punishment didn't hurt.' He became defiant. 'I got the knife. Then I punished the man too.' He laughed again.

*He got the scalpel away from the killer, and mutilated the body.*

'Do you remember taking a bus?'

A nod.

'The bus driver remembers he let you off in Dardilly two days ago, near the hotel.'

'Who could forget him?' Saint Jacques muttered.

'What did you do then?' Silence. 'What did you do for two days, Alexandre? Did you sleep in the woods? What did you eat?'

No response. And then he raised his hands and showed us what covered them, and with a demented smile, he licked his palms.

Saint Jacques let out a guffaw. My stomach heaved and I turned away. The idea was too disgusting. But I was putting the pieces together.

'Emile, here's my scenario. Toussaint's been living in the woods for a few days, watching people come and go. He saw the victim arrive at the hotel and then the killer too. He may have been standing outside the window and witnessed the murder taking place; it affected him, excited him. As we would say in Texas, it riled him up. On a whim, he decided to steal the victim's car, went to get the keys and confronted the killer. The killer realized there was a witness and

256

tried to kill him, sliced him on the face and arms, stabbed him in the shoulder. He defended himself and got the scalpel away. The killer realized the man was incoherent and not really a threat, so she left.'

'She was probably too sickened by the smell to get close to him,' Saint Jacques added.

'Could be,' I said, turning to glare at him. What was his problem?

'So this psychotic just happened upon the scene and added to it?' Emile said, with disappointment.

'Yes, our prime suspect is still a woman.'

'*Incroyable*,' said Chapelle, impressed.

Emile told him, 'A witness in Toulouse spotted two women near the scene, and samples of women's hair have been found at three of the scenes. Some samples match the ones found in Dardilly last night.'

An officer came in and handed Chapelle computer readouts of crimes against animals. There had been a rash of animal killings in Lyon, most of them in Toussaint's neighbourhood, starting three years ago and continuing as recently as last week. He handed me the sheet. 'I guess these will stop now.'

'Do you think he can describe the woman at the scene he mistook for his maman?' Emile asked. 'If he can, that's our killer.'

Chapelle shook his head. 'It takes an excellent memory and a clear mind to work with an artist. He couldn't possibly do it.'

I agreed. 'But we'll get evidence from his clothes: sweat, or blood, and hair. We know the killer touched him.'

'Ugh,' Saint Jacques said.

Chapelle was as annoyed with him as I was. 'I feel sorry for the officers who must test his clothing,' he said. 'We put it in the basement to dry out and the odour comes up through the pipes.'

'Any more questions?' I said to Emile.

He shook his head and said to Chapelle, 'Inspector, you can move the man to a hospital and sedate him.'

We followed Chapelle back to his office with Saint Jacques trailing behind. But I closed the door on him and turned to Emile.

'We've got a weapon, Emile. It's our first major break!'

He nodded, reading from the weapons report. 'It's made of German steel, manufactured by a French company outside Tours called Anteil. They only sell to surgical supply companies or hospitals. So that narrows the field. We've requested the company's sales records for the last six years.'

'The scalpels aren't numbered by any chance?'

'No but they can be traced through lot numbers.' Emile's spirits were improving rapidly. He lifted a plastic bag holding the scalpel and actually grinned. 'The murder weapon!'

I gave him a thumbs up sign and then raised my cup of coffee. 'To her first mistake and to outside forces. May they always intervene!' Chapelle and Emile raised theirs and toasted with me.

Chapelle said, 'Do you want us to continue gathering statements from family, business associates, witnesses?'

'Yes,' Emile said, 'and be thorough.'

Chapelle shuffled papers until he found the medical report. 'The victim's throat was cut from the left carotid artery, through the jugular and larynx, by a right-handed unknown. All wounds to the body were done by a scalpel as were the cuts on the genitalia.'

Emile took a folder from his briefcase and handed it across. 'These are the results of our investigation so far, including all pornographic video tape dealers from three other cities. We will be adding anyone

258

with a record who has access to medical equipment, works in a hospital, or is currently employed. The manufacturer of the murder weapon will tell us where these scalpels were sold, then we'll add medical techs, doctors, nurses, and people employed in related professions employed in those locations.'

'We're not positive the killer is a woman, but witness sightings and a footprint from the scene in Toulouse indicate that it is.'

'Also,' I added, 'the killer has a source of income that allows her to travel and drive expensive cars. In Toulouse it was a Mercedes, here in Lyon it was a Jaguar or Maserati. Maybe she owns them all, which means she's really wealthy.'

'Why couldn't she have rented them or stolen them from other locations?' Chapelle asked.

'Everyone who's rented this calibre of car during the time of the murders has checked out,' Emile told him. 'Nor have there been any expensive cars stolen in the vicinity of the killings.'

'What if the killer stole a car in a distant city and then travelled to commit the crime?'

'It's possible, but we think she owns it,' I said.

'She could be in the used car business,' Chapelle offered, lamely.

'What information do you have on the porno tapes?' I asked, staying with more important matters. Chapelle gave a blank stare. 'I want to know where Lepic rented his machine.'

'Oh, at a local video company. But we found no tape in the room or the area.'

'Lepic brought the tape with him,' I said. 'The killer took it back with her.'

'But Lepic was an upstanding citizen,' Chapelle said. 'Not the type to hire whores or watch pornography.'

'Not only did he watch it, it got him killed,' I said.

'What if the tapes were not sexual?' Chapelle said. 'But depicted something else that turned him on.'

'Like silk weaving in the orient,' Emile scoffed, 'or computer military training.'

'Wait,' I said. 'Maybe he's right. What if it's a torture or snuff film, or neo-Nazis saying *Sieg Heil*. That might be the link we're looking for.'

Emile slammed his coffee cup down on the desk. 'I've checked out snuff films, torture, Nazis, massacres, everything I can think of, James. I cannot find a link, damn it! I've tried school affiliations, both theirs and their children's, their wives' schools, even their ancestors'. I've tried bridge games, gambling, visits to spas, and political affiliations: some of them were conservative, others were liberal, and some independent. They have dissimilar war records, they don't belong to the same clubs or organizations, and they have different religions – three are Catholic, the others Protestant. They are not connected! I'm sure of it. These men are being stalked by someone with her own agenda, who knows them independently of one another.'

It was getting close to lunch and I was hungry, but I set it aside. In my work, creature comforts have to wait. To me, heaven is a place where I could eat when I was hungry, or go to the bathroom when nature called and not postpone them until neither mattered nor brought relief.

Just then loud voices outside the office interrupted us and we all heard Saint Jacques say, 'Emile Laurent is a fucking kike lover! I'll see him in hell before he gets my badge.'

The look of shock on Emile's face was enough to make my temper flare. I leaped from my chair and flung open the door, shouting, 'I've had enough of your crap.' Then I grabbed the man's shoulder, swung him around and punched him right in the gut. It felt great!

Emile pulled me off him. And suddenly I recognized him. He was Solange Monod's boyfriend, the cop who'd been with her in Lourdes. No wonder he had it in for Emile.

# Chapter 14

I shouted at Saint Jacques, 'You fuckhead. Watch your mouth!' Then I said to Emile, 'I saw this joker two nights ago with Solange in Lourdes, I swear it.' I turned to him. 'What were you doing there?'

'He's crazy!' Saint Jacques insisted, as Chapelle helped him to his feet. 'He attacked me!'

'You were there, weren't you?' I persisted.

Emile was starting to believe me. 'Saint Jacques . . . I remember you. You were with the Michel Leveque team in Paris at the same time as Solange. You transferred here to Lyon when she came over to my group. Were you with her in Lourdes?'

He shrugged but didn't reply. I noticed how big he was, nearly four inches taller than I. It didn't matter, I could still wipe the floor with him.

Chapelle said, 'He was in Lourdes. I sent him to question some witnesses on a smuggling case that's still on the books. We got a call from a woman that she had some information for us. I assigned it to Saint Jacques.'

'It's an old case of Solange's,' Saint Jacques admitted. 'I thought she should be in on it.'

'So she was there!' I said to Emile, who now looked as if he'd been the one hit in the stomach. She had lied to him.

'Why didn't she tell me?' he asked Saint Jacques.

'Your team is working on the Boardroom Killings,

she didn't want to ask for time away from the case.'

I knew the real reason. She wanted to see her lover.

Emile was glaring at him.

'We all like to finish what we start,' I said, trying to make Emile feel better. He'd had enough disappointments for one day.

Without another glance at Saint Jacques, he left the building and I followed. But the press was waiting for us, shoving forward, shouting questions, trying to get past Chapelle's officers who shielded us. I gave them as little as possible. One of them dubbed me 'Clint' for being as close-mouthed as Eastwood. 'No, Serpico,' someone else said. No one called me Maigret.

Then Emile gave a brief interview to a respectful audience, who allowed him to answer one question before they asked another. When he explained that the man in custody was not the Boardroom Killer, they all groaned with disappointment. Everybody wanted this fucker caught.

'What about porno tapes?' someone asked.

'We're checking on it,' I replied.

When we finally got away from there, Emile said, 'Thanks for coming to my defence.'

'That guy really pissed me off,' I told him.

'I want to buy you a present,' he insisted.

'Emile, it's not necessary.'

'It's not just for today,' he said. 'It's for everything.'

We commandeered one of the police cars parked at the kerb and drove off, leaving behind the crowd of gawkers, the press and police, past the suburb of Villeurbanne where Toussaint lived and into the centre of the city where Emile found a garage.

Then we walked along the shopping street to a boutique where they sold men's sportswear. Emile insisted on buying me a pair of Regarde jeans, a silk

264

shirt and a bomber jacket to match in a dark green colour.

'It's the least I can do for almost getting you killed on your vacation, Clint,' he said, teasing me. Then he tossed my old clothes into the bag and took me back to the hotel so I could take a shower.

Emile was depressed by what had happened – to have a suspect in custody and find that he wasn't the one, was a blow. And Solange's deceitfulness on top of it did not help.

'Let's go to lunch,' I said.

He didn't seem to care.

We went to a café in the old city where the narrow cobblestoned streets wove their way around the base of a hill. Above us loomed Lyon's sixteenth-century cathedral with its four towers in the air, looking like a grey elephant on its back, or so the Lyonnais describe it.

'What you need is a chilli dog or a burrito,' I told Emile. 'That always improves my mood.'

But instead I found myself eating a spicy Gazpacho made with cream that almost tasted Tex-Mex. The Salade Lyonnaise with croûtons, bacon, poached egg and potatoes was like nothing I'd ever eaten before, and neither were the famous potatoes Lyonnaise, baked in a casserole with a creamy cheese sauce, that accompanied our fish. After that, I could have slept for a week. The food seemed to revive Emile enough for him to order coffee and apple tart.

'Do you think the smuggling case Solange and Saint Jacques were investigating is the one that involved your friend, Pierre Fontelle?'

'How do I know?' he said. 'She doesn't confide in me; it could have been anything. But I'm going to find out.'

'I didn't believe her story,' I told him. 'I was sure I

265

saw her in Lourdes. I even asked Lillianne Reneau to check the flights from Paris that night. She hasn't got back to me yet.'

'Thanks for telling me,' he snapped. 'You must think I'm a real fool!'

'No, just blinded by good sex. Not the best state to be. But I understand it.'

'How was it for you when you saw Catherine?' he asked.

'She's not the same person,' I told him. 'But how could she be, living in that place? You'd think with all the advances of modern medicine, they could help her.'

'Certainly Paul has spared no expense. He visits her, provides her with a special companion. It's a difficult situation, enough to tear a family apart,' he said.

'Are you talking about the d'Aumants or you and Claudine?' I asked him.

'Sometimes I think Claudine knows about Solange, and it kills me. I've got to break it off. I don't want to hurt my wife, but Solange is impossible to shake.'

'Maybe now you can do it,' I said.

'Yes. This might be my chance.' But from the look on his face, I could see how upset he was.

At two o'clock when we returned to Chapelle's office, some of the lab reports were in. There were two samples of blood on Toussaint's clothes: his own, from the wound in his shoulder, and Lepic's. Samples of excrement and urine were Toussaint's. Beige fibres were found from a Burberry-type raincoat, and saliva samples were not Toussaint's or Lepic's so they must be the killer's. Fingerprints and footprints in the hotel room in Dardilly were all Toussaint's. No one had found a porno tape.

We left the Prefecture and headed for the headquarters of Interpol, across the boulevard from the Rosarie of the famous Parc De La Tête d'Or, with its hundreds of varieties of roses. Interpol headquarters is a sprawling modern complex surrounded by a twelve-foot-high iron fence, with huge flood lights, and enough antennae and cameras on the roof and surrounding acreage to furnish a rock concert. Even we had difficulty getting admitted, but finally we found our way to the Department of Investigation and Research, and requested cooperation on checking out surgical supply companies and hospitals who received shipments from Antiel throughout Europe over the last six years.

When we were finished at Interpol, Emile said, 'Now we're going to see the sights.' And he drove me to the top of Montée du Rosaire to see the panoramic view of the city bisected by two rivers. Immediately below us were the red-tiled roofs of the old city, behind that the lighter roofs of the last century, and then the modern city skyscrapers spread out beyond.

'The Lyonnais say that actually three rivers flow through the city – the Saône, the Rhône and the Beaujolais,' Emile said.

'Do you want to talk about Saint Jackass?' I asked him as we got into the car and headed out of the city, wondering if he suspected Solange of cheating on him.

'He's not worth our time,' Emile said, smiling at the name I'd given him. 'There are worse things than being called a kike lover. I have frequent arguments with right-wing extremists on the force who doubt that the Holocaust ever happened. What can I do? The French can be bigoted, even my own family. Lineage is crucial to getting ahead. Even in my work, top positions are appointed by the government, not awarded from within. Friends of the officials get ahead, not a farmer's son married to a Jewess.'

It was the first time I'd heard him so bitter. 'Aren't things improving here?'

'Yes, but it's slow. Right now there's a debate raging

as to whether Mitterrand should place a memorial wreath on the tomb of Marcel Pétain. In the past, nobody gave a damn. But now, people don't want the President to honour the memory of a man responsible for the murder of so many Jews. Especially on the anniversary of Vel d'Hiv, the night the Jews of Paris were rounded up by the French police and given to the Nazis. Our government blamed the Germans, said they made us do it. And we dumb citizens believed them.'

'You mean, "I'm just following orders?" '

'That's it.'

'What happened to change public opinion?'

'New evidence. The Paris police were actually responsible, more zealous in turning over their fellow Jews than the Germans required. The Nazis instructed French officials to round up Jews who were sixteen and over, take them to the Vélodrome d'Hiver where they would be sent to Germany. But the French turned over every Jew they could find, even small children and babies, on the pretext of not separating families. It's a national embarrassment that we're just beginning to face.

'People are searching their souls, trying to do the right thing. Unfortunately, Claudine and others who have suffered directly relive the anguish all over again.'

'No wonder she kept her religion hidden for years,' I said. 'Victoria's lifestyle affects me too, only in a different way. Other wives we know stay home or work part-time. My buddies kid me about having a rich wife who can support herself.

'Where are you taking me?' I asked as we drove through the countryside with its ubiquitous vineyards and beautiful green fields alongside the river.

'You'll see,' he said. 'It's a surprise.'

Not far from the restaurant of Paul Bocuse, we entered the village of Rochetaillée and Emile turned in at our destination, the museum of antique cars.

'This is it,' he said.

I paid the entry fee and we entered a converted château filled with nearly two hundred examples of antique vehicles. Like any grown boy, I'm in awe of the old automobiles, horseless carriages, antique motorcycles, and bicycles dating back two hundred years. The racing cars weren't bad either. For a moment I was absorbed in this fabulous place, not thinking about Victoria, or Chloe, or Catherine. And certainly not about Shithead.

'This is what I brought you to see,' Emile said, leading the way to a nearby warehouse filled with more treasures. He led me directly to a long black Mercedes touring sedan with an open chauffeur's section. 'This was Hitler's car,' he said. And I stared.

It was in perfect condition except for several holes in the driver's window. 'That's where somebody shot at him,' Emile commented. 'Too bad they missed.'

The reality made an impact. I could touch with my own hand the car owned by the Shithead of all Shitheads. I got a sudden, clear image of him sitting in the back seat against the padded black leather, surveying his domain, an evil Horseman of the Apocalypse or Prince of Darkness, overseeing his mass destruction and annihilation.

'This man's mania is still alive in the world. In Germany, in France, in America. We French discuss the war as though it was yesterday,' Emile said.

'I should have wiped the floor with Saint Jackass, the bastard!'

'You're a good friend,' Emile said, putting an arm around me. And I didn't feel the least uncomfortable.

He was quiet on the ride back. As we re-entered the city he said, 'I've decided you're right, James. I'm going to institute proceedings against Saint Jacques.

We've got to fight prejudice wherever we can.'

I was glad. The bastard deserved whatever he got.

At Chapelle's office he handed Emile a file. 'Here's the list of hospitals and surgical supply offices in France where scalpels have either been stolen or misplaced in the last two years: seven locations in all, three in Paris, one in Bordeaux, two here in Lyon, and one in Lourdes.'

'I'll take the one in Lourdes,' I told Emile, who understood why I wanted to go there.

Chapelle cleared his throat, looking uncomfortable. 'Inspector Laurent, please accept my apology for Officer Saint Jacques. He is reprimanded, and if you wish to institute disciplinary action, you have my cooperation.'

'I do,' Emile told him. 'You'll be hearing from me.' And Chapelle nodded.

Emile and I parted company; he was heading back to Paris. But I was too tired to drive to Eugénie, so I returned to the hotel, ordered room service and slept the night through. The next morning, I took a commercial flight to Pau, picked up my car and arrived in Eugénie by afternoon.

Tacked to my door at the pension was a note forwarded from Prés d'Eugénie: '*They wouldn't tell me where you were staying, only that they'd deliver a note. So, when you read this, come see me. I'm in room 207.*'

Victoria was here. Impossible!

I hurried over to the hotel, amazed that she had followed me. First I was furious. She can't afford to stay there. She's invaded my privacy. Then I was flattered. What gall, what nerve, what guts.

Once I got used to the shock, I realized I should have expected it, knowing Victoria.

I headed up the stairs to her room but no one was

270

there. So I began to search. She was not in the dining room, or the strong-smelling sulphur spa, or on the tennis courts.

I found her lying by the pool reading a novel, wearing a black bikini and tanned to a caramel colour. The blazing heat of the sun made her raven hair sparkle and I felt a rush of excitement to see her.

With that first glimpse all I wanted was for us to start over again, banish all the hurts and misunderstandings and irritations that had piled up between us.

She saw me and lowered her book, watching to see what kind of reception she'd get, deciding to be cheerful no matter what. She smiled and waved and my spirits lifted even more.

'Hi there! Surprise, surprise. Isn't this the most glorious place?'

She stood and gave me a full view; Victoria in a bikini is really something. Then she put her arms around me and kissed me passionately. Amazingly, something happened. We both felt it right away.

'So you're glad to see me, huh?' She took my hand and smiled into my eyes. It was almost like old times. 'Wanna go upstairs and fool around? I'm paid up for the night.'

I kissed her nose. 'Let's talk for a while, all right?' I peeled off my shirt and took a chair next to hers.

'Are you all right? You look tired.' A policeman's wife knows when not to worry, so she let it go. She stretched back on the lounger and I pulled my chair closer to hers. A waiter came to offer us drinks and I ordered two of their specialities.

The pool is in the middle of acres of green lawn at the edges of which is the lush foliage of Michel Guerard's herb garden.

'Look at that,' exclaimed Victoria, pointing to a basil plant that was over five foot tall. 'And there's fennel and rosemary too, and those heavenly roses.' She took a breath of the fragrant air. 'I could get used to this,' she said, sipping her drink.

'How did you get here so quickly?' I was a touch annoyed, yet excited. I still couldn't believe she was actually sitting beside me. Her presence was out of context, as though she'd arrived from a trip in a time machine.

'I told you if you weren't home in a week, there'd be consequences to pay.' She smiled.

'But that was just two days ago.'

'I didn't want to spoil the surprise.'

'Well, you surprised me,' I admitted. 'How can we afford it?'

'I borrowed money from the teachers' union against my summer bonus. Then I called Mama and she came up from Baton Rouge to stay with the kids. My dad's going to join her at the weekend. Everybody's happy, especially the kids. No more'n five minutes after Gramaw got there they were saying, "hush my mouth", and "y'all", and "whatshadoin?" '

Her mother, Lucille, had been born in L'usiana. Her drawl was so heavy it affected everyone around her, even me. 'It was good of her to help out.'

'I told her it was important. Besides, I wanted to see France too, though this little bitty corner isn't much to talk about.'

I agreed with her, though it was growing on me. 'I thought you were going to get a new car with your summer bonus money?'

'Seeing you was more important.'

I was flattered, but her Ford wagon was barely hanging on.

'Have I seen those clothes before?' she asked.

I explained to her that Emile had bought me an outfit.

272

'It's the least he can do, after all you've done for him.' Her concern for me made me feel guilty, as though I didn't deserve it.

'What's new with the kids?'

'Lindsay loves her ballet lessons. She's got the build for it, but her little elbows stick out like crow's wings. You should see her. She screws up her mouth every time she points her toes, but she's got the muscles to do pliés and go up on demi-point. And she loves to do bâtements, the big kicks. The teacher has to scold her for daydreaming and talking in class, but I think she's got a talent for it. I only signed her up for a series of six. It's expensive.'

'How much?'

'Fifteen dollars a class, but when you buy a series the lessons are twelve-fifty.'

I heard the wistfulness in her voice. Neither of us had been able to afford extras like ballet lessons when we were kids; we both wanted our children to have those advantages.

'I know what you're thinking – that the money it's costing for this trip could have paid for a whole lot of lessons, both for Lindsay and Adam, as well as a new car. But I'd rather spend it on us than a divorce lawyer.'

'Are things that bad?' I asked her.

'You tell me, Jimmy.'

'I don't want a divorce, for Christ's sake. I want to work things out. I just had to get away.'

'You told me enough times. So how are you now?'

'Let's not get into it yet, okay? Let's enjoy being together and allow the future to take care of itself.'

I saw her shoulders stiffen and knew what she was thinking. Again, I was refusing to face the problems in our relationship, putting things off. But it felt good to take time out from the fighting. This was the perfect place for it. And since she'd already spent the money, I might as well enjoy it.

And then she said, 'What was it like seeing Catherine after all this time?' I hesitated. 'Jimmy, be honest. Don't lie to me. Do you have feelings for her?'

God, this was hard. I felt myself shying away from the truth; wanting to be anywhere but here. Yet she deserved an answer. 'It's hard to say what my feelings are. The woman is sick. I talked to her doctor. She'll probably never get well. But being here in all our old haunts has brought back memories I've been avoiding for a long time.'

'I see.'

'I promised myself to be honest with you, Victoria. Not being able to tell you that I wanted to see Catherine put a distance between us.' I was amazed to see her smile.

'I never thought I'd hear you say that,' she said. 'You know I've always believed that if we faced our problems head-on, things would get better between us.' She gazed deeply into my eyes. 'I've missed you so much, darlin',' she said, taking my hand and placing it on her breast, moving my fingers so that they caressed her nipple which sprang erect. That simple touch shot a fire through me and I leaned over and kissed her, reaching inside the silky jersey of her bathing suit to touch her bare skin. Desire for her exploded through me. And I was ready.

'Let's go to your room,' I said, taking her hand and pulling her to her feet.

She grabbed her towel and bag and wrapped her arm around my waist. The bare skin of her back was warm to my touch. We walked with our arms wrapped around each other, back into the hotel and up to her room.

In the past, when passion consumed us, we would

tear off our clothes and go to it. But being in France, where the art of lovemaking had been perfected, I wanted to take my time.

Slowly, I untied her bra straps so that I could look at her and touch her, fondling her breasts, rubbing her nipples, sliding her bikini bottoms off her hips, down her thighs until she stepped out of them, touching her body, revelling in it, and then undressing myself as she touched me.

Victoria's lovemaking is an extension of her personality; she's direct and sure of what she wants, not at all shy. And she puts herself into it wholeheartedly. I'd forgotten what it was like to be with her. After my fiasco with Jeanette in Paris, and my fantasies about Catherine and Chloe, it was wonderful to feel her in my arms.

I took the lead and it felt like the first time for us. I couldn't get enough of her, maybe because my ardour matched hers for a change. Every part of her seemed new to me, and I was starved for the taste of her skin. Licking under her arms, smelling her, feeling her, I was lost in the magic of making love to a woman I loved. And I did love her. Whatever it was that had kept me from these feelings was gone; in fact, I couldn't remember why I'd ever had any trouble at all. Maybe seeing Catherine and mourning the past had worked. Maybe I just needed time away, a change of scene, to act out a few fantasies, for my manhood was back, halleluiah, full and throbbing and ready to go.

It was hot in the room and our bodies were sweating in spite of the air from the overhead fan, but her slippery skin felt wonderful. I pulled her over on top of me and her hair fell forward, shielding our faces from the afternoon light. Her breasts were right where I could see them, and taste them, and touch them to my heart's content. I was about to slide into her when she

275

whispered, 'Are you going to use protection?'

'Why?' I asked. 'Aren't you taking your pills?'

'I just thought, in case you've been with someone else.'

'With someone else?' I nearly exploded. 'I haven't!' I said, wondering if she had.

'Are you sure?' she asked, poised over me, like a magnificent sea creature flying on a wave.

'Yes, damn it!' I insisted, knowing that she had the right to ask. Jesus, at this moment, I wished I hadn't even tried – damn that moment of weakness with Jeanette! The fantasies of Catherine and Chloe didn't count. And suddenly, in my moment of guilt, everything that infuriated me about Vickie came rushing back.

'I'm so glad,' she said, and I could see tears in her eyes. It had been hard for her to ask me such a question (what if I'd said yes?) but I was too angry and embarrassed to feel compassion. And as she lowered herself on to me, her eyes gazing into mine, we both discovered at the same time with that terrible sinking feeling, that there was nothing there.

My eyes shot fury at her, blaming her. If only she'd kept her mouth shut! She looked as if I'd slapped her. We stared at one another for a heart-stopping moment.

Then she moved off me, lifting her leg over my body from where she was straddling me, and sat back on her haunches gazing off into space. Finally, with resignation, she rolled over on her hip, on to her back, and lay there, her hand thrown over her head.

I pulled up the sheet to cover me. 'I'm sorry' stuck in my throat. In the past, when this happened – and it sickened me to recall how many times – I would get up, take a shower and leave. But not this time. The frustration was so intense I wanted to pound the wall.

It was not going to happen again. I could perform. I

knew it! I would try something else.

The image of Chloe came to my mind, that pink tongue licking her lips, the outline of her body through her dress.

Instantly, I felt a reaction.

I kept going: the way she lowered her eyelids and gazed at me knowingly, the way she tilted her head and appraised me, how her tongue would feel touching my prick.

My erection was full blown again.

I pulled back the sheets so Victoria could see. For a moment, she was startled and then looked at me with surprise.

I wasted no time and sat up to straddle her; she opened herself to me and we stared into each other's eyes as I entered her and began the rhythm that grew stronger and stronger. But I kept thinking about Chloe, her body, her face, her mouth welcoming mine. I moved harder and harder, stronger and stronger, not caring about Victoria's pleasure, not noticing her reaction, wanting to perform, for God's sake, thinking only of doing it, finally doing it, especially to that forbidden image. And as I came, instead of saying *I love you* out loud as I usually did, a silent voice cried out in my head, *God forgive me!*

# Chapter 15

I'd fucked up again.

I rolled on to my back, suffocating in Victoria's silence. But I didn't care. I'd done it, God damn it! I'd actually screwed my wife for the first time in over six months. That counted for something.

Victoria reached over to touch my head and I flinched, but didn't move away. If she'd said anything like, *Congratulations*, or *It's about time*, or *What about my turn?* I would have lost it; wisely she kept quiet.

Guilt bored into me. We lay there staring at the ceiling, watching the fan revolve, while I wondered what she was thinking. Where do we go from here? I thought. Could I ever make love to her for real, without pretending she was someone else? The idea of repeating this performance was repugnant, too mortifying even to think about, so I gave myself up to the relaxation that follows orgasm.

The phone rang and I jerked awake. 'Who could be calling you here?' I asked. 'The kids?'

'I've spoken to them already,' she said, reaching for the phone on her side of the bed. 'Hello? Yes this is Mrs Barton. Oh yes.'

I decided it was the front desk.

'Tonight? No, I have no particular plans, that would be lovely.' *It wasn't the front desk.* 'Did you want me to include my husband? Yes, he's back from Lyon. In fact, he's here with me now. Would you like to talk to him? Oh, all right. Eight-thirty will be fine.' And she hung up. 'That was your girlfriend's brother, Paul d'Aumant. He invited us for dinner.' Then she said sarcastically, 'Isn't that nice?'

'I'd rather not go.'

'Why don't you want to?'

'I'm beat, I've had a helluva few days. I thought we'd be alone tonight, just the two of us. We could dine here at the hotel, it's one of the finest restaurants in the world.' A lame excuse. We both knew that being alone would only cause us to rehash our problems or stare silently at each other as we'd been doing for months. And yet I couldn't tell her my real concerns. I did not want to be around Chloe. I didn't know why the girl had run out on me at dinner the other night. She might even pull one of her seductive tricks in front of Victoria. And after fantasizing about her the way I had, I didn't trust my reactions around her. I also didn't want to have Victoria comparing me to rich, handsome, sophisticated and eligible Paul d'Aumant.

'Shall I go alone?'

'No, we'll both go,' I agreed. 'I wouldn't want you to miss seeing the *castelle*.' But reluctance dogged me.

'Fine,' she said, turning over to go to sleep.

'Do you want to stay here or at my place tonight?' I asked.

'Which is better?' she mumbled.

'No contest, this is.'

'Fine, then we'll stay here.'

'Okay. I'll shower and change in my room and pick you up at eight-fifteen,' I told her, leaning over to kiss her before I left.

Despair accompanied me down the stairs and the long driveway to the road, out of the front gates and all the way up the street to my pension, the heavy kind, like the grinding of gravel in my guts. I needed to talk to Paul about Catherine and Chloe, but a social dinner wouldn't give me the opportunity. And now the feeling that I'd hoped to shed by coming to France was back with full force. Why the hell wasn't I happy being married to a beautiful, intelligent woman? What was wrong with me, or with her? Nothing. That was the stupid, damned fact of it all. Like a cloud of smog that hung over my life, I couldn't blow it away and it was poisoning me. Emile's words came back to me: somewhere inside was anger.

Tonight, our faltering marriage, our middle-class lives, our rather unimportant reasons for existing, would be placed centre stage to be spotlighted by the most piercing light of all, the judgements of all-seeing Paul d'Aumant, and his far too sensuous niece. I couldn't hide from those two how my life had turned out. Seeing me and Victoria together would reveal that our marriage was in trouble.

A nap and a shower revived me. I threw some toiletries into a bag for my one night in a luxury hotel and was about to pick up Victoria when Emile called. The excitement in his voice lifted my spirits. 'We've finally got a connection between two of the victims: Fontelle in Paris, and Patrick Richard in Bordeaux. Both were involved in the smuggling of nuclear devices and selling them to a Middle East buyer.'

'So it was Solange's old smuggling case! I was right.'

'Yes. She and Saint Jacques met a representative of a third member of the syndicate in Lourdes. Naturally, he's terrified. Two of his associates have been killed and he might be next.'

'Why didn't she tell us?'

'She didn't think the cases were related. Fontelle had been cleared of charges and she didn't know about Richard's involvement.'

'She should have told us what she was doing in Lourdes.'

'You're right. But the go-between wouldn't identify herself or the third man. They insisted on anonymity.'

'So when did it break?'

'The woman called again. Even though the man is still frightened, he's willing to turn himself in for protection, but he's worried that the killer is a member of the police.'

'The police?'

'Yes. Fontelle bribed someone in the department to bury the proof against him.'

'Does Solange know who it is?' I asked.

'No. If she did, we might have the killer.'

'What do you mean, might?'

'The killer could also be the Middle East buyers. We know an Arab syndicate ordered the illegal goods, paid half the money for the shipment and never got delivery.'

'I hope that's who it is and not someone in the department.'

'So do I. It disgusts me to imagine that the killer might be someone in the Paris Prefecture. Someone who knows enough procedure to make the murders look like serial killings.'

The worst kind of feeling for us is when one of our own is dirty. Who can you trust then?

'When are you bringing in this source?'

'As soon as we can. He's scared shitless. The officer in charge of his safety could be the one trying to kill him. I'm wary of confiding in anyone in the department, except for you. And of course, Solange knows.'

'What about Saint Jackass?'

'He's still on suspension for insulting me: off the case.'

'Well, if you need me to guard your caged bird, I will.'

'I was hoping you'd say that. But we have to set it up first. His intermediary, whom I suspect is his wife, says if we don't guarantee his safety, he'll leave the country.'

'So guarantee it. Lie if you have to, but get him in.'

'I'm trying! I have to wait for them to call.'

'Emile, I hate to say this, but maybe the Boardroom Killings are unrelated to the smuggling case. Only two of the victims are connected so far, but there have been five murders. What about the other three? Your source didn't implicate them.'

'Maybe he doesn't know all the investors. A deal like that requires a lot of capital.'

'I'll feel better when all the names are tied in.'

'So will I. The informant is the key. He's calling us within twenty-four hours.'

'Emile, Arab assassins kill people with *plastique* or guns.'

'I know,' he sighed. 'The killings look more like an inside job. We'll find out soon enough,' he said.

'Good luck, my friend. Let me know.'

'I will.'

My mind was on Emile's case but I still got a kick out of the way Victoria's eyes lit up when we turned in at the gates and drove along the five-mile approach to the *castelle*. When she saw the place for the first time, I chuckled.

'Oh my God! Is that it? Oh my God! It's so beautiful it makes me want to cry. I can't believe people really live in places like this.'

It was magnificent, all lit up like a birthday cake. There was a footman to open our car door and another fo open the front door. Victoria's eyes drank it all in and she gave exclamations like 'Oh!' Once she even said, 'Dear Lord!'

We were escorted through the great hall and into the library where I'd been taken by Catherine that first time to meet her family. I half expected to see them all sitting there. But it was only Paul. I dared not look for Chloe, hoping she wouldn't be here.

Paul was wearing a black suit made of sand-washed silk, the kind I coveted but couldn't afford; the jacket was open, casually, the sleeves rolled up Italian-style. He wore a round necked T-shirt tucked in at the waist around which was a belt whose gold buckle was shaped like an alligator. 'Boss' was the GQ word for how he looked. Even in my new silk shirt and jacket I looked like a poor Texan.

I don't usually notice men's clothes and never take much time with mine either, plain stuff is what I wear and can afford – blue short-sleeved shirts in the summer or else the Sears version of a polo shirt, khaki cotton pants, cords in the winter, a sports jacket, a suit now and then. But this guy was so turned out, you couldn't help but notice. He smelled of money, of breeding, of assurance. And when a man dresses like that and looks at my wife the way he was looking, it makes my stomach turn.

Victoria had been wearing a shawl flung over one shoulder. So when she removed it, both Paul and I got an eyeful. Her bodice was of transparent white lace that clung to her voluptuous shape like a glove and you could see her breasts as clearly as if she were nude. The rest of the outfit was a long white skirt with a slit in the side that let too much leg show, from her ankle to the hip. It was the kind of outfit men notice, especially when a woman has breasts and legs like Victoria's, slender smooth thighs, round muscular calves. I wanted to cover her up and hustle her out of there.

She wore her hair pulled to one side with a white sparkling comb so the loose strands fell over one eye. And around her neck was the diamond on a chain I'd given her for our tenth anniversary. We hadn't been able to afford an engagement ring when we got married, and this diamond was over a carat. Tonight it really sparkled. I'd made payments on it for over a year. She'd never looked more beautiful or more sexy.

Paul came oiling towards us and took her hand, kissing the air above it like some French Duc, which he was. A waiter brought us champagne in tall crystal glasses, not the flat clumsy kind I'd thought were for champagne.

'Your home is so magnificent it takes my breath away,' said Victoria, giving her Vivien Leigh smile.

'Your beauty puts it all to shame,' Paul had the gall to reply. 'Your husband is a lucky man.'

I recalled what our marriage had been like for the past six months, topped by today's fiasco in bed, and gall rose in my throat so high it nearly blocked my jealousy.

Paul turned to me. 'I was interested to hear what happened in Lyon. How is the investigation going?'

I was surprised he knew what I'd been doing, but then, this was a small town.

'I suppose you read about it? We had a promising suspect who turned out to be a false lead.'

'I saw it on the news. The police bungled it again. These abominable murders will never be solved. And the country talks of nothing else. All my business associates are afraid of who will be next.'

'Any wealthy male over sixty-five should be careful,' I said, wondering why only his business associates were worried and not his friends. Maybe he didn't have any friends?

'It's terrifying,' he exclaimed, 'that some fiend is

285

murdering the best of us.' He raised his eyes upwards as if it were all too much for him.

I was dying to tell the supercilious bastard about our recent break in the case, but all I said was, 'We're getting close.'

Paul led Victoria to a sofa and sat her down, keeping hold of her hand. Then he took the seat next to her so that I had to sit opposite them in a hard-backed chair. It annoyed me that he still had hold of her hand, but then she carefully withdrew it so as not to offend. She was handling herself well; must be her southern breeding.

'Tell us what happened in Lyon,' Paul said.

'A mentally deranged tramp surprised the killer in the act of murdering Monsieur Lepic. The killer stabbed him in the shoulder and fled, leaving the tramp to mutilate the body.'

'How horrible!' Victoria exclaimed. 'You didn't tell me that.'

'How do you know it was the Boardroom Killer who stabbed him?' asked Paul.

This was beginning to sound like an Abbott and Costello routine. 'From various details only we know.'

'Isn't it possible that this deranged person wounded himself? Don't clever criminals do things like that?' He looked to Victoria for corroboration. She nodded.

A smile tugged at the corners of my mouth. This was my turf now and I was rubbing my hands together. 'No. The man's wound wasn't self-inflicted. And he couldn't be the killer because he doesn't fit the profile of the person we're looking for.' *First of all, he's a man*, I thought. *And second, we have information that points in another direction.*

'A man who mutilates dead bodies is capable of anything,' said Paul, sounding truly appalled. 'What kind of monster would do such a thing?'

'Not so bad a monster as the one who lured the victim to jeopardy and then slit his throat,' I said.

'What do you mean by that?' asked Paul.

But before I could reply, Victoria suggested, 'Let's change the subject.'

But Paul wanted an answer to his question, so I gave him one.

'We're further along on this case than we've revealed, Paul. We know this tramp is not the killer because we're looking for a wealthy, intelligent, clever person whose enormous ego allows him to underestimate the police. Now that we've got the murder weapon, we'll make quick progress.' What I didn't reveal was that the murders might not be serial killings at all.

'You have the weapon?' He sounded proud of me. 'That should lead you to him.'

'Most likely,' I said, feeling positive.

'It's too bad that deranged witness couldn't give you a description of the killer,' Victoria said.

'Oh, but he did,' I lied, just because I felt like it. 'And there's new physical evidence. We'll tie this one up soon.'

'Really?' Paul said. 'How exciting! Can you tell us about this new evidence?'

'You know I can't.'

'Of course,' he said. 'But it's taking so long. I should think you'd want to go back to America.'

'Not until it's finished,' I replied.

'Good for you!' he exclaimed.

Victoria didn't look pleased.

'Maybe there's a real chance that you'll catch this person now,' Paul said. 'But why does he pick on men in the prime of life, who have worked hard to enjoy their later years? The best of us are being snuffed out! I'm glad my parents didn't live to see such things.'

'There does seem to be a connection between the type of victim and the identity of the killer,' I commented, not surprised by his concern. His *kind* was being killed. If someone was murdering FBI agents, I'd feel skittish, too. 'In my opinion, these are societal killings. The killer is sick, but also a product of your culture. When the killer is caught, I believe that assumption will be proven.'

Paul watched me thoughtfully. 'One thing is certain – I want the world to be a place where my young niece can feel safe, where such things don't happen to innocent people.'

'Paul's niece Chloe is Catherine's child,' I said to Victoria.

'The girl you told me about?' she said, and I nodded.

'We've hardly had time to be grateful for the good things that have happened lately,' Paul continued. 'Like the end of Communism, the removal of the Berlin Wall, the forming of the Common Market, because our best citizens are being slaughtered like beef cattle.'

I was amused at his evoking social change; surely only the formation of the Common Market would affect him. He lived in a fortress like a feudal lord, with a bank balance that could finance a country.

Unfortunately, Victoria seemed impressed by him. This was going to be some evening. I wanted her to be on my side, no matter what.

And then, to make matters worse, two hands covered my eyes and I heard Chloe say, 'Guess who?' as she breathed in my ear.

Even as I pried her hands away, I was electrically aware of her touch. She was wearing something long and sophisticated with white flowers in her hair. I kept my eyes averted from Victoria but it was like having my mistress walk into the room. I knew Victoria sensed something.

But when Paul said, 'Chloe, this is Mrs Barton, James's wife. Victoria, this is my niece, Chloe,' Victoria smiled warmly and gave the affectionate greeting she usually gives young people.

'Hi, sweetheart. I'm happy to meet you. Jimmy's told me about you.'

I swear my ears turned red.

Trying to gain control, I said to Paul, 'Chloe and I had dinner together the other night at the hotel, when you were called away unexpectedly.'

'Yes, I know. Sorry about that. I should have told you I had to go to Bordeaux instead of letting this thoughtless girl deliver my message. I understand she forgot to tell you?'

Chloe had crossed the room and was now standing behind her uncle on the sofa; she draped her arms around his neck and winked at me. 'James was a lovely companion. We shared the Chocolate Decadence.'

The way she said it made it sound suggestive. Besides, it wasn't true. She'd left before dessert. I gave her a look to remind her of our agreement not to flirt, but she ignored me and gave me her sultry smile, the one that affects me. I fought my reaction and shook my head to tell her to stop. This was a different Chloe from the one I'd seen the other night when she'd been ambivalent about her role, half child, half temptress. Inviting herself to my room had been only partly serious. I'd believed she'd really prefer me as a surrogate father. But tonight, because of Victoria, I was truly the target of her attention.

Still smiling, she came around to the front of the sofa, stepped over Victoria's legs and pushed herself into the space between her uncle and his female guest. Both of them had to move to let her in. Paul was amused, and instead of reprimanding her rudeness, put his arm around her and let her snuggle against him.

If Victoria was surprised, she didn't show it. This was a child, no matter how sophisticated she tried to be, and Victoria understood this age group.

She moved over to give Chloe room. 'So tell me, Chloe, how are you enjoying your summer?'

'It has its moments.' Another glance my way.

'Are you reading?'

'Of course. *The Effects of Psychosexual and Social Mores on Aboriginal Peoples* by Avery Kellerman. Have you heard of it?'

That stopped Victoria. 'No-oo, I haven't. But I'd love you to tell me about it.'

Wanting to forestall that conversation, I said, 'Chloe's also familiar with Hawthorne and Poe.'

'And Anne Rice and Clive Barker,' she added, switching from one topic to another. 'One of my favourite books is *The Silence of the Lambs*. The character of Doctor Lecter is so interesting, the way he eats his victims and outsmarts the police. Of course, in France that isn't difficult to do. In fiction the FBI solves the crimes, but that doesn't happen in real life. Not when they're up against a brilliant mind. Criminals are far more clever than the police.'

'Chloe,' Paul interrupted, 'don't be rude to James. He's helping our Brigade Criminelle and they are making progress on their case.'

'Of course they are.' She suppressed a yawn.

'Why don't you play something for us?' he suggested. 'Chloe is an excellent pianist.'

'Would you like to hear me play?' she asked, trying for a double meaning.

'I'd love to,' I told her, staying neutral, and then offered Victoria my arm to make a point.

Chloe led the way through the foyer, across the large

290

entry, through the Grand Salon and into the music room, whose walls were upholstered in blue silk. A grand piano, a harp, a violin and cello were arranged in a group for musical evenings, and there were music stands piled with music.

Chloe turned on a standard lamp nearby that cast a sheen on her pale blonde hair, then took her seat. Paul lit candles that cast a flickering glow.

'How beautiful this is,' Victoria exclaimed. 'The blue silk walls glow like a butterfly's wing.'

Chloe smiled, but I could tell she wanted Victoria to disappear. Victoria knew it too, but refused to be caught in the game. I was grateful for her strength.

Out beyond the open french doors, the trees of the surrounding forest were outlined against a twilit sky.

Paul offered us chairs facing the instruments.

Chloe sat poised, her hands above the keys as she gazed into space. I suppressed a smile at her flair for the dramatic. Then she tossed her hair over her shoulders and said, 'Tchaikovsky's Piano Concerto,' before she began to play.

A listener is supposed to know what the pianist is playing, or discreetly ask about it after the performance. But I was glad she'd told us, for even though the music was extraordinary, I had no idea what it was. However, she was brilliantly talented. Music filled every corner of the room, reaching into my soul; one moment uplifting, the next making me sad. For a cynic like me, who knows nothing about classical music, it was an amazing experience. I felt I would never tire of listening. Victoria had tears in her eyes. And I thought of how Chloe was wasting herself by focusing on stupid seductions when she could further a talent like this. I remembered how the touch of her fingers on my hand had been featherlight; now I understood the true magic they could perform. I forced myself away from the fantasy of what that touch could do to me.

When Chloe finished with an extraordinary crescendo, the three of us applauded loudly.

Then Victoria, the softie, went over and gave her a hug which she suffered stiffly until it was withdrawn. 'That was so wonderful, Chloe! You could be a concert pianist. Are you aware how good you are?'

'Uncle Paul doesn't want me to perform in public,' she said, giving me a look filled with pathos.

He said, rather stiffly, 'Chloe has other obligations right now that keep her from performing. But she might appear in public someday.' I had been right about that conflict between them. This was definitely not Chloe's choice.

Paul offered Victoria his arm and escorted her in to dinner.

Chloe and I followed.

'Did you really like my music?' she asked.

'You're extraordinary,' I told her, genuinely thrilled. 'What a talent.'

'I played just for you,' she said, taking my hand.

I almost jerked it away, but when I saw the wounded look in her eyes, I let her hold my hand and offered her my arm. She walked beside me possessively, almost like a date, and I tried my damnedest not to let my body react from the nearness of her.

We entered the dining room and the images firing my mind were impossible to ignore. I was right back where I'd started. The table where Catherine and I had eaten lunch, all those years ago, sparkled with golden utensils, crystal glasses, and an elaborate flower arrangement. But, luxurious accompaniments didn't dispel the bitter memories. Victoria gave me a look as I seated Chloe, who made matters worse by deliberately caressing my hand. Sitting there looking up at me, she reminded me even more of Catherine.

*Damn.* I couldn't take my seat. I stood behind my chair, keeping my memories at bay, while three faces, lit by candlelight, awaited me. There was an overwhelming urge to run away from all this, get the hell out of here, out of this town, even this country, and go home as fast as I could.

Three people watched me hesitate, particularly Victoria. What would she do if I ran out of here? I couldn't leave her behind. Neither could I explain my inappropriate feelings for a young girl who reminded me of her own mother. Come on, Barton, get real.

I sat.

Immediately, as though I'd tripped some wire, a string quartet began to play in another room and some of the tension eased, as though our mood was orchestrated by the music. But to me it had a sinister undertone, as though it was being played by concentration camp inmates forced to perform for their captors.

Waiters served the first course of an extravagant French meal for which, again, I had no appetite. In front of me they placed a silver egg holder embossed with the family crest; in it sat a soft-boiled goose's egg, cut open and topped with caviar, the kind that costs a fortune.

Victoria took a spoonful. I became aware that she'd been talking and her voice contained a strident note, that out-to-change-the world tone I so disliked. I'd forgotten how it set me on edge.

'Of course I'm Pro-choice and a strong advocate of women's rights,' she said to Paul. 'Frenchwomen have the abortion pill but we're still haggling over it.'

'Yes,' said Chloe with a touch of glee. 'It's unfortunate for you.'

'I'm surprised you are able to have this pill in a Catholic country,' Victoria said.

293

'Why?' I interrupted. 'Didn't the French invent sexual freedom?'

Her eyes flashed, as if to say, What do you know? and I felt my anger rising.

And yet, when Paul said, 'He's right, we've been practising sexual freedom for centuries, right under the noses of the Catholic clergy,' she laughed as though he'd said something wonderful. Damn her.

'It's truly engrained in our history,' he continued. 'A Frenchman allows nothing to curtail his pleasure.'

'You Frenchmen do have a reputation,' Victoria said.

'What Uncle Paul doesn't admit,' Chloe explained, 'is that we French think our country is superior to all others. "France for the French." And we go to confession to be forgiven everything, even abortion, don't we, Uncle Paul?'

He didn't reply.

Victoria was trying to like Chloe, but finding it difficult. 'In America, anti-abortionists are bombing medical centres in the name of God,' she said. 'I've demonstrated for free choice for years and volunteered my time in clinics, but lately it's become much more dangerous.'

'Victoria,' I said, stopping short of telling her to shut up. She got the message and glanced down for a moment to compose herself. Then she raised her eyes but avoided mine. I was choking back memories of all the hours, the phone calls, the meetings, the Saturdays, Victoria spent defending her ideals. She always had time for everybody but me. And having Chloe across the table, a time bomb ready to explode, wasn't helping.

Chloe said, 'In France, the right wing is concerned with keeping France pure for the French and keeping the Arabs out. They realize that abortion helps control immigrant birthrate.' Unaware what an abhorrent concept this was to Victoria, she took a dainty bite of her *pissaladière*, an onion tart that looked like a pizza.

I wasn't eating that either.

Victoria's mouth grew tight.

'It's true,' Paul said. 'The National Front Party wants to get rid of the Arabs.'

'Why don't we talk about something else?' I suggested.

'Oh no,' Chloe said. 'I want to hear more about Mrs Barton's demonstrations. How violent are they?'

Victoria was appalled. 'A doctor was shot and killed recently by an anti-abortionist! Is that violent enough?'

'Don't they refer to themselves as Right-to-Life?'

'I don't care! I call them what they are, anti-abortionists.'

'Does that make you a pro-abortionist?' asked Chloe sweetly.

'No, I am pro-choice, I'm not against life. Most of us dislike abortion, I wouldn't have one myself. But we support a woman's right to choose, and we never advocate violence,' my wife replied. 'We think sex education, non-violent demonstrations, and elected representatives who support our cause, is the way to go. If more women were elected to national offices, we could make our voices heard.'

'You'd make a good candidate,' Paul said.

And her eyes took on a defiant glint. 'It's funny that you mention it. I've been thinking about running for state representative,' she said, nearly blowing me away. 'A group of teachers at the high school, where I work as a guidance counsellor, are willing to back me. But I haven't decided yet.' Her triumphant expression made me explode.

'You knew how I'd feel about this!' I shouted,

disregarding all social etiquette. 'Is that why you brought it up here, so I wouldn't say anything? And if I waited 'til later, you'd just say, "You should have said something before. I thought you liked the idea." Well, I'm not falling for it this time. You want my opinion? Here it is. If you run for political office it will be over my dead body!' I let go all the tension of the evening. 'And I don't care if it's for flea-catcher!'

My father used to raise his voice like that with my mother, and sometimes his hand. For the first time, I understood why.

Red spots of fury rose on Victoria's cheeks. She gave me a withering look. Then slowly, deliberately, she put down her fork, wiped the corners of her mouth with her napkin and placed it on the table. Then she turned to Paul. 'Will you excuse me? Thank you for your kind invitation, but I'm leaving now. It's been an interesting evening.' And she stood up from her chair, ignoring me.

'Oh, Madame Barton,' he pleaded. 'Please stay and finish your dinner. I'm sure James didn't mean anything.' He couldn't hide how pleased he was by our distress. We were more diverting than television.

'Don't leave on my account,' I said. 'Maybe you'd like to finish your lecture about how you have all the answers? Madam Representative, please tell us what's wrong with today's society? Is there anything else you'd like to spout off about, some other cause only *you* can solve?'

Chloe looked triumphant, she couldn't have planned this any better, and seeing her face I realized how badly I was behaving and felt like a fool.

Victoria saw it too and stepped away from her chair, her head held high, her back ramrod straight. 'I'll walk if I have to, but I am leaving this minute. Is that clear?'

I'd never seen her so angry.

'Then I will drive you,' said Paul, getting up and following her out. 'Chloe, entertain our guest for me, will you?' Said the spider to the fly.

The angry echo of Victoria's heels crossing the marble floor broke the silence until it receded into stillness. I wanted to run after her and apologize, but I was ashamed to play out any more family drama in front of Paul and Chloe. And, unfortunately, I had meant most of what I'd said.

As the front door slammed the musicians started up again. Perfect timing. Music to get angry by.

*Damn her*, I thought. Not only had her ridiculous idea of running for office infuriated me, but now I was alone with Chloe who probably thought I'd arranged it. *Shit*. This was not what I'd planned.

Chloe had fake tears in her eyes. The girl knew every trick. 'She's horrible to you. You don't deserve such a woman. It makes me so sad. You should not have married her. You should have married my mother. Now you can stay in France and help her get well again. Your wife won't even miss you.'

'But my children would, Chloe. Listen, I know you think she's wrong to have left, but it's not her fault. I shouldn't have said what I did.' Now I was embarrassed and angry with myself. I always said things I regretted. And I should never have let Chloe bother me, she was only a child.

The fake tears were real now, running down her face.

'You are the first one of my uncle's friends I have ever met.'

'Oh? That can hardly be true,' I said.

'It is,' she said, with a finality that suggested the subject was closed. She seemed overly upset about it. Then she gave a look full of pleading. 'I care for you. Do you care for me?'

'Very much,' I told her, trying to sound parental.

'What if I wanted you to stay here with me?'

'I can't, my dear. I have another life with my family.'

'Won't you even try?'

The girl was squeezing my heart.

The waiter brought us our main course, described as a leg of veal stuffed with wild mushrooms in a truffle sauce. It was delicious, but I could swallow only a few bites. We sat there awkwardly picking at our food while she stole glances at me.

Finally, Chloe broke the spell by getting up from the table. 'Come with me,' she said. 'I have something to show you.'

Before I could object, she'd run out of the open french doors on to the patio and I had to hurry after her. I followed her around the side of the *castelle* past the office where the old stables used to be and around the new stable building which housed Paul's office. We were at the edge of the lake as I ran to keep up with her. Her hair undulated and the fabric of her narrow skirt bounced around her calves. We were like characters in a medieval romp having a merry chase across the grass. I was the satyr and she the forest nymph, but of course I would not ravish her.

She disappeared around the back of the stables and I followed, smelling the wet grass and rich earth mixed with the pungent odour of horses. But just as I turned the corner, I stopped in surprise. For behind the stables was an elaborate kennel I hadn't known existed, and it was far too large to miss. At least fifty separate cages were filled with dogs, most of whom yelped or barked as we approached. These must be the ones she'd mentioned.

Chloe trailed ahead of me along the wire fence of the cages, calling to dogs of all ages in the pens. The puppies were the most excited, jumping and barking,

298

but the older dogs were eager for attention too.

'Raising poodles and Yorkies is my hobby,' she said. 'When Uncle Paul built this kennel for me, he said I could choose whatever kind of dog I wanted. He wanted me to raise Sharpeis but I like fluffy dogs the best. They're so cuddly.'

She was crooning and kissing the air, putting her fingers into the openings in the fence, petting them through the wire spaces or scratching their ears. Her normal behaviour gave me hope that she could be like any other girl.

The dogs were separated by age, from the smallest newborns to full-grown animals, and they were all fluffy and appealing. She explained which were the parents of each litter and told me their ages and their histories. Some of them had been champions many times over.

'This is the first year I will be able to show them myself. There are rules about age. I don't think that's fair, do you? I'm the one who hires the trainers and makes the breeding decisions. Even when I started three years ago, I helped the accountant set up my books, watched my investment turn into a profit. In my first year I had to fire two trainers for not doing their job, and when I went with Uncle Paul to buy my dogs, I decided what to buy. You should see how those stuffy men reacted to me.' She laughed. 'They thought I was a child, but I showed them! D'Aumant dogs are going to be the best in the world. Want to hold one?' she asked.

Little dogs were not my thing, but these were irresistible with their pleading eyes and lolling pink tongues. The cages were made of wire mesh and covered over as well, to make enclosures the size of a small room. The floors were covered with shredded newspaper and sawdust and there was an unmistakably doggy odour.

Four champagne poodle puppies in one section

caught Chloe's eye; she opened the door, picked up two and handed one to me. It wriggled and squirmed and licked my hand in a frenzy. Hers she held by the scruff of the neck, cradling its rear in her hand.

'Come on,' she said, closing the door and leading me into an elaborate grooming shed where blue ribbons and awards lined the walls. There were three grooming tables in the centre of the room and several dogs, asleep in cages, scheduled to be groomed in the morning.

'I've told Hervé not to let the groomers leave dogs here overnight!' she said angrily. 'If he does it once more, then ffffht!' She made a gesture of her finger across her throat, like 'Off with his head'. I felt a touch sorry for Hervé.

She saw my expression. 'He knows better, but he's a good trainer. Ex-dancers are the best. They fly around the ring when they're showing a dog, put on a wonderful show.'

I could just picture it.

'Hervé is a well-known trainer in Europe; he's shown dogs in America too. I heard Queen Elizabeth wanted to hire him for her kennel, her dogs are worth a fortune, but Uncle Paul convinced him to stay with us.'

The grooming shed was spotless and pristine, even though it smelled of dog. Long pointed scissors and other grooming instruments were neatly laid out on a side table, like a medical surgery.

I held my wriggling dog firmly against my coat to calm him down. 'Are those dangerous-looking scissors used for grooming?' I couldn't imagine how one could cut the hair on a restless animal with them. The dog's tiny tender body vibrated with tension and pleasure as I cradled him. It was easy to see why they were so lovable.

'An expert groomer never makes a mistake, even

with something like this,' Chloe said, picking up an evil-looking pair of shears. 'They'd better not if they want to work for me! It takes a long time to scissor a poodle, and to fluff and buff them. Sometimes we have to chalk them to whiten their fur. We're not supposed to dye them, but some people do. I can always tell. Their skin gets extra pink and the regrowth looks like a prickly beard. You'd better be careful he doesn't make pee-pee on you,' she cautioned, and I thrust the dog away from me while she laughed.

'Poodles and Yorkies and wire fox terriers are the best show dogs of the miniature breeds,' she told me. 'But I only have poodles and Yorkies.'

'What makes them so good?' My children would have loved this place, which made me think of Victoria and wonder what she was doing right now; if she'd ever speak to me again. Even coming all the way to France, we hadn't escaped from our problems, two people who argued too much.

'The best dogs know when they're winners. You could tell too if you saw them in the ring. They're stars; they lap up the spotlight. Usually a trainer has to stack his dog – you know, make him stand properly. But a good show dog will stack himself to show his blood lines. In any litter of puppies, you can tell which one will be a champion. They're the ones who are afraid of nothing, who have electric personalities. Not like these two,' she said, indicating the ones we were holding.

'That's what I like about raising animals,' she said. 'I give them life and I can take it away just as easily.'

'That's not funny, Chloe,' I said. 'And it isn't true. You're only the breeder. God gives them life.'

She ignored me. 'You're wrong,' she said. 'I can do anything I want. Right now, it's dogs. Later on it may be other animals, like prize cattle. But an owner mustn't get attached to her product,' she said. 'Animals

301

get sick and die. It's not like they're pets, they're an investment. And if the investment doesn't pay off, they become a liability.

'Do you see what I can do?' she said. Still holding the puppy by the skin of its neck she raised the fiercely pointed shears and snapped at the squirming creature as though it was no more than a piece of paper. The animal was terrified by the dangerous sounds and whined frantically, kicking his paws, fighting the air for a foothold.

'Chloe, stop that!' I said, watching the hands that had played such magnificent music, now terrifying a helpless animal.

'I'm trying to make a point here, James. This one will never be a star and he'll never be a show dog, will you?' she teased the puppy. 'You cost me two hundred and twenty-five francs a month don't you, you greedy little thing?'

Snap snap.

'Chloe, you're frightening him.' I tried to take the dog away from her, but she swung him out of my reach. In the moment it took me to set my animal down, she had her puppy's head between the jaws of those awful shears.

'Chloe! Don't!' I yelled, grabbing for the dog but she eluded me by turning away. And then, with all her strength, she shoved me back and with a quick *clacking* motion, severed the dog's head from its body. 'There,' she said. 'All gone.'

Blood spurted everywhere.

'Chloe!' I shouted. 'My God!'

I jumped back so as not to be splattered by the severed body which she let fall to the ground; it was still twitching. Then she turned and dropped the tiny fluffy head into the waste basket next to her.

Shocked beyond belief, I wanted to slap her, but she

held those bloody shears like a weapon. Her jaw was slack, as though she had lost her senses. And then she eyed the other dog as though it was next.

I placed myself between her and the remaining puppy to protect it. She'd have to go through me. How many of these massacres had she performed before? She was dangerously disturbed. More than I'd suspected. Just like her mother.

'Put the shears down, Chloe,' I commanded her in an authoritative voice, keeping my control. For a breathless moment she stood there, staring at the body of the dead dog, and then at me as though in a daze. Only a monster could have done what she'd done.

Her eyes glazed over and I could see she was going into shock.

'Put the shears down,' I commanded again, more forcefully.

She looked down as if noticing the bloody things in her hand for the first time. Then, docilely, she set them on the table.

'That's right,' I told her. When she raised her eyes to mine they were filled with sheer pain. But it didn't take the edge off my fury and disgust. Then she took a step towards me and collapsed, her knees buckling under her. I caught her just before she reached the ground and held her up like a dead weight. I couldn't tell if this was real or not, but when she started to whimper and then to cry, I could see that it was. She had shocked herself even more than me. Close to hysteria, I thought she might pass out or convulse. But I had no sympathy for her. The thought of that soft, fluffy thing, so alive one moment and cruelly massacred the next, made me sick.

She could not stand on her own. Each time I lifted under her arms so that her feet touched the ground, they buckled. Finally, I picked her up like a child and

303

she lay cradled against my chest, curled there like a little bird. In a moment the keening had turned to cries and whimpers, and then to sobs so deep and awful that they shook her whole body. I've never felt such a desperate pain. This time my anger melted away. The girl was sick.

The other puppy was crying as it gave a few sniffs at its dead brother and then wandered in circles. Still holding Chloe, I made soothing sounds and stroked her back while she continued to sob, growing heavier in my arms. I leaned back against the table for support.

We stood there for a long time while she cried as though her heart was breaking. I could not imagine what had injured her so terribly that it had turned her into a beast. Yet her remorse seemed genuine, her pain excruciating; she cried from the depths of her soul.

Eventually, she calmed down. I handed her some paper towels to blow her nose and dry her face; she dabbed at my sopping shirt and tie in a vain attempt to dry them. But each time I shifted my weight to put her down, she clung to my neck even harder, so I continued to hold her and rock her, trying to heal both of us.

'Shh,' I kept saying, over and over. And when I thought my arms couldn't hold her a moment longer, she came back to life; an imperceptible movement of her cheek against mine alerted me. I felt her hair brush my arm like caress, and she shifted her weight against me. Suddenly, I was aware of her sensuality; again I tried to let her go, but she clung to me.

In amazement, I wondered how anyone could be this quixotic. One moment she was a madwoman, then near collapse, and the next she was a chrysalis emerging from a dormant cocoon. In a moment she would beat her wings to be released.

And even though I was numb and in shock from what I'd witnessed, my damned body responded in spite of myself. She had been viciously cruel, sick beyond imagining, and still a flush of intense heat shot through me. *Oh God*. I wanted to drop this tiger's tail, let her stand on her own! But she clung to me and I could not put her down.

I bargained with myself. *I'll hold her just a few seconds more*. She was so alive in my arms, so desirable, she was a drug I needed to survive, yet I knew never to get hooked. I toyed with danger, one moment longer, then one moment more. And of course, the longer I held her, the more she held me.

Then slowly she shifted her weight in my arms until she faced me, her chest pressing against mine, her breath on my cheek. Slowly, so slowly, she moved her head and brushed my cheek with her lips until her mouth was next to mine, breathing with a sweet honeyed smell. One millimetre more and our mouths would meet, one infinitesimal moment and the fire in my loins would burst into flames, one millisecond and everything would be lost. I would be stepping into that maggot-infested pile of rotten humanity I so despised. I would be one of them. *Pedophile!* my brain screamed at me. But I'd never wanted anyone as much in my life as I wanted this girl.

Finally, with an agonized cry, I shouted out loud, 'Chloe, no!' It shocked us both and broke the spell. I pulled her arms away from my neck and put her down, even though she held on with all her might.

Over and over she repeated, *'Je t'aime, je t'aime,'* as I pried at her hands. Her fingers were everywhere, featherlight, exquisite touches on my body, my lips, my face; still, I fought her off. Finally, I took her by the wrists and held her at arm's length away from me.

'No!' I told her, staring into her eyes. 'I told you before not to do this!' I was rough with her, but I was scared. No normal girl would have killed that little dog.

Slowly, she accepted my refusal. 'It's your wife's fault. She should not have come here. I hate her! Tell her to go away and then you will love me. I know you do, I can tell you do. Please, James. Don't you want to love me?'

'Chloe, you're a young girl, half my age. There can't be anything between us. You've got to stop. I'm your friend. I'll never be anything more than that. Do you understand?'

She stared at me as though transfixed, unable to act. 'I'm going to let go of your wrists now, all right?'

No reply.

'And you're not going to hurt your dogs any more, are you? Ever again! Is that clear?'

'Yes,' she whispered. 'You won't tell Uncle Paul, will you? Please don't tell him.' This time her request was not perfunctory, she seemed terrified of his reaction.

Of course I planned to tell him, but I didn't say that. 'Why did you kill that poor little dog, Chloe? What made you act so cruelly? I still can't believe what you did.'

She looked up at me with those innocent clear blue eyes, horrified by what she'd done. 'Oh God,' she cried. 'Forgive me. I don't know why I did it. Help me, please!'

'I will,' I promised. 'Tell me why you did it?'

'I went crazy. Like Maman. I must be crazy like her.'

'You're not!' I insisted, thinking she was.

'All the time I have to be so grown up, so wise and so careful. It gets too much for me, I can't explain. I must be crazy like Maman, that is all.'

I was completely drained by the events of this evening and wanted to get away from her. This incident would never resolve itself. I didn't want to be involved, but I was.

'Here,' I said, handing her some newspaper. Then I

made her scoop up the body of the dog, reunite it with its head, and wrap it up. I kept hold of her shoulder, in case she tried to bolt, then found a shovel and walked her out to the lakeside where I began digging a grave.

After we had buried the poor thing, I knelt and pulled her down beside me. I didn't know what was appropriate, but we both needed this to begin the healing process.

'Dear Lord, hear our prayer,' I began. 'We beg your forgiveness for what happened here tonight, the unfortunate killing of this animal.' She tried to pull away, but I kept her next to me. 'In all humility, we give thanks for the miracle of life you bestowed upon this tiny creature, even though short. We commend his innocent soul to your keeping. And now, the person responsible for his cruel death has something to say to you.'

I turned to Chloe who could not look at me. 'Go on, Chloe,' I said. 'Tell God how you feel.'

She was crying again, but I didn't touch her. Instead, I kept a vigil over her pain. We knelt there for some time before she whispered, '*Mon Dieu, pardonnez-moi, pardonnez-moi. Je suis désolée. Je suis triste. Je suis pauvre et méchante!*' I could hear from her protestations that she truly regretted her actions. '*Jamais, jamais non plus,*' she said. Never, never again.

I helped her to her feet and handed her another paper towel to dry her eyes before I escorted her back to the house.

'God will not forgive me, will he?' she cried. 'I should be dead too. You should kill me, that's what you should do.'

I whispered comforting words to her while this disturbed waif leaned against me, and I wondered what the hell I was going to do now.

# Chapter 16

I sat for hours in the lobby of Victoria's hotel waiting for her to return while I tried to make sense of everything that had happened tonight. Since I wasn't registered, the damned clerk wouldn't give me the key to her room. Both he and Victoria were punishing me. I deserved it. But her anger was minor compared to what had happened after she left.

I called Dr Guillaud from the hotel to tell him about Chloe, but tonight of all nights he wasn't on call. I left word for him to call me. I really wanted Victoria to return so I could apologize and tell her what had happened. She would have good advice.

What could I have done differently with Chloe? Nothing, I supposed. Hindsight is a worthless pastime. But someone had to help her. I blamed Paul for her behaviour. He had failed as a parent, allowing her to get too close to the edge. He never set limits with her, and look what had happened. I recalled the way he had slapped her and she'd kneed him in the groin that day I'd had lunch with them. There was something really sick about it, too familiar. But I had to let it go. Now, I was at a loss to know what to do. I hated the idea of interfering in their lives. I'd resent it like hell if anyone tried it with me.

To get my mind off them, I thought about the case. At least we'd made some progress. The scalpel that killed Lepic should provide good leads, and Emile's informant would give us proof that two of the victims were associated. Hopefully, we could prevent any more killings. By now, Emile might even know the identity of the Boardroom Killer.

It would not be a total surprise if Shithead turned out to be some sicko cop, killing people to cover her tracks. The serial killer profile had never really fit.

But several things continued to bother me: the staged aspect of the murders, as if they were posed. It was all so neat. And the time difference between them seemed odd. Six months between the first two, and only a matter of weeks between the next three. I wondered if it had something to do with the seasons, or merely opportunity?

I thought it was time for Emile to give the media all that we knew about the killer and warn the public, but then Shithead might go underground. She wasn't driven by psychopathic motives, so she could bide her time. And a potential victim would never turn himself in and ask for protection. I wouldn't. They'd take their chances.

I ought to be with Emile right now. Better there than here, trying to figure out what to do about Chloe.

I needed to get some sleep, and the lobby was uncomfortable. So in the early hours of the morning, I went back to Madame Cretier's and passed out.

The image of Chloe killing that puppy was repeated in my dreams. And each time a nightmare woke me, I had a hard on. I was as sick as she was. Thank God I had stopped myself from doing anything with her. But what about the next time? If Victoria and I separated, I might fall into a precipice with no return. Like Adam, one taste of forbidden fruit would damn me forever.

I kept telling myself, *There's a difference between wanting and doing*. But at this moment, as I fought not to masturbate to that image again, the differences were hardly there. Obsession was unfamiliar and frightening.

By morning, Dr Guillaud hadn't called and neither had Emile. I was worried about Victoria. Chloe was a disturbed young woman; her jealousy could erupt in terrible ways. And she blamed Victoria for my refusal to play.

I called Paul. 'Where did you take my wife last night?'

'Back to her hotel,' he said.

'She's not there. Do you know where she went?'

'No,' he insisted. 'Just that she was quite angry.'

'I need to speak to you about Chloe. Something happened last night.'

'You mean about the puppy? I know all about it.'

'She told you?' I was amazed.

'Yes, we had a long talk. She begged my forgiveness, promised me it wouldn't happen again. I know she regrets what she did, James. She just got carried away. I think we should forget about it, don't you?'

'No, I don't. She needs help, Paul. You should take her to see Catherine's doctor.'

There was a telling pause. 'Chloe is not crazy like her mother. I know what's best for my niece, not you,' he said sharply, and hung up.

*What an ass!*

I placed a call to Paris, but Emile was on the road. Lucien brought me up to date.

'He's in Biarritz, waiting to bring the informant to a safe house. There's been a delay. Naturally, the man is frightened. I would be too.'

'It will be all right,' I assured him. But delicate negotiations like these could fall apart. Informants could disappear or be killed. I've seen it happen. Sometimes you get close enough to smell their breath, and they vanish. Even the most careful planning and sophisticated procedure can't prevent it.

'Tell Emile to call me as soon as he hears anything,' I said. Then I took a run past the fields and farms, trying to burn off steam, letting the sweet faces of the white cows soothe me. I came back by way of the café.

There were my two buddies Alfonse, and Marcel the baker, whose croissants and baguettes were responsible for my thickening waist.

Pagnol the mayor of Duhort-Bachen, a tall bear of a man with a swooping black moustache, had joined the two men and greeted me warmly. '*Ça va?*'

'*Ma femme est ici, mais pas ici.*' I tried to explain by my hangdog expression that my wife was here in Eugénie but not with me at the moment, flicking my fingers to show it was too hot to handle. They commiserated.

'*Dis-nous alors,*' tell us, Alfonse asked, ready to give advice.

'She's furious with me. The Duc dropped her off and he won't tell me where she is.'

A cryptic look passed between them when I mentioned the Duc. 'What's on your minds, fellas?' I asked. 'Something I should know.'

They gave Gallic shrugs but wouldn't elaborate.

I ordered a bottle of cognac and poured generous shots, listening to them discuss the truckers' strike tying up the highways of France.

'Those crazy bastards,' Marcel said. 'They drive too fast and kill people. You take your life in your hands when they're around.'

'There should be a point system on their licence for safety violations,' Pagnol said. 'Other countries have it.'

'Our produce is rotting on the trees and they don't care,' Marcel countered.

'Nobody can get to the Art Festival in Avignon.

312

Hotels and restaurants will suffer,' Alfonse said.

'Italy and Spain will sue us if they don't get their fruit!' Pagnol added.

Three cognacs had loosened their tongues and I brought up the subject from before. 'What were you going to say about Paul d'Aumant? Should I worry about my wife?'

They smiled into their drinks.

'Is he gay?'

'No,' Pagnol insisted. 'He doesn't go with men or women.'

'Who then, his poodles?' I joked.

Everybody laughed. Alfonse leaned closer and the rest of us followed. 'He lost interest a long time ago.'

The others nodded.

'What happened?' I asked Pagnol. 'Is he a sicko?'

'No!' Alfonse assured me. 'He is *rien*, nothing. My brother and his wife worked at the *castelle* and the Duc never had anyone, man or woman.'

'I don't believe it!' I declared. 'He's virile.'

'The laundress knows what's on the sheets,' said Marcel.

'Maybe he was injured.'

'Only here,' Marcel tapped his head. 'And here.' He touched his heart. 'Now, this doesn't work so good.' He put his hand on his crotch.

'Jeez, the whole family needs a psychiatrist,' I blurted out.

But only Americans take their troubles to a shrink. And who was I to talk? I hadn't gone to one either. I had more in common with Paul than I'd realized.

We drank another round and the room began to tilt, but nothing fazed these guys. 'Will somebody tell me what happened?'

Marcel started the story. 'In the sixties, things were really wild. Paul's father, Charles, loved the ladies.'

'Even our wives weren't safe from him,' Pagnol added, angry and envious.

Marcel continued, 'Parties at the *castelle* lasted for days.'

'You mean orgies,' said Pagnol. 'He invited his rich friends, not us. But we heard about them.'

'From your brother?' I asked Alfonse.

'No. My father made extra money working at the *castelle*. He was there one night to help serve an eight-course dinner, a different wine with each course, the chef flown in from Paris, and porno movies.' He winked. 'Duc Charles brought in women to entertain the men. Everybody was drunk and they had a prick contest, pulled them out of their tuxedos to compare.'

'That must have been a sight,' I agreed.

'This one woman was lying on that big table.' He spread wide his arms.

'The one that's as big as a skating rink?' I commented.

'You've seen it,' Marcel nodded.

'Go on,' Pagnol urged him, and we shifted closer.

'The whore offers to take on everybody. Come get your turn. So they oblige her, keeping score, you know. "Give it to her, Henri. That's four, that's five." Things like that. This was some woman. And then she says, "Is that all you've got? I want a man to satisfy me! Come on, give me more." But everybody was finished. Once you've had a whore you don't want to do it again. Nobody was left.'

'And Charles announces, "There is one more." ' Marcel started to laugh. 'He points to Alfonse's father, who is backing out the door.' We all laughed, now.

'He didn't want to be the last one in,' Alfonse said, showing his distaste. 'My father was a respected man in his town, the Duc would not fool with him. But the woman wanted more! The Duc tells my father, "Go and get Master Paul." He was a boy of fourteen, still a virgin. My father didn't like the idea, and dragged his feet. But the Duc and his friends pushed him aside and went upstairs to wake Paul. They were laughing and shouting and falling down on each other.

'Finally they brought him down to the party. Everyone was clapping and pounding on the table. They stripped the boy nude; he was yelling and cursing. The women were whistling and kissing his behind, pinching his prick. Then the men hoisted him in the air and lowered him down over the woman.' His hands drew pictures in the air.

I was titillated but sorry for the kid.

'It's true!' Alfonse insisted.

'So what happened?'

'The worst thing. Paul can't get it up. They kept lifting him up and lowering him down on her while she lay there pointing to the place where everybody's been. She kissed him and grabbed him, telling him, "Come on, pretty baby, give it to me. Do it good like your old man. Stick it right in there." And Paul tried, but he couldn't do it.

'And he started to cry.' Alfonse threw up his hands in disbelief.

'What a shame,' Pagnol stated. 'He failed the honour of every Frenchman in this town. I would have performed like a man,' he boasted. 'By fourteen, I'd already fucked half the countryside.'

'Sure you did,' Marcel said. This was the biggest lie of all. Now we were really laughing. The whole story smacked of a whopper.

'Wait a minute,' I said. 'Are you telling me that's the reason Paul doesn't have sex at home? Did it ever occur to you that he does it somewhere else so guys like you won't find out?'

They looked as though they'd never thought of that.

'Maybe he does,' Alfonse declared, laughing. 'But it's a damned good story, eh?' And I realized they had been putting me on.

The next morning I woke up with a pounding headache, anxious to talk to Emile. Dr Guillaud and I had been missing each other and Victoria hadn't called either. I was about to call her hotel again when she appeared at my door. I was so glad to see her I wanted to hug her, but anger took over.

'You took your time,' I said, ignoring the way she looked in her jeans and white T-shirt. 'I was worried about you.'

'Then you know how it feels for a change.' Her anger matched mine.

'I've been imagining you hurt somewhere, or killed.'

'What the hell do you think I imagine every day of our lives?'

'Okay,' I sighed. 'Your point. I just wanted to tell you how sorry I was about the other night.' I tried to put my arms around her but she deflected me as only a woman who doesn't want to be touched can do, especially by someone as lowly as I. The knot in my stomach tightened.

'You were really obnoxious. It's taken me this long to cool off.'

'Where were you?'

'At the hotel. I checked in to another room and left instructions not to tell anyone where I was.'

'You weren't with Paul?'

'With that horrible man, I should hope not!'

I was relieved. 'Well, you taught me a lesson,' I countered.

'Yes. And I had a grand time.'

'You're pleased with yourself.'

'Why not. I lay in the sun, took a long walk, went to

dinner by myself. Just what I needed. You're right. The food's incredible here.'

'How nice for you.' I was angry, but the way she took care of herself made me respect her. She would never be in the mess I was in.

We sat down on my bed and I wanted to put my arms around her, make everything all right again. But nothing was right between us, not our lovemaking, or what we wanted out of life. I could feel my protective shield rising.

'Do you know why I really left in the middle of dinner?'

'I don't blame you, I behaved like an ass.'

'No, it was because of Chloe. That girl is one of the most disturbed people I've ever seen. The relationship between her and her uncle is sick. Remember when you asked me what could make a young girl overly sexy? I asked my friend Millie, who's a psychologist, and she said it can be from being molested.'

'What?'

'She explained that when a child's sexual behaviour is inappropriate, it's possible that an adult taught her what to do.'

'But who would have done such a thing?'

'It could be anyone, a servant, a relative.'

'You don't mean her uncle?' I was getting a sick feeling inside.

'If not him, someone else in her life. Look at the way she comes on to old men like you, and he does nothing about it.'

'I'm not old!'

'Come off it. You're old enough to be her father. Maybe you are!'

'That's ridiculous. That's really sick!'

She studied me for a moment. And then she said, 'Don't tell me you have a *thing* for her the way she has

317

for you? Like mother, like daughter?' Her guess sent a chill through my bones.

She was staring at me as though I was disgusting. 'Of all these disturbed people, you may be the one who needs the most help.' Her voice was barely audible. The colour had drained from her face. 'It's like incest, James! Chloe might have been your daughter, yours and Catherine's.'

'Well, she's not,' I insisted. 'She was born years after I knew Catherine. Her father died in a car accident. And don't try to tell me that Catherine was pregnant when she got married. She wasn't. Your accusations are disgusting and irresponsible.'

She turned to me with an even deader expression on her face than she'd had before. 'If she's not your child, does that make it all right?'

'That's not what I said!'

'I pity you.'

'Don't be so damned sanctimonious,' I shouted. 'You're making something out of nothing.' Every ounce of me needed her to believe this so I could believe it too. *Molested?* I couldn't stand the thought. Catherine might have been molested too. Some of the things she said to me began to make sense. 'I'm being punished for having too much sex. I did bad things.'

'I'm not making this up,' Victoria interrupted my thoughts. 'Everybody in that family is sick but you won't see it.'

'I see it,' I admitted quietly.

'Then do something about it,' she said staring at me. 'When did it go bad between us, James? Was it when I took on that volunteer work for the National Abortion Rights League?' She looked up at me wanting my reassurance.

'You know I agree with you on abortion,' I insisted.

'If it's not our politics, then it must be that you don't

318

want me to be independent from you.'

'That's not true!' I insisted, embarrassed to admit she was partly right, unable to acknowledge how much I needed her. 'It's just that you're never there any more.'

'What do you mean, never there? I come home every night, don't I? You're the one who's not there.'

'That's the nature of my work, Victoria.' The truth was that I needed more of her than I got and I couldn't tell her that. She used to be available, around the house. When the kids were little she was at home, only worked part-time. Now she was off somewhere, looking after other people's needs, damn it. She had no idea what her presence meant to me, how I depended on her, how her ebullience kept me going, almost like a lifebelt keeping me afloat. When she wasn't there, I sank to the bottom.

'I know about the nature of your work,' she said. 'And I have a need to pursue my goals too. But I'm there, don't ever say I'm not! We earn the same amount of money, but I do twice the work. I go to the market, I cook the dinner, I drive the kids, I hire the sitter when they're sick, I help them with their homework when you're not there, I do the laundry, I make our social plans – what do you mean I'm never there!' Her voice grew louder, showing her frustration. And I wanted to shout, *Not like you used to be*. But it made me feel like a child. I had no right to demand more from her than she gave, but I wanted it. And that made me wrong. Being wrong was hell to live with.

'Keep it down, will you?' I pleaded, knowing Madame Cretier was downstairs listening to us, and would repeat every word in the café later on. Then everyone would know.

'I don't care who hears,' she insisted. 'Just tell me what you want from me? Should I stop having interests

319

of my own? Should I wait for you after work like Mirabelle Morgan?'

'Is it wrong to want my wife to be a wife?'

'It's archaic!' she shouted, the neighbours be damned. 'I have interests just as you do. And if I don't pursue them, James, my soul will shrivel and die. Can't you see that? I won't allow you to do that to me. I wouldn't do it to you. What kind of example would we be for our children?'

My feelings were irrational, but damn it, that's exactly what I wanted her to be, a wife for Christ's sake! Not some glorified patriot leading marches in the streets. Or at least, that's what I told myself I wanted. For something had to fill up this hole inside when she turned away her attention.

She waited for me to say something, but I would only indict myself.

'I shouldn't be surprised at how you feel, given the way you were raised. But I'm not like your parents, you knew that when you married me. And I'm not a fantasy, like Catherine, a pampered little rich girl who doted on you. I won't fall apart when I have to face harsh realities.'

'That's not fair,' I shouted, defending Catherine. 'Losing your parents and then having your husband killed is more than harsh reality; it's shattering.'

'Come on, James. A lot of people suffer terrible tragedies and don't end up in a mental ward. She's not a wronged saint. She's a woman with a mental imbalance who might have gone bonkers even if you'd married her. Who can say you two would have lived happily ever after?'

'This is off limits,' I snarled. I might not have saved Catherine from her tragic fate, but I could defend my memories. She was my ideal for when Victoria let me down.

'Fine. Keep her perfect image alive, I don't give a damn any more. Except that it's ruining our lives. You've got some screwed-up idea of what life should have been, only it's not real. What's real are your two beautiful, healthy, well-adjusted children at home who love you and need you. Yet you come over here and beat your breast and fawn all over that sick brat Chloe who's headed down the same path as her mother. In fact, her mother might have been mentally ill when you knew her, but your brains were so far at the end of your prick you couldn't see it.'

'Chloe has nothing to do with this,' I shouted, terrified that she would discover my feelings about the girl.

She stood up and faced me. 'Don't you see what you're doing? Throwing our lives away over nothing. I could just kill you for what you've done to our children. They don't deserve this, James! And neither do I.'

She glared at me, her fists clenched, her body rigid. 'When is this going to stop? I've waited for the man I love to come back to me. I thought this trip would do it, but it hasn't. You're still stuck in the mire of your own crap, and it stinks. I don't know what to do any more.' She shook her head. 'But we can't go on, James. We can't.'

Now her eyes filled with tears. 'I never wanted to be one of those people who got a divorce,' she said. 'I hate divorce. It's such a shame when people give up. I still think we can work this out, if you'll try. Won't you come home and see a counsellor with me?'

The idea nearly made me explode. 'God damned psychiatrists again! That's not the answer!' I yelled. 'This is my life and I'll fix it by myself!'

'If you wait too long, you won't be able to, and I won't be there any more,' she said, sinking down on the bed again, her head in her hands.

Then she looked up at me. 'This is enough. I can't stand this fighting any more, James. I'm leaving. I had hoped that we could talk this through. I was going to stay here until you were ready to come home. But I can't help you, you have to do it alone. I hope to God you do.

'You know where I'll be if you want me. Come and find me when you're ready.'

She was almost at the door when I called to her, 'Vickie, would you still take me back, after all this?'

'I don't know, James,' she said. 'Maybe if you got help. But even then, I don't know.'

'Are you going back to Houston?'

'No, I'm staying in France a while. I need a vacation. I'm going to see the sights you've always talked about.'

She glanced at me once before she walked out the door.

I let her go. There was no way I could follow her now, not until I had settled everything here. And Chloe was first on my list.

# Chapter 17

The minute she left I realized what an ass I was. Victoria was more important to me than Chloe. The sight of her car turning the corner out of sight made me feel helpless. I couldn't bear to lose her.

I wanted to go after her, but I could not bring myself to drive around the countryside again looking for a lost love. When we got back to Houston, I'd see a counsellor with her, if she'd give us a chance.

I was halfway out of the door on my way to see Paul about Chloe, when the phone rang. My heart leaped as I grabbed it. 'Vickie?'

'No, it's me,' Emile said. 'I've got bad news. We lost our witness. He was killed before we could get to him.'

'What happened?'

'He called us from his office after eleven last night. He told us he'd come to us, that he was waiting for a late appointment and then he'd pick up his wife and come over.'

'Don't tell me; the appointment was with a woman about a video tape!'

'Yes. When I asked him about it, he was shocked that I knew. I warned him immediately to get out of there, that the killer lured her victims with a video tape. He admitted that he had the tape; he even agreed to bring it to us. But the killer got to him in the hall right outside the door of his private office. This time there was a struggle. He suffered defensive cuts on his upper arms. And he had a gun, too, but the killer disarmed him, left the gun there. There were stab wounds on the upper body. His throat was cut and an X carved across his face.'

'So she really lost her cool this time.'

'Yes. We have footprints that match the ones in Toulouse and skin fragments under the victim's nails. If we catch her, we have enough on her now to send her away.'

'We'll catch her, Emile.'

'God, it was maddening. Knowing he was on his way to us, not knowing who he was, sitting there waiting.'

'What about a trace?'

'He wasn't on the phone long enough. We had to sit and wait, praying he'd get out of there in time. He didn't. We were so close, James. So close!'

'Who was he?'

'A hotelier named Antoine Terraille, sixty-eight years old. Owned the St Jean de Biarritz, one of those luxury highrise hotels like Loewe's in Monte Carlo. He was going to tell us who Fontelle was paying in the department, and identify his connections in the Middle East, plus give us the other names of his syndicate. We could have protected people. Now we're helpless again. We didn't even ID him until his wife found the body after midnight and reported it.

'She was hysterical, blames us of course. I can understand. She was the go-between who met Solange in Lourdes, begged her husband to get protection. But he waited too long. Imagine how she feels, trying so hard to save her husband's life and not being able to. And, of course, he didn't tell her about the tape.'

'It's rough,' I commiserated, 'but it's Solange's fault. She should have had the wife followed the moment she met her in Lourdes. If she'd told the wife how the killer lures her victims, we'd have caught the killer by now and Terraille would be alive.'

'You're right,' he said. 'Solange didn't warn them.'

'Why, for God's sake?' This incompetence was making me furious. 'What does Solange have to say for herself? She let a material witness get killed; she cleared Fontelle of smuggling charges. Sounds irresponsible to me. Or else stupid. And we know she's not stupid.'

There was silence. Then he said, 'Solange is missing. We're afraid she might be dead.'

'Dead? Who would want to kill her?'

'The same person who's been killing elderly businessmen to cover up her involvement in the smuggling of illegal goods. Solange was getting too close.'

'Emile, you're blind! Solange could be the one taking the bribes, that's why she's missing. She might be the killer.'

'No!'

'It makes sense. She took a bribe from Fontelle, then joined your group to remove herself from the case. But something happened. Maybe the investment syndicate wanted something more from her. They might have threatened her career, so she decided to get rid of them all. When your group was assigned to find the killer, she was able to cover her tracks. That's why you've been making so little progress, she's been sabotaging you. No wonder she didn't warn Terraille. Either she killed him, or she wanted him dead.'

'I don't believe it!' he insisted. 'She could be dead herself and you're insulting her.'

'Emile, for God's sake, wake up! Check out her files. Talk to Saint Jacques in Lyon. I'll bet he knows where she is.'

'I've spoken to him. He admits nothing. And her files are nearly empty.'

*So it was Solange!*

'What are you going to do?'

'Find her! Bring her in for questioning. The Minister called the Chef de Brigade Criminelle, who said if I don't arrest someone in two days, I'm off the case and he'll demand my resignation!'

'That won't happen. This case is ready to break.'

'James, if Solange is the killer, then I'm responsible. I couldn't keep my prick in my pants.'

'I always suspected her motives,' I said.

'I can't believe it. Bribery maybe, but killing, never!'

'Emile, she fits the description. She had access to the victims, they all knew her. She could talk her way into their lives. She could fool the police. She's tall and strong. And she lies about where she's been. And I saw her in a blonde wig.'

'It's impossible,' he said.

'Sometimes, impossible things happen.' Like the idea of Chloe being molested. I understood how he felt. 'We'll find out the truth,' I assured him. 'Any other physical evidence?'

'I haven't had all the reports back yet.'

'Do you want me to join you in Biarritz, or look for Solange?'

'Neither. I want you to check out the theft of medical supplies in that hospital in Lourdes.'

Frustration made my temper flare. 'That should have been done already. We got that list from Chapelle two days ago!'

'Damn it, James. I entrusted it to Solange.'

'Oh, Christ. No wonder you haven't made any progress. I'll go as soon as I take care of something here in Eugénie.' Namely, Chloe.

'I need you there now, James!' he shouted, stopping me.

'Okay,' I said, 'calm down. I'll go right away.'

326

'Fine. Once we eliminate the hospital in Lourdes, there are only four more: one in Marseille reported a loss of supplies in the last three years, one in Switzerland and two in Germany.'

'Tell Interpol to give those priority,' I said.

'They know.'

I was about to hang up when he said, 'James, the evidence will clear Solange.'

'Sure,' I said. But I recalled the testimony of friends and family of murderers who'd had no idea how sick the killer was. Some killers are perfect at masking their behaviour.

'Inspector Raspail in Lourdes has been assigned to you,' he told me. 'Call me through the Prefecture in Biarritz. I'll be waiting to hear from you.'

I took a change of clothes with me and headed out of town. But I couldn't go without seeing Paul. If there was the slightest chance that he had molested his niece, I'd tear him apart.

I tore down the winding road to the *castelle*, roared up to the entry, jumped out of the car and ran up the steps. The footman looked askance as I approached him.

'Monsieur le Duc and Mademoiselle are not here,' he said, taking a step back when he saw my expression.

'When will they return?'

He shrugged. It wasn't his place to know, only to answer the door.

I could barely contain my anger. I'd expected them to be there. I asked to see Paul's secretary.

'Just a moment,' he said.

'I know the way,' I told him, getting back in the car and driving around the side of the *castelle* to the office.

When I entered the reception area, Paul's assistant was standing at the desk. 'When will the Duc be back?'

'Not for some time. He's taken Mademoiselle Chloe

to Switzerland to visit universities.'

'When you hear from him, give him a message. Tell him to contact me through Chief Inspector Laurent in Paris. I have an urgent matter to discuss with him concerning Mademoiselle Chloe.'

He nodded. If Paul didn't contact me, I would ask for Emile's help.

The drive back to Lourdes was tedious and hot and I longed for a helicopter or an air-conditioned car. But it gave me time to go over details of the case. Solange had been absent from the Prefecture in Paris at the times of most of the murders. I remembered how Emile tried to find her when we were in Toulouse. She could have been there committing the crime, wearing a blonde wig. We needed to find her female accomplice. I hoped the evidence to convict her would be in Lourdes.

At the un-airconditioned Prefecture, I met Inspecteur Raspail, a no-nonsense woman in her late-twenties, medium height with an attractive figure; she had large green eyes and sandy-coloured hair. I did not keep the admiration out of my smile.

She smiled back. 'You seem glad to have been assigned to me, instead of to a man.'

'You guessed it,' I laughed. The excellence of her English comforted me. Emile was counting on me to pick up nuances of rapid conversation. With Raspail to interpret, I wouldn't worry.

I left my car and we took hers through the crowded streets, both of us frustrated by the delay. 'When I was a girl I hated all the tourists and invalids in this city,' she confided. 'I even resented the shrine to Saint Bernadette. Then I went to Marseille which doesn't have busloads of tourists and pilgrims. It was so ordinary I began to appreciate my city. It's like living in Monte Carlo, there's action all the time.'

'Speaking of action,' I told her, 'the Boardroom Killer might be a female officer from the Paris branch of the Brigade Criminelle.'

Tendons tightened in her jaw as she clenched her teeth. 'That's infuriating.'

'I know how you feel,' I told her. 'But we'll get her. Tell me about the hospital theft here in Lourdes.'

'Two years ago, a large quantity of drugs was stolen from Our Lady of Lourdes, along with high quality surgical knives. We caught the thieves with the drugs in their possession. The knives were never recovered. Now I wish we'd pursued them.'

'One never knows when a small detail will make an enormous difference.'

'How do you know the Boardroom Killer uses stolen knives?'

'Surgical instruments purchased from legitimate sources can be traced. Stolen goods are not traceable.'

'But it's been two years.'

'That's not such a long time when planning a crime of this magnitude.' I remembered the staged quality of the murders. If only I could figure out why.

'I've brought you the jackets on the drug thieves.' She handed me some files from the back seat. 'They've been in prison a year-and-a-half.'

I read through their statements and found something interesting. 'This Jean-Luc Marat claims he didn't steal any drugs, that he bought them from a blonde woman who stole them from the hospital. He gave her cash and stolen jewellery as payment.'

'Of course he would say that,' Raspail insisted.

I read a bit further. 'This Marat claims that the woman sold him the drugs at such a bargain price, he couldn't say no. He made an enormous profit on what he sold, but he never used them himself.'

'What do his specimen tests show?' she asked.

I leafed through the file until I found them. 'Urine and blood shows no traces of drug use, in either of the accused.'

'That doesn't mean they didn't steal the drugs.'

'Was the blonde woman ever caught?'

'There was no woman,' she insisted.

'Then how did they pull off the burglary? The report says there was no evidence of a break-in to the hospital. Neither of the men was employed at the hospital and there were no witnesses. It had to be an inside job, an accomplice working in the hospital, or they're telling the truth. They didn't commit the burglary.'

'The blonde woman!' she concluded.

'Yet they were convicted of this crime only on the evidence of possessing stolen goods.'

'I suppose so,' she said. 'This all happened before I joined the force. I think you're right, it was an inside job.'

'And their accomplice was never caught or named.'

'Don't feel sorry for them. Jean-Luc and his partner had prior records for stealing electronic equipment, cars, jewellery. Besides the drugs, some of those goods were recovered. And they confessed.'

'To stealing cars and jewellery, not stealing drugs. Nobody listened.'

She pulled into the parking lot of the hospital, stopped the car and turned to me. 'If a blonde woman stole the drugs, she must have done it to cover up the theft of the scalpels.'

'For what reason?'

'Why else would she sell top quality drugs for a fraction of what she could get on the open market? She sold them to two greedy thieves with a police record who were bound to get caught. She knew no one would believe their story or care about missing surgical knives when the stolen drugs were recovered. Clever woman.

Something a cop would do.'

'It fits, doesn't it?'

I noticed a note on the bottom of a page. 'It says here, your department received an anonymous tip about the burglary. The blonde woman probably made the call. It's too bad you weren't an investigator back then. Your department could have used you.'

She smiled at the compliment. 'Maybe this Jean-Luc and his friend can give us a description of the woman who sold him the drugs. She might still have the stolen jewellery. Women keep things like that.'

'Call your office and tell them to send an artist to the prison in Lyon to do a sketch. Maybe Jean-Luc and his friend know where she is.'

Raspail phoned her request into the Prefecture, and I placed a call to Emile in Biarritz to tell him my theory.

He agreed with me. 'Good work, James,' he told me. 'I'm glad I sent you there. Tell Lourdes to fax me the file on this case and I'll go over it.' Raspail agreed to have that done.

'What did Terraille's wife say?' I asked.

'Not much. She only knew the names of two men who financed the arms deal with her husband: Fontelle and Richard. And if that's true, it means Solange is not guilty. She'd have no reason to kill Sourais, Lepic or de Saint Robert if they weren't involved in smuggling. We've gone over their files again, re-questioned the witnesses. There's no evidence that any of those three were connected to the deal.'

'It has to be there. You just haven't found it.'

'Why?'

'Because everything else fits,' I told him. 'Any word on Solange?'

'She's been spotted in Morocco. We've contacted Interpol.'

'If Solange isn't the killer, why did she run?'

'To evade bribery charges,' he insisted, 'which are bad enough.'

I still believed she was guilty. 'Emile, I'm sorry.'

'Thanks,' he said as he disconnected.

Raspail and I left her car and entered the large city hospital overlooking the Grotto of the Virgin.

The hospital administrator was expecting us and gave us the employee and patient records for the years in question. Then we ran them through the computer looking for any young blonde female patients or employees who'd been in the hospital at the time of the theft. There were over seventy names to check out. But one of them jumped out at me: Véronique Desault.

Catherine's companion at the sanitarium had been an administrative assistant at Our Lady of Lourdes prior to working for Catherine. She'd left the hospital shortly after the theft. Perhaps she would have information about the theft. I was anxious to talk to her, but it was also an excuse to see Catherine.

Checking out the seventy names we'd collected at the hospital would be tedious work. But Raspail's team would do it. She took the printouts back to the Prefecture and dropped me at my car. I promised to stop by before I left the city and tell her if I learned anything from Véronique Desault.

For lunch, I bought a grilled sausage on a baguette from a vendor and ate it as I headed over to Catherine's sanitarium. But when I asked to speak to Mademoiselle Desault, the woman at the desk told me that she and Madame Jolibois had gone out to lunch and would be back shortly. I decided to wait in the courtyard under a tree, to escape the heat of the afternoon.

As I sat there, I wondered where Victoria was right now, whether she'd reached Paris or if she'd stopped to visit the châteaux I'd never seen. Now that Emile had nearly solved his case, he wouldn't be needing me any more and I could join her. The idea brought mixed feelings. I wanted to settle our differences, but I still felt an attachment to Catherine. The thought of seeing her today filled me with nervous excitement. And I still had to deal with Chloe and Paul.

It was nearly an hour before Catherine's car pulled into the driveway with Mademoiselle Desault seated next to her. I marvelled at how in control she looked, like an ordinary woman out to lunch with a friend. Maybe I could take her out sometime. She'd said she liked to drive.

And then, something clicked in my mind – gold jewellery, a dark green Mercedes and two blonde women. Véronique Desault wore an expensive gold necklace and had been employed at the hospital where scalpels were stolen. Maybe I was making too many connections, but she was a short blonde woman. She could have been Solange's accomplice, or involved in this somehow. Maybe she'd been using Catherine's car!

*Barton, you're grasping at nothing*, I told myself. But it was worth checking out. The two elements, hot jewellery and stolen scalpels, made it more than coincidence.

I got up from my bench and went back through the salon across the entry hall to the front desk.

A woman in her mid-fifties looked at me. '*Oui?* Mademoiselle Desault has not returned.'

'I know,' I told her, staying calm, not hurrying, even though the two women were getting out of the car by now.

'Perhaps you could tell me something? When an employee leaves the premises, are they required to sign in and out?'

'Of course,' she said. 'Every time, day or night. Right here.' She patted a black record book on her

333

desk. 'That's what I was told.' She was wearing a badge that read, *Je suis stagiare*. I am temporary.

'My name is James Barton, of the American FBI.' Véronique and Catherine were halfway up the drive by now, nearly at the garden entrance. 'I'm on a special assignment with the French National Police. If you will call Inspector Raspail at the Prefecture in Lourdes, she will verify that fact. I'd like to look through your record book.'

'Do you have identification?' she asked.

I showed her my ID.

They were crossing the garden now, entering the salon.

'I don't need to call,' she said, turning the book around to face me. 'Go ahead.'

I opened the book and turned the pages back to each date of a Boardroom Killing. And each time, there was an entry for Véronique Desault's name; she had been out of the sanitarium with Catherine.

A chill went through me. Sometimes it's so simple when you know where to look. I ran my finger down the entries to check their destinations. They were different from where the killings occurred, and the dates weren't exact. But still, the two women had been away! When Richard was killed in Bordeaux, they'd been to Paris, they were in Eugénie when both Sourais and Fontelle were killed in Paris. They'd gone to Pau when Lepic was killed in Lyon, and to Bordeaux when de Saint Robert was killed in Toulouse. And last night, when Terraille was killed in Biarritz, they'd been in Lannemezan. Too coincidental! Véronique and Solange might have been using Catherine as a dupe to commit murder. And if it wasn't Solange, Véronique may have assisted someone else.

The connections were there: stolen scalpels, a dark green Mercedes, two women, one tall, one short, gold jewellery, and these damned dates.

I heard their voices behind me.

'Here she is now,' the temp said, pushing the book over for them to sign. 'Mademoiselle Desault, there's an American agent to see you.'

I turned to face them. Véronique Desault saw that I'd been looking in the record book and her expression became cold. Catherine saw her friend's expression and then fear accompanied by guilt crossed her face.

'Hello, ladies. I came for another visit. Why don't we go into the garden?' I gave them a gentle push. 'I'll be right with you,' I said, waving them away.

Then I turned to the woman at the desk. 'Call Inspector Raspail at the Prefecture and tell her to get here immediately with back-up officers!'

Her eyes grew wide with fear. 'What's wrong? Why the police?'

'Just make the call now!'

She hurried to comply.

Catherine and Véronique were watching me and I gave them a friendly smile as I joined them, taking each of their arms, so they wouldn't go off in opposite directions. I herded them into the walled garden.

Véronique eyed me nervously.

'I just want to talk to you,' I said gently.

But my presence unnerved Catherine. 'What does he want, what does he want?' she asked Véronique, alerted to danger.

Her face had grown pale, her eyes wide with alarm, and she was shaking. But she seemed more normal than the last time I'd seen her. Even though her eyes moved restlessly, I could sense her enhanced awareness. Was she cogent enough to be an accomplice to murder? Not likely.

'I'm just here on a visit,' I said soothingly.

'I'm sure you want to be alone,' Véronique offered, moving away.

'Sit down!' I ordered her sharply.

She sat. Catherine began to whimper. 'Don't be angry, James. I've been good. Tell him I've been good. Haven't I been good?' She turned to Desault for agreement. Véronique patted her hand.

'What is it you want, Monsieur Barton?'

At the moment, I wanted the city traffic to disappear so that Inspector Raspail could get here instantly. And I wanted to be totally wrong about Véronique Desault; that she hadn't had anything to do with six grisly murders.

'Just to talk,' I replied.

'About what?'

'About the trips you take when you go on outings with Catherine, and other things.' If she told me anything incriminating, I had no authority to make an arrest or hold Catherine as a material witness. If Desault wanted to leave, I couldn't drag her to a room and lock her in. And I didn't know the rules of interrogation in France. If I infringed on their rights, I might ruin a potential case. But neither could I sit there and wait for Raspail.

'Tell me about the administrative job you had at Our Lady of Lourdes,' I said to Véronique.

'Oh, that was long ago. I got tired of office work.'

'So you took a job as Catherine's companion?'

Catherine was shifting uneasily on the bench. Véronique took her hand to quiet her.

I gave her a smile to reassure her and she smiled back. In that moment she looked nearly normal and it tugged at my heart. It was like trapping a wild animal who had no chance of evading my well-sprung trap.

'I left the hospital job when Paul d'Aumant hired me.'

'How did he choose you?'

'We met socially.'

'Who introduced you?'

'You are making me afraid,' Catherine said. 'Do you hurt people?' Tears were rolling down her cheeks.

'No!' I insisted, wishing Raspail would get here.

'It's all right,' Véronique assured her. 'No one's going to hurt you.' She turned to me. 'My father owns a restaurant in Lourdes. He buys wine from the d'Aumant vineyards. The Duc mentioned to my father that his sister needed a companion.'

'But didn't you make more money as an administrator?'

'The Duc is a generous employer, and Catherine is my friend. I like a job that gives me freedom.'

'Did generosity get you that beautiful gold necklace you were wearing when I met you?' Her hand strayed automatically to her throat and her eyes grew wary. 'I wish I could afford one like that for my wife.'

'It came from Italy. I bought it myself when I went on holiday.'

'A holiday in Italy and gold jewellery, all on your salary?'

She blushed. 'Yes,' she said, speaking low.

'It's true,' Catherine said. 'I was there, in Florence.'

'You went to Italy? I thought you were too sick to leave this place, or to care for your own child?'

'I can go sometimes,' she insisted, twisting her hands.

'How much does d'Aumant pay you?'

Véronique told me she made $200,000 francs, which was about $40,000 dollars a year. She obviously realized I would find out anyway.

'You must be an excellent companion to earn that kind of money. Do you do anything else for the Duc?'

'He doesn't touch her, she doesn't let him.' Catherine was terribly agitated.

The words sent a shock through me. I'd heard her say things like that before, but they didn't mean anything 'til now. 'Catherine, did Paul ever do anything bad to you? Did he touch you when you didn't want him to?' I asked softly.

Her eyes grew wide and filled with tears. 'No, no!' she insisted. Only I could tell she meant yes. I wanted to kill him. If he'd been standing there, I would have.

'Oh, Catherine, I'm so sorry. I should have known. If only I hadn't been so young, so blind.'

Her azure eyes gazed at me sadly. Then she touched my cheek and I saw the woman she might have become. 'You were the most wonderful person I'd ever known,' she said. 'I didn't deserve you.'

I felt a knife in my heart and an overwhelming hatred for Paul.

'Véronique, did you know about this?'

'No!' she said, looking nearly as shocked as I. I almost believed her.

'Are you involved in anything illegal?'

'No, no, no, no,' Catherine repeated. 'She's not. No, she's not.' She was trying too hard, as though she wanted to protect her friend but couldn't. They were being found out. *Oh God, Catherine. What do you know, how are you involved?*

'Do you know Solange Monod?'

'I don't know anyone by that name!' Véronique insisted.

'Did she ask you to steal scalpels and drugs from Our Lady of Lourdes hospital when you were employed there?'

'*Absolument, non!*' she insisted.

'Catherine,' I said, turning to her, keeping my voice calm, 'wouldn't you like to leave this place?'

Slowly she nodded.

'Why do you stay here if you're well enough to go on outings with Véronique?'

'She helps me, you see. And I help her. I'm not always well,' she whispered. I could see it was true. 'And where would I go? Back to *him*?' She shook her head. 'Never again. Never, never, never.'

'But what about Chloe?' I asked. 'How could you leave her with him?'

'Chloe?' It was the name of a stranger.

I understood. She could not protect herself and her daughter, so she'd opted out. Madness was her protection.

We heard sirens approaching like the ones in a WWII film when the Nazis are about to capture people in hiding. The two women grew agitated, looking around for escape.

'Stay calm,' I said, taking their hands. 'The police are coming to ask you some questions, that's all. I want you to co-operate now, will you?'

'Why do they want me? I can't tell them, I can't!' Catherine said. 'I need permission to go. We always get permission, you know. We go on trips all the time. This week and last week. Sometimes I don't even want to go, but Véronique says we have to.'

She rolled her eyes as though Catherine shouldn't have said that and it sickened me. I knew how Emile felt, finding out that Solange was a suspect. The coincidence of both the women we loved being somehow involved was incredible.

I wished with all my heart that it wasn't true. But the more I discovered, the worse it looked. Even if Catherine had been duped to go along, it's possible that she witnessed those awful slayings, she might have taken part in some way. I was so filled with despair, I wanted to toss my badge over the fence and quit my job here

339

and now. But there was no one to accept my resignation.

It was all so unreal. Especially my role in it. Two totally separate parts of my life had somehow converged. I couldn't imagine what the odds were of this happening.

I held on to Catherine's hand, moved by the depth of her sadness; it tore at my heart. *Please don't let this be true!*

Raspail came through the front door looking sane and solid. When all else fails there's procedure. She spotted me in the garden and strode into the sunlight, followed by two male officers.

'What's going on, Barton?'

'I'd like you to take these two women in for questioning. They may have important information concerning the Boardroom Killings. And then notify Emile Laurent in Biarritz of the developments.'

'The Boardroom Killings?' Véronique exclaimed, her voice shrill. '*C'est impossible! C'est folle!*' She was incredulous as two officers took her arms. 'I will give you information about Our Lady of Lourdes Hospital. But I don't know anything about those horrible killings! They have nothing to do with us! With me! Tell them, Catherine! Tell them!'

But Catherine was in a world of her own. She just looked at me with all the anguish of betrayal in her eyes. It was the same expression I'd seen in the eyes of that puppy before Chloe killed it. Then she got up from the bench and went with the other officers while I followed.

I sat in my car and watched the two police cars drive away. Not since that day nineteen years ago, when I'd lost her the first time, had I felt this kind of pain. But this time it was for both of us, for what she'd gone

340

through, and the loss of an ideal. It had been an illusion, destroyed before I ever knew her.

The pain I'd protected myself from all this time ripped through me. I wanted to scream with the agony of it. What a putrid mess Paul had made of our lives. We'd never had a chance. And now I might have lost Victoria because of it. I'd never fully committed myself to her because of Catherine. What a fool I'd been.

But no more. It was over, finally over. I didn't belong here, and I didn't belong with Catherine. Paul had seen to that. And I would destroy him for it.

I arrived at the Prefecture in time to witness Raspail process the women, issue them prison smocks, take their belongings and place them in glassed-in holding cells. Emile called to tell me he was en route; they hadn't found Solange, but he had made arrangements with the *juge d'instruction* in Paris to work with the *juge* in Lourdes. Procedure would be followed rigorously. Both *juges* needed to be convinced of our reasons for wanting these women in custody, we needed permission to proceed.

The forty-eight-hour rule was in effect and we could conduct questioning without council or notification. For a private citizen it is scary; for the police, ideal.

'It's a crazy mistake, James,' Emile assured me when he arrived. 'Catherine got dragged into this by Desault. We'll prove her innocence.' Then he said, 'Bring this man a scotch.'

I took a swallow, grateful that the French police were allowed to have liquor in their offices.

Raspail's group left to search both women's residences. Véronique lived in a garage apartment behind her parents' house. Catherine had several rooms at the *maison de repos*.

Then Dr Guillaud strode through the door and I couldn't restrain myself. I grabbed him by the lapels.

'You stinking bastard. You knew about her brother and you didn't do anything about it! That monster ruined her life, and now he's ruining her daughter, and you sit on your privileged ass doing nothing. I can't stand you guys, you're all alike. How do you feel about this?' I asked, mimicking the standard psychiatric question. Then I grabbed him between the legs and squeezed until he yelled. His eyes stared wildly for help. But no one stopped me. 'Is this how Paul d'Aumant has been keeping you in line? He pays you to keep your mouth shut about his filthy perversions, doesn't he?'

'What are you talking about?' he yelled. 'Let go of me!'

I released him.

I wanted to spit in his face. 'I'll bet you have a number where you can reach the Duc in case of emergency, don't you? Well, call him. We want to arrest him, Doctor! And maybe you too.'

'James,' Emile said, in my ear, 'we need Dr Guillaud to question Catherine. She still trusts him.'

'Don't leave him alone with her,' I insisted.

'We won't,' he promised.

I watched Guillaud limp into the other room.

'Nothing Catherine says can be used in court,' Emile told me. I nodded and followed him into the holding cells.

Emile questioned Véronique. The interrogation was in French, but I understood her denial that she knew anything about the killings. When pressed on the dates of her outings with Catherine away from the sanitarium, she insisted that they were legitimate trips and offered to provide hotel receipts.

'How can Catherine leave the *maison de repos* so often when she's so mentally ill?' Emile asked.

'I am capable of caring for her,' Véronique said.

342

'Catherine has periods of lucidity.'

Every time I thought that Catherine might have witnessed those murders, my stomach turned over. I wished Victoria was here. I needed her with me now. And then I thought of what Chloe had been through. I didn't know how she'd survive, knowing her mother might have assisted in butchering people.

Catherine sat there calmly, her hands folded in her lap, her head bowed. Looking at her, I couldn't believe she'd done anything to anyone. But she was so much taller than I'd remembered.

And then Raspail came back from searching the houses. One look at her face and I knew the worst.

'What did you find?'

She dumped the contents of a box on the table in her office, everything marked and labelled and encased in plastic. There were several blonde wigs, the expensive kind made of human hair. There was a room key with blood on it from the hotel in Dardilly where Henri Lepic was found, and a tie clip, matching the description of one belonging to François Saurais. I could hardly breathe. There was an empty video cassette holder with bloody prints on it. Even a pair of women's shoes, size 40, with a rounded toe and stacked heel. The right shoe had dried blood on it. 'All this evidence has to be tested against our other samples,' Raspail said, trying to make me feel better. But her eyes wouldn't meet mine.

The most damning of all was a package they'd found taped under the toilet cover in Catherine's bathroom. Three other scalpels exactly like the murder weapon. Two had blood on them.

'Catherine?' I whispered.

The sight of the scalpels made me feel sick. I dashed for the men's room and barely made it in time.

343

# Chapter 18

I grabbed Emile's arm and made him look at me. 'Solange and Véronique committed these murders, not Catherine!'

'It wasn't Solange,' he said softly. 'She's connected only to Fontelle, Richard, and Terraille. She may be guilty of taking a bribe, but she's not guilty of murder. When Fontelle was killed, she assumed it happened because of the arms deal, so she sabotaged our investigation to keep her cover. But no physical evidence links her to the other murders. Her apartment in Paris is clean. Her hair and blood samples do not match any found at the scenes. Now, look at this evidence.' He pointed to the table. 'It is too much to ignore.'

'Then why did she run?'

'To keep from going to jail!'

'But why would Catherine commit murder? She has no motive. And she couldn't have planned it all, she's crazy!'

'Only a crazy person could do something like this. Remember your theory, the killer hated her father?'

'It's her brother she hates. And he's younger than the victims.'

'But the evidence is too damning.'

I couldn't argue. As a trained agent, I knew that. Even if Desault proved to be the more guilty of the two, it didn't exonerate Catherine. 'I'm out of here,' I said, backing towards the door. Invisible hands gripped my throat, making it impossible to swallow. 'Send me the transcripts of the trial.' I would have run if he hadn't grabbed my arm and pulled me back into an embrace, holding me tightly as if to stop the madness. I wanted to smash someone, kill the bastard, beat the shit out of someone. I nearly passed out from the rage building inside me.

Finally, he let me go. 'Take it easy, James. It will get better.'

I just stood there.

'Where will you go now?'

'Christ, I don't know. Back to fucking Eugénie, pack my bags, take the first flight out of Paris for home. But first I'm going to kill Paul d'Aumant. I might quit my job. I've lost the stomach for investigation.'

'Why would you kill Paul d'Aumant?' he asked.

I realized I hadn't told him. I described Catherine and Chloe's sexual behaviour and explained Victoria's theory. He stared at me, unable to make sense of it. Then tears came to his eyes. 'Oh God,' he said. 'Not those two beautiful women? That stinking bastard! It will give me great pleasure to bring him down!'

'Chloe will be devastated. Her mother a murderer, and her uncle arrested for molesting them both. I'd better be the one to tell her.'

'I'll keep Catherine's identity a secret from the press until we find Paul.'

'She couldn't have done it!' I insisted. And then I yelled, 'Fuck it!' as I started to fall apart. He put his arm around me and squeezed. My thoughts were full of Catherine with that scalpel in her hand, slicing, killing. How could someone I had loved have done that?

Raspail had tears in her eyes when I said goodbye to her. Emile had told her of my relationship with Catherine. Everyone in the office was upset. They'd captured the most vicious killer in French history but it had brought no satisfaction. Even the Minister couldn't believe it when Emile told him that the killer was a woman from one of the finest families of France. French society is never good at blaming their own; protectionism is a matter of honour. Look at the Dreyfuss affair. They'd prefer it to be some lowly scum, hopefully an Arab, not a Grace Kelly look-alike.

'She wants to see you,' Dr Guillaud told me when he came back from Catherine's holding cell.

That was one thing I couldn't do, see her again.

'If you knew anything about the murders, you're an accessory,' I told him. 'I hope you lose your licence.'

The man's face was white. Evidently he was realizing how stupid he'd been. 'She did not commit murder,' he insisted. 'I would have known it. I never saw any sign of violence in her.'

'No violence, huh? Well, her daughter is violent. She slaughtered an innocent puppy in front of my eyes. Cut his head off with a pair of shears. Did you know her uncle was molesting her too?'

'No, but I suspected it.' He did not flinch from my gaze.

'You never reported it.'

'You are right. He paid me well.'

'You're disgusting.'

'Yes. I'm glad it is over. But Catherine did not kill anyone. Nor did her companion, Véronique, though she stole the scalpels.'

Emile and I exchanged glances. He didn't believe Guillaud, but I did. Somehow, I had known it couldn't be Catherine. Then who was the Boardroom Killer? It must be Solange. I would force Emile to hurry her extradition.

'Here,' Guillaud said, handing me a letter from Catherine. It had my name on it.

'She said you would understand. She is terrified of her brother. But she wrote this to help her daughter, Chloe.' The letter burned my fingers. I stuck it in my pocket.

'We're going to arrest him for child abuse. Will she testify against him for her daughter's sake?' I asked Guillaud.

'It wouldn't be admissible because of her mental condition.'

'Then I'll find the proof to convict that filth. I'll convince Chloe to do it.' I said to Emile, 'I'll wait for you in Eugénie. We'll get Paul together.'

'I'll be there as soon as I finish here.'

I hated to leave Emile, he was my lifeline to sanity. Out of his sight, I didn't know what I would do.

The drive back to Eugénie from Lourdes was the longest of my life. When I arrived I stuffed my things into my suitcase and settled my bill with Madame Cretier. The woman had never been friendly but since I was leaving she tried to engage me in conversation. When she noticed my expression, she fell silent.

I called Emile at the Prefecture in Lourdes but he was on his way. So I drove over to the *castelle*.

Paul and Chloe had not returned from Switzerland but were expected sometime in the morning. The office was closed, the assistant and the receptionist gone for the night. When I told the footman there had been a tragedy with Madame Catherine, he let me into Paul's office. I assumed Emile would arrive with a search warrant so I began to look around.

The place was as opulent as rich cream gone sour. I didn't know where to start looking for evidence of sexual perversion. The scars were all on the victim's soul.

I sat at Paul's desk and removed Catherine's letter from my pocket. The familiar handwriting brought back the memory of her, the distinctive way she made the J of my name with fancy calligraphy. How well I remembered it from the love notes we wrote to each other; but everything else was altered. She'd written a poem, not a letter.

## BEING SAFE

### 12

We gave ourselves to youth
Through miles of rivers flowing
In wild flowers overgrowing
Thistles, whistles, missiles

Exploring caverns that weren't mine
Drowned in wine
Unwinding vines of ivy through our toes
I've loved you more than you can know

### 24

My lips have traced a pattern
Not of choice,
Glistening like the snowflakes on my eyes
A saving balm that flowed from me to you
From right to left and tongue to tongue

### 78

I wanted us forever, you and I
Joined more than a smile, a touch, a twist of a dial
Or the root at the source of evil

Changeling, foundling, newborn
Once of love
Architect, archetype, blood oath
And smoke of exploding memory

Never give up!

I had no idea what she meant. The numbers of the stanzas followed no order, but the sexual innuendo was clear. The cavern we'd explored wasn't hers because it had been claimed by Paul. Her lips traced a pattern not of her choice, but of his. And he owned the root of the source of evil. I could guess what that was.

My eyes burned and I rubbed them. I couldn't remember when I'd last rested peacefully. Even now, I longed to lay my head down on the desk and sleep. But I would only continue this nightmare.

I had to remember that the poem was the product of a disturbed mind and not take it too seriously. Yet she wanted me to remember what we'd once had, especially the trust. Never give up? I won't! I promised her. I'll get him for you.

I propelled myself from the desk, away from her poem, and walked the room, corner to corner, not knowing what I was looking for.

The awards on the wall mocked my quest. Excellence and depravity in the same person. The awards for the champion dogs and horses were even worse. He'd treated his animals like people and his people like animals. I came to a wall of family photographs and searched the faces for a clue. The parents were stony, the children unsmiling, their wealth like poison sprinkled on a birthday cake.

The first photo was a colour-tinted portrait of the d'Aumant family when Paul was about sixteen and Catherine only a toddler. The colours had faded, making the once handsome family look as if they'd never been alive. The father was in uniform with gold braid and epaulettes, impressive; the mother looked like Catherine now, and Catherine was a butter-smooth baby. I moved over to a Kodacolour snap of Paul and Catherine a bit older, she was about eleven, he was in his early-twenties. Paul had his arm around her and she leaned against him. I wanted to rip it in two, just to separate them.

Next to that was a Polaroid picture of Paul and Chloe in the same pose. I could imagine him posing her, like mother like daughter. Fury rose to my throat. My stomach turned over and my skin began to crawl. And then, something surfaced in my mind.

Staged murders and posed photographs. They seemed connected.

There were many more of Charles or Paul being given ribbons by men in top hats. And a series of Paul seated in fancy cars. Then there was an old black and white photograph of a party of men, taken by a professional who'd signed at the bottom 'Jean Martine'. It showed a much younger Charles d'Aumant and his friends in evening clothes, vintage fifties. They were seated at one end of the enormous d'Aumant dining table, some in their shirtsleeves, ties untied, shirts unbuttoned. Others had on tuxedo jackets. All of them were grinning.

At the end of the table stood Paul, aged fourteen, his head down to hide his face. In fact, he was nude, standing there with his hands covering his privates, his shoulders hunched forward over his adolescent chest, utterly miserable.

This photo must have been taken that infamous night when Paul was forced to have sex with a whore. So the story was true! And Paul had kept the record of his shame hanging in his office all this time. He must get off on it. Or else it was the start of his perversion. The party had been the stuff of legends. The town still talked about it. And Paul had never lived it down.

I studied the men grinning at the camera, laughing hilariously at the boy's failure. One man pointed at Paul's genitals, making fun, his smile huge and wide; including Paul's father, there were six other men.

The back of my neck began to prickle. The smiles on their faces reminded me of something, the way they were seated, all grinning. One had his head back, one was turned to the side, one had his hand on his prick.

And then I figured it out. These men were all victims of the Boardroom Killer who had posed them in death exactly this way.

They were younger then, had all their hair, but I recognized them. This was the connection we'd been looking for. These men had all known Charles d'Aumant and had all insulted Paul. Catherine wasn't the Boardroom Killer and neither was Solange. It was Paul d'Aumant. He had killed everyone who'd laughed at him, and probably his father too!

I reached to lift the photo off the wall but it wouldn't budge. Instead, it swung away, revealing a wall safe behind it. What a sick mind, to hide his safe behind the one photo that constantly reminded him of his humiliation. It probably kept him motivated.

*Catherine's poem!* It was entitled, BEING SAFE. Was this the safe she meant? Perhaps the numbers of the stanzas were the combination? She knew I would come for Paul and if I found the picture, I'd find the safe.

I felt as though her hand was guiding me.

I crossed back to the desk and re-read the poem. Now, certain phrases stuck out, like twisting a dial, left to right, to the root of evil.

I carried the poem back to the safe and tried a combination of numbers from the stanzas, making a note of each failed attempt. Most wall safes open in a similar fashion. I tried the standard turns, clearing the dial by turning left to the first number, then three turns to the right, stopping on the next, and then left again past the third number, until the tumbler stopped. But all the while, I didn't have much hope. This poem could be a paranoid fantasy of Catherine's. Still, I kept trying – there was a limited number of possibilities.

On the twelfth try I heard something click, and the safe opened. It was small with only a few files inside and several video tapes.

*These must be the missing tapes used to lure the victims.*

My hands trembled as I opened the files first. There were clippings about the barge explosion that killed the Duc and Duchesse d'Aumant, with pictures of them alive and smiling, and Paul and Catherine at the funeral, looking shocked and alone. Across the article was written a sarcastic '*Au revoir!*'

I was right. He had killed his parents!

The next file contained articles about the death of Catherine's husband, Antoine Jolibois, killed in a car crash. One of the headlines asked: 'Murder or Suicide?' The article speculated that there had been a malfunction in the automobile. Was it Paul again? I wondered if Catherine knew about this. She must. That's why she was so terrified of him, why she'd been unable to protect her daughter. Controlling Chloe was his way of keeping her silence. And besides, who would believe a mad woman?

The last item in the file was a letter from Paul to Catherine, addressed to her at the *maison de repos* shortly after her husband's death.

My Darling One,
I'm sorry you're suffering but you brought this on yourself. You alone know the depth of my love. I proved it with the boat, you know I did! I told you something else might happen, yet you stayed with Antoine though he mistreated you. I couldn't allow it to go on. I had to stop it just as I stopped

353

them. Now you see how much I love you? Don't
worry, my precious. You'll feel better soon. Then,
come back to me. I ache for you.

P

Here was his admission of guilt! I was lucky he'd only
betrayed me to his parents. If I'd stayed in France, he
would have killed me too.

With shaking hands, I reached into the safe and took
out another file. This one contained a stack of photographs. Polaroids of all the murdered men; they were
nearly like the ones in the police files, only in these the
victim's heads had been posed exactly as they'd been in
the group photo from that long ago party. This time
their sardonic grins were underscored by the addition
of a grotesque slash across the throat.

I remembered the times Paul had questioned me
about this case, acting as though he knew nothing,
when all along he was the killer.

I put the files back and took out a tape marked
C–1963.

The TV monitor and VCR were in an entertainment
unit in the corner next to the french windows that
overlooked the grounds. It was pitch black outside and
I could see my hollow-eyed reflection in the glass. I
looked like one of Paul's victims.

I inserted the tape in the VCR and swivelled Paul's
chair to the right, facing it.

The tape was poor quality with lines across it that
cleared a bit when I adjusted the tracking with the
remote unit. A black and white interior of the *castelle*
appeared, as it was when I first saw it in 1974. The
camera panned jerkily back and forth. Children's
voices argued: Catherine and Paul.

'Let me do it, I want a turn,' Catherine pleaded.

'No, it's my present,' he insisted, keeping control.

'I want to do it!'

'You'll break it.'

'I won't!' she said, starting to cry.

He told her to shut up.

The film was 8mm transferred to tape. The jumpy shots made me dizzy as the novice tried to work his new toy. Young Paul d'Aumant had a state of the art movie camera with sound before the advent of video tape.

I fast forwarded through more footage of the house and the grounds, shots of Paul's parents, stiff and obnoxious, of the servants coming and going. Paul's camera skills got better as he recorded the history of their lives, Catherine as a little girl, chubby and angelic-looking, with the universal appeal of all beautiful children.

Then there was a stationary interior shot of Catherine's bedroom. The camera was on a tripod, aimed at her small bed piled with dolls and stuffed animals. Next to the bed was a doll's carriage. Off camera Paul's voice directed his sister.

'Hurry up,' he insisted. 'I haven't got all day.'

'I don't want to,' she said.

'Get over there!' What an autocrat.

She came into view, a child of five, and climbed on the bed. The camera adjusted to her and focused.

Sitting there, she looked like a porcelain doll with her long blonde hair and her white dress, reminding me of Lindsay.

'I don't want to do this again,' she whined in a child's voice.

'You'd better or I'll tell Maman and Papa,' he threatened – the way I did when I bullied my younger brother.

'Right now!' he insisted.

'You have to help me.' She got off the bed and stepped out of frame, bumping the tripod which caused the picture to go out of focus.

'Watch out!' he yelled.

'I can't do it myself,' she insisted. 'Mademoiselle unfastens me.'

'Next time wear something you can take off by yourself. That's part of the show.'

When she came back and climbed into the camera frame she had taken off her dress and was wearing her underwear, a sleeveless T-shirt, panties, white socks and ankle strap shoes.

'Okay,' he said. And then he began to narrate. 'This is Catherine, aged five. We are beginning her history now. This is the first day.' He said to her, 'Do as I showed you, Catherine.'

And I watched as she removed her T-shirt and then her pants, wriggling out of them until she was nude.

'Move down here a little bit more,' he said, 'over this way. That's right.' She did as she was told.

He aimed the camera at her body. Then he said. 'Okay, now.'

And before my horrified eyes, she spread open her legs revealing that tiny little rosebud between them. Her childish eyes looked straight at the camera, deep pools of curiosity, as though she could see beyond this moment.

'Now move around as I showed you,' he directed, the little shit.

And she moved her hips in a grotesque parody of a sexually aroused woman.

Paul moved over and stood next to the bed so that he was in the camera's view. But since it was aimed at Catherine, his head was out of shot and only his torso was visible. He had removed his clothes. He had an erection.

'Now take hold of it,' he told her. And she did. 'And say it,' he instructed.

'Oh, baby,' her little voice repeated from previous coaching. 'You're the biggest man I ever saw. You can give it to me any time, right in here.' And she pointed to her vagina.

He moved against her hand, thrusting himself along the side of the bed. It only took a few quick strokes before he ejaculated.

'Ugh,' she said, with repugnance.

'Don't say that,' he yelled, punching her in the arm. 'Say that you liked it.'

'I liked it,' she said, starting to cry.

He gave her another punch on the arm, walked over to the camera and the screen went blank.

I turned it off and sat there stunned. This was what he'd been doing to her all her life until Chloe came along. And he'd planted all that evidence in her room, worn blonde wigs and women's shoes, to put the blame on his disturbed sister. He had almost got away with it. But he kept the photos and tapes as mementoes, and Catherine helped me find them. Payback time!

I turned the tape back on and fast forwarded through a lifetime of abuse, not stopping as the incidents got more graphic, more elaborate. Paul had obsessively chronicled Catherine's physical development throughout the years, to the point of measuring the growth of her breasts and her pubic hair with close ups ad nauseam. Although there was no intercourse, he'd had her sitting and standing and exposing herself, as well as fondling and having oral sex with him for her whole life. Some life. The porno king of Aquitaine.

I had seen all I could stand and was about to turn it off when a familiar location appeared.

The camera was shooting down from a ceiling location focused on a narrow bunk bed in a small room – maybe a servant's quarters.

The bed looked familiar.

Then I recognized it; it was the bedroom on the barge where Catherine and I had made love. The barge Paul had blown up to kill his parents.

Almost immediately, I heard my own voice and there I was, twenty-two years old, boyish and perfectly at ease, sitting on the bed, talking to my girl, kissing her on the lips, fondling those incredible breasts. And then we were having sex, my body moving up and down as I made love to Catherine. Paul must have had a fit when he saw this!

The range of emotions that shot through me was like nothing I'd ever known. How young we were and how beautiful she was! And though having films of it was sick and depraved, it was amazing to see the reality of it. These events had taken on mythic proportions in my mind so that nothing could possibly compare. But it was just sex. If only I could reach into the picture and change the way things had turned out.

Catherine wasn't aware of the camera as she ran the gamut of her performance, pre-taught, pre-tested and family-approved filmographic sex. Paul had schooled her to do everything he liked, and she did it so well.

Afterwards we lay on the bunk looking up, whispering our plans, talking of things I had forgotten. It was really sweet, except that someone was watching. How many people had seen this over the years?

*What if he'd sold it, the bastard!*

Every enticement Chloe performed had also been orchestrated by an incestuous, murdering pedophile. No wonder Shithead didn't have other sexual play mates; he had his sister and his niece. Catherine's husband and I were his only competition. But he'd got rid of us and had her all to himself. No one interfered with Chloe. I remembered how he'd insisted on Catherine being a virgin, though he'd never had intercourse with her. He couldn't after that night with the prostitute. But I had. The film of me and Catherine must have driven him crazy. Catherine had defied him and loved me in spite of the consequences. No wonder he hated me.

Had Catherine been his accomplice? Was she the one who sat in the chair and helped entice those men to their death, or was it Véronique? Someone had to take the polaroids of dead men while Paul held their heads.

*And then I knew. It was Chloe. Oh, God, no!*

That would explain the time delay between the first and second killing. The first one took place when Chloe was home on Christmas holiday, the others had occurred when she was home for the summer. When I thought of what he'd done to that brilliant talented girl, I could hardly stand it. 'Chloe has other obligations to fulfil right now,' he'd said. Helping him murder six men. No wonder she'd killed that puppy, it was her cry for help.

I went back to the safe and took another tape, dated C–1991, but as I pulled it out, something fell to the floor. Chloe's birth certificate. I was afraid to look. What if I was her father? I glanced down and saw the date of her birth – years after I'd left France. The name of her father was Antoine Jolibois. I hadn't expected anything else, but I was relieved.

I despised Paul for everything he'd done, but his criminal manipulation of Chloe put me beyond fury.

I reached under my jacket and patted my gun for reassurance. Then I inserted the next tape into the machine and turned it on.

# Chapter 19

This video was in colour with a musical score. How professional. The scene opened on a country road in late-spring, the fields were newly sown and the trees had their leaves. Birds were chirping, insects buzzed, ambient sounds of nature. Chloe walked through a field of wildflowers in her white, gauzy dress. A breeze played through her hair. She turned and waved at the camera while her voice narrated: 'Monsieur Lepic. Monsieur Henri Lepic. Where are you? I'm looking for you. This film was made especially for you, the man I dream about.'

Pretty potent stuff; a porno video made specifically for you. Imagine receiving that in the mail. What man wouldn't respond? And no one would ask where it came from if they were cautioned against it. Not if they wanted another one.

Next was a close-up of Chloe. Seeing her on film made it seem playful, less horrible than it was.

'All my life, I've looked for you, my handsome man. Am I the girl of your dreams? I hope so, my darling, for I was created just for you. Only for your pleasure. Show me how much I mean to you. Can you feel how much I want you? Show me. Ah, yes, unzip your pants. Take it out. Oh, I see how wonderful you are. Soon I will come to you in person and do all the things you have ever wanted, pleasure you in every way possible.

You will tell me what to do. I will be yours to command. I can't wait for that day to arrive.'

When she looked at the camera with that expression of smouldering desire in her eyes and licked her mouth so suggestively with her tongue, any man would be turned on. Especially an older man with a history of sowing wild oats who hasn't had excitement in years.

The camera pulled back to a long shot of her walking forward so that the sunlight outlined her body through the diaphanous fabric of her dress, just as she'd done it for me, only this time she ran her hands lightly over her body and down between her legs in a sensual gesture. 'I can feel you touching me like this,' she said, her expression filled with longing. Then she beckoned for the camera to follow her.

She entered a tree-covered glade on the banks of the river, like the places Catherine and I used to go. On the ground was a lace and satin quilt, and to add to the depravity, some children's toys and a music box. She backed away from the camera, smiling, enticing, picked up a stuffed toy and rubbed it on her body as though enjoying the wicked sensation before tossing it aside. I could see she was acting, there was no life in her eyes. I remembered how her eyes had been so bright when she'd played the piano for us and that deepened my despair.

She thrust her arms forward, her lips trembling. 'My dearest Monsieur Lepic, my body aches to find you, to give you the pleasure you deserve, the exquisite pleasure that you've longed for all your life. Only I can adore you. Only I can make you happy. I was created for it. Until the moment when I come to you in person, I want to show you what I can do for you.'

She sank down on the quilt on her knees and then lay down on her stomach, slowly pulling up her dress to reveal her nakedness. Then she bent her legs at the

362

knee, crossing her ankles in their black patent-leather ankle strap shoes exactly like the photograph I'd seen in the newspaper a week ago.

The camera panned up and I was amazed to see that she was not alone. Her upper body, perched on her elbows, lay between the bent hairy legs of a man with an erection. He was draped by a black cloth so that only his legs and genitals were visible. That way, the viewer could imagine it was himself.

She turned her head and spoke to the camera with faked sincerity. 'This is a poor substitute for you, my dearest Monsieur Lepic, but it's the only way I can show you what I want to do to you. I know your penis is much better than this. I know it's sweeter and so much larger. And it will taste so good. Mmm,' she cooed, and began to lick, as though it was a lollipop. I recognized every calculated movement; it was exactly the way Catherine used to do it to me. And in spite of my disgust, my body throbbed, wanting to be the man in that pose, only with Catherine doing it to me, not Chloe.

Suddenly, a searing pain in my scalp made me cry out, jerking me back to reality as strong fingers grabbed my hair, yanking my head back and jamming it against the chair. A scalpel dug into my throat under my left ear, piercing my skin. My brain screamed in terror and I waited to die, not moving a muscle.

A deep female voice said, 'Don't move or I'll cut your throat before you swallow!' Then the voice became Paul's. 'Isn't she delicious?' he asked, exactly the way he used to speak about Catherine.

*Emile*, I thought. *Where the fuck are you?* Adrenaline pumped through me and my pulse rate shot through the ceiling as my heart flailed against my ribs. My gun was under my left arm. If only I could reach it . . . But if I so much as twitched, that knife would slice my throat as it had done all the others.

'It's so easy to sneak up behind someone when he's watching Chloe on tape,' he said, his voice rasping in my ear. 'It gets one's full attention, doesn't it? And when Chloe arrives in person, and sits down in front of them and flashes her privates, it's powerful. You've seen her do it, haven't you? Hard to resist. Makes you want to touch.

'You can imagine how these old fools felt seeing that video, hearing her calling their name. And when she was sitting there in person right in front of them, their tongues were hanging out, not to mention their limp old pricks. They thought she was going to do to them what she did to me in the video; couldn't believe their luck. They were so turned on they didn't know what to watch, the real Chloe or the video.'

'That's when you killed them,' I said.

He tightened his grip until my scalp ripped, but I didn't scream.

'You didn't have your prick in your hand. Why not? Don't you like young girls? They're so much better than older ones. Their skin is smooth, their breasts are taut. They don't give you any trouble. When you get them really young, they don't even have any odour.'

I wanted to ram that scalpel into his guts, after I sliced off his prick.

He yanked on my hair again and I could feel a clump of my scalp really tear. This time I screamed and jerked, and the knife cut my throat. I froze and held my breath.

'Get up, James.' His voice was terrible in my ear. 'We're leaving.' Then he changed his voice to sound like a woman's again, and I heard how adept he was at impersonation. 'I was a beautiful woman, dear, you should have seen me. I don't want to kill you here,' he

364

said in his female voice. 'The evidence would be too much to hide.'

'You're an expert at fixing the evidence, aren't you?' I asked, sounding braver than I felt.

He jerked me up out of the chair and walked me backwards, forcing me around the desk. 'Reach into your holster and take out your gun. Now.' He dug in the knife again. 'Use two fingers; put it on the desk. Do exactly as I say, or you're dead in an instant.'

I had been trained to disarm an attacker holding me like this, but I needed to be clear of the furniture so I could get my balance. He was taller than I, but I was five years younger. In a fair fight, I could take him, but this was not a fair fight. I removed my gun and laid it on the desk, safety off.

'Put your hands in your pockets,' he demanded. I did as he asked.

'Catherine's been arrested,' I told him.

'Good. That means you followed my clues and found all the evidence, even the dates when she was away from the *maison de repos*.'

'Véronique Desault will testify that you hired her to steal the scalpels and take Catherine on outings.'

'Véronique will be dead before the trial. What a stroke of luck that you, of all people, came to France for this case. It made everything perfect. The only one I wanted to kill who was difficult to reach. And then you arrived in Eugénie, the answer to a prayer. I'm surprised how long you resisted Chloe, but you're younger than the rest. Still, you were so helpful. I asked you a few key questions, and found out exactly what the police knew. You were too stupid to figure out who the killer was, so I led you to her.'

He noticed his safe was open. 'How did you do that?'

'Catherine told me the combination. She knows you set her up. She's co-operating with the police.'

He laughed. 'My sister's a crazy bird, her testimony doesn't count. And if she ever opens her mouth about me, she knows I'll kill Chloe.'

Another voice spoke up. 'What did you say?'

I felt Paul stiffen. He hadn't expected anyone to hear him. But Chloe was standing there. She had come in through the french doors. 'You would kill me, Uncle Paul? You can't kill me, you need me! I've done everything you asked. I made the tapes for all those men. I went with you and sat in those chairs. I even kept my eyes open and watched one time. Why would you kill me? Is it because I hurt the dog?'

'Don't be stupid. I don't care about the dog.' He was flustered by this confrontation. Her interference wasn't in the equation.

I felt an infinitesimal loosening of his grip on my hair and tried to slide my hands out of my pockets, but he tightened his hold and jerked my head back again, exposing my throat. 'Don't make me do this here, or it will be slow and painful.' And he gave a deep cut this time to prove his point. I could feel the blood flowing down my neck into my shirt. The scalpel was so sharp it didn't hurt at first, and then it did. Pain shot through me like an electric shock.

'Don't!' Chloe cried. 'Don't hurt him. He's not one of the men from the photograph.'

'But he's the most important one. The one who spoiled Catherine for me.'

'Let him alone,' she said.

'Oh, little one, do you care about him?' He was gleeful. He gave my neck another slice. 'See what I do to people you care about. I won't have my sweet little bird spreading her wings for anyone but me.'

I clenched my jaw to keep from crying out in pain while my mind raced. Chloe's feelings for me were real after all. She could be a reluctant ally. She hadn't known who I was in Paris that first time she'd flirted with me. I was just some stranger she'd admired. Then she saw me in Eugénie and flirted again. But when she realized that Paul wanted her to lure me, so he could kill me too, she'd fought with him not to do it. That's why she didn't want to have lunch with me that day, and she'd struggled with herself when we'd had dinner, not wanting to seduce me, asking me questions about being a father. I had to get her on my side.

'Chloe, go and call the police,' I said.

She wavered for a moment then changed her mind. 'I don't give a damn about you. Uncle Paul, kill him if you want to.'

'Chloe,' I said, 'once I am dead, he will kill you too.'

'Never, my darling bird. You know I love you,' Paul insisted.

'Chloe, listen. He wants to find a younger girl. He's tired of you, he told me so. You're getting too old.'

'Shut up!' Paul said, cutting me again.

'That's not true!' she insisted, with doubt in her voice.

Paul cut me once more. 'I warned you,' he said.

'No!' Chloe cried.

'If he kills me here, in this room, the police will find out. Right now, fibres from my clothing are everywhere, my fingerprints too, and strands of my hair. Emile Laurent is on his way. He'll know I died here. If Paul doesn't kill you, you'll go to prison. You don't want that, do you? Your mother will tell them that Paul killed all those men and you helped him.'

'No, she won't,' Chloe said. 'She's never told anyone about Uncle Paul, and she never will. And she won't save you either, she never saved me!'

'She told me about the safe with the photographs of dead people in it, and the video tapes. The tapes of you.'

'You saw them?'

'Yes, Chloe. I'm sorry. I know he made you do it.'

'Don't be sorry for me,' she said, furious. 'I was good!'

'That's enough,' Paul said, dragging me towards the door. I did not want to leave this room. Out in the grounds, he could kill me and toss me into the lake, or bury me in the woods. If I was going to die, I wanted to leave as much evidence as I could.

'Your mother told me something else about you, Chloe. That you're my child, my own little girl,' I lied, hoping it would get to her. 'Antoine's not your father. I am. Isn't that wonderful! Now we can really love each other, as father and daughter.'

'That's a lie!' she insisted. 'My father died in a car crash when I was a baby.'

'No. There's a birth certificate in the safe. Go and look for yourself.'

'Stay where you are!' Paul insisted. He was getting nervous. He knew this wasn't true, but I'd planted doubt. Spontaneous moments threw him off and he made mistakes, like when he'd stabbed Toussaint in Dardilly and lost the scalpel. That's what led us to him. He got rattled under pressure.

'It's true,' I kept insisting. 'I am your real father. I came here to take you back to America with me. Would you like to go? We could travel together, see all the wonderful sights.'

'What about your wife?'

'I'll divorce her and you and I can live together, just the two of us. We've wasted too much time already.' I was counting on the fact that she'd meant it when she told me she loved me.

'Enough!' Paul shouted, thrusting the knife into the top of my shoulder, near the base of my neck, and twisting it. I screamed and almost passed out as the

368

pain shot up and down my arm, searing through my skull like a hot poker. In another moment, all my strength would be gone and I couldn't make a break if I got the chance.

'Chloe,' I gasped, 'don't let him kill me. He killed Antoine, and your grandparents. He'll kill you too, or else you'll end up in an institution like your mother. He's trying to send her to prison for his crimes. But you can stop him. There's a gun on the desk. Go and get it.'

Paul shouted. 'Don't move.' But she ignored him and started for the desk. His attention was on her and he loosened his grip on me just a fraction.

I made my move; in one motion I slammed my head back hitting him square on the nose as I pulled down on his arm and up with my knee. I was trying to force the knife out of his hand, but I was weakened by my wounds and couldn't get control. Then I broke away from him.

He lunged after me slashing with the knife; I leaped back, but he sliced through my abdomen. A superficial wound, but it hurt like hell. Then he jabbed again, moving for the advantage. I side-stepped and swung around behind him as the momentum of his body threw him forward. Lacing my fingers together and using my arms as a weapon, I slammed him across the upper back. Pain shot through me, but a loud crack pierced the air and he cried out. I think one of his vertebrae snapped and he fell forward against the desk, but it didn't stop him. Pushing off from the desk, he swung around, slashing at me with the knife. This time he hit home again, inflicting a deep cut across my forearm. I felt the flesh give way, flapping against itself. It was like being cut by a threshing machine, every way I turned another blade. I felt no pain which meant I was probably in shock; my right arm was nearly useless and hung there gushing blood. I looked at it stupidly, leaving him an opening for my heart.

Chloe screamed, 'Stop or I'll kill you!' I didn't know which of us she meant. But when I looked she was pointing the gun at both of us, pivoting it from one to the other, her hand shaking so badly she could barely aim.

'Go ahead, shoot him,' Paul said, the knife poised in the air. 'I don't care about the blood any more. We'll burn the carpet; there won't be any evidence. Go on, shoot him. I know you want to, the way you wanted your turn with Terraille in Biarritz. And I let you, didn't I? I let you make the X in his face. And you enjoyed it! You're just like I am, aren't you, little one? You're my love. You belong to me. I know you so well. Go on, shoot him.'

'Chloe,' I pleaded, 'don't listen to him. I know you're good in your soul, you're not like him. You feel sorry when you do something wrong, but he never does. You're still young. You can change your life. I'll help you, I'll take care of you. We'll go away from here together.'

Pleading with her was using up my remaining strength; the room began to spin. My knees were going. I'd lost so much blood I could barely stand. I gripped the wound in my arm and tried to stop the flow. Then I began to lose consciousness as I pitched forward.

Chloe screamed; I heard the roar of the gun and felt the searing pain of a bullet hitting my shoulder. Somewhere far away was the muffled sound of another shot.

# *Epilogue*

Throbbing pain pulsated, edged its way into my consciousness. And then it slammed through my body. I hurt so bad I couldn't even cry out. I lived in pain, I was wrapped in it; I breathed it, exuded it.

*But I was alive.*

I had been cut and stabbed and shot, I remembered. This pain had to stop; I begged it to stop, had to stop, had to stop. I couldn't take it. My body was in a vice that shot fire through every nerve ending; it annihilated me, first here and then there, then everywhere. The unbearable ache in my shoulder shot needle scrapes down my arm. The other arm had a tearing, searing feeling from the fingertips to the shoulder. Jesus God, I hurt. My eyelids were stuck together. I forced them open to grey flannel.

A sound. My own voice whimpering, moaning, crying.

Consciousness again, more pain than I could stand. 'Oh God!' I cried out. Cool hands touched my face.

'I'm here, darlin'.'

Vickie's voice.

'You're gonna live, Jimmy. Go to sleep.'

It went on like that for a long time, until I was able to sip some water instead of ice chips and then some beef broth, even Jello. They make you sit up as soon as the stitches congeal but you think you're going to tear into pieces.

371

Chloe's bullet had gone through my shoulder just above my left armpit. Paul had slashed my right arm to the bone, so I was really out of commission. Then there were the cuts and gouges in my neck; just lying on the pillow was excruciating. I was so shaky I was almost weeping, especially seeing Victoria's face.

'How did they find you?' I asked.

'I was in Paris visiting Claudine. Emile called us the moment he arrived at the *castelle*. The French papers, the *International Tribune*, the entire press covered the story. It's been on television for days. When I heard Catherine had been arrested I tried to find you, but you'd checked out of your pension. Everyone is relieved that it's over. You're a national hero. They're going to give you a medal. You found the real killer.'

'Where are we?'

'In a hospital, in Mont de Marsan. They air-lifted you here. Don't you remember?'

It was a blank. 'I'm sorry for what I put you through.'

'It's over, isn't it?'

'Damn straight,' I told her, trying to smile, but the gashes in my neck pulled like crazy and I sucked in air through my teeth.

'What that man did to you!' she exclaimed.

'What happened? I remember being shot. I thought I was dead.'

'No, Paul is dead. Chloe shot him.'

'She shot us both.'

'She was aiming at him, but she'd never shot a gun before and you fell into her line of fire. Then she shot him. Luckily the servants heard the shots and called an ambulance just as Emile arrived. You lost a lot of blood. Chloe was in shock.'

'Poor kid. What kind of a life can she possibly have now?'

'She may never forget this, but there are good people

372

and programmes to help her. She's not schizophrenic like her mother. I talked to Catherine. She made them bring her here. She insisted on seeing you.'

'That must have been difficult for you. I have no memory of it.'

'I watched her sit by your side. She stroked your face, studied you for a long time as though trying to memorize you. She's so sad, Jimmy. We cried together. I felt so badly for what's been done to her. She loved you very much. She let you go because she was afraid of what her brother would do to you. She was no match for him. He controlled her whole life. Mental illness was her way of getting away from him. But I don't think she could help it. It's not something we choose.'

'You're a remarkable woman, Victoria Barton,' I said.

'Not really. I just love you too.'

'Did you know Paul killed his parents and Catherine's husband?'

'Yes. She only married Antoine to get away from her brother, but it didn't work. After Antoine died, she knew that wherever she went, Paul would find her. He controlled her finances. Not being able to care for Chloe made things worse. She tried to be a mother to the child, but couldn't do it.'

'What's going to happen to Chloe?' I asked.

'She has a great-aunt in Switzerland who loves her.'

'She's going to need help,' I said.

'Do you want her to come to us?' Victoria asked.

I looked at her in amazement. I knew what that offer had cost her, especially after the way I had treated her .

'Maybe for a visit sometime,' I said. 'Not right away. We have to work out things between us first. And I have a long way to go.'

'Only an eight-hour flight to Houston,' she said, kissing me lightly on the cheek.

'There's someone here to see you,' she told me, and went to the door. Emile came in.

He took my hand and held it in both of his, grinning at me. 'We've been saying prayers for you. To both Gods.'

'Did you find Solange?'

'Yes,' he said, giving me a look so that I wouldn't say too much. 'She was arrested in Morocco and extradited. She admitted taking bribes from Fontelle but she's been cleared of any involvement in the murders. It was just a coincidence that Fontelle, Richard and Terraille were in business together and also knew Charles d'Aumant. But when Fontelle and Richard were murdered, Solange panicked. She was conducting her own investigation separate from ours, trying to keep herself in the clear.'

'What about Véronique Desault?'

'She was just a pawn. She did whatever Paul told her for money, stole some scalpels from the hospital, took Catherine on outings on the dates he specified. She had no idea what he was doing. It was an elaborate plan to build a case against Catherine. He never counted on you.'

'I got him,' I said. 'How are you doing?'

From the way he squeezed my hand, I knew he had settled his mid-life crisis. 'I've been given a citation by the government and a bonus when I retire.'

'Good for you.'

'They're giving you the Medal of Honour.'

'Hey, that's great,' I said, smiling just enough to keep my stitches from pulling.

'I'll let you get some rest,' he said. 'We'll see you later.' And he left.

Victoria came back to sit beside me. 'Emile said you threatened to leave your job,' she said. 'Lost the stomach for investigation?'

374

'I haven't decided,' I told her. 'But I promise things are going to change. I don't want to be dragged through life's sewer any more. And I also know how much you mean to me. I'll go to a counsellor with you if you want. As long as it's not Dr Guillaud.'

She laughed. 'I think it's a good idea,' she said. 'But you're not the only one who's to blame. I'm going to devote more time to you, more attention, not be so fierce about my independence. We'll compromise.' She smiled at me. 'And if I run for flea-catcher, I could use you on my team.' She was waiting for my reaction.

I gave her the best smile I could muster. 'Ma'am, not only would you make the finest flea-catcher Houston has ever seen, you could scratch my bites any time. I'd even be proud to work for you.'

She kissed me then and darted her tongue between my lips. Not only was Catherine d'Aumant the farthest thing from my mind, but I could feel my flagpole coming right to attention.

# A selection of bestsellers from Headline